bridge *of* clay

Also by Markus Zusak

The Book Thief

I Am the Messenger

markus zusak

bridge of clay

Alfred A. Knopf
New York

THIS IS A BORZOI BOOK PUBLISHED BY ALFRED A. KNOPF

Jacket design by Isabel Warren-Lynch and Ericka O'Rourke

Visit us on the Web! GetUnderlined.com

Educators and librarians, for a variety of teaching tools, visit us at RHTeachersLibrarians.com

Library of Congress Cataloging-in-Publication Data
Names: Zusak, Markus, author.
Title: Bridge of Clay / Markus Zusak.
Description: New York : Alfred A. Knopf, 2018. | Summary: Upon their father's return, the five Dunbar boys, who have raised themselves since their mother's death, begin to learn family secrets, including that of fourth brother Clay, who will build a bridge for complex reasons, including his own redemption.
Identifiers: LCCN 2018013864 (print) | LCCN 2018021166 (ebook) | ISBN 978-1-9848-3015-9 (hardcover) | ISBN 978-0-375-84559-8 (hardcover signed ed.) | ISBN 978-0-375-94559-5 (lib. bdg.) | ISBN 978-0-375-89699-6 (ebook) | ISBN 978-1-9848-3016-6 (intl. tr. pbk.)
Subjects: CYAC: Brothers–Fiction. | Abandoned children–Fiction. | Secrets–Fiction. | Family life–Fiction. | Bridges–Design and construction–Fiction.
Classification: LCC PZ7.Z837 (ebook) | LCC PZ7.Z837 Bri 2018 (print) | DDC [Fic]–dc23

The text of this book is set in 10.5-point Goudy Old Style.

Printed in the United States of America
May 2019
10 9 8 7 6 5 4 3 2

First Edition

For Scout, Kid, and Little Small,
for Cate,
and in loving memory of K.E.:
a great lover of *language*

before the beginning

the old tw

In the beginning there was one murderer, one mule and one boy, but this isn't the beginning, it's before it, it's me, and I'm Matthew, and here I am, in the kitchen, in the night—the old river mouth of light—and I'm punching and punching away. The house is quiet around me.

As it is, everyone else is asleep.

I'm at the kitchen table.

It's me and the typewriter—me and the old TW, as our long-lost father said our long-lost grandmother used to say. Actually, she'd called it the *ol'* TW, but such quirks have never been me. Me, I'm known for bruises and levelheadedness, for height and muscle and blasphemy, and the occasional sentimentality. If you're like most people, you'll wonder if I'd bother stringing a sentence together, let alone know anything about the epics, or the Greeks. Sometimes it's good to be underestimated that way, but even better when someone sees it. In my case, I was lucky:

For me there was Claudia Kirkby.

There was a boy and a son and a brother.

Yes, always for us there was a brother, and he was the one—the one of us amongst five of us—who took all of it on his shoulder. As ever, he'd told me quietly, and deliberately, and of course he was on the money. There *was* an old typewriter buried in the old backyard of an old-backyard-of-a-town, but I'd had to get my measurements right, or I might dig up a dead dog or a snake instead (which I did, on both counts). I figured if the dog was there and the snake was there, the typewriter couldn't be far.

It was perfect, pirateless treasure.

I'd driven out the day after my wedding day.

Out from the city.

Right through the night.

Out through the reams of empty space, and then some.

The town itself was a hard, distant storyland; you could see it from afar. There was all the straw-like landscape, and marathons of sky. Around it, a wilderness of low scrub and gum trees stood close by, and it was true, it was so damn true: the people sloped and slouched. This world had worn them down.

It was outside the bank, next to one of the many pubs, that a woman told me the way. She was the uprightest woman in town.

"Go left there on Turnstile Street, right? Then straight for say two hundred meters, then left again."

She was brown-haired, well-dressed, in jeans and boots, plain red shirt, an eye shut tight to the sun. The only thing betraying her was an inverse triangle of skin, there at the base of her neck; it was tired and old and crisscrossed, like the handle of a leather chest.

"You got it, then?"

"Got it."

"What number you lookin' for, anyway?"

"Twenty-three."

"Oh, you're after the old Merchisons, are you?"

"Well, to tell you the truth, not really."

The woman came closer and I noted the teeth of her now, how they were white-and-gleaming-but-yellow; a lot like the swaggering sun. As she approached, I held my hand out, and there was she and I and her teeth and town.

"My name's Matthew," I said, and the woman, she was Daphne.

By the time I was at the car again, she'd turned and come back, from the money machine at the bank. She'd even left her card behind, and stood there now, with a hand at center-hip. I was halfway into the driver's side and Daphne nodded and knew. She knew near to almost everything, like a woman reading the news.

"Matthew Dunbar."

She said it, she didn't ask.

There I was, twelve hours from home, in a town I'd never set foot in in all my thirty-one years, and they'd all been somehow expecting me.

It was a long time we looked at each other then, a few seconds at least, and all was broad and open. People appeared, and wandered the street.

I said, "What else do you know? Do you know I'm here for the typewriter?"

She opened the other eye.

She braved the midday sun.

"Typewriter?" Now I'd totally confused her. "What the hell are you talkin' about?"

Almost on cue, an old guy started shouting, asking if it was her bloody card holding up bloody traffic at the bloody bank machine, and she ran back up to retrieve it. Maybe I could have explained—that there *was* an old TW in all this story, back when they used typewriters in doctors' surgeries, and secretaries bashed at the keys. Whether or not she was interested, I'll never know. What I do know is that her directions were spot-on.

Miller Street:

A quiet assembly line of small, polite houses, all baking in the heat.

I parked the car, I shut the door, and crossed the crispy lawn.

It was right about then I regretted not bringing the girl I'd just married—or actually, the woman, and mother of my two daughters—and of course, the daughters themselves. Those kids, they would have loved this place, they'd have walked and skipped and danced here, all legs and sunny hair. They'd have cartwheeled the lawn, shouting, "And don't go lookin' at our knickers, right?"

Some honeymoon:

Claudia was at work.

The girls were at school.

Part of me still liked that, of course; a lot of me liked it a lot.

I breathed in, and out, and knocked.

* * *

Inside, the house was oven-like.

The furniture all was roasted.

The pictures just out of the toaster.

They had an air conditioner. It was broken.

There was tea and Scotch Fingers, and sun clapped hard at the window. There was ample sweat at the table. It dripped from arm to cloth.

As for the Merchisons, they were honest, hairy people.

They were a blue singlet of a man, with great big sideburns, like fur coat meat cleavers on his cheeks, and a woman named Raelene. She wore pearl earrings, tight curls, and held a handbag. She was perennially going to the shops, but stayed. From the moment I mentioned the backyard and that something might be buried there, she'd had to hang around. When the tea was done and the biscuits reduced to a nub, I faced the sideburns, front-on. He spoke to me fair and squarely:

"Guess we should get to work."

Outside, in the long dry yard, I walked left, toward the clothesline, and a weathered, dying banksia. I looked back for a moment behind me: the small house, the tin roof. The sun was still all over it, but reclining, leaning west. I dug with shovel and hands, and there it was.

"Goddamn!"

The dog.

Again.

"Goddamn!"

The snake.

Both of them nothing but bones.

We combed them close and careful.

We placed them on the lawn.

"Well, I'll be!"

The man said it three times, but loudest of all when at last I'd found the old Remington, bullet-grey. A weapon in the ground, it was wrapped in three rounds of tough plastic, so clear I could see the keys: first the Q and the W, then the midsection of F and G, H and J.

For a while I looked at it; I just looked:

Those black keys, like monsters' teeth, but friendly.

Finally, I reached in and hauled it out, with careful, dirty hands; I filled in all three holes. We took it out of the packaging, and watched and crouched, to examine it.

"A hell of a thing," said Mr. Merchison. The fur coat cleavers were twitching.

"It is," I agreed, it was glorious.

"I didn't think *this* was going to happen when I woke up this morning." He picked it up, and handed it across.

"You want to stay for dinner, Matthew?"

That was the old lady, still half astonished. Astonishment didn't trump dinner.

I looked up from my crouching stance. "Thanks, Mrs. Merchison, but I'm hurting from all those biscuits." Again, I eyed the house. It was parceled up now, in shade. "I should actually get going." I shook the hand of each of them. "I can't thank you enough." I began to walk on, the typewriter safe in my arms.

Mr. Merchison was having none of it.

He called out a forthright "Oi!"

And what else could I do?

There must have been good reason for unearthing the two animals, and I turned from under the clothesline—the tired old Hills Hoist, just like ours—and waited for what he would say; and he said it.

"Aren't you forgetting something there, mate?"

He nodded to the dog bones and the snake.

And that was how I drove away.

In the back seat of my old station wagon that day were the skeletal remains of a dog, one typewriter, and the wiry boneline of a king brown snake.

About halfway, I pulled over. There was a place I knew—a small detour, with a bed and proper rest—but I decided not to take it. Instead, I lay in the car with the snake there at my neck. As I drifted off, I thought how before-the-beginnings are everywhere—because before and before so many things there was a boy in that old-backyard-of-a-town, and he'd kneeled on the ground when the snake had killed that dog, and the dog had killed that snake . . . but that's all still to come.

No, for now, this is all you need:

I made it home the next day.

I made it back to the city, to Archer Street, where everything *did* begin, and went many and varied ways. The argument about just why in the hell I'd brought back the dog and the snake dissipated hours ago, and those who were to leave have left, and those to stay have stayed. Arguing upon return with Rory about the contents of the car's back seat was the icing on the cake. Rory, of all the people. He, as much as anyone, knows who and why and what we are:

A family of ramshackle tragedy.

A comic book *kapow* of boys and blood and beasts.

We were born for relics like these.

In the middle of all the back-and-forth, Henry grinned, Tommy laughed, and both said, "Just like always." The fourth of us was sleeping, and had slept the whole time I was gone.

As for my two girls, when they came in, they marveled at the bones and said, "Why'd you bring those home, Dad?"

Because he's an idiot.

I caught Rory thinking it, immediately, but he'd never say it in front of my kids.

As for Claudia Dunbar—the former Claudia Kirkby—she shook her head and took my hand, and she was happy, she was so damn happy I could have broken down again. I'm sure it's because I was glad.

Glad.

Glad is a stupid-seeming word, but I'm writing and telling you all of this purely and simply because that's exactly how we are. I'm especially so because I love this kitchen now, and all its great and terrible history. I have to do it here. It's fitting to do it here. I'm glad to hear my notes get slapped to the page.

In front of me, there's the old TW.

Beyond it, a scratchy wooden tableland.

There are mismatched salt and pepper shakers, and a company of stubborn toast crumbs. The light from the hall is yellow, the light in here is white. I sit and think and hit here. I punch and punch away. Writing is always difficult, but easier with something to say:

Let me tell you about our brother.

The fourth Dunbar boy named Clay.

Everything happened to him.

We were all of us changed through him.

part one

cities

portrait of a killer as a middle-aged man

If before the beginning (in the writing, at least) was a typewriter, a dog, and a snake, the beginning itself—eleven years previously—was a murderer, a mule, and Clay. Even in beginnings, though, someone needs to go first, and on that day it could only be the Murderer. After all, he was the one who got everything moving forward, and all of us looking back. He did it by arriving. He arrived at six o'clock.

As it was, it was quite appropriate, too, another blistering February evening; the day had cooked the concrete, the sun still high, and aching. It was heat to be held and depended on, or, really, that had hold of *him*. In the history of all murderers everywhere, this was surely the most pathetic:

At five-foot-ten, he was average height.

At seventy-five kilos, a normal weight.

But make no mistake—he was a wasteland in a suit; he was bent-postured, he was broken. He leaned at the air as if waiting for it to finish him off, only it wouldn't, not today, for this, fairly suddenly, didn't feel like a time for murderers to be getting favors.

No, today he could sense it.

He could smell it.

He was immortal.

Which pretty much summed things up.

Trust the Murderer to be unkillable at the one moment he was better off dead.

* * *

For the longest time, then, ten minutes at least, he stood at the mouth of Archer Street, relieved to have finally made it, terrified to be there. The street didn't seem much to care; its breeze was close but casual, its smoky scent was touchable. Cars were stubbed out rather than parked, and the power lines drooped from the weight of mute, hot and bothered pigeons. Around it, a city climbed and called:

Welcome back, Murderer.

The voice so warm, beside him.

You're in a bit of strife here, I'd say. . . . In fact, a bit of strife doesn't even come close—you're in desperate trouble.

And he knew it.

And soon the heat came nearer.

Archer Street began rising to the task now, almost rubbing its hands together, and the Murderer fairly caught alight. He could feel it escalating, somewhere inside his jacket, and with it came the questions:

Could he walk on and finish the beginning?

Could he really see it through?

For a last moment he took the luxury—the thrill of stillness—then swallowed, massaged his crown of thorny hair, and with grim decision, made his way up to number eighteen.

A man in a burning suit.

Of course, he was walking that day at five brothers.

Us Dunbar boys.

From oldest to youngest:

Me, Rory, Henry, Clayton, Thomas.

We would never be the same.

To be fair, though, neither would he—and to give you at least a small taste of what the Murderer was entering into, I should tell you what we were like:

Many considered us tearaways.

Barbarians.

Mostly they were right:

Our mother was dead.

Our father had fled.

We swore like bastards, fought like contenders, and punished each other at pool, at table tennis (always on third- or fourth-hand tables, and often set up on the lumpy grass of the backyard), at Monopoly, darts, football, cards, at everything we could get our hands on.

We had a piano no one played.

Our TV was serving a life sentence.

The couch was in for twenty.

Sometimes when our phone rang, one of us would walk out, jog along the porch and go next door; it was just old Mrs. Chilman—she'd bought a new bottle of tomato sauce and couldn't get the wretched thing open. Then, whoever it was would come back in and let the front door slam, and life went on again.

Yes, for the five of us, life always went on:

It was something we beat into and out of each other, especially when things went completely right, or completely wrong. That was when we'd get out onto Archer Street in evening-afternoon. We'd walk at the city. The towers, the streets. The worried-looking trees. We'd take in the loudmouthed conversations hurled from pubs, houses, and unit blocks, so certain this was our place. We half expected to collect it all up and carry it home, tucked under our arms. It didn't matter that we'd wake up the next day to find it gone again, on the loose, all buildings and bright light.

Oh—and one more thing.

Possibly most important.

In amongst a small roster of dysfunctional pets, we were the only people we knew of, in the end, to be in possession of a mule.

And what a mule he was.

The animal in question was named Achilles, and there was a backstory longer than a country mile as to how he ended up in our suburban backyard in one of the racing quarters of the city. On one hand it involved the abandoned stables and practice track behind our house, an outdated council bylaw, and a sad old fat man with bad spelling. On the other it was our dead mother, our fled father, and the youngest, Tommy Dunbar.

At the time, not everyone in the house was even consulted; the mule's arrival was controversial. After at least one heated argument, with Rory—

("Oi, Tommy, what's goin' on 'ere?"

"What?"

"What-a-y' mean *what,* are you shitting me? There's a donkey in the backyard!"

"He's not a donkey, he's a mule."

"What's the difference?"

"A donkey's a donkey, a mule's a cross between—"

"I don't care if it's a quarter horse crossed with a Shetland bloody pony! What's it doin' under the clothesline?"

"He's eating the grass."

"I can see that!")

—we somehow managed to keep him.

Or more to the point, the mule stayed.

As was the case with the majority of Tommy's pets, too, there were a few problems when it came to Achilles. Most notably, the mule had ambitions; with the rear fly screen dead and gone, he was known to walk into the house when the back door was ajar, let alone left fully open. It happened at least once a week, and at least once a week I blew a gasket. It sounded something like this:

"Je-sus *Christ*!" As a blasphemer I was pretty rampant in those days, well known for splitting the Jesus and emphasizing the Christ. "If I've told you bastards once, I've told you a *hun*dred Goddamn times! *Shut* the back door!"

And so on.

Which brings us once more to the Murderer, and how could he have possibly known?

He could have guessed that when he got here, none of us might be home.

He could have known he'd have to decide between using his old key and waiting on the front porch—to ask his single question, to make his proposition.

It was human derision he expected, even invited, sure.

But nothing like this.

What a broadside:

The hurtful little house, the onslaught of silence.

And that burglar, that pickpocket, of a mule.

At somewhere near quarter past six, he went footstep for footstep with Archer Street, and the beast of burden blinked.

And so it was.

The first pair of eyes the Murderer met inside belonged to Achilles, and Achilles was not to be trifled with. Achilles was in the kitchen, a few steps from the back door, in front of the fridge, with his customary what-the-hell-you-lookin'-at look parked on his long, lopsided face. Flare-nostriled, he was even chewing a bit. Nonchalant. In control. If he was minding the beer he was doing a bloody good job.

Well?

At this point, Achilles seemed to be doing all the talking.

First the city, now the mule.

In theory, it made at least some semblance of sense. If something of the equine species might turn up anywhere in this city, it would be here; the stables, the practice track, the distant voice of race callers.

But a mule?

The shock was indescribable, and the surroundings certainly didn't help. This kitchen was a geography and climate all of its own:

Overcast walls.

Parched floor.

A coastline of dirty dishes stretching toward the sink.

And then the heat, the heat.

Even the mule's vigilant belligerence eased momentarily in consideration of this terrible, heavyweight heat. It was worse in here than outside, and that was an achievement not to be sniffed at.

Still, it didn't take Achilles long to be back on task, or was the Murderer so dehydrated he was hallucinating? Of all the kitchens in all the world. He thought fleetingly of shoving his knuckles into his eyes, to wring the vision out, but it was futile.

This was real.

He was sure this animal—this grey, patchy, ginger, light brown, thatch-faced, wide-eyed, fat-nostriled, casual bastard of a mule—was standing steadfast, on the cracked flooring, victorious, making one thing known, and irrefutably clear:

A murderer should probably do many things, but he should never, under any circumstances, come home.

warming up the clay way

ACROSS TOWN, WHILE THE MURDERER MET THE MULE, THERE WAS CLAY, AND Clay was warming up. Truth be told, Clay was always warming up. At that moment he was in an old apartment block, with stairs at his feet, a boy on his back, and a storm cloud in his chest. His short dark hair was flat on his head, and there was fire in each eye.

Running next to him, on his right, was another boy—a blond one, a year older—struggling to keep up, but pushing him all the same. On his left was a sprinting border collie, which made it Henry and Clay, Tommy and Rosy, doing what they always did:

One of them talked.

One of them trained.

One of them hung on for dear life.

Even the dog was giving her all.

For this training method, they had a key, they'd paid a friend; it guaranteed entry to the building. Ten dollars for a stuffed lump of concrete. Not bad. They ran.

"You miserable piece-a shit," said Henry (the moneymaker, the friendly one) at Clay's side. As he struggled, he loped and laughed. His smile swerved off his face; he caught it in his palm. At times like these, he communicated with Clay through tried and tested insults. "You're nothing," he said, "you're soft." He was hurting but had to talk on. "You're soft as a two-minute egg, boy. Makes me sick to watch you run like this."

It also wasn't long before another tradition was observed.

Tommy, the youngest, the pet collector, lost one of his shoes.

"Shit, Tommy, I thought I told you to tie 'em up better. Come on, Clay, you're weak, you're ridiculous. How 'bout havin' a bloody go?"

They reached the sixth floor and Clay dumped Tommy sideways and tackled the mouth on his right. They landed on the musty tiles, Clay half smiled, the other two laughed, and they all shrugged off the sweat. In the struggle, Clay got Henry in a headlock. He picked him up and ran him round.

"You really need a shower, mate." Typical Henry. We always said that to do Henry in we'd have to kill his mouth twice. "That's shockin', that is." He could feel the wire in Clay's arm as it wrung his smart-mouth neck.

To interrupt, Tommy, thoroughly thirteen, took a running jump and brought all three of them down, arms and legs, boys and floor. Around them, Rosy leapt and landed; her tail was up, her body forward. Black legs. White paws. She barked but they fought on.

When it was over, they lay on their backs; there was a window on this, the top floor of the stairwell, and grubby light, and rising-falling chests. The air was heavy. Tons of it, heaping from their lungs. Henry gulped it good and hard, but his mouth showed true heart.

"Tommy, you little bastard." He looked over and grinned. "I think you just saved my life, kid."

"Thanks."

"No, thank *you*," and he motioned now to Clay, who was already up on an elbow. His other hand down in his pocket. "I don't get why we put up with this lunatic."

"Me neither."

But they did.

For starters, he was a Dunbar boy, and with Clay you wanted to know.

What was it, though?

What was there to know when it came to Clayton, our brother?

Questions had followed him for years now, like why did he smile but never laugh?

Why did he fight but never to win?

Why did he like it so much on our roof?

Why did he run not for a satisfaction, but a discomfort—some sort of gateway to pain and suffering, and always putting up with it?

Not one of those inquiries, however, was his favorite.

They were warm-up questions.

Nothing more.

After lying on their backs, they did three more sets, Rosy cleaning up the stray shoe on the way.

"Oi, Tommy."

"Yeah?"

"Put 'em on tighter next time, right?"

"Sure, Henry."

"Double knots, or I'll cutcha in half."

"Okay, Henry."

At the bottom, he gave him a slap on the shoulder—the signal to get on Clay's back again—and they ran the stairs and came down in the lift. (Cheating in some people's minds, but actually much harder: it shortened the recovery.) After the last climb, Henry, Tommy, and Rosy took one more ride down, but Clay was taking the stairs. Outside, they walked over to Henry's iron slab of a car and went through the old routine:

"Rosy, get out of the front seat." She sat there at the wheel, her ears perfect triangles. She looked ready to adjust the radio. "Come on, Tommy, get her out of there, do us a favor."

"Here, girl, stop muckin' round."

Henry pocketed a hand.

A fistful of coins.

"Clay, here it is, we'll see you up there."

Two boys drove, the other ran.

Out the window: "Oi, Clay!"

He pushed on. He didn't turn around, but he heard all right. The same thing, every time.

"Get daisies if you can, they were her favorite, remember?"

As if he didn't know.

The car pulled out, blinker on. "And don't get done on the price!"

Clay ran faster.

He hit the hill.

In the beginning it was me who trained him, then Rory, and if I did it with an old-school brand of foolish integrity, Rory bludgeoned but never broke him. As for Henry, he'd made a scheme of it—he did it for the cash, but also because he loved it, which we'll witness soon enough.

From the outset, it was straightforward, yet stupefying:

We could tell him what to do.

He would do it.

We could torture him.

He'd endure it.

Henry could boot him out of the car because he'd seen a few mates walking home in the rain, and Clay would get out, he'd break into a jog. Then, when they drove past and shouted "Stop bludging!" out the window, he'd run faster. Tommy, guilty as all buggery, would look out the back, and Clay watching till the car dropped out of sight. He'd see the bad haircut getting smaller and smaller, and that was how it was:

It might have looked like we were training him.

But really, we weren't even close.

Through time the words became less and less, the methods more and more. We all knew what he wanted, but not what he was going to do with it.

What the hell was Clay Dunbar training for?

At six-thirty, tulips at his feet, he leaned forward, into the cemetery fence. It was nice and high, this place; Clay liked it. He watched the sun, grazing amongst the skyscrapers.

Cities.

This city.

Down there, the traffic was herded home. The lights changed. The Murderer came.

"Excuse me?"

Nothing. He tightened his grip on the fence.

"Young man?"

He looked over now and an old woman was pointing, sipping her lips. They must have been tasty.

"Would you mind?" She had shapeless eyes, a tired dress, and she was wearing stockings. The heat meant nothing to her. "Would you mind if I asked for one of those flowers?"

Clay looked into the deep wrinkle, a long streak above her eyes. He handed her a tulip.

"Thank you, thank you, young man. For my William."

The boy nodded and followed her through the open gate; he navigated the graves. When he got there he crouched he stood he folded his arms he faced the evening sun. He had no idea how long it took for Henry and Tommy to be either side, and the dog, tongue out, at the epitaphs. Each boy stood, slouched yet stiff, hands in pockets. If the dog had pockets, she'd have had her paws in them, too, for sure. All attention was then given to the gravestone and the flowers in front of it, wilting before their eyes.

"No daisies?"

Clay looked over.

Henry shrugged. "Okay, Tommy."

"What?"

"Hand it over, it's his turn."

Clay held out his hand. He knew what to do.

He took the Mr. Sheen and sprayed the metal plate. Next he was handed the arm of a grey T-shirt and gave the memorial a good rub, a good wipe.

"You missed a bit."

"Where?"

"Are you blind, Tommy, right there, in the corner, *look* there, are your eyes painted on?"

Clay watched them speak, then gave it a circular polish, and now the sleeve was black; the city's dirty mouth. All three of them were in singlets and old shorts. All three of them tightened their jaws. Henry gave Tommy a wink. "Good work, Clay, time to go, huh? Don't want to be late for the main event."

Tommy and the dog followed first, always the same.

Then Clay.

When he joined them, Henry said, "Good cemeteries make good neighbors." Honestly, his crap was endless.

Tommy said, "I hate coming here, you know that, don't you?"

And Clay?

Clay—who was the quiet one, or the smiler—only turned, one last time, and stared across the sunlit district of statues, crosses, and gravestones.

They looked like runners-up trophies.

Every last one.

barbarians

Back at 18 Archer Street, relations were at a stalemate in the kitchen.

The Murderer backed slowly away, into the rest of the house. Its silence was something awesome—an enormous playground for the guilt to wreak havoc, to work him over—but it was also a deception. The fridge hummed, the mule breathed, and there were more animals in there, too. Now that he'd reversed into the hallway, he could sense the movement. Was the Murderer being sniffed out and hunted down?

Not likely.

No, the animals didn't remotely pose a threat; it was the two eldest of us he feared most.

I was the responsible one:

The long-standing breadwinner.

Rory was the invincible one:

The human ball and chain.

Around six-thirty, Rory was across the street, leaning against a telegraph pole, smiling wry and rueful, smiling just for laughs; the world was filthy, and so was he. After a short search, he pulled a long strand of girls' hair from his mouth. Whoever she was, she was out there somewhere, she lay open-legged in Rory's head. A girl we'll never know, or see.

A moment earlier, he'd run into a girl we *did* know, a girl named Carey Novac. It was just beyond her driveway.

She smelt like horse, she'd called out hi.

She'd jumped off her old bike.

She had good-green eyes and auburn hair—miles of it down her back—and she gave him a message, for Clay. It had to do with a book; one of three important to everything. "Tell him I'm still loving Buonarroti, okay?"

Rory was taken aback, but didn't move. Only his mouth. "Borna-*who*?"

The girl laughed on her way to the garage. "Just tell him, okay?" But then she took pity, she tilted back, all freckly-armed and sure. There was a kind of generosity to her, of heat and sweat and life. "You know," she said, "Michelangelo?"

"What?" Now he was even more confused. The girl's mad, he thought. Sweet but totally mad. Who gives a shit about Michelangelo?

But somehow the thought endured.

He found that pole, he leaned a while, then crossed the road for home. Rory was a bit on the hungry side.

As for me, I was in there, out there, trapped in traffic.

Around, in front, and behind, thousands of cars were all lined up, all pointed the way of assorted homes. A steady wave of heat came through the window of my station wagon (the one I still own), and there was an endless cavalcade of billboards, shopfronts and people portions. With every movement, the city plowed inside, but there was also my signature smell of wood, wool and varnish.

I let my forearm poke from the car.

My body felt like lumber.

Both my hands were sticky with glue and turpentine, and all I wanted was to get home. I could have a shower then, and organize dinner, and maybe read, or watch an old movie.

That wasn't too much to ask for, was it?

Just get home and relax?

Not a Goddamn chance.

bernborough

On days like these, Henry had rules.

First, there had to be beer.

Second, it had to be cold.

For those reasons, he left Tommy, Clay, and Rosy at the cemetery and would meet them later, at Bernborough Park.

(Bernborough Park, for those unfamiliar with this neighborhood, is an old athletics field. Back then it was a crumbling grandstand, and a good car park's worth of broken glass. It was also the venue of Clay's most infamous training days.)

Before Henry got in the car, though, he felt it necessary to give Tommy some last-minute instructions. Rosy listened, too:

"If I'm late getting down there, tell 'em to hold their horses, right?"

"Sure, Henry."

"And tell them to have their money ready."

"Sure, Henry."

"Are you right with the 'Sure bloody Henrys,' Tommy?"

"I'm right."

"Keep going like this and I'll put you out there in front of him as well. Do you want that?"

"No thanks, Henry."

"Don't blame you, kid." A short smile at the end of a playful, well-exercised mind. He slapped Tommy's ear, soft and sure, then grabbed ahold of Clay. "And you—do me a favor." He gripped his face, a hand each side. "Don't leave these two bastards behind."

In the post-car wave of dust, the dog looked at Tommy.

Tommy looked at Clay.

Clay looked at neither one.

As he checked his pocket, there was so much in him that wanted to—to break again, into a run—but with the city splayed out in front of them, and the graveyard by their backs, he took two steps at Rosy, and tucked her under his arm.

He stood and the dog was smiling.

Her eyes like wheat and gold.

She laughed at the world below.

They were on Entreaty Avenue—the great hill he'd just ascended—when finally he put her down. They trod the rotten frangipanis, onto Poseidon Road: the racing quarter's headquarters. A rusted mile of shops.

While Tommy was aching for the pet store, Clay would die for other places; of streets, and monuments of *her*.

Lonhro, he thought.

Bobby's Lane.

The cobblestone Peter Pan Square.

She had auburn hair and good-green eyes, and was apprenticed to Ennis McAndrew. Her favorite horse was Matador. Her favorite race was always the Cox Plate. Her favorite winner of that race was the mighty Kingston Town, a good three decades before. (The best stuff happens before we're born.)

The book she read was *The Quarryman*.

One of three important to everything.

In the heat of Poseidon Road, the boys and the dog turned eastwards, and soon, it loomed: the athletics track.

They walked till they blended beside it, and in through a gap in the fence.

On the straight, in the sun, they waited.

Within minutes, the usual crowd appeared—boy vultures on a sports field carcass; the lanes were awash with weeds. The red Tartan Track peeled from the surface. Its infield had grown to a jungle.

"Look," said Tommy, and pointed.

More and more boys were arriving, from all directions of their peak pubescent glory. Even from a distance you could see their sunburn smiles, and count the suburban scars. You could also sense their odor: the smell of never quite men.

For a while, from the outside lane, Clay watched them. Drinking, scratching armpits. Throwing bottles. A few kicked at bedsores on the track—till soon enough, he'd seen enough.

He put a hand on Tommy's shoulder, and walked to the shade of the grandstand.

Its darkness ate him up.

the greeks got him

For the Murderer, it was an embarrassing consolation to find the rest of them in the lounge room—what we often referred to as Tommy's roster of shithead pets. And then, of course, the names. Some would say sublime, others again, ridiculous. He saw the goldfish first.

He'd followed a sideways glance, over toward the window, where the tank was on a stand, and the fish lunged forward and reeled itself back, butting the sheet of glass.

Its scales were like plumage.

Its tail a golden rake.

AGAMEMNON.

A peeling sticker along the bottom announced him in green marker pen in crowded, boyish lettering. The Murderer knew the name.

Next, on the eroded couch, asleep between the remote and a dirty sock, was a big grey brute of a cat: a tabby with giant black paws and a tail like an exclamation mark, who went by the name of Hector.

On many counts, Hector was the most despised animal in the house, and today, even in such heat, he was curled up like a furry fat C, except for his tail, which was stuck into him like a shaggy sword. When he changed positions, fur flew off him in droves, but he slept on, undiminished, and purring. Someone need only go near him to set the motor running. Even murderers. Hector was never very discerning.

Last, on top of the bookshelf, sat a long, large birdcage.

Inside it was a pigeon, waiting sternly still but happy.

The door was completely open.

Once or twice, when he stood and walked, his purple head bobbed with great economy, he moved in perfect rhythm. That was what the pigeon did, each and every day, as he waited to perch on Tommy.

These days we called him Telly.

Or T.

But never, no matter the occasion, his full, infuriating name:

Telemachus.

God, how we hated Tommy for those names.

The single reason he got away with it was that we all understood:

That kid knew what he was doing.

A few steps in now, the Murderer looked.

This appeared to be the lot:

One cat, one bird, one goldfish, one murderer.

And the mule, of course, in the kitchen.

A pretty undangerous bunch.

In the weird light, in the hung heat, and amongst the other articles of the lounge room—a used and abused old laptop, the coffee-stained couch arms, the schoolbooks in cairns on the carpet—the Murderer felt it loom, just behind his back. The only thing it didn't do was say *boo:*

The piano.

The piano.

Christ, he thought, the piano.

Wooden, walnut and upright, it stood in the corner with its mouth closed and a sea of dust on top:

Deep and calm, sensationally sad.

A piano, that was all.

If it seems innocuous enough, think again, for his left foot began to twitch. His heart ached with such force that he could have burst back out the front door.

What a time for first feet on the porch.

* * *

There was key, there was door, there was Rory, and not a moment to straighten up. Any words the Murderer might have prepared had vanished from his throat, and there wasn't much air in there, either. Just the taste of beating heart. He was only able to glimpse him, too, for he was through that hallway like a streak. The great shame was that he couldn't tell who it was.

Rory or me?

Henry or Clay?

It wasn't Tommy, surely. Too big.

All he'd sensed was a moving body, and now a roar of delight from the kitchen.

"Achilles! You cheeky bastard!"

The fridge opened and shut, and that's when Hector looked up. He thumped down onto the carpet and stretched his back legs in that shaky cat-like way. He wandered into the kitchen from the other side. The voice immediately changed.

"What the hell do you want, Hector, you heavy heap of shit? Jump on my bed again tonight and it's all bloody over for you, I swear it." The rustle of bread bags, the opening of jars. Then another laugh. "Good old Achilles, ay?" Of course, he didn't get rid of him. Get Tommy to deal with it, he thought. Or even better, he'd just let me find him later. That'd be pure gold—and that was it.

As fast as he'd come in, there was another glimpse in the hallway, a slam of the front door, and he was gone.

As you might imagine, it took a while to recover from that.

Many heartbeats, many breaths.

His head sank, his thoughts gave thanks.

The goldfish butted the tank.

The bird watched him, then marched, end to end, like a colonel, and soon the return of the cat; Hector entered the lounge room, and sat, as if in audience. The Murderer was sure he could hear his pulse—the din of it, the friction. He could feel it himself in his wrists.

If nothing else, one thing now was certain.

He had to sit down.

In quick time he got a stronghold on the couch.

The cat licked its lips and pounced.

The Murderer looked back and saw him in full flight—a thick grey chunk of fur and stripes—and he braced himself and took it. For a moment, at least, he wondered; should he pat the cat or not? It didn't matter to Hector—he was purring the house down, right there on his lap. He even started happy paws, he butchered the Murderer's thighs. And now came someone else.

He almost couldn't believe it.

They're coming.

They're coming.

The boys are coming, and here I am with the heaviest domesticated cat in history sitting on me. He might as well have been stranded under an anvil, and a purring one at that.

This time it was Henry, wiping hair from his eyes and walking purposefully to the kitchen. For him it was a lot less hilarious, but certainly no more urgent:

"Yeah, good one, Achilles, thanks for the memories—Matthew's sure to blow another stack tonight."

Would I ever!

Next he opened the fridge, and this time there were some manners. "Can you just move your head there, please, mate? Thanks."

He clinked, reaching and lifting, throwing beer cans into a cooler—and soon he was on his way again, bound for Bernborough Park, and the Murderer, again, remained.

What was going on here?

Could no one intuit the killer?

No, it wasn't going to be that easy, and now he was left, this time crushed on the couch, to contemplate the term of his natural invisibility. He was caught—somewhere between the relief of its mercy and the shame of its impotence—and he sat there, simple and still. Around him, a cyclone of loose cat hair whirled in the evening light. The goldfish resumed its war with the glass, and the pigeon hit full stride.

And the piano watched him from behind.

the human ball and chain

At Bernborough Park, when the last of them turned up, they shook hands, they laughed. They reveled. They drank in that adolescent way, all greedy-mouthed and wide open. They said "Oi!" and "Hey!" and "Where the hell have you been, you dopey deadshit?" They were virtuosos of alliteration and didn't know it.

As soon as he'd stepped from his car, Henry's first order of business was to make sure Clay was in the grandstand dressing sheds. Down there he'd meet today's batch; there'd be six boys, all waiting, and what would happen was this:

They'd walk back out the tunnel.

Each of those six boys would then position himself around the 400-meter track.

Three at the 100-meter mark.

Two at the 200.

And one anywhere from the 300 to the finish.

Last, and most importantly, all six would do everything in their power to stop Clay running a single lap. Easier said than done.

As for the mob who watched, they guessed at the result. Each would call out a specific time, and that's where Henry came in. Henry, very willingly, handled the bets. A stump of chalk in his hand, an old-school stopwatch round his neck, and he was set.

* * *

Today, several boys were at him immediately, down at the foot of the grandstand. To Henry, many of them weren't even real—they were nicknames with boys attached. As for us, for all but two of them, we'll see them here, we'll leave them here, they'll be fools like this forever. It's kind of nice, when you think of it.

"Well, Henry?" asked Leper. You can only pity a guy with a nickname like that; there were scabs of various shapes, sizes, and colors all over him. Apparently he'd started doing stupid things on his bike when he turned eight, and never stopped.

Henry very nearly took pity on him, but opted instead for a smirk. "Well, what?"

"How tired is he?"

"Not very."

"Has he run up Crapper's stairwell yet?" This time it was Chugs. Charlie Drayton. "And up the hill to the graveyard?"

"Look, he's good, all right, he's in mint condition." Henry rubbed his hands together, in warm anticipation. "We've got six of the best down there, too. Even Starkey."

"*Starkey!* That bastard's back, is he? That's worth at least another thirty seconds, I reckon."

"Oh, come on, Trout, Starkey's all talk. Clay'll run right past him."

"How many floors in that apartment block again, Crapps?"

"Six," said Henry, "and that key's getting a bit rusty, too, old boy. Fix us up for a new one and I might even let you bet free."

Crapper, curly-haired, curly-faced, licked his curly lips. "What? Really?"

"Okay, maybe half."

"Hey," said a guy named Spook, "how come *Crapps* gets a free bet?"

Henry interrupted before there was anything *to* interrupt. "*Unforchantly*, Spook, you pale, poor bastard, Crapps has got something we can use; he's use*ful*." He walked with him, he mentored. "You, on the other hand, are use*less*. Get it?"

"Okay, Henry, how about this?" Crapper tried for more. "You can have *my* key if you give me three bets gratis."

"*Gratis?* What are you, bloody French?"

"I don't think the French say gratis, Henry. I think it might be German."

That voice had come from out of the pack; Henry sought it out. "Was that you, Chewie, you hairy bastard? Last I heard you couldn't speak fucking English!" To the rest of them: "Can you believe that awful prick?"

They laughed. "Good one, Henry."

"And don't think a 'Good one, Henry'll do *you* any extra favors."

"Hey, Henry." Crapper. One last try. "How about—"

"Oh, *Jesus*!" His voice erupted in fury, but Henry did mock-anger, not anger itself. At seventeen, he'd endured much of what life as a Dunbar could throw at him, and he always came up smiling. He also had a soft spot for Wednesdays here at Bernborough, and the boys who watched from the fence. He loved that all of this was their midweek main event, and to Clay it was one more warm-up. "All right, you bastards, who's up first? It's ten up front or piss off!"

He jumped to a splintery bench.

From there the bets went this way and that, from 2:17 to 3:46 to a resounding 2:32. With his stump of green chalk, Henry wrote the names and times on the concrete at their feet; next to bets from previous weeks.

"All right, come on, Showbag, enough's enough."

Showbag, also known as Vong, or Kurt Vongdara, had agonized a long time. He took few things very seriously, but this, it seemed, was one of them. "Okay," he said. "With Starkey out there, make it, shit—5:11."

"Jesus." Henry smiled from his crouching stance. "And remember, boys, no mind-changing, either, or messing with the chalk—"

He saw something.

Someone.

They'd missed each other by minutes, back home in the kitchen, but now he saw him—hard and unmistakable, of dark-rust hair, and scrap-metal eyes, and chewing a piece of gum. Henry was utterly delighted.

"What's up?" A collective question, a chorus. "What is it? What's—" and

Henry nodded upwards, to coincide with the voice, which landed amongst the chalk.

"Gentlemen—"

And for just a moment, each boy wore an oh-shit look that was utterly priceless, then all burst into action.

Everyone changed their bets.

smoke signal

All right, that's it.

He'd had enough.

Grim and guilty and regretful as he was, the Murderer had come to a point; we could despise him, but we wouldn't ignore him. Then again, his next move also felt like good manners—that since he'd entered the house without permission, he really should have warned us:

He extracted Hector from his lap.

He walked toward the piano.

Rather than open the lid to the keys (no way could he face doing *that*), he exposed the strings from above, and what he found was possibly worse—for lying there, inside, were two charcoal-colored books, on an old blue woolen dress. In a pocket was one of its buttons, and beneath the dress what he'd gone there for: a packet of cigarettes.

Slowly, he took it out.

His body folded up.

He fought hard to lift and straighten.

It took an effort to close the piano again, and walk back into the kitchen. He fished a lighter from out of the cutlery drawer, and stood before Achilles.

"Bugger it."

For the first time, he dared to speak. He'd realized now that the mule wasn't fit for attack, and so the Murderer lit up, and made his way toward the sink.

"I might as well do the dishes while I'm at it."

the idiots

INSIDE, THE WALLS OF THE DRESSING ROOM WERE SAD WITH GRAFFITI—THE kind of amateur work that was nothing short of embarrassing. Clay sat barefoot, he ignored it. In front of him, Tommy was picking knots of grass from Rosy's stomach, but the border collie soon came over. He clamped a hand down gently on her snout.

"Dunbar."

As expected, there were six other boys, each in his own small region of the graffiti. Five of them talked and joked with each other. One paraded a girl: the animal-boy named Starkey.

"Hey, Dunbar."

"What?"

"Not you, Tommy, y' bloody nitwit."

Clay looked up.

"Here." Starkey lobbed a roll of masking tape, hitting him in the chest. When it landed on the floor, Rosy scooped it up and held it in her jaws. Clay watched her wrestle it, as Starkey ranted on.

"I just don't want you having any excuses when I tidy you up out there, that's all. That, and I've got vivid memories of you pulling that sticky tape shit when we were younger. *And* there's a lot of broken glass out there. Wouldn't want you hurting your pretty little feet."

"Did you say *vivid?*" asked Tommy.

"A thug can't have vocab? I said *nitwit*, too, and that applied brilliantly to the likes of you." Starkey and the girl enjoyed that one, and Clay couldn't help quite liking her. He watched her lipstick and grimy grin. He also liked her bra strap, flopping over her shoulder the way it did. He didn't mind the way they touched and sort of smudged each other, either—her crotch on his thigh, a leg each side. It was a curiosity, but nothing more. First, she was no Carey Novac. Second, this was nothing personal. To those outside, the boys in here were cogs in a beautiful machinery; a tainted entertainment. To Clay, they were colleagues of a particular design. How much could they damage him? How much could he survive?

He knew it was soon they'd be walking out, so now he leaned back, he closed his eyes, he imagined Carey beside him; the heat and light of her arms. In her face the freckles were pinpricks—so deep and red, but minuscule—like a diagram, or even better, a schoolkid's connect-the-dots sheet. In her lap was the pale-covered book they shared, with its bronze and fractured lettering: THE QUARRYMAN.

Under the title it said, *Everything you've ever wanted to know about Michelangelo Buonarroti—an infinite quarry of greatness*. Inside, at the very front, was the torn-off line of a missing page; the one with the author's biography. The bookmark was a recent betting slip:

Royal Hennessey, Race 5
#2—Matador
Win only: $1

Soon, she stood, then leaned at him.

She smiled in that interested way she had, like facing front-on at everything. She came closer and began; she put her bottom lip on his top one, and held the book between them. *"He knew right then that this was the world, and all it was was a vision."*

As she quoted a favorite page, her mouth kept touching his—three times, four times, make it five—and now just slightly away:

"Saturday?"

A nod, for on Saturday night, just over three more days, they'd meet in reality, in his other favorite, forgotten field. A place called The Surrounds. There, in that place, they'd lie awake. Her hair could itch him for hours. But never would he move it, or adjust.

"Clay." She was fading. ". . . It's time."

But he didn't want to open his eyes.

In the meantime, a bucktoothed kid they called Ferret was out, and Rory, as always, was in. Whenever he showed up for old times' sake, that was how it went.

He walked down the tunnel and entered the depressing dressing room, and even Starkey stopped showboating with the girl. Rory held a finger up, hard against his lips. He gave Tommy an almost unfriendly rummage of the hair, and stood now, over Clay. He examined him, smiling, casually, with his priceless, scrap-metal eyes.

"Oi, Clay." He couldn't resist. "Still mixed up in this bullshit, huh?"

And Clay smiled back, he had to.

He smiled but didn't look up.

"Ready, boys?"

Henry, stopwatch in hand, let them know.

As Clay stood up, Tommy asked him; all just part of the ritual.

He pointed casually toward his pocket.

"You want me to mind it for you, Clay?"

Clay said nothing but told him.

The answer was always the same.

He didn't even shake his head.

From there, they left the graffiti behind.

They walked back out the tunnel.

They shaped up to the light.

In the arena were approximately two dozen idiots, half each side, to clap them out. Idiots clapping idiots, it was tremendous. It was what this mob did best.

"Come on, boys!"

The voices were warm. Clapping hands.

"Run hard, Clay! Dig 'em in, son!"

The yellow light persisted behind the grandstand.

"Don't kill 'im, Rory!"

"Hit him hard, Starkers, y' ugly bastard!"

Laughter. Starkey stopped.

"Oi." He pointed a finger and quoted the movies. "Maybe I'll practice on you first." *Ugly bastard* he didn't mind one bit, but he couldn't abide *Starkers*. He looked behind and saw his girl venture to the firewood seats in the grandstand. She had no business with the rest of this riffraff; surely one was bad enough. He shuffled his big frame to catch up.

Briefly they were all on the straight, but soon the dressing room boys drifted away. The first three would be Seldom, Maguire, and Tinker: two with agility and strength, and one brick outhouse to smother him.

The pair at the 200 would be Schwartz and Starkey, of which one was a perfect gentleman, and one a certified beast. The thing with Schwartz, though, was that while he was completely, emphatically fair, he'd be devastating in the contest. Afterwards, he'd be all white-tooth smiles and pats on the back. But at the discus net, he'd hit him like a train.

The gamblers were now on the move as well.

They spilled upwards, to the highest row of the grandstand, to see out past the infield.

The boys on track were prepared:

They punched the meat of their quadriceps.

They stretched and slapped their arms.

At the 100 mark, they stood a lane apart. They had great aura, their legs were alight. The falling sun behind.

At the 200, Schwartz was moving his head, side to side. Blond hair, blond eyebrows, focused eyes. Next to him, Starkey spat on the track. The whiskers on his face were dirty and alert, perpendicular to his cheeks. His hair was like a doormat. Again, he stared and spat.

"Hey," Schwartz said, but he didn't take his eyes from the 100. "We might land in that in a sec."

"So?"

Then, lastly, down on the straight, maybe fifty meters from the end, Rory stood, quite easily, as if moments like these were reasonable; it was how they were meant to be.

the magician's handkerchief

FINALLY, THE NOISE OF AN ENGINE:

The car door sound like a stapler.

He tried to fend it away, but the Murderer's pulse churned that little bit extra, most notably at the neck. He was almost desperate enough to ask Achilles to wish him luck, but at long last the mule looked a little vulnerable himself; he sniffed, and shifted a hoof.

Footsteps on the porch now.

The keyhole entered and turned.

I instantly smelt the smoke.

In the doorway, a long list of blasphemy fell silently from my mouth. A magician's hanky of shock and horror, it was followed by miles of indecision, and a pair of bloodless hands. What do I do? What the hell do I do?

How long did I stand there?

How many times did I consider turning and walking back out?

In the kitchen (as I learned much later), the Murderer stood quietly up. He breathed the sultry air. He looked gratefully at the mule:

Don't even think about leaving me now.

the smiler

"THREE . . . TWO . . . ONE . . . NOW."

The stopwatch clicked, and Clay was on his way.

Lately they always did it like this; Henry loved how skiers were sent down the mountain on TV, and adopted the same method here.

As usual, Clay had started the countdown a distance from the line. He was impassive, blank-faced, and his barefoot feet felt great. They hit the line nicely for the *now*. Only when he started to run did he feel a pair of tears, bitten and burning, swell inside his eyes. Only then did his fists tighten; he was ready for it now, this idiots' brigade, this terrifically teenaged world. He would never see it or be it again.

The weeds at his feet swung left and right, they swayed to get out of his way. Even his breath seemed to come out of him only to escape. Still there was no feeling on his face. Just the two arching tear lines, drying as he took the first bend, toward Seldom, Maguire, and Tinker. Clay knew how to hurt them. He had one or two of most things, but also a thousand elbows.

"Here."

Business-like, they converged.

They met him in Lane Four with noxious sweat and forearms, and his legs continued to run, diagonally in the air. Momentum, somehow, was his. His right hand dug into the rubber, then a knee, and he threw Maguire behind him; he fended Seldom's face. In an instant he could see the poor guy fog up, and he brought him down next, and hard.

By then, the rotund Brian "Tinker" Bell—with the secondary nickname of Mr. Plump—came in with a gluttonous thump. It was a fist across the throat, an ample chest against his back. He whispered, hot and hoarsely, "I gotcha now." Clay didn't like being whispered to like that. He also didn't care much for *gotcha,* and very soon there was a very sad sack lying amongst the weeds. A sack with a bleeding ear. "Fark!" The boy was gone.

Yes, Tinker was forgotten, but the other two came back, one hurt, one strong; it wasn't enough. Clay pushed away. He strode out. He took hold of the worn back straight.

Now he eyed the next two, and they hadn't expected him so soon.

Schwartz steadied himself.

Starkey spat again. The guy was a Goddamn fountain. A gargoyle!

"Come on!"

That was the creature in Starkey's voice box now, crying a call to arms. He should have known better, that Clay wouldn't be threatened, or inflamed. In the background, the first three boys were hunched, all just blurry shapes, as he swung out wide, then changed. He aimed more for Starkey, who by now wasn't spitting, but veering. He reacted barely in time to get a finger onto the very top thread of Clay's shorts, and then, of course, came Schwartz.

As promised, Schwartz hit him like a train.

The 2:13 express.

His neat fringe came over the top as he buried him, half into Lane One, half in the wall of weeds, and Starkey followed with his knees. He gored Clay's cheek with that facial hair. He even pinched him as they went kicking and a-gouging in the blood and the shove and Starkey's beer breath. (God, that poor girl up in the bleachers.)

As if in suffocation, their feet kicked at the Tartan.

Seemingly miles away, a complaint arrived from the grandstand. "Can't see a bloody thing!" If it went any longer in the infield, they'd have to run to the bend.

Inside the Bernborough Park greenery, there was a lot of grappling, but

Clay always found a way. To him, there was no win at the end of this, or a loss, or a time, or the money. It didn't matter how much they hurt him, they couldn't hurt him. Or how much they held him, they couldn't hold him. Or at least, they couldn't quite hurt him *enough*.

"Pin that knee!"

A prudent suggestion by Schwartz, but too late. A free kneecap was a free Clay, and he was able to push himself off, hurdle the hundred kilos at his feet, and accelerate.

There were cheers now, and whistles.

A herd of nicknames came charging down, grandstand to track. From that distance their calls were very vague—more like the songs in his bedroom when the nighttime southerly came—but they were there, all right, and so was Rory.

For 150 meters, Clay had the ochre-red surface to himself. His heart clanged, the dry tear lines cracked apart.

He ran at the refusing light, at its stubborn, bulky rays.

He looked into his gait, at the elastic width of Tartan.

He ran at the cheers of boys, who called from the grandstand shade. Somewhere in there was that red-mouthed girl and her careless, wayward shoulder. There was no sex in the thought, just that similar thread of amusement. He wondered about her deliberately, for a suffering was soon to begin. It didn't matter that this was the fastest he'd ever got here. Nothing. It meant nothing, because there, fifty meters from the finish, Rory now stood like a rumor.

Leading in, Clay knew he should be decisive. To hesitate would ruin him. Timidity could kill him. Not long before they met, at the far right margin of his sight, there was twenty-four boys' worth of miscellaneous shouts. They damn near brought the grandstand down, and before them a glimpse of Rory. He was typically raw and wry.

And Clay?

He fought every urge, to sidestep, left or right. He virtually climbed into him and somehow made it over. He felt his brother's anatomy: his love and lovable anger. There was collision between boy and ground, and just the one foot was held now. One arm locked around his ankle was the only thing standing between Clay and something long considered unachievable. There was no getting past Rory. Never. Yet there he was, dragging him behind. He was stretching back to palm him off. His arm stiffened, but an inch or two from Rory's face, a hand rose up like a titan out of the deep. A handshake from hell, he crushed Clay's fingers with one effortless clinch, and with it, he ripped him downwards.

Ten meters short, he hit the track completely, and what was it about Rory's weightlessness? That was the irony of the nickname. A human ball and chain implied an unbearable heaviness, but here he was more like a mist. You turned and he was there, but when you reached out, nothing was left. He was already somewhere else, causing danger up ahead. The only things of mass and weight were the depth and rust of his hair, and those hard grey metal eyes.

Now he had a good hold of him, on the red and buried track. Voices were climbing down to them, from boys and folding sky.

"Come on, Clay. Jesus, ten meters, you're almost there."

Tommy: "What would Zola Budd do, Clay? What would the Flying Scotsman do? Fight him to the line!"

Rosy barked.

Henry: "He really surprised you, Rory, huh?"

Rory, looking up, gave him a quizzical smile of the eyes.

Another non-Dunbar voice, to Tommy: "Who the hell's Zola Budd? And the Flying Scotchman, for that matter?"

"Scotsman."

"Whatever."

"Would you lot please shut up? There's a stoush on here!"

It was often like this when the struggle set in.

The boys lingered, watching and half wishing they had the heart for it themselves, but grateful like hell they didn't. The talk was a security measure, for there was something slightly gruesome about them, scissored on the track, with paper lungs and breath.

Clay twisted, but Rory was there.

Only once, several minutes in, he nearly pulled loose, but again he was held up short. This time he could see the line, he could almost smell the paint.

"Eight minutes," Henry said. "Hey, Clay, you had enough?"

A rough but certain corridor was formed; they knew to show respect. If a boy might pull a phone out, to film or take a photo, he'd be set upon and duly thrashed.

"Hey, Clay." Henry, marginally louder. "Enough?"

No.

It was said, as always, without being said, for he wasn't smiling yet.

Nine minutes, ten, soon it was thirteen, and Rory was thinking of strangling him; but then, close to the fifteen-minute mark, Clay eventually relaxed, threw back his head, and very slackly, grinned. As a faint reward, right through all the boys' legs, he saw the girl up in the shade, bra strap and all, and Rory sighed, "Thank Christ." He fell to the side, and watched as Clay—very slowly, with one good hand, and one trailing—dragged himself over the line.

murder music

I GOT MYSELF TOGETHER.

I entered the kitchen with force—and there, by the fridge, stood Achilles.

Beside the mountain of clean dishes, I looked from murderer to mule and back again, deciding who to take first.

The lesser of two evils.

"Achilles," I said. There had to be great control in that annoyance, that fed-up-ness. "For Christ's sake, did those bastards leave the back door open again?"

The mule, true to form, toughed it out, deadpan.

Bluntly, boredly, he asked the usual pair of questions:

What?

What's so unusual about this?

He was right; it was the fourth or fifth time that month. Probably close to a record.

"Here," I said, handling him quickly, holding the thatch of his neck.

At the door I spoke back to the Murderer.

Back but matter-of-fact.

"Just so you know, you're next."

like a hurricane

THE CITY WAS DARK BUT ALIVE.

The car, inside, was quiet.

There was nothing now but homecoming.

Earlier, the beer had come out, it was shared around.

Seldom, Tinker, Maguire.

Schwartz and Starkey.

They all took some cash, as did the kid called Leper, who'd bet fourteen minutes flat. When he'd started gloating, they all told him to go get a skin graft. Henry kept the rest. All of it was performed under a pink and grey sky. The best graffiti in town.

At one point, Schwartz was telling them about the spitting shenanigans at the 200, and the girl had asked the question. She loitered with Starkey in the car park.

"What the hell's wrong with that guy?" That wasn't the question in question, though; it would be here in moments to come. "Running like that. Fighting like that." She thought about it and scoffed. "What sort of stupid game is it, anyway? You're all a bunch of dumbshits."

"Dumbshits," said Starkey, "thanks a lot." He put his arm around her like it was a compliment.

"Hey, love!"

Henry.

Both girl and gargoyle turned, and Henry swerved a smile. "It's not a game, it's just training!"

She put a hand on her hip, and you know what she asked next, the lacy-limp girl, and Henry would do his best. "Go on, Clay, enlighten us. What the hell are you training for?"

But Clay had turned from her shoulder this time. He felt his pulse in the graze on his cheekbone—courtesy of Starkey's whiskers. With his good hand, he searched his pocket, very deliberately, then crouched.

It bears mentioning now that exactly what our brother was training for was as much a mystery to him. He only knew that he was working and waiting for the day he'd find out—and that day, as it was, was today. It was waiting at home in the kitchen.

Carbine Street and Empire Lane, and then the stretch of Poseidon.

Clay always liked this ride home.

He liked the moths gathering tall and tight-knit at their various street-light postings. He wondered if the night excited or soothed and settled them; if nothing else, it gave them purpose. These moths knew what to do.

Soon they came to Archer Street.

Henry: driving, one-handed, smiling.

Rory: feet up on the dash.

Tommy: half asleep against the quick-panting Rosy.

Clay: unknowing this was it.

Eventually, Rory couldn't take it any longer—the calmness.

"Shit, Tommy, does that dog have to pant so bloody loud?"

Three of them laughed, short and stout.

Clay looked out the window.

Maybe it would have been fitting for Henry to drive the car ramshackle, to rampage onto the driveway, but it wasn't like that at all.

The blinker on at Mrs. Chilman's, next door.

A tranquil turn at our place—as clean as his car could be.

Headlights off.

Doors opened.

The only thing betraying total peace was the closing of the car. With four quick shots, the doors were fired at the house, and all went straight for the kitchen.

Together, they crossed the lawn.

"Any of you bastards know what's for dinner?"

"Leftovers."

"That'd be right."

Their feet all plowed the porch.

"Here they come," I said, "so you might as well get ready to leave."

"I understand."

"You understand nothing."

Right then I was trying to work out why I'd let him stay. Just a few minutes earlier, when he'd told me why he'd come, my voice had ricocheted off the dishes and gone right for the Murderer's throat:

"You want *what*?"

Maybe it was the belief that this was already in motion; it was going to happen anyway, and if the moment was now, so be it. Also, despite the Murderer's pitiful state, I could also sense something else. There was resolve there as well, and sure, throwing him out would have been such a pleasure—oh, grabbing his arm. Standing him up. Pushing him out the door. Jesus H. Christ, it would have been bloody beautiful! But it would also leave us open. The Murderer could strike again when I wasn't around.

No. Better like this.

The best way of controlling it was to have all five of us together in a show of strength.

Okay, stop.

Make that four of us, and one betrayer.

This time, it was instant.

Henry and Rory might have failed to sense the danger earlier, but now the house was rich with it. There was argument in the air, and the smell of burnt cigarette.

"Shh." Henry slung an arm back and whispered. "Careful."

They walked the hallway. "Matthew?"

"Here." Pensive and deep, my voice confirmed everything.

For a few moments, the four of them looked at each other, alert, confused, all rifling through some internal catalogue, for their next official move.

Henry again: "You all right, Matthew?"

"I'm brilliant, just get in 'ere."

They shrugged, they open-palmed.

There was no reason now not to go in, and one by one, they stepped toward the kitchen, where the light was like a river mouth. It changed from yellow to white.

Inside, I was standing at the sink, arms folded. Behind me were the dishes; clean and gleaming, like a rare, exotic museum piece.

To their left, at the table, was him.

God, can you hear it?

The hearts of them?

The kitchen was its own small continent now, and the four boys, they stood in no-man's-land, before a kind of group migration. When they made it to the sink, we stayed close in together, and Rosy somewhere between us. It's funny that way, how boys are; we don't mind touching—shoulders, elbows, knuckles, arms—and all of us looked at our killer, who was sitting, alone, at the table. A total nervous wreck.

What was there to think?

Five boys and scrambled thoughts, and a show of teeth from Rosy.

Yes, the dog knew instinctively to despise him as well, and it was she who broke the silence; she snarled and edged toward him.

I pointed, calm and mean. "Rosy."

She stopped.

The Murderer's mouth soon opened.

But nothing at all came out.

The light was aspirin-white.

The kitchen began to open then, or at least it did for Clay. The rest of the house broke off, and the backyard dropped, into nothingness. The city and suburbs and all the forgotten fields were razed and chopped away, in one apocalyptic sweep—black. For Clay there was only here, the kitchen, which in one evening had grown from climate to continent, and now this:

A world with table-and-toaster.

Of brothers and sweat by the sink.

The oppressive weather remained; its atmosphere hot and grainy, like the air before a hurricane.

As if pondering that, the Murderer's face seemed far away, but soon he hauled it in. Now, he thought, you have to do it now, and he did, he made a colossal effort. He stood, and there was something terrifying about his sadness. He'd imagined this moment countless times, but he'd arrived here hollowed out. A shell of all he was. He might as well have tumbled from the wardrobe, or appeared from under the bed:

A meek and mixed-up monster.

A nightmare, suddenly fresh.

But then—abruptly, it was enough.

A silent declaration was made, and years of stable suffering was intolerable for another second; the chain was cracked, then broken. The kitchen had seen all it could that day, and ground to a halt at *here:* five bodies facing *him.* Five boys were joined, but now one was alone, standing, exposed—for he wasn't touching a brother anymore—and he liked it and he loathed it. He welcomed it, he mourned it. There was nothing else but to take that step, to the only black hole of the kitchen:

He reached inside his pocket again, and when he pulled it back up, there were pieces; he held them out in his hand. They were warm and red and plastic—the shards of a shattered clothes peg.

And what, after that, was left?

Clay called over, his voice in the quiet, from the dark toward the light:

"Hi, Dad."

part two

cities + waters

the mistake maker

Once, in the tide of Dunbar past, there was a many-named woman, and what a woman she was.

First, the name she was born with: Penelope Lesciuszko.

Then the one christened at her piano: the Mistake Maker.

In transit they called her the Birthday Girl.

Her self-proclaimed nickname was the Broken-Nosed Bride.

And last, the name she died with: Penny Dunbar.

Quite fittingly, she'd traveled from a place that was best described by a phrase in the books she was raised on.

She came from a watery wilderness.

Many years ago, and like so many before her, she arrived with a suitcase and a scrunched-up stare.

She was astounded by the mauling light here.

This city.

It was so hot and wide, and white.

The sun was some sort of barbarian, a Viking in the sky.

It plundered, it pillaged.

It got its hands on everything, from the tallest stick of concrete to the smallest cap in the water.

In her former country, in the Eastern Bloc, the sun had mostly been a toy, a gizmo. There, in that far-off land, it was cloud and rain, ice and snow, that wore the pants—not that funny little yellow thing that showed its face every now and again; its warmer days were rationed. Even on the boniest, barren afternoons there was a chance of moisture. Drizzle. Wet feet. It was communist Europe at its slow-descending peak.

In a lot of ways it defined her. Escaping. Alone.

Or more to the point, lonely.

She would never forget landing here in sheer terror.

From the air, in a circling plane, the city looked at the mercy of its own brand of water (the salty kind), but on the ground, it didn't take long to feel the full force of its true oppressor; her face was dappled immediately with sweat. Outside, she stood with a flock, a herd—no, a rabble—of equally shocked and sticky people.

After a long wait, the lot of them were rounded up. They were corralled into a sort of indoor tarmac. The light globes were all fluorescent. The air was floor-to-ceiling heat.

"Name?"

Nothing.

"Passport?"

"*Przepraszam?*"

"Oh, Jesus." The man in uniform stood on his toes and looked above the heads and hordes of new immigrants. What a mob of sorry, sweltering faces! He found the man he wanted. "Hey, George! Bilski! I got one here for you!"

But now the woman who was nearly twenty-one but appeared sixteen gripped him firmly in the face. She held her grey-colored booklet as if to strangle its edges of air. "Parshporrt."

A smile, of resignation. "Okay, love." He opened it up and took a stab at the riddle of her name. "Leskazna-*what?*"

Penelope helped him out, timid but defiant. "*Less-choosh-ko.*"

She knew no one here.

The people who'd been in camp with her for nine months in the Austrian mountains had broken away. While they were sent, family after family, west across the Atlantic, Penelope Lesciuszko would make a longer journey, and now she was here. All that remained was to get to camp, learn English better, find a job and a place to live. Then, most importantly, buy a bookshelf. And a piano.

Those few things were all she wanted from this new world laid searingly out in front of her, and as time went by, she got them. She got them, all right, and a whole lot more.

I'm sure you've met certain people in this world and heard their stories of lucklessness, and you wonder what they did to deserve it.

Our mother, Penny Dunbar, was one of them.

The thing is, she would never have called herself unlucky; she'd have placed a blond bunch of hair behind her ear and claimed no regrets—that she'd gained a lot more than she ever lost, and a big part of me agrees. The other part realizes that bad luck always managed to find her, most typically at various milestones:

Her mother died giving birth to her.

She broke her nose the day before her wedding day.

And then, of course, the dying.

Her dying was something to see.

When she was born, the problem was age and pressure; her parents were both quite old to be having children, and after hours of struggle and surgery, her mother's shell was shattered and dead. Her father, Waldek Lesciuszko, was shattered and alive. He brought her up best he could. A tram driver, he had many traits and quirks, and people likened him not to Stalin himself, but a statue of him. Maybe it was the mustache. Maybe it was more. It could easily have been the stiffness of the man, or his silence, for it was a silence larger than life.

In private, though, there were other things, like he owned a grand total of thirty-nine books, and two of them he obsessed over. It's possible it was because he'd grown up in Szczecin, near the Baltic, or that he loved the Greek mythologies. Whatever the reasons, he always came back to them—a pair of epics where the characters would plow into the sea. In the kitchen, they were stationed, midrange, on a warped but lengthy bookshelf, filed there under *H:*

The Iliad. The Odyssey.

While other children went to bed with stories of puppies, kittens, and ponies, Penelope grew up on *the fast-running Achilles*, *the resourceful Odysseus*, and all the other names and nicknames.

There was *Zeus the cloud-compeller.*

Laughter-loving Aphrodite.

Hector the panic maker.

Her namesake: *the patient Penelope.*

The son of Penelope and Odysseus: *the thoughtful Telemachus.*

And always one of her favorites:

Agamemnon, king of men.

On many nights, she'd lie in bed and float out on Homer's images, and their many repetitions. Over and over, the Greek armies would launch their vessels onto the *wine-dark sea*, or enter its *watery wilderness*. They'd sail toward the *rosy-fingered dawn*, and the quiet young girl was captivated; her papery face was lit. Her father's voice came in smaller and smaller waves, till finally, she was asleep.

The Trojans could return tomorrow.

The long-haired Achaeans could launch and relaunch their ships, to take her away the following night, again.

Next to that, Waldek Lesciuszko gave his daughter one other life-affirming skill; he taught her to play the piano.

I know what you might be thinking:

Our mother was highly educated.

Greek masterpieces at bedtime?

Lessons in classical music?

But no.

These were remnants of another world, a different time. The small book collection had been handed down as nearly the sole possession of her family.

The piano was won in a card game. What neither Waldek nor Penelope knew just yet was that both would turn out to be crucial.

They would bring the girl ever closer to him.

Then send her away for good.

They lived in a third-floor apartment.

A block like all the others.

From a distance, they were one small light in a concrete Goliath.

Up close, it was spare but closed-in.

At the window stood the upright instrument—both black and brawny, and silky smooth—and at regular times, morning and night, the old man sat with her, with a strict and steady air. His paralyzed mustache was camped firmly between nose and mouth. He moved only to turn the page for her.

As for Penelope, she played and concentrated, unblinking, on the notes. In the early days it was nursery rhymes, and later, when he sent her for lessons he couldn't afford, there was Bach, Mozart, and Chopin. Often, it was only the world outside who blinked, in the time it took to practice. It would alter, from frosty to windswept, clearing to grim. The girl would smile when she started. Her father cleared his throat. The metronome went click.

Sometimes she could hear him breathe, somewhere amongst the music. It reminded her that he was alive, and not the statue people joked about. Even when she could feel his anger rising at her newest foray of errors, her father was always trapped, somewhere between po-faced and thoroughly pissed off. Just once she'd have loved to see him erupt—to slap his thigh, or tear at his aging thicket of hair. He never did. He only brought in a branch of a spruce tree and whipped her knuckles with an economic sting, every time her hands dropped, or she made another mistake. One winter's morning, when she was still just a pale and timid-backed child, she got it twenty-seven times, for twenty-seven musical sins. And her father gave her a nickname.

At the end of the lesson, with snow falling outside, he stopped her playing and held her hands, and they were whipped and small and warm. He clenched them, but softly, in his own obelisk fingers.

"*Już wystarczy*," he said, "*dziewczyna błędów* . . . ," which she translated, for us, as this:

"That's enough, mistake maker."

That was when she was eight.

When she was eighteen, he decided to get her out.

The dilemma, of course, was the communism.

A single great idea.

A thousand limits and flaws.

Growing up, Penelope never noticed.

What child ever does?

There was nothing to compare it to.

For years, she didn't realize what a guarded time and place it was. She didn't see that while everyone was equal, really they were not. She never looked up at concrete balconies, and the way the people watched.

As the politics gloomed above, the government handled everything, from your job to your wallet to all you thought and believed—or at least what you *said* you thought and believed; if you were even vaguely suspected of being part of *Solidarność*—the Solidarity Movement—you could count on paying the cost. As I said, the people watched.

The truth is, it had always been a hard country, and a sad one. It was a land where the invaders had come from all sorts of directions, across all sorts of centuries. If you had to choose, though, you'd say it was harder than it was sad, and the communist era was no different. It was a time, in the end, where you moved from one long queue to another, for everything from medical supplies to toilet paper, and vanishing stocks of food.

And what could people do?

They stood in line.

They waited.

The temperature fell below freezing. It changed nothing.

People stood in line.

They waited.

Because they had to.

* * *

Which brings us back to Penelope, and her father.

For the girl, none of that mattered so much, or at least it didn't yet.

To her this was just a childhood.

It was a piano and frozen playgrounds, and Walt Disney on Saturday nights—one of the many small concessions from the world that lay wayward and west.

As for her father, he was careful.

Vigilant.

He kept his head down, and held all political ideas in the shadows of his mouth, but even that wasn't much comfort. Keeping your nose clean while an entire system broke down around you guaranteed only that you would survive longer, not that you would survive. An endless winter would finally break, only to return in record time, and there you were again, at work:

Small, allotted hours.

Friendly without friends.

There you were at home:

Quiet but wondering.

Is there any way out at all?

The answer was formed, and worked on.

Definitely not for him.

Maybe, however, for the girl.

In the years between, what else can be said?

Penelope grew up.

Her father grew visibly older, his mustache the color of ash.

To be fair, sometimes there were good times, there were great times—and old and dour as he was, Waldek surprised his daughter maybe once a year and raced her to the tramline. It was usually for one of those paid music lessons, or a recital. At home, in her early years of high school, he played stiff-and-steady partner, in the dance hall of the kitchen. Pots would clamor. A rickety stool was felled. Knives and forks would hit the floor, and the girl would laugh, the man would crack; he'd smile. The smallest dance floor in the world.

For Penelope, one of the strongest memories was her thirteenth birthday, when they came home via the playground. She felt far too grown-up for such things, but she sat on a swing there anyway. Many decades later, she would recount that memory, one more time, to the fourth of her five boys—the one who loved the stories. It was in the last few months of her life, when she was half-dreaming, half-high on morphine, on the couch.

"Now and again," she'd said, "I still see the melting snow, the pale unfinished buildings. I hear the noisy chains. I can feel his gloves on the small of my back." Her smile was hoisted up by then, her face was in decay. "I remember screaming with that fear of going too high. I begged for him to stop, but I didn't want him to, not really."

And that's what made it so hard:

The heart of color in all that grey.

To her, in hindsight, leaving wasn't so much a breaking free as an *abandonment*. Much as he loved them, she didn't want to leave her father with only his Greek cast of seafaring friends. After all, what good was the fast-running Achilles in this land of ice and snow? He'd freeze to death eventually. And how could Odysseus be resourceful enough to give him the company required to keep him alive?

The answer was clear to her.

He couldn't.

But then, of course, it happened.

She hit eighteen.

Her escape was set in motion.

It took him two long years.

On the surface, all was going well: she'd left school with good results and worked in a local factory, as a secretary. She took notes at all the meetings, she was responsible for every pen. She shuffled all the papers, and accounted for all the staplers. That was her position, her slot, and there were definitely many worse ones.

It was also around that time when she became more involved with various musical outfits, accompanying people here and there, and playing solo pieces as well. Waldek actively encouraged it, and soon she was traveling to perform. Restrictions had slowly become less monitored, due to general disarray, and also (more menacingly) to the knowledge that people could always leave, but had family members who *stayed*. Either way, sometimes Penelope was approved to cross borders, and even once to slip through the Curtain. At no point did she ever consider that her father was planting a seed for her defection; within herself, she was happy.

But the country, by then, was on its knees.

Market aisles were closer to completely bare.

The queuing had intensified.

Many times, in ice, then sleet and rain, they'd stood together, for hours, waiting for bread, and when they got there, nothing was left—and soon he realized. He knew.

Waldek Lesciuszko.

The statue of Stalin.

It was ironic, really, for he didn't say a word; he was deciding *for* her, forcing her to be free, or at least, thrusting the choice upon her.

He'd nursed his plan, day after day, and now the moment came.

He would send her to Austria, to Vienna, to play in a concert—an eisteddfod—and make it clear that she was never to return.

And that, to me, was how us Dunbar boys began.

the surrounds

So there she was, our mother.

Ice and snow, and all those years ago.

And look here, at Clay, in the far-flung future.

What can we say about him?

Where and how did life begin again the next day?

It was pretty simple, really, with a multitude lying in wait:

He woke up in the biggest bedroom in the city.

For Clay, it was perfect, another strange but sacred site: it was a bed, in a field, with the ignition of dawn and distant rooftops; or, more accurately, it was an old mattress, lying faded in the earth.

In truth, he went often (and always on Saturday nights), but it was many months since he'd stayed till morning, in the field behind our house. Even so, it was still an oddly comforting privilege; this mattress had survived much longer than it had the right.

In that spirit all appeared normal when he'd first opened his eyes.

Everything was quiet, the world was still as a painting.

But then it all came stumbling up, and falling down.

What have I gone and done?

Officially it was called The Surrounds.

One practice track, and one adjoining stables.

But that was years ago, another life.

Back then, this was where all the cash-strapped owners, struggling trainers, and two-bit jockeys came to work and pray:

One lazy sprinter. One honest stayer. Please, for the love of God, could just one of them rise above the heap?

What they got was a special gift from the National Jockey Club.

Foreclosure. Devastation.

The plan was to sell it off, but that took the better part of a decade, and typically, as far as the city went, nothing yet had come of it. All that remained was an emptiness—a giant, uneven paddock, and a sculpture garden of household waste:

Troubled televisions. Battered washing machines.

Catapulted microwaves.

One enduring mattress.

All of that and more was stationed, sporadically, across the terrain, and while most people viewed it as just another scene of suburban neglect, to Clay it was keepsake, it was memory. After all, this was where Penelope had peered over the fence and decided to live on Archer Street. It was where we'd all stood together one day, with a burning match in a westerly.

Another point of note was that ever since its abandonment, the grass at The Surrounds hadn't much grown; it was the anti–Bernborough Park: low and gaunt in some areas, knee-high and stringy in others, the latter of which where Clay had just woken up.

Years later, when I asked him about that, he stayed silent for quite a while. He looked over, across this table. "I don't know," he said, "maybe it just got too sad to grow—" but he cut the idea off there. For him that was a tirade of sentimentality. "Actually, forget I ever said that."

But I can't.

I can't forget, because I'll never comprehend:

One night he would find pure beauty there.

And commit his greatest mistake.

* * *

But let's get back to that morning; the first day beyond the Murderer, and Clay lay curled, then straightened. The sun didn't so much rise as carry him up, and there was something light and lean, in the left-hand pocket of his jeans, beneath the broken peg. He chose for now to ignore it.

He lay across the mattress.

He thought he felt he heard her—

But it's morning, he thought, and Thursday.

At times like this, thinking of her ached:

The hair against his neck.

Her mouth.

Her bones, her breast, and finally, her breath.

"Clay." A bit louder now. "It's me."

But he would have to wait for Saturday.

she cried all the way to vienna

In the past, she's there again, utterly unknowing—for Waldek Lesciuszko didn't so much as breathe in a way that might suggest what he was planning.

The man was meticulous.

Absolutely dormant.

A concert in Vienna?

No.

Often, I wonder what it must have been like for him—to buy the mandatory return ticket, knowing she was only going one-way. I wonder how it was to lie and make her reapply for her passport, as had to be done, every time you left, even if briefly. So Penelope did it, like always.

As mentioned earlier, she'd been in concerts before.

She'd gone to Kraków. Gdańsk. East Germany.

There was also the time she'd traveled to a small city by the name of Nebenstadt, west of the Curtain, but even that was spitting distance from the East. The concerts were always high but not-too-high affairs, because she was a beautiful pianist, and a brilliant one, but not a *brilliant* one. She usually made the trips alone, and never failed to return at the allotted hour.

Until now.

This time her father encouraged her to take a bigger suitcase, and another jacket. In the night he added some extra underwear and socks. He also fed an envelope inside the pages of a book—a black hardcover, which was one of a pair. The envelope held words and money:

A letter and American dollars.

The books were then wrapped in brown paper.

On top, in weighty handwriting, it said, *FOR THE MISTAKE MAKER, WHO PLAYS CHOPIN BEST OF ALL, THEN MOZART, AND BACH*.

When she picked up her luggage in the morning, it was immediately, obviously heavier. She'd started to unzip it and check, when he said, "I added a small gift, for the road—and you're in a rush." He hurried her out the door. "You can open it on the train."

And she believed him.

She was in a blue woolen dress with fat, flat buttons.

Her blond hair reached the middle of her back.

Her face was certain and soft.

Lastly, her hands were crisp and cool, and perfectly clean.

She looked nothing like a refugee.

At the station it was odd, for the man who'd never shown a spark of emotion was suddenly shaky and wet in the eyes. His mustache was vulnerable for the first time in its steadfast life.

"*Tato?*"

"This damn cold air."

"But it's not so cold today."

She was right, it wasn't, it was mild, and sunny. The light was high, silvering the city in all its glorious grey.

"Are you arguing with me? We should not argue when someone is leaving."

"Yes, *Tato*."

When the train pulled in, her father pulled away. Looking back, it's so clear he was barely holding himself together, tearing out his pockets from within. He was working away at them to distract himself, to keep the emotion at bay.

"*Tato*, it's here."

"I can see that. I'm old, not blind."

"I thought we weren't supposed to argue."

"Now you're arguing with me again!" Never would he raise his voice like that, not at home, let alone in public, and he wasn't making sense.

"Sorry, *Tato*."

From there, they kissed, both cheeks, a third time on the right.

"*Do widzenia*."

"*Na razie*. See you later."

No you won't. "*Tak, tak. Na razie*."

For the rest of her life, she was relieved beyond measure that when she boarded the train, she turned and said, "I don't know how I'll play without you hitting me with that branch." She'd said the same thing every time.

The old man nodded, barely allowing her to see his face chop and change, as watery as the Baltic Sea.

The Baltic.

That was how she always explained it. She claimed her father's face had turned to a body of water. The deep wrinkles, the eyes. Even the mustache. All of it drowned in sunshine, and cold, cold water.

For a good hour, she looked out the window of the carriage, at Eastern Europe passing her by. She thought of her father many times, but it wasn't till she saw another man—something like a Lenin—that she remembered the gift. The suitcase.

The train trotted on.

Her eyes met the underwear first, and the socks, and then the brown package, and still she hadn't pieced it together. The extra clothing was possibly explained by the eccentricities of an older man; a happiness came over her when she read the note about Chopin, Mozart and Bach.

But then she opened the package.

She saw the two black books.

The print on their covers was in English.

Both had *Homer* written at the top, and then respectively, *The Iliad*, *The Odyssey*.

When she thumbed through the first one and found the envelope, the realization was sudden, and severe. She rose to her feet and whispered "*Nie*" to the half-crowded train.

Dear Penelope,

I imagine you reading this letter on your journey to Vienna, and I say from the outset—do not turn around. Do not come back. I will not receive you with open arms, but rather push you away. I think you can see that there is another life for you now, there's another way to be.

Inside this envelope are all the documents you need. When you get to Vienna, do not take a taxi to the camp. It is overpriced and you will arrive far too early. There is a bus, and that will get you there. Also, don't say you are seeking to leave for economic reasons. Say only this: you are afraid of reprisals from the government.

I expect it will not be easy, but you will make it. You will survive and live, and one day I hope we will see each other again, and you will read these books to me in English—for I expect that to be the language you will speak. If it turns out that you never come back, I ask you to read it to your own children, if that is to be what happens out there, on the wine-dark sea.

The last thing I will say is that I taught only one person in this world to play the piano, and although you were a great mistake maker, it was my pleasure and privilege. It is what I've loved best, and most.

Yours sincerely, with much love,
Waldek Lesciuszko

Well, what would you do?

What would you say?

Penelope, the Mistake Maker, stayed standing a few seconds longer, then sagged slowly back to her seat. She kept quiet and shivery, with the letter in her hands, and the two black books in her lap. Without a sound, she started to cry.

Into the passing face of Europe outside, Penelope Lesciuszko cried her stray, silent tears. She cried all the way to Vienna.

the forces are displayed

He'd never been drunk, and therefore never hungover, but Clay imagined this was probably what it was like.

His head was next to him, he gathered it up.

He sat awhile, then crawled from the mattress and found the heavy plastic sheet next to him, in the grass. With tired bones and shaking hands, he made his bed with it, he tucked it in, then walked toward the fence line—an obligatory white sports field divider, all rail and no palings—and rested his face on the wood. He breathed the burning rooves.

For a long time, he tried to forget:

The man at the table.

The quiet background noise of brothers and felt betrayal.

It came from many moments, that bridge of his, but there, at The Surrounds that morning, it came from last night most of all.

Eight hours earlier, when the Murderer left, there were ten minutes of uncomfortable silence. To break it, Tommy said, "Jesus, he looked like death warmed up." He held Hector over his heart. The cat purred, a lump of stripes.

"He deserved to look a lot *worse*," I told him.

"What a shocker of a suit" and "Who gives a shit, I'm going down the pub," said Henry and Rory, in sequence. They stood like melded elements, like sand and rust combined.

Clay, of course, famous for saying all but nothing, said nothing. He'd probably spoken enough for one night. For a moment he wondered, why now? Why had he come home *now*? But then he realized the date. It was February 17.

He put his injured hand in a small bucket of ice, and kept the other from the graze on his face, tempting as it was to touch it. At the table it was he and I, at silent loggerheads. For me, this much was clear: there was only one brother to worry about, and that was the one in front of me.

Hi, Dad, for Christ's sake.

I looked at the ice, bobbing around his wrist.

You'll need a bucket big as your body, boy.

I didn't say it, but I was sure Clay read it on my face, as he lost the battle and placed two trigger-like fingers on the wound below his eye. The mostly mute little bastard even nodded a bit, just before the clean pile of dishes, in all its outlandish altitude, collapsed into the sink.

It didn't stop the standoff, though, oh no.

Me, I went right on staring.

Clay carried on with his fingers.

Tommy placed Hector down, cleaned up the crockery, and soon returned with the pigeon (T looking on from his shoulder), and couldn't get out of there fast enough. He would check on Achilles and Rosy—both exiled, out back, to the porch. He made a point of closing the door.

Of course, earlier, when Clay had said those two fateful words, the rest of us stood behind him, like witnesses at the scene of a crime. A grisly one. Caught and swollen, there were many things to be thought, but I only remember one:

We've lost him now for good.

But I was ready to fight it out.

"You've got two minutes," I said, and the Murderer slowly nodded. He slipped against his chair; it ground into the floor. "Well, go on then. Two minutes aren't long, old man."

Old man?

The Murderer queried and resigned himself to it in the same breath. He *was* an old man, an old memory, a forgotten idea—and middle-aged though he might have been, to us he was all but dead.

He put his hands down on the table.

He resurrected his voice.

It came out in installments, as he awkwardly addressed the room.

"I need, or, actually, I was wondering . . ." He didn't sound like him anymore, not to any of us. We'd remembered him slightly left, or right. "I'm here to ask—"

And thank God for Rory, because in a broiled voice that sounded just like it always had, he unloaded a full-blooded reply, to our father's timorous stutterings. "For Christ's sake, spit the fucking thing out!"

We stopped.

All of us, temporarily.

But then Rosy barked again and there was me and a bit of shut-that-bloody-dog-up, and somewhere, in the middle, the words:

"Okay, look." The murderer found a way through. "I won't waste any more time, and I know I've got no right, but I came because I live far from here now, in the country. It's a lot of land, and there's a river, and I'm building a bridge. I've learned the hard way that the river floods. You can be locked either side, and . . ." The voice was full of splinters, a fence post in his throat. "I'll need help to build it, and I'm asking if any of you might—"

"No." I was first.

Again, the Murderer nodded.

"You've got some fucking neck, haven't you?"—Rory, in case you didn't guess.

"Henry?"

Henry took my cue and remained his affable self, in the face of all the outrage. "No thanks, mate."

"He's not your mate—Clay?"

Clay shook his head.

"Tommy?"

"No."

One of us was lying.

From there, there was a sort of bashed-up quiet.

The table was arid between father and sons, and a hell of a lot of toast crumbs. A pair of mismatched salt and pepper shakers stood in the middle, like some comedy duo. One portly. One tall.

The Murderer nodded and left.

As he did so, he took out a small piece of paper and gave it to that company of crumbs. "My address. In case you change your mind."

"Go now." I folded my arms. "And leave the cigarettes."

The address was torn up straightaway.

I threw it into the wooden crate next to the fridge that held assorted bottles and old newspapers.

We sat, we stood and leaned.

The kitchen quiet.

What was there to say?

Did we have a meaningful chat about uniting even stronger at times like these?

Of course not.

We spoke our few sentences, and Rory, pub-bound, was first to leave. The Naked Arms. On his way out he put a warm and humid hand, just briefly, on Clay's head. At the pub, he'd likely sit where we'd all sat once—even the Murderer—on a night we'd never forget.

Next, Henry went out back, probably to arrange some old books, or LPs, which he'd amassed from weekend garage sales.

Tommy followed soon after.

Once Clay and I had sat for a while, he'd quietly walked to the bathroom. He showered, then stood at the basin. It was cluttered with hair and toothpaste; held together by grit. Maybe it was all he needed to prove that great things could come from anything.

But he still avoided the mirror.

Later, he went to where it all began.

His hoarding of sacred sites.

Sure, there was Bernborough Park.

There was the mattress at The Surrounds.

The cemetery on the hill.

Years earlier, though, for good reason, it all started here.

He made his way up to the roof.

Tonight he walked out front, then around to near Mrs. Chilman's house—fence, to meter box, to tiles. As was his habit, he sat about halfway, blending in, which was what he did more as he got older. In the early days he went up mostly in daylight, but now he preferred not to be seen by passersby. Only when someone climbed up with him did he sit on the ridge or the edge.

Across the road, diagonally, he watched the house of Carey Novac.

Number 11.

Brown brick. Yellow-windowed.

He knew she'd be reading *The Quarryman*.

For a while he watched the varied silhouettes, but soon he turned away. Much as he loved seeing just the slightest sight of her, he didn't come to the roof for Carey. He'd sat up here well before she'd even arrived on Archer Street.

Now he moved over, a dozen tiles to the left, and watched the length of the city. It had clambered from its previous abyss, big, broad and street-lit. He took it all steadily in.

"Hi, city."

At times he liked to talk to it—to feel both less and more alone.

* * *

It might have been half an hour later when Carey came out, fleetingly. She put one hand on the railing, and held the other, slowly, aloft.

Hi, Clay.

Hi, Carey.

Then back in.

Tomorrow, for her, was a brutal start like always. She'd wheel her bike across the lawn at quarter to four, for trackwork at the McAndrew Stables, down at Royal Hennessey.

Toward the end, Henry came up, straight from the garage, with a beer and a bag of peanuts. He sat at the edge, near a *Playboy* in the gutter; a dead and dying Miss January. He gestured for Clay to follow, and when he arrived, he made his offerings; the nuts and the sweating beer.

"No thanks."

"He speaks!" Henry slapped his back. "That's twice in three hours; this really *is* a night for the books. I'd better get down to thc newsagent's tomorrow and do another lotto ticket."

Clay looked silently out:

The dark compost of skyscrapers and suburbia.

Then he looked at his brother, and the surety of his beer sips. He enjoyed the thought of that lotto ticket.

Henry's numbers were one to six.

Later, Henry gestured to the street, where Rory came laboring upwards, a letterbox over his shoulder. Behind him, the timber pole dragged along the ground; he swung it to our lawn, triumphant. "Oi, Henry, throw us a nut, y' weak lanky prick!" He thought for a moment but forgot what he was saying. It must have been funny, though, it must have been sidesplitting, because he laughed on his way to the porch. He angled up the steps and lay noisily down on the deck.

Henry sighed. "Here, we better get him," and Clay followed, to the other side, where Henry had propped a ladder. He didn't look at The Surrounds, or the immense backdrop of slanted rooves. No, all he saw was the yard, and Rosy running laps of the clothesline. Achilles stood chewing in the moonlight.

As for Rory, he weighed a drunken ton, but they somehow slung him to bed.

"Dirty bastard," said Henry. "Must have twenty schooners in 'im."

They'd never seen Hector move so quickly, either. His look of alarm was priceless, as he leapt, mattress to mattress, and out the door. On the other bed, Tommy slept against the wall.

In their bedroom, later, much later, it said 1:39 on Henry's old clock radio (also bargained for at a garage sale), and Clay was standing, his back to the open window. Earlier, Henry had sat on the floor, writing a quick-fire essay for school, but now he hadn't moved for minutes; he lay on top of the sheets, and Clay was safe to think it:

Now.

He bit down hard.

He made his way to the hallway, aiming for the kitchen—and faster than expected, he was next to the fridge, his hand in the assorted recycling.

From nowhere there was light.

Jesus!

It was white and heavy and belted him across the eyes like a football hooligan. He brought his hands up as it was turned off again, but still it throbbed and stung. In the new drowning dark was Tommy; he was standing in just his underpants, with Hector at his flank. The cat was a shifting shadow of himself, and eyes in shock from the light.

"Clay?" Tommy wandered toward the back door. His words drooled, mid-sleep and walk. "Kil' nee' s' fee' . . ." With a second attempt, he nearly cracked the full code of his sentence. "Achilles knees some feed."

Clay took his arms and turned him, watching as he ambled the hall. He even bent down and gave the cat a small pat, triggering a few short purrs. For a moment, he expected Rosy to bark, or Achilles to let loose a bray, but they didn't, and he reached for the crate.

Nothing.

Even when he gambled and opened the fridge—just a crack, to borrow some light—he couldn't find a single scrap of the murderous paper. What a shock to walk back in then, and find it patched up, with sticky tape, on his bed.

the birthday girl

Needless to say, Penelope never went to the eisteddfod; she never rehearsed, or walked the city of aqua rooftops. She remained at the Westbahnhof, on the platform, sitting on her suitcase, elbows on her knees. With her crisp, clean fingers, she played with the buttons on her blue woolen dress, and traded her return ticket for an earlier one home.

Hours later, when the train was set to leave, she rose to her feet. A conductor leaned from the train's doorway, unshaven, overweight.

"Kommst einer?"

Penelope only looked at him, stricken with indecision, twirling one of those buttons, center-chest. Her suitcase stood in front of her. An anchor at her feet.

"Nah, kommst du jetzt, oder net?" There was something charming in his dishevelment. "You coming now or not?" Even his teeth were loosely stowed. He leaned like a schoolboy, and he didn't blow a whistle but called to the front of the train. *"Geht schon!"*

And he smiled.

He smiled his jangle-toothed grin, and Penelope held the button now, in front of her, in the palm of her right hand.

As forecast by her father, though, she made it.

She was all suitcase and vulnerability, but exactly as Waldek predicted, she got through.

There was a camp in a place called Traiskirchen, which was an army of bunk beds and a wine-dark toilet floor. The first problem was finding the end of the line. Lucky she'd had plenty of practice; Eastern Europe had taught her to queue. The second problem, once inside, was negotiating the ankle-deep pool of refuse at your feet. Some watery wilderness, all right, it was a test of nerve and stamina.

People in line were blank-faced and tired, and each feared many outcomes, but one of them most of all. They could not, under any circumstances, be sent home.

When she'd arrived, she was questioned.

She was fingerprinted, she was interpreted.

Austria was essentially a holding ground, and in most cases, it took twenty-four hours to be processed and sent to a hostel. There you would wait for approval from another embassy.

Her father had thought of many things, but not that Friday was a bad day to arrive. It meant you had to last out the weekend at the camp, which was no picnic, but last it out she did. After all, in her own words, it wasn't hell on earth, either. Not compared to what other people endured. The worst was the not-knowing.

The next week she took another train, this time to the mountains, to another set of bunk beds, and Penelope started the wait.

I'm sure in nine months there, we could dig around, but what do I really know about that time? What did Clay know? As it turned out, Penelope's life in the mountains was one of the few periods she didn't talk about as much—but when she did, she spoke simply and beautifully, and I guess what you'd also call mournfully. As she explained it once to Clay:

There was one short phone call, and one old song.

A few small parts to tell the whole.

In the first couple of days, she'd noticed other people making calls from an old phone booth by the roadside. It stood like a foreign object, by the vastness of forest and sky.

It was obvious the people were calling home; there were tears in their eyes, and often, after they'd hung up, they struggled to walk back out.

Penelope, like many, hesitated.

She wondered if it was safe.

There'd been enough rumors of government phone taps to make anyone second-guess. As I mentioned earlier, it was people left behind who'd be punished.

What most of them had on their side was that they'd left for supposedly longer time frames. Why wouldn't they call home in their weeks away? For Penelope, it wasn't that simple—she should have already returned. Would a call put her father at risk? Luckily, she'd loitered long enough for a man named Tadek to find her. He had a voice, and body, like the trees.

"You want to call home, young girl?"

At her reluctance to speak, he went and touched the phone booth, to prove it couldn't hurt her. "Is anyone from your family in the movement?" And then, even more specific. "*Solidarność?*"

"*Nie*."

"Have you ever bent the wrong nose out of shape, if you know what I mean?"

Now she shook her head.

"I didn't think so." He grinned, like he'd borrowed the teeth from the Austrian train conductor. "Okay, then, let me ask. It's your parents?"

"My father."

"And you're sure now. You've caused no trouble?"

"I'm sure."

"And him?"

"He's an old tram driver," she said, "who barely speaks."

"Oh, well then, I think you're okay. The Party's in such a pitiful state right now, I don't think they've got time to worry about an old *Tramwaj* man. It's hard to be sure of anything these days, but of that, I'm totally certain."

It was then, she'd said, that Tadek looked out through the pine trees, and corridors of light. "Was he a good father to you?"

"Tak."

"And he'll be glad to hear from you?"

"Tak."

"Well, here." He turned and threw her some change. "Say hi from me," and walked away.

Of the phone conversation, there were ten small words, in translation:

"Hello?"

Nothing. Just static.

He repeated it.

That voice, like cement, like stone.

"Hello?"

She was lost in pine and mountainside, her knuckles bony white.

"Mistake Maker?" he asked. "Mistake Maker, is that you?"

And she imagined him in the kitchen, and the shelf of thirty-nine books—her head now against the window, somehow saying "Yes."

Then hung the phone up lightly.

The mountains all gone sideways.

Now to the song, a few months in, in the evening, in the guesthouse.

The moon against the glass.

The date was her father's birthday.

In the East, name days were given more significance back then, but out of country, you felt things harder. She'd let it slip, to one of the women.

They had no *wódka*, but there was always plenty of schnapps in that place, and a tray came out with glasses. When they were handed around, the owner held his own glass up, and looked at Penelope, in the parlor. A good dozen or so people were there, and when she heard the words, in her own language, "To your father," she looked up, she smiled, and it was all to keep herself together.

At that moment, another man stood.

Of course it was Tadek, and he started, very sadly—and beautifully—to sing:

“Sto lat, sto lat,
niech żyje, żyje nam.
Sto lat, sto lat,
niech żyje, żyje nam . . .”

It was all too much now.

Since the early days of her phone call it had been storing up, and she couldn’t hold it any longer. Penelope stood and sang, but inside her, something collapsed. She sang her country’s song of luck and companionship and wondered how she’d left him. The words came in great surges of love and self-loathing, and when it was over, many of them wept. They wondered if they’d see their families again; should they be grateful or condemned? The only thing they knew for sure was that now it was out of their hands. It was begun and had to end.

As a side note, the opening words from that song are these:

A hundred years, a hundred years,

May you live one hundred years.

As she sang, she knew, he wouldn’t.

She would never see him again.

For Penelope, it was hard not to relive that feeling, and become it, in all her remaining time there, especially living in such ease.

Everyone treated her so well.

They liked her—her quietness, her polite uncertainty—and they referred to her now as the Birthday Girl, mostly behind her, and at the sides. Every now and then, the men, especially, would say it directly, in various tongues, when she cleaned up, or did the laundry, or tightened the shoelace of a child.

“Dzięki, Jubilatko.”

“Vielen Dank, Geburtstagskind.”

“Děkuji, Oslavenkyně . . .”

Thank you, Birthday Girl.

A smile would struggle through her.

* * *

In between, all there was was the waiting, and recollections of her father. Sometimes it felt like she was getting by in spite of him, but that was in her darker moments, when the rain slew in from the mountains.

On those days especially, she worked longer, and worked hard.

She cooked and cleaned.

She washed dishes and changed the sheets.

In the end it was nine months of regretful hope and no piano, when finally a country agreed. She sat at the side of her bunk bed, the envelope in her hand. She looked out the window at nothing; the glass was white and smoky.

Even now, I can't help seeing her back there, in those alps I often imagine. I see her as she was, or as Clay had once described her:

The future Penny Dunbar, joining one more line, to fly far and south, and somewhat straight, to the sun.

the killer in his pocket

Penelope crossed worlds, and Clay crossed the fence:

He walked the small laneway between The Surrounds and home, where the palings were ghostly grey. There was a wooden gate there these days, for Achilles—for Tommy to walk him out, and in. In the backyard, he was grateful he hadn't had to climb over; morning-afters were obviously pretty awful, and the next few seconds would be telling:

First, he took on the slalom course of mule apples.

Then the labyrinth of dog shit.

Both culprits were still asleep; one was upright on the grass, the other sprawled out, on a porch-lit couch.

Inside, the kitchen smelt like coffee—I'd beaten him to it, and clearly in more ways than one.

Now it was Clay's turn to face my music.

As I did every now and again, I was eating breakfast out the front.

I stood at the wooden railing with cooked sky and cold cornflakes. The streetlights were still on. Rory's letterbox lay on the lawn.

When Clay opened the front door and stood a few steps behind me, I went on finishing my cereal. "Another letterbox, for Christ's sake."

Clay smiled, a nervous one, I felt it, but that was the extent of my niceties. After all, the address was in his pocket; I'd taped it my very best.

Initially, I didn't move.

"So, you got it?"

Again, I felt him nod.

"I thought I'd save you the trouble of fishing it out yourself." My spoon clanked in the bowl. A few drops of milk jumped the rail. "It's in your pocket?"

Another nod.

"You're thinking of going?"

Clay watched me.

He watched but said nothing while I tried, as I'd often done lately, to somehow understand him. In looks, he and I were most alike, but I was still a good half foot taller. My hair was thicker, and my body too, but it was only the extra age. While I worked on hands and knees on carpet, floorboards, and concrete each day, Clay went to school and ran his miles. He survived his regime of sit-ups and push-ups; he was tense, and tight-looking—lean. I guess you could say we were different versions of the same thing, most notably in the eyes. Both of us had fire in our eyes, and it didn't matter what color they were, because the fire in them was everything.

In the middle of it all, I smiled, but hurtly.

I shook my head.

The streetlights flickered off then.

I'd asked what had to be asked.

Now to say what needed to be said.

The sky widened, the house tightened.

I didn't move close, or aim up, or intimidate.

All I said was "Clay."

Later on, he told me that that was what unnerved him:

The peace of it.

In the midst of that strangely dulcet tone, something in him tolled. It lowered itself, steadily, from throat to sternum to lungs, and full morning hit the street. On the other side, the houses stood ragged and quiet, like a gang of violent mates, just waiting for my word. We knew I didn't need them.

After a moment or two, I took my elbows off the rail and placed a look down on his shoulder. I could ask him about school. What about school? But both of us knew the answer. Who was I, of all the people, to tell him to stay in school? I'd left before the end myself.

"You can leave," I said. "I can't stop you, but—"

The rest was broken off.

A sentence as difficult as the job itself—and that, in the end, was the truth of it. There was leaving and coming back. There was crime, then facing punishment.

Returning and being let in:

Two very different things.

He could walk away from Archer Street, and trade his brothers for the man who left us—but coming home meant getting through me.

"Big decision," I said, more directly, then, in his face and not by his shoulder. "And, I guess, one hell of a consequence."

And Clay looked, first in my face, then away.

He recognized my toil-hardened wrists, my arms, my hands, the jugular in my neck. He noticed the reluctance in my knuckles, but the will to see it through. Most importantly, though, he saw that fire in each eye, pleading as they were:

Don't leave us for him, Clay.

Don't leave us.

But if you do.

The thing is, these days I'm convinced.

Clay knew he had to do it.

He just wasn't sure if he could.

When I walked back inside, he stayed awhile, stranded on the porch, with the fullest weight of the choice. After all, what I'd promised was something I couldn't even bring myself to say. What *was* the worst thing you could do to a Dunbar boy, anyway?

For Clay, that much was clear, and there were reasons to leave, and reasons to stay, and all of it was the same. He was caught somewhere, in the current—of destroying everything he had, to become all he needed to be—and the past, ever closer, upon him.

He stood watching the mouth of Archer Street.

paper houses

AND THE TIDE COMES IN WITH VICTORY, AND STRUGGLE ALONG THE WAY—FOR likely the fairest thing to say about Penelope's entrance to life in the city was that she was constantly torn and astonished.

There was great gratitude to this place for taking her.

Then fear of its newness, and heat.

And then, of course, the guilt:

A hundred years he'd never live.

So selfish, so callous to leave.

It was November when she got here, and although not normally the hottest time of year, occasionally it produced a week or two of brutal reminders that summer was drawing near. If ever there was a time not to arrive, it was one like this—a binary weather chart of that heat, humidity, heat. Even the locals seemed to be suffering.

On top of that, she was obviously an intruder; her room at the camp clearly belonged to a squadron of cockroaches, and God almighty, she'd never seen such terrifying things. So big! Not to mention relentless. They fought her each day for territory.

Not surprisingly, the first thing she bought here was a can of Baygon.

Then a pair of flip-flops.

If nothing else, she understood you could go a long way in this country with crap footwear and a few good cans of fly spray. It helped her get by. Days. Nights. Weeks.

* * *

The camp itself was buried deep in the unruly rug of suburbs.

She was taught there, from the absolute basics, to speak the language. Sometimes she walked the streets outside, and the rows of peculiar houses—each one set in the middle of giant, lawn-mowered lawns. Those houses seemed made of paper.

When she asked the English teacher about them, by sketching a house and pointing to the paper, he burst forth loudly with laughter. "I know, I know!" But soon he gave her an answer. "No, not paper. *Fibro*."

"Fi-bro."

"Yes."

Another note about the camp and its many small apartments was that it was much like the city; it sprawled, even in such a tight space.

There were people of every color.

Every speech.

There were high-headed proud types, and then the worst offenders of foot-dragging disease you could ever hope to meet. Then there were people who smiled the whole time, to keep the doubt within. What they did all have in common was that they all seemed to gravitate, in varying degrees, to people of their own nationality. Country ran thicker than most things, and that was how people connected.

In that regard, Penelope did find others from her own part of the world, and even her own city. Often they were very hospitable, but they were families—and blood ran thicker than country.

Every now and then, she was invited to a birthday or a name day celebration—or even just a cobbled-together get-together of *wódka* and *pierogi*, *barszcz* and *bigos*—but it was strange how quickly she'd leave. The smell of that food in the stifling air; it belonged here as much as she did.

But that wasn't what really bothered her.

No, the one thing she truly dreaded was the sight and sound of men and women standing up, and loosening their throats, for another rendition of "*Sto Lat*." They sang for home like a perfect idea—like there weren't any reasons to leave. They called on friends and family, as if the words could bring them near.

But then, like I said, there was the gratitude, for other times, like New Year's Eve, when she walked through the camp at midnight.

Somewhere close by there were fireworks; she could see them between the buildings. There were great plumes of red and green, and distant cheers, and soon she stopped and watched them.

She smiled.

She saw the workings of light in the sky, and sat on the stony road. Penelope held her arms, either side, and rocked herself, just lightly. *Piękne*, she thought, it's beautiful, and this was where she would live. The thought of it made her eyes close, hotly, and talk to the simmering ground.

"*Wstań*," she said. And again. "*Wstań, wstań*."

Stand up.

But Penelope didn't move.

Not yet.

But soon.

the arsemover and the minotaur

"Wake up, for Christ's sake."

While Penny comes in, Clay begins the process of wading, gradually, out.

On the first day, after my front porch ultimatum, he made his way to the bread bags and remaining coffee. Later, he dried his face in the bathroom, and heard me on my way out to work. I was standing over Rory:

Me in my dirty old work gear.

Rory still half asleep, half dead from the night before.

"Oi, Rory." I shook him. "*Rory!*"

He tried to move, but couldn't. "Oh, shit, Matthew, what?"

"You *know* what. There's another Goddamn letterbox out there."

"Is that all? How do you know it was me?"

"I'm not answering that. What I *am* saying is that you're taking it back and reinstalling the bloody thing."

"I don't even know where I got it from."

"It's got a number on it, doesn't it?"

"Yeah, but I don't know what *street*."

Now the moment Clay was waiting for:

"Je-sus C*hrist*!" He felt me seething, right through the wall, but then the practicality. "Okay, I don't care what you do with it, but when I get back home later, I expect it gone, you got that?"

Later, when Clay went in, he discovered the whole conversation was had with Hector wrapped like a wrestler around Rory's neck. The cat lay molting and purring, simultaneously. The purrs were hitting pigeon-pitch.

When he noticed a new presence in the doorway, Rory spoke, a muffled tone. "Clay? Is that you? Can you do me a favor and get this bloody cat off me?" after which he waited for the last two stubborn claws, and then, "Ahh*hhh*!" He breathed a great, relieving breath. Cat hair floated up; it showered down. Rory's phone alarm now bleating—he'd been lying on it, trapped by Hector.

"I guess you heard Matthew, the cranky bastard." Despite his appalling headache, he gave the tired suggestion of a smile. "You wouldn't mind throwing that letterbox over to The Surrounds for me, would you?"

Clay nodded.

"Thanks, kid, here, help us up, I better get to work." First things first, though, he walked over and slapped Tommy, hard across the head. "And you—I told you to keep that cat of yours"—he found the extra strength—"OFF MY FUCKING BED!"

It was Thursday, and Clay went to school.

On Friday he left it for good.

That second morning he went to a teacher's room, where there were posters fixed to the wall, and writing all over the board. The posters were both quite comical. Jane Austen in frilly dress, holding a barbell with weights overhead. The caption said *BOOKS ARE FRIGHTFULLY TOUGH*. The other one was more like a placard, saying *MINERVA McGONAGALL IS GOD*.

She was twenty-three years old now, that teacher.

Her name was Claudia Kirkby.

Clay liked her because these days, when he went to see her, she broke ranks with proper politeness. The bell would ring and she'd look at him. "Go on, kid, get out of here . . . get your arse to class." Claudia Kirkby was good with poetry.

She had dark brown hair and light brown eyes and a sunspot center-cheek. She had a smile for putting up with things, and calves, nice calves, and heels, and was quite tall and always well-dressed. For some reason, she'd liked us from the start; even Rory, who'd been nightmarish.

When Clay went in before school that Friday, she was standing over the desk.

"Hey there, Mr. Clay."

She was going through some essays.

"I'm leaving."

She stopped, abruptly, and looked up.

No get-your-arse-to-class on that day.

She sat down, looked worried, and said, "Hmm."

By three o'clock I was sitting at the school, in Mrs. Holland's office, the principal, and I'd been there a few times before—the lead-up to Rory's expulsion (in waters still to come). She was one of those stylishly short-haired women, with streaks of grey and white, and crayoned-under eyes.

"How's Rory going?" she asked.

"He's got a good job, but he hasn't really changed."

"Well, um, say hi from us."

"I will. He'll like that."

Of course he would, the bastard.

Claudia Kirkby was there as well, in her dignified heels and black skirt, cream shirt. She smiled at me, like always, and I knew I should have said it—it's good to see you—but I couldn't. After all, this was a tragedy. Clay was leaving school.

Mrs. Holland: "So, um, as I said, um, on the phone." She was one of the worst *ummers* I'd ever known. I knew bricklayers who *ummed* less than her. "We've, um, got young Clay here wanting, to, ahh, leave us." Damn it, she'd hit us with an *ahh* now, too; this wasn't looking good.

I glanced at Clay sitting next to me.

He looked up but didn't speak.

"He's a good student," she said.

"I know."

"Like you were."

I didn't react.

She went on. "He's sixteen, though. By, um, law we can't really stop him."

"He wants to go and live with our dad," I said. I'd wanted to add *for a while*, but somehow it didn't come out.

"I see, well, um, we could find the closest school to where your father lives. . . ."

Suddenly it came:

I was hit by a terrible numbing sadness in that office, in its sort-of-dark, sort-of-fluorescent-light. There'd be no other school, no other anything. This was it, and we all knew it.

I turned away, past Claudia Kirkby, and she looked sad, too, and so dutifully, damningly sweet.

Afterwards, when Clay and I walked to the car, she called out and chased us down, and there were her soundless, fast-running feet. She'd abandoned her heels near the office.

"Here," she said, with a small stack of books. "You can leave, but you've gotta read these."

Clay nodded, he spoke to her gratefully. "Thanks, Ms. Kirkby."

We shook hands and said goodbye.

"Good luck, Clay."

And they were nice hands, too; pale but warm, and a gleam in her sad-smiling eyes.

In the car, Clay faced his window and spoke, casual but also flatly. "You know," he said, "she likes you."

He said it as we drove away.

Strange to think, but I'd marry that woman one day.

Later, he went to the library.

He was there by four-thirty, and by five he sat between two great pylons of books. Everything he could find on bridges. Thousands of pages, hundreds of techniques. Every type, each measure. All jargons. He read through them and didn't understand a thing. He liked looking at the bridges, though: the arches, suspensions, and cantilevers.

"Son?"

He looked up.

"Would you like to borrow any of those? It's nine o'clock. It's time to close."

At home, he struggled through the door, he didn't turn on the light. His blue sports bag flowed over with books. He'd told the librarian he'd be gone a long time, and was given a lengthy extension.

As luck would have it, when he came in, I was the first one he saw, prowling the hallway like the Minotaur.

We stopped; we both looked down.

A bag that heavy announced itself.

In the half darkness, my body was blunt, but my eyes were lit. I was tired that night, much older than twenty; I was ancient, stricken and grizzled. "Come on through."

On his way past, he'd seen I was holding a wrench; I was fixing the tap in the bathroom. I was no Minotaur, I was the Goddamn *maintenance man*. And still we both watched that book bag, and the hallway felt tighter around us.

Then, Saturday, and waiting for Carey.

In the morning Clay drove around with Henry, for his books and records at garage sales; he watched him talk them down. In one converted driveway there was a collection of short stories called *The Steeplechaser*, a nice paperback, with a hurdler embossed on the cover. He paid a dollar and handed it to Henry, who held it, opened it, and smiled.

"Kid," he said, "you're a gentleman."

From there, the hours fell.

But they also needed conquering.

In the afternoon he went to Bernborough, for several laps of the track. He read his books up in the grandstand, and started to comprehend. Terms like *compression*, *truss*, and *abutment* were slowly making sense.

At one point, he sprinted the channel of stairs, between the splintery benches. He remembered Starkey's girl there, and smiled because of her lips. A breeze shuffled through the infield, as he left and quickened on the straight.

It was down to not much longer.

He would soon be at The Surrounds.

the spoils of freedom

Penelope made it through summer.

Its test was the choice of enjoying it.

Her first effort at the beach was a typical double hit; a mix-up of sunburn and southerly. She'd never seen so many people move so fast, or be swept with so much sand. On the bright side, it could have been worse; at first, when she saw the bluebottles floating serenely in the water, they looked so pure and otherworldly. Only when children came running up the beach, in varied states of distress, did she realize they'd all been stung. *Biedne dzieci*, she thought, poor children, as they sprinted toward their parents. While most of them shivered under the showers, and cried and sobbed unedited, one mother, especially, kept her daughter from rubbing sand in. She'd reached down for panicked handfuls of it and raked it over her skin.

Penelope watched helplessly on.

The mother took care of everything.

She calmed her and kept her close, and when she had her and knew she had her, she looked up, at the immigrant close at hand. No more talk, just a crouch, and stroking the girl's tangled hair. She saw Penelope and nodded, and carried the child away. It would be years before Penelope learned that bad bluebottle days were rare.

The other fact that amazed her was that most of the children went back in the water, but this time not for long, on account of the howling wind; it came up seemingly from nowhere, carrying darkening lumps of sky.

To top it all off, she lay awake that night, throbbing hotly amongst her sunburn, and the pitter-patter of insect feet.

But things were looking up.

The first momentous event was that she found herself a job.

She became a certified unskilled laborer.

The camp was linked to what was then known as the CES—the government-run job center—and when she visited their office, she was fortunate. Or at least, fortunate in her usual way. After a long interview and a sea of governmental forms, she was granted permission for the uglywork.

In short, it was public amenities.

You know the ones.

How could so many men piss with such inaccuracy? Why did people paint and smear and decide to shit anywhere but in the toilet? Were these the spoils of freedom?

In the stalls, she read the graffiti.

Mop in hand, she'd recall a recent English class, and chant it into the floor. It was a great way to pay her respects to this new place—to get amongst its heat, to scrub and clean its filthy bits. Also, there was a personal pride in knowing that she was willing. Where once she'd sat in a frozen, frugal storeroom, sharpening up the pencils, now she lived on hands and knees; she breathed the breeze of bleach.

After six months, she could almost touch it.

Her plan was coming together.

Sure, the tears still welled up each night, and sometimes during the day, but she was definitely making progress. Out of sheer necessity, her English was forming nicely, although it was often that calamitous, jumbled-up syntax of false starts and broken endings.

Decades later, even when she was teaching English at a high school across the city, she sometimes summoned a stronger accent at home, and always we couldn't help ourselves, we loved it, and cheered, then called for it. She never did manage to teach us her original language—it was hard enough practicing piano—but we loved that ambulance could be *umboolunce*, and that she told us to *shurrup* rather than shut up. And juice was often *chooce*. Or "Quiet! I can't even hear myself *fink*!" Somewhere in the top five, also, was unfortunately. We liked it better as *unforchantly*.

Yes, in the early days, it all came down to those two religious things:

The words, the work.

She wrote letters to Waldek now, and called him when she could afford it, realizing, at last, he was safe. He confessed all he'd done to get her out, and how standing on the platform that morning was the highlight of his life, no matter what it cost him. Once, she even read to him, from Homer, in broken English, and was certain she felt him crack; he smiled.

What she couldn't know was that the years would pass by, almost too quickly, in that way. She would scrub a few thousand toilets, and clean chipped tiling by the acre. She'd withstand those bathrooms' felonies, and work newer jobs as well, cleaning handfuls of houses and apartments.

But then—what she *also* couldn't know:

That her future would soon be determined, by three connected things.

One was a hard-of-hearing music salesman.

Then a trio of useless piano men.

But first, it was a death.

The death of the statue of Stalin.

carey and clay and matador in the fifth

He'd never forget the day he first saw her on Archer Street, or actually, the day she'd looked up, and seen *him*.

It was early December.

She'd driven seven hours from the country with her mum and dad, and they arrived late afternoon. A removalist truck was behind them, and soon they carted boxes, furniture, and appliances, to the porch and into the house. There were saddles there, too, a few bridles and stirrups; the horseworks important to her father. He'd been a jockey once as well, in a family of jockeys, and her older brothers, too; they rode in towns with awkward names.

It must have been a good fifteen minutes after they got there when the girl stopped and stood, midlawn. Under one arm she held a box, under the other, the toaster, which had somehow come loose on the trip. The cord hung down to her shoes.

"Look," she'd said, and she'd pointed—casually across the road. "There's a boy up there on that roof."

Now, a year and a few months later, on Saturday night, she came to The Surrounds with a rustle of feet.

"Hey, Clay."

He felt her mouth and blood and heat and heart. All in a single breath.

"Hi, Carey."

It was nine-thirty or so, and he'd waited on the mattress.

Moths were there, too. A moon.

Clay lay on his back.

The girl paused a moment at the edge, she put something down, on the ground, then lay on her side, with a leg strapped loosely over him. There was the auburn itch of hair on his skin, and just like always he liked it. He could sense she'd noticed the graze on his cheek, but knew too much to ask, or to look for further injuries.

But still, she had to do it.

"You boys," she said, and touched the wound. Then waited for Clay to speak.

"Are you enjoying the book?" The question felt vaguely heavy at first, as if somehow pulleyed up. "Still good the third time round?"

"Even better—Rory didn't tell you?"

He tried to remember if Rory had said something along those lines.

"I saw him on the street," she said, "a few days ago. I think it was just before—"

Clay almost sat up, but quelled it. "Before—what?"

She knew.

She knew he'd come home.

Clay, for now, ignored it, preferring to think about *The Quarryman*, and its faded old bookmark betting stub, of *Matador in the fifth*. "Where are you up to, anyway? Has he gone to work in Rome yet?"

"Bologna, too."

"That's fast. You still in love with his broken nose?"

"Oh yeah, you know I can't help it."

He gave her a short, broad grin. "Me too."

Carey liked the fact that Michelangelo had had his nose broken as a teenager, for being too much of a smart mouth; a reminder that he was human. A badge of imperfection.

For Clay, it was slightly more personal.

He knew of another broken nose, too.

* * *

Back then—way back then, a few days after she moved in—Clay was out front on the porch, eating toast, a dinner plate up on the rail. It was just as he finished when Carey crossed Archer Street, in a flannelette shirt and well-worn jeans; the shirt rolled up at the elbows. The last piece of sun beside her:

The glow of her forearms.

The angle of her face.

Even her teeth, they weren't quite white, they weren't quite straight, but they had something nonetheless, a quality; like sea glass, eroded smooth, from grinding them in her sleep.

At first she wondered if he'd even seen her, but then he walked, timidly, down the steps, the plate still in his hands.

From that close-but-careful range, she surveyed him; interested, happily curious.

The first word he ever said to her was "Sorry."

He spoke it downwards, into the plate.

After a comfortable, customary silence, Carey spoke again. Her chin touched his collarbone, and this time she'd make him face it.

"So," she said, "he came. . . ."

Their voices were never whispered there—just quiet, like friends, unthreatened—and now she confessed, "It was Matthew who told me."

Clay felt it in his graze.

"You saw Matthew?"

She nodded, just slightly, against his neck, and went on to reassure him. "I was coming in Thursday night when he was taking out the garbage. It's hard to avoid you Dunbar boys, you know."

And Clay could have almost broken then:

The name Dunbar, and soon to be gone.

"It must have been pretty rough," she said, "seeing—" She adjusted. "Seeing him."

"There are rougher things."

Yes, there were, and they both knew it.

"Matthew said something about a bridge?"

She was right, I had. It was one of the more unsettling traits of Carey Novac; you seemed to tell her more than you should.

Silence again. One twirling moth.

Closer now when she spoke, he could feel the actual words, as if put there, on his throat. "Are you leaving to build a bridge, Clay?"

That moth wouldn't go away.

"Why?" she'd asked; that long-ago front lawn. "Why are you sorry?"

The street had all gone dark.

"Oh, you know, I should've come over and helped you unpack the other day. I just sat there."

"On the roof?"

He liked her already.

He liked her freckles.

Their positioning on her face.

You only saw them if you really looked.

Now Clay navigated, to a place well clear of our father.

"Hey," he said, he looked over. "Can you finally show me your tips tonight?"

She curled in more intensely, but let him get away with it. "Don't talk to *me* like that. Be a gentleman, for God's sake."

"*Tips*, I said, not . . ." His voice faded, and this was all part of it, each time at The Surrounds. It didn't matter that Saturday night was the worst time to ask for betting advice, since all the big races had been run and won that afternoon. The other, less prestigious race day was Wednesday, but as I said, the question was only a ritual. "What are they saying down at trackwork?"

Carey half smiled now, happy to play. "Oh yeah, I got tips all right. I got tips you can't even handle." Her fingers touched his collarbone. "I got Matador in the fifth."

He knew that despite being happy to say it, her eyes were close to tears then, and he held her that extra piece tighter—and Carey used the momentum, to slip down, to put her head upon his chest.

His heart was out of its gate.

He wondered how hard she could hear it.

On the lawn, they'd talked on. She was getting onto statistics.

"How old are you?"

"Pretty much fifteen."

"Yeah? I'm pretty much sixteen."

She stepped closer then, and nodded, just slightly, toward the roof. "Why aren't you up there tonight?"

He quickened—she'd always had him quickening, but not in a way he minded. "Matthew told me to take a day off. He yells at me about that a lot."

"Matthew?"

"You might have seen him. He's the oldest. He's good at saying Jesus Christ." And now Clay had smiled, and she took the opportunity.

"Why do you go up there, anyway?"

"Oh, you know." He thought how best to explain it. "You can see a pretty long way."

"Can I come up one day?"

It shocked him that she'd asked, but he couldn't help starting to joke with her. "I don't know. It's not that easy to get up there."

And Carey laughed; she bit the hook. "Bullshit. If you can climb it, I can, too."

"Bullshit?"

They both half grinned.

"I won't distract you, I promise." But then she got the idea. "If you let me come up, I'll bring binoculars."

She seemed always to be thinking ahead.

When he was there with Carey, sometimes The Surrounds felt bigger.

The household junk stood like distant monuments.

The suburbs felt further away.

That night, after Carey's tips and Matador, she spoke evenly, about the stables. He asked if she was due for a run on race day, and not just trackwork and barrier trials. Carey answered that McAndrew had said nothing, but knew what he was doing. If she pestered him, it would set her back months.

The whole time, of course, her head lay on his chest, or up against his neck, his favorite of favorite things. In Carey Novac, Clay had found someone who knew him, who *was* him, in all but one life-defining way. He also knew that if she could have, she'd have traded anything to share that with him as well:

The reason he carried the peg.

She'd have traded her jockey's apprenticeship for it, or her first Group One winner, let alone a ride in a listed race. She'd even have traded a mount in the Race That Stops the Nation, I'm sure, or the race she loved even more: the Cox Plate.

But she couldn't.

What she *could* understand, though, without a moment's hesitation, was the way to see him off, and quietly, she pleaded. Gentle but matter-of-fact:

"Don't do it, Clay, don't go, don't leave me . . . but go."

Had she been a character in one of Homer's epics, she'd have been *the clear-eyed Carey Novac*, or *Carey of the valuable eyes*. This time she let him know exactly how much she'd miss him, but also that she expected—or more so, demanded—that he do what he had to do.

Don't do it, Clay, don't leave me . . . but go.

As she left back then, she realized:

In the middle of Archer Street, the girl turned.

"Hey, what's your name?"

The boy, from in front of the porch. "It's Clay."

A silence.

"And? You don't want to know *my* name?"

But she spoke like she'd known him always, and Clay remembered himself, and asked, and the girl came walking back.

"It's Carey," she said, and left again, when Clay called out an afterthought.

"Hey, how do you spell that?"

And now she jogged over, she took the plate.

With her finger, she wrote her name, carefully, amongst the crumbs, then laughed when it was hard to decipher it—but they both knew the letters were in there.

Then she smiled at him, brief but warmly, and crossed the road for home.

For twenty minutes more, they stayed and they were quiet; and The Surrounds was quiet around them.

And this was always the worst of it:

Carey Novac leaned away.

She sat at the edge of the mattress, but when she stood to leave, she crouched. She kneeled at the side of the bed, where she'd paused upon arrival, and held a package now, wrapped in newspaper; and slowly, she put it down, she placed it against his ribs. Nothing more was spoken.

There was no *Here, I brought you this*.

Or *Take it*.

Or a *Thank you* said from Clay.

Only when she was gone did he lift himself up and open it, and reel at what lay within.

death in the afternoon

For Penelope, everything was going nicely.

The years flowed in, and by.

She'd been out of the camp a long time now, living alone in a ground-floor unit, on a road called Pepper Street. She loved the name.

She worked with other women now, too: a Stella, a Marion, a Lynn.

They worked in different pairings, traveling the city to clean. Of course, she'd been saving for a used piano in that time, too, waiting patiently to go and buy it. In her small apartment on Pepper Street, she kept a shoebox under the bed, with the rolled-up cash inside.

She continued mastering the English language as well, feeling it closer every night. Her ambition of reading both *The Iliad* and *The Odyssey* from cover to cover seemed an increasingly real possibility. Often she sat well beyond midnight, with a dictionary by her side. Many times she fell asleep like that, in the kitchen, her face all creased and sideways, against the warmth of pages; it was her constant immigrant Everest.

How typical, then, and perfect.

This, after all, was Penelope.

As the feat loomed up before her, the world came down in front of it.

It was like that pair of books, really.

Just when a war was there to be won, a god would get in the way. In this case, obliteration:

A letter arrived.

It informed her; he'd died outside.

His body was toppled next to an old park bench. Apparently, his face was half-covered in snow, and his hand was a fist, and sunken across his heart. It was not a patriotic gesture.

The funeral predated the letter.

A quiet affair. He was dead.

Her kitchen was full of sun that afternoon, and when she dropped it, the letter swayed, like a pendulum made of paper. It skimmed beneath the fridge, and she spent many minutes, hands and knees, reaching under, and in, to retrieve it.

Jesus, Penny.

There you were.

There you were with your knees all pinched and stretched, and the table cluttered behind you. There you were with your blurry eyes and crestfallen chest, your face on the floor—a cheek and an ear—your bony backside up in the air.

Thank God you did what you did next.

We loved what you did next.

bridge of clay

It was like this that night, when Carey left The Surrounds, and Clay unraveled the paper:

He peeled off the sticky tape gently.

He folded the *Herald*'s racing section flat, and tucked it under his leg. Only then did he look at the present itself—an old wooden box—and hold it in both hands, chestnut-brown and scuffed. It was the size of an old hardcover book, with rusty hinges and a broken latch.

Around him, The Surrounds was airy, and open.

Barely a breeze.

A weightlessness.

He opened the small wooden door on top, and it creaked like a floorboard, and dropped.

Inside was another gift.

A gift within a gift.

And a letter.

Usually, Clay would read the letter first, but to get to it he lifted the lighter; it was a Zippo, made of pewter, about the size and shape of a matchbox.

Before he even thought to take it, he was holding it in his hand.

Then turning it.

Then steering it toward his palm.

It surprised him how heavy it was, and when he flipped it onto its back, he saw them; he ran his finger across the words, engraved on its metal chest:

Matador in the fifth.

That girl was something else.

When he opened the letter, he was tempted to flick the Zippo open, to light its light, but the moon was enough to read by.

Her handwriting small and precise:

Dear Clay—

By the time you read this we'll have talked anyway . . . but I just wanted to say that I know you'll be leaving soon, and I'll miss you. I miss you already.

Matthew told me about a far-off place and a bridge you might be building. I try to imagine what that bridge will be made of, but then again, I don't think it'll matter. I wanted to claim this idea for myself, but I'm sure you know it anyway, from the jacket of The Quarryman:

"EVERYTHING HE EVER DID WAS MADE NOT ONLY OF BRONZE OR MARBLE OR PAINT, BUT OF HIM . . . OF EVERYTHING INSIDE HIM."

One thing I know:

That bridge will be made of you.

If it's okay with you, I'm hanging on to the book for now—maybe to make sure you come back for it, and come back as well to The Surrounds.

As for the Zippo, they say you should never burn your bridges, but I offer it to you anyway, even if only for luck, and to remember me by. Also, a lighter sort of makes sense. You know what they say about clay, don't you? Of course you do.

Love,
Carey

PS. Sorry about the state of the wooden box, but somehow I think you'll like it. I figured it couldn't hurt, to keep some treasured things in. Take more than just a peg.

2nd PS. I hope you like the engraving.

Well, what would you do?

What would you say?

Clay sat, stock-still, on the mattress.

He asked himself:

What *do* they say about clay?

But then, very quickly, he knew.

Actually, he understood before he'd finished asking, and he stayed at The Surrounds a long time. He read the letter over and over.

Finally, when he did break his stillness, it was only for the small heavy lighter; he held it against his mouth. For a moment he almost smiled:

That bridge will be made of you.

It wasn't so much that Carey did things largely or commanded attention or love, or even respect. No, with Carey it was her little moves, her easy touch of truth—and in that way, as always, she'd done it:

She'd handed him the extra courage.

And she'd given this story its name.

the removalists

On the kitchen floor, Penelope made up her mind.

Her father had wanted her to have a better life, and that was what she would do:

She would shed her meekness, her politeness.

She would go and pull out the shoebox.

She'd take the money out and clench it.

She'd stuff her pockets and walk to the railway—all the while remembering the letter, and Vienna:

There's another way to be.

Yes, there was, and today she would take it.

Bez wahania.

No delay.

She already had the shops mapped out in her mind.

She'd been before, and she knew each music shop by its location, prices, and varying expertise. One shop, in particular, had always called her back. The pricing was the first part; it was really all she could afford. But she'd also enjoyed the shambolic nature of it—the curled sheet music, the grimy bust of Beethoven scowling in the corner, and the salesman hunched at the counter. He was pointy-faced and cheerful, eating orange quarters almost always. He shouted through his deafness.

"Pianos?" he'd boomed the first time she went in. He fired an orange peel at the bin and missed. ("Shit, from one meter!") Deaf as he was, he picked up on her accent. "What would a traveler like yourself want a piano for? It's worse than a lead weight around your neck!" He stood and reached for the nearest Hohner. "Slim girl like you needs one of these. Twenty bucks." He opened the small case and ran his fingers along the harmonica. Was this his way of explaining she couldn't afford a piano? "You can take it anywhere."

"But I am not leaving."

The old man changed tack. "Of course." He licked his fingers and slightly straightened. "How much have you got?"

"So far, not much. I think, three hundred dollars."

He laughed his way through a cough.

Some orange flesh hit the counter.

"See, love, you're bloody dreaming. If you want a *good* one, or at least half-decent, come back when you've got a grand."

"Grand?"

"Thousand?"

"Oh. Can I try one?"

"Certainly."

But till now she never did play any of the pianos, not in that shop or the others. If she needed a thousand dollars, she needed a thousand dollars, and only then would she find a piano, play it, and buy it, all on the same day.

And that day, as it was, was today.

Even if she was fifty-three dollars short.

She walked into the shop and her pockets were bulging.

The shopkeeper's face lit up.

"You're here!"

"Yes." She was breathing heavily. Sweating soggily.

"You got a thousand dollars?"

"I have . . ." She took out the notes. "Nine hundred . . . and forty-seven."

"Yes, but—"

Penny slapped her hands on the counter, making paw prints in the dust, her fingers and palms all clammy. Her face was level with his; her shoulder blades threatened to dislocate. "Please. I must play one today. I will pay the rest as the money comes—but I must try one, please, today."

For the first time, the man didn't force his smile on her; his lips parted only to speak. "Okay then." He waved and walked, simultaneously. "Over here."

Of course, he'd directed her to the cheapest piano, and it was nice, the color of walnut.

She sat at the stool; she lifted the lid.

She looked at the boardwalk of keys:

A few were chipped, but through the gaps of her despair, she was already in love, and it hadn't yet made a sound.

"And?"

Penny turned slowly to look at him, and she was close to collapsing, within; she was the Birthday Girl again.

"Well, come on then," and she nodded.

She focused on the piano and remembered an old country. She remembered a father and his hands on her back. She was in the air, high in the air—a statue behind the swings—and Penelope played and wept. In spite of such a long piano-playing drought, she did it beautifully (one of Chopin's nocturnes) and she tasted the tears on her lips. She sniffed them up and sucked them in, and played everything right, and perfectly:

The Mistake Maker made no mistakes.

And next to her, the smell of oranges.

"I see," he said, "I see." He was standing at her side, on the right. "I think I see what you mean."

He gave it to her for nine hundred, and organized delivery.

The only problem was that the salesman didn't only have atrocious hearing and a shambles of a shop—his handwriting was shocking, too. Had it been even slightly more legible, my brothers and I wouldn't even exist—for instead of reading 3/7 Pepper Street from his own pen, he sent the delivery men to 37.

As you can imagine, the men were miffed.

It was Saturday.

Three days after she'd bought it.

While one knocked at the door, the other two started unloading. They lowered the piano from the truck and had it standing on the footpath. The boss was talking to a man on the porch, but soon he shouted down at them.

"What the hell are you two doin'?"

"What?"

"We're at the wrong bloody house!"

He went inside and used the man's phone, and was muttering on the way back out. "That idiot," he said. "That stupid, orange-eating *prick*."

"What is it?"

"It's an apartment. Unit three. Down there at number seven."

"But look. There's no parking down there."

"So we'll park in the middle of the road."

"That won't be popular with the neighbors."

"*You're* not popular with the neighbors."

"What's that s'posed to mean?"

The boss maneuvered his mouth into several shapes of disapproval. "Right, let me go down there. You two pull the trolley out. The piano wheels'll die if we roll it on the road, and so will we. I'll go and knock on the door. Last thing we need is taking it down and no one's home."

"Good idea."

"Yes, it *is* a good idea. Now don't so much as *touch* that piano again, right?"

"All right."

"Not till *I* tell you."

"All right!"

In the boss's absence, the two men looked at the man on his porch:

The one who didn't want a piano.

"How's it going?" he called down.

"A bit tired."

"Want a drink?"

"Nah. The boss prob'ly won't like that."

The man on the porch was normal height, had wavy dark hair, aqua eyes, and a beaten-up heart—and when the boss came walking back, there was a quiet-looking woman with a white face and tanned arms, out in the middle of Pepper Street.

"Here," said the man; he came off the porch, as they shifted the piano to the trolley. "I'll take an end there if you like."

And that was how, on a Saturday afternoon, four men and a woman rolled a walnut-wooden piano down a sizable stretch of Pepper Street. At opposite corners of the rolling instrument were Penelope Lesciuszko and Michael Dunbar—and Penelope could have no idea. Even as she noticed his amusement for the movers, and his care for the welfare of the piano, she couldn't possibly know that here was a tide to the rest-of-her-life, and a final name and nickname.

As she said, to Clay, when she told it:

"Strange to think, but I'd marry that man one day."

last wave

As you might expect, in a household of boys and young men, it wasn't so much spoken that one of us was leaving. He just was.

Tommy knew.

The mule, too.

Clay had stayed the night at The Surrounds again, waking Sunday morning, with the box still in his hands.

He sat and reread the letter.

He held the lighter and *Matador in the fifth*.

At home he brought the box inside and put the Murderer's sticky-taped address in, placed it deep beneath his bed, then quietly did his sit-ups, on the carpet.

About halfway through, Tommy appeared; he could see him from the edge of his sight, each time he came back down. The pigeon, T, was on his shoulder, and a breeze flapped Henry's posters. They were musicians, mostly; old ones. A few actresses; young and womanly.

"Clay?"

Tommy triangled each time into sight.

"Can you help me later with his feet?"

He finished up and followed to the backyard, and Achilles was near the clothesline. Clay walked over and gave him a sugar cube, open hand, then crouched and tapped a leg.

The first hoof came up; it was clean.

Then the second.

When the job was done on all four, Tommy was hurt in his usual way, but there was nothing for Clay to do. You can't change the mind of a mule.

To cheer him up, he took two more small white sugar cubes out.

He handed one over to Tommy.

The yard was full of morning.

An empty beanbag lay flat on the porch; it had slid off the ledge of the couch. In the grass was a bike with no handlebars, and the clothesline stood tall in the sun.

Soon Rosy came out from the shelter we'd built for Achilles at the back. She got to the Hills Hoist and started rounding it up, and the sugar lay melting on their tongues.

Near the end, Tommy said it:

"Who'll help me with this when you're gone?"

To which Clay did something that caught even himself by surprise:

He grabbed Tommy by the scruff of his T-shirt, and threw him on Achilles, bareback.

"Shit!"

Tommy had quite a shock, but soon gave himself over; he leaned in at the mule and laughed.

After lunch, as Clay started out the front door, Henry held him back.

"And where the hell do you think *you're* going?"

A brief pause. "The cemetery. Maybe Bernborough."

"Here," said Henry, grabbing his keys, "I'll come with you."

When they got there, they leaned forward, into the fence, they navigated the graves. At the one they wanted they crouched they watched they folded their arms they stood in the afternoon sun; they looked at the corpse of tulips.

"No daisies?"

They half laughed.

"Hey, Clay?"

Both were slouched yet stiff, and Clay now came to face him; Henry was affable as ever, but different in some way, too, looking out across the statues.

At first he just said, "God." A long silence. "*God*, Clay." And he pulled something out of his pocket. "Here."

Hand to hand:

A nice big slice of money.

"Take it."

Clay looked closer.

"It's yours, Clay. Remember the bets at Bernborough? You wouldn't believe how much we made. I never even paid you."

But no, this was more, it was too much, a paperweight of cash. "Henry—"

"Go on, take it," and when he did, he held its pages in his hand.

"Hey," said Henry. "Oi, Clay," and he met him, properly, in the eyes. "Maybe buy a Goddamn phone, like someone normal—let us know when you actually get there."

And Clay, a smile, of scorn:

No thanks, Henry.

"Okay—use every bloody cent for a bridge then." The wiliest of boyish grins. "Just give us the change when you're done."

At Bernborough Park, he did some laps, and after rounding the ruin of the discus net, he was given a nice surprise—because there, at the 300-meter mark, was Rory.

Clay stopped, his hands on quadriceps.

Rory watched with his scrap-metal eyes.

Clay didn't look up, but smiled.

Far from angry or betrayed, Rory was somewhere between amusement for the oncoming violence, and a perfect understanding. He said, "I gotta give it to you, kid—you've got heart."

And Clay stood fully upright now, first silent as Rory went on.

"Whether you're gone three days or three years . . . You know Matthew'll kill you, don't you? When you come back."

A nod.

"Will you be ready for him?"

"No."

"Do you want to be?" He thought about it. "Or maybe you never *will* come back."

Clay bristled, internally. "I'm coming back. I'll miss these little heart-to-hearts of ours."

Rory grinned. "Yeah, good one, look—" He was rubbing his hands together now. "Do you want some practice? You think I was tough down here? Matthew's a whole other thing."

"It's okay, Rory."

"You won't go fifteen seconds."

"But I know how to take a beating."

Rory, a single step closer. "That much I know, but I can at least show you how to last a bit longer."

Clay looked at him, right in the Adam's apple. "Don't worry, it's too late," and Rory knew better than anyone—that Clay was *already* ready; he'd been training for this for years now, and I could kill him all I wanted.

Clay just wouldn't die.

When he came back home, cash in hand, I was watching a movie, the first *Mad Max*—talk about suitably grim. At first, Tommy had been with me, and begged to watch something different.

"Can't we just once watch a movie not made in the eighties?" he said.

"We are. This was 1979."

"That's just what I was going to say! Eighties or even earlier. None of us were even *born*. Not even close! Why can't we just—"

"You *know* why," I cut him off. But then I saw that look on him, like he might even start to cry. ". . . Shit—sorry, Tommy."

"No you're not."

He was right, I wasn't; this was part of being a Dunbar.

When Tommy walked out, Clay walked in, once the money was deposited in the box. He came to the couch and sat.

"Hey," he said, he looked over, but I didn't take my eyes off the screen.

"You still got the address?"

He nodded, and we watched *Mad Max*.

"The eighties again?"

"Don't even start."

We were silent right up to the part when the scary gang leader says, "*And Cundalini wants his hand back!*" and I looked at my brother beside me.

"He means business," I said to him, "doesn't he?"

Clay smiled, but didn't react.

So do we.

In the night, when everyone else was in bed, he stayed up and left the TV on, with the sound completely down. He looked at Agamemnon, the goldfish, who watched him calmly back, before a last good headbutt at the tank.

Clay walked to the birdcage, and quickly, no warning, he took him. He squeezed him in his hand, but gently.

"Hey, T, you okay?"

The bird bobbed a little, and Clay could feel him breathe. He felt his heartbeat through the plumage. "Just hold still, boy—" and quick, like that, he snapped at his neck, he held the tiny feather; it was clean and grey with an edge of green, in the palm of his still left hand.

Then he put the bird back in.

The pigeon watched him seriously, then walked from end to end.

Next, the shelves and the board games:

Careers, Scrabble, Connect Four.

Beneath them, the one he wanted.

He opened it up and was distracted, momentarily, by the movie on TV. It looked like a good one—black-and-white, a girl arguing with a man in a diner—but then, the riches of Monopoly. He found the dice and hotels till he handled the bag he wanted, and soon, in his fingers, the iron.

Clay, the smiler, smiled.

* * *

Close to midnight, it was easier than it might have been; the yard was free of dog and mule shit, God bless Tommy's cotton socks.

Soon he stood at the clothesline, with the pegs pegged up above him, in rows of shifting color. He reached up and gently unclipped one. It was once bright blue, now faded.

He kneeled then, near the pole.

Of course, Rosy came over, and Achilles stood watch, with his hooves and legs beside him. His mane was brushed but knotted—and Clay reached over and leaned—a hand at the edge of a fetlock.

Next he held Rosy, very slowly, by a single black-and-white paw:

The gold in her eyes, goodbye to him.

He loved that sideways dog-look.

Then he headed further back, for The Surrounds.

As it was, he didn't stay very long; he was already gone, so he didn't remove the plastic. No, all he did was say goodbye, and promise to return.

At home, in the house, in his and Henry's room, he looked inside the box; the peg was the final object. In the dark, he saw the contents, from the feather to the iron, the money, the peg, and the Murderer's patched-up address. And, of course, the metallic lighter, inscribed from her to him.

Instead of sleep, he turned on the lamp. He repacked his suitcase. He read from his books, and the hours swept him by.

At just past three-thirty, he knew Carey would soon come out:

He got up and put the books back in the sports bag, and held the lighter in his hand. In the hallway he felt the engraving again, cut slimly into the metal.

He noiselessly opened the door.

He stood at the railing, on the porch.

Eons ago he'd been here with me. The front door ultimatum.

Soon, Carey Novac emerged, a backpack on her back and a mountain bike beside her.

First he saw a wheel: the spokes.

Then the girl.

Her hair was out, her footsteps fast.

She was in jeans. The customary flannel shirt.

The first place she looked was across the road, and when she saw him she put the bike down. It lay there, stuck on a pedal, the back wheel whirring, and the girl walked slowly over. She stood, dead center, on the road.

"Hey," she said, "you like it?"

She was quiet but it came out shouted.

A delighted kind of defiance.

The stillness of predawn Archer Street.

As for Clay, he thought of many things to say to her then, to tell her and have her know, but all he said was "Matador."

Even from a distance he could see her not-quite-white, not-quite-straight teeth, as her smile laid open the street; and finally, she held a hand up, and her face was something strange to him—at a loss for what to say.

When she left, she walked and watched him, then watched a moment longer.

Bye, Clay.

Only when he imagined her well down Poseidon Road did he look again into his hand, where the lighter dimly sat. Slow and calm he opened it, and the flame stood straightly up.

And so it was.

In the dark he came to all of us—from me lying straight in bed, to Henry's sleepy grin, and Tommy and Rory's absurdity. As a final act of kindness (to both of them) he pulled Hector from Rory's chest, and clamped him across his own shoulder, like one more part of his luggage. On the porch he put him down, and the tabby was purring, but he, too, knew Clay was leaving.

Well?

First the city, then the mule, now the cat did all the talking.

Or maybe not.

"Bye, Hector."

But he didn't leave, not yet.

No, for a long time, a few minutes at least, he waited for dawn to hit the street, and when it did it was gold and glorious. It climbed the rooves of Archer Street, and a tide came calling with it:

There, out there, was a mistake maker, and a distant statue of Stalin.

There was a birthday girl rolling a piano.

There was the heart of color in all that grey, and floating paper houses.

All of it came through the city, across The Surrounds and Bernborough. It rose in the streets, and when finally Clay left, there was light and gathering floodwater. First it reached his ankles, then his knees, until, by the time he made the corner, it was up to the height of his waist.

And Clay looked back, one last time, before diving—in, and outwards—to a bridge, through a past, to a father.

He swam the gold-lit water.

part three

cities + waters + criminals

the corridor

So THIS WAS WHERE HE WASHED UP.

In the trees.

For years now, Clay had imagined a moment like this—that he'd be strong, he'd be sure and ready—but those images were swept away; he was a shell of all he was.

Trying to recapture his resolve, he stood motionless, in this corridor of strapping eucalypts. He felt the pressure in his lungs: a sense of oncoming waves, though they were made now only of air. It took reminding to breathe them in.

Out here somewhere was where waters led.

Out here somewhere was where murderers fled.

Behind him, there was sleeping and reading, and the city's distant subdivisions. A lazy chain of metal, and countless miles of pure, ragged land. In Clay's ignorance, it was a place of great simplicity. There was train line and earth, and reams of empty space. There was a town called Silver, and no, it wasn't the town you might think (of dog, TW, and snake)—it was a town halfway between.

Small houses. Tidy lawns.

And winding past all of it, dry and cracked, was a broad, misshapen river. It had a strange name, but he liked it:

The Amahnu.

In the afternoon, when he arrived, he considered having the river lead him to his father, but opted for the town instead. He bought a foldout map from the petrol station. He walked the rusty street signs, and the drunken, sprawled-out beer cans. He found a road, north and west; he left the town behind.

Around him, as he walked, the world grew emptier still; it seemed to surge, continuously out, and then there was the other feeling—that it was also coming *at* him. There was an obvious, slow-approaching quiet, and he felt it, every step. The emptier it became, the closer the way, to our father's lonely home.

Somewhere, nowhere, there was a right turnoff from the road. A mail drum said the number, and Clay knew it, from the address in the wooden box. He took the dirt road driveway.

Initially it was stark and open, but after a few hundred meters and a gently sloping hill, he arrived in the corridor of trees. At eye level, the trunks were more like muscled thighs—like giants standing around. On the ground there were knots of bark, and long streaks of shedding, crumbling beneath his feet. Clay stayed; he wouldn't leave.

Beyond it, a car was parked, but still on this side:

A Holden, a long red box.

Further away, across the dry river, was a gate, in the light. And beyond the gate was a house; a hunchback, with sad eyes and a mouth.

Out amongst the tall bony weeds, there was life. Crouched in the heather and scrub and the Bernborough-like grass, the air was overrun. There was a teeming noise of insects, electric and erudite. A whole language in a single note. Effortless.

Clay, on the other hand, was laboring. He'd found in himself a fresh hemorrhage of fear and guilt, and doubt. It weaved through him, triple-tiered.

How many procrastinations could he work through?

How many times could he open the small wooden chest, and hold each item within?

Or rifle through the sports bag?

How many books could he reach for, and read?

How many letters to Carey could he formulate, but not yet write?

Once, his hand fell onto a long belt of late-afternoon sun.

"Go on."

He said it.

It shocked him that the words came out.

Even more so a second time.

"Go on then, boy."

Go on, Clay.

Go and tell him why you came. Look him in his weathered face and sunken murderous eyes. Let the world see you for what you are:

Ambitious. Stubborn. Traitorous.

Today, you're not a brother, he thought.

Not a brother and not a son.

Do it, do it now.

And he did.

the murderer wasn't always the murderer

Yes, Clay walked out and on, but who exactly was he walking to that afternoon? Who was he really, and where did he come from, and what decisions and indecisions had he made to become the man he was, and wasn't? If we imagine Clay's past coming in on the tide, then the Murderer had traveled toward it from a constant, distant dry land, and he was never the strongest swimmer. Maybe it's best summed up like this:

In the present, there was a boy walking toward what was so far only a wondrous, imagined bridge.

In the past, there was another boy, whose path—across longer distance and further years—had also ended here, but in adulthood.

Sometimes I have to remind myself.

The Murderer wasn't always the Murderer.

Like Penelope, he also came from far away, but it was a place in *this* place, where the streets were hot and wide, and the land was yellow and dry. Around it, a wilderness of low scrub and gum trees stood close by, and the people sloped and slouched; they lived in constant states of sweat.

Most of what it had, it had one:

One primary school, one high school.

One river, one doctor.

One Chinese restaurant, one supermarket.

And four pubs.

At the far end of town, a church hung in the air, and the people simmered inside it: men in suits, women in flower-patterned dresses, kids in shirts, shorts, and buttons, all dying to take their shoes off.

As for the Murderer, when he was a boy he wanted to be a typist, like his mother. She'd worked for the town's one doctor and spent her days punching away in the surgery, on the old Remington, bullet-grey. Sometimes she took it home with her, too, to write letters, and asked her son to carry it. "Here, show us your muscles," she'd tell him. "Can you help with the ol' TW?" The boy smiled as he lugged it away.

Her glasses were receptionist-red.

Her body was plump at the desk.

She had a prim voice, and her collars were stout and starched. Around her, patients sat with their sweat and their hats, their sweat and printed flowers, their sweat and sniffling children; they sat with their sweat in their laps. They listened to Adelle Dunbar's jabs and left hooks, as she worked that typewriter into a corner. Patient for patient, old Dr. Weinrauch emerged, like the pitchforked farmer in that painting *American Gothic*, then beamed to them, every time. "Who's next on the chopping block, Adelle?"

Out of habit, she looked at her chart. "That'd be Mrs. Elder," and whoever it was—whether a limping woman with a bum thyroid, a pub-drenched old man with a pickled liver, or a scab-kneed kid with a mystery rash in his pants—they each rose and sweated their way in, they lodged their various complaints . . . and sitting amongst the lot of them, on the floor, was the secretary's young boy. On the threadbare carpet, he built towers, he careered through countless comic books, and their crimes and chaos and *kapows*. He warded off the scowls of each freckle-faced tormentor from school, and flew spaceships around the waiting room: a giant, miniature solar system, in a giant, miniature town.

The town was called Featherton, though it was no more bird-like than any other place. Certainly, since he lived on Miller Street, near the river, his bedroom was filled—at least during times of rain—with the sound of flocking birds, and their various shrieks and laughters. At midday, crows made lunchtimes out of roadkill, hopping away for the semitrailers. In late afternoon, the cockatoos screeched—black-eyed and yellow-headed, and white in the blistering sky.

Still, birds or no birds, Featherton was famous for something else.

It was a place of farms and livestock.

A series of deep-holed mines.

More than anything, though, it was a place of fire:

It was a town where sirens howled and men of all descriptions, and a few women, zipped up orange overalls and walked out into the flames. Mostly, with the landscape stripped and stiffened black, they all returned, but every once in a while, when the fire roared that extra piece more, thirty-odd people would go in, and twenty-eight or twenty-nine would stagger back out; all sad-eyed, cough-ridden, but quiet. That's when boys and girls with skinny arms and legs, and old faces, were told, "I'm sorry, son" or "I'm sorry, darl."

Before he was the Murderer, he was Michael Dunbar.

His mother was an only parent, and he was an only child.

As you can see, in many ways, he was almost the perfect other half of Penelope; they were identical and opposite, like designed or destined symmetry. Where she came from a far-off watery place, his was remote and dry. Where he was the single son of an only mother, she was the only daughter of a single man. And lastly, as we're about to see—and this was the greatest mirror, the surest parallel of fate—while she was practicing Bach, Mozart, and Chopin, he was obsessing on an art form of his own.

One morning, spring holidays, when Michael was eight, he sat in the surgery waiting room and it was 39 degrees Celsius; the thermometer on the door frame said so.

Close by, old Mr. Franks smelt like toast.

His mustache still had jam in it.

Next was a girl from school named Abbey Hanley:

She had limp black hair and powerful arms.

The boy had just fixed a spaceship.

The postman, Mr. Harty, was struggling at the door, and Michael left the small grey toy near the girl's feet and helped the ailing postie, who stood like a hapless messiah, with the hellish light behind him.

"Hey, Mikey."

For some reason he hated to be called Mikey, but the young murderer-to-be squashed himself to the door frame and let him in. He turned back just in time to witness Abbey Hanley stand for her appointment, and crush the spaceship underfoot. She had a mighty pair of flip-flops.

"*Ab*bey!" laughed her mother. A few embarrassed notes. "That wasn't very nice."

The boy, watching the whole sad event, closed his eyes. Even at eight he knew what *fucking bitch* meant, and he wasn't afraid to think it. Then again, thinking it was no accomplishment, and he knew what that meant, too. The girl smiled out a pretty shameless "Sorry" and trudged toward old Weinrauch.

A meter away, the postman shrugged. A button was missing where his guts surged forward with great determination. "Girl trouble already, huh?"

Bloody hilarious.

Michael smiled, he spoke quietly. "Not really. I don't think she meant it." The fucking bitch.

Harty pressed him. "Oh, she meant it, all right."

Toast-and-Jam Franks coughed up a smirk of agreement, and Michael tried to move on. "What's in the box?"

"I just deliver, kid. How 'bout I put it down here and you do the honors? It's addressed to your mother, at home, but I figured I'd just bring it here. Go ahead."

When the door closed, Michael took another look.

He circled the box with suspicion, for it dawned on him what it was—he'd seen these boxes before:

The first year it was delivered in person, with condolences, and a stale pile of scones.

The second year it was left on the front porch.

Now they just shoved it in the post.

Charity for charred children.

Of course, Michael Dunbar himself wasn't charred at all, but his life, supposedly, was. Each year, start of spring, when rogue bushfires often began, a local philanthropy mob called the Last Supper Club took it upon themselves to prop up the lives of fire victims, whether they were physically burnt or not. Adelle and Michael Dunbar qualified, and this year all was typical—it seemed almost tradition that the box be both well-meaning and full to the brim with absolute shit. Soft toys were always despicably maimed. Jigsaw puzzles were guaranteed to be a few pieces short. Lego men were missing legs, arms, or heads.

This time around, when Michael went for a pair of scissors, he did so without enthusiasm, but when he returned and cut the box open, even Mr. Franks couldn't help peering in. The boy pulled out a sort of plastic roller coaster with abacus beads at one end, then some Lego—the giant kind, for two-year-olds.

"What, did they rob the bloody bank?" said Franks. He'd finally cleared out the jam.

Next was a teddy bear with one eye and half a nose. See? Brutalized. Beaten up in some kid's dark alleyway between bedroom and kitchen.

Then came a collection of *Mad* magazines. (Okay, fair enough, that was pretty good, even if the final fold-over page was already done, on every single one.)

And lastly, strangely—what was this?

What the hell *was* this?

Were these people having a laugh?

Because there, at the very bottom of the box, keeping the foundations together, was a calendar, and it was titled *Men Who Changed the World*. Was Michael Dunbar to choose a new father figure here?

Sure, he could go straight to January and John F. Kennedy.

Or April: Emil Zátopek.

May: William Shakespeare.

July: Ferdinand Magellan.

September: Albert Einstein.

Or December—where the page turned to a brief history and the work of a small, broken-nosed man, who would become, through time, everything the murderer-to-be admired.

Of course it was Michelangelo.

The fourth Buonarroti.

The oddest part about the calendar wasn't so much the contents but the fact that it was outdated; it was last year's. It most likely *was* just there to give added support to the box, and clearly it was well used: when each page opened to a photo or sketch of the man of the month, the dates were often scrawled with events, or things to do.

February 4: *Car registration due*.

March 19: *Maria M.—Birthday*.

May 27: *Dinner with Walt*.

Whoever owned the calendar had dinner with Walt on the last Friday of every month.

Now a small note about Adelle Dunbar, the red-rimmed receptionist:

She was a practical woman.

When Michael showed her the box of Lego and the calendar, she frowned and tilted her glasses. "Is that calendar . . . *used*?"

"Yep." Suddenly there was a kind of pleasure in it. "Can I keep it?"

"But it's last year's—here, give us a look." She flipped through the pages. She didn't overreact. It may have crossed her mind to march down to the woman responsible for sending this charity shitbox, but she didn't. She swallowed the glint of anger. She packed it into her prim-and-proper voice and, like her son, moved on. "You think there's a calendar of *women* who changed the world?"

The boy was at a loss. "I don't know."

"Well, do you think there *should* be?"

"I don't know."

"There's a lot you don't know, isn't there?" But she softened. "Tell you what. You really want this thing?"

Now that there was a chance he might lose it, he wanted it more than anything. He nodded on fresh batteries.

"Okay." Here came the rules. "How about you come up with twenty-four women who changed the world as well? Tell me who they are and what they did. Then you can keep it."

"Twenty-*four*?" The boy was outraged.

"There's a problem?"

"Here it's only twelve!"

"Twenty-four women." Adelle was really enjoying herself now. "Have you finished blowing up, or should we make it thirty-six?" She readjusted her glasses, and got straight back to work, and Michael returned to the waiting room. After all, there were some abacus beads to shove in a corner, and the *Mad* magazines to defend. The women would have to wait.

After a minute, he wandered back over, to a good solid round for Adelle, at the typewriter.

"Mum?"

"Yes, son?"

"Can I put Elizabeth Montgomery on the list?"

"Elizabeth who?"

It was his favorite repeated TV show, every afternoon. "You know—*Bewitched*," and Adelle couldn't help herself. She laughed and finished things off with a powerhouse full stop.

"Sure."

"Thanks."

In the middle of the small exchange, Michael was too preoccupied to notice Abbey Hanley return, sore-armed and teary, from the doctor's infamous chopping block.

If he *had* noticed, he'd have thought:

Well, one thing's for sure, I'm not putting *you* on the list.

It was a moment a bit like a piano, or a school car park, if you know what I mean—for it was strange to think, but he'd marry that girl one day.

the boyish hand

NOW HE APPROACHED THE RIVER AND IT WAS CUT AND DRY, CARVED OUT. IT turned through the landscape like a wound.

At the edge, as he made his way down, he noticed a few stray beams of wood, tangled in the earth. They were like oversized splinters, angled and bruised, delivered like that by the river—and he felt another change.

Not more than five minutes earlier he'd told himself he wasn't a son or brother, but here, in the last scraps of light, in what felt now like a giant's mouth, all ambitions of selfhood had vanished. For how do you walk toward your father without being a son? How do you leave home without realizing where you're from? The questions climbed beside him, up the other side of the bank.

Would our father hear him coming?

Would he walk to the stranger by his riverbed?

When he made it up, he tried not to think about it; he shivered. The sports bag was heavy across his back and the suitcase shook in what was suddenly just a boy's boyish hand.

Michael Dunbar—the Murderer.

Name, and nickname.

Clay saw him, standing in a darkened field, in front of the house.

He saw him, as we do, from far away.

men and women

You had to give it to the young Michael Dunbar.

He had a healthy sense of resolve.

He got his calendar of great men, but only after enlisting his mother to help him find the requisite twenty-four women—including Adelle herself, who he said was the world's greatest typist.

It had taken a few days, and a pile of encyclopedias, but they found the world-changing women easily:

Marie Curie, Mother Teresa.

The Brontë sisters.

("Does that count as three?")

Ella Fitzgerald.

Mary Magdalene!

The list was endless.

Then again, he was eight, and sexist as any young boy could be; only the men made it to his bedroom. Only the men were hung on the wall.

But still, I have to admit it.

It was nice, in a strange kind of way—a boy living a real life to a sweaty town's ticking clock, but also having another time frame, where the closest thing he had to a father was a paper trail of some of the greatest figures in history. If nothing else, those men, over the years, would make him curious.

At eleven, he got to know Albert Einstein, he looked him up. He learned nothing about the theory of relativity (he just knew it was genius), but he loved the old guy with the electric hair, poking his tongue out, midpage, of the calendar. At twelve, he'd go to bed and imagine himself training at altitude with Emil Zátopek, the legendary Czech long-distance runner. At thirteen, he wondered at Beethoven in his later years, not hearing a note he played.

And then—at fourteen:

The real breakthrough came, early December, taking the booklet from the nail.

A few minutes later, he sat down with it.

A few minutes later again, he was still staring.

"My God."

In previous years, on this last page of the calendar, he'd looked at the Giant, better known as *Il David*, or the statue of David, many mornings, many nights—but for the first time now, he saw it. He decided instantly with whom his true loyalties lay. By the time he stood again, he couldn't even be sure how long he'd been there, watching the expression on David's face—a statue in the grip of decision. Determined. Afraid.

There was also a smaller picture in the corner. *The Creation of Adam*, from the Sistine Chapel. The curvature of the ceiling.

Again, he said it.

"My God . . ."

How could someone create such things?

He borrowed books then, and there was a grand total of three titles on Michelangelo in the Featherton public and high school libraries combined. The first time he read them one by one, then a couple simultaneously. He read them each night, with his lamp burning long into the morning. His next goal was to trace some of the work, then memorize it, and draw it again.

Sometimes he wondered why he felt like this.

Why Michelangelo?

He'd catch himself crossing the street, saying his name.

Or listing his favorite works, in no particular order:

Battle of the Centaurs.

David.

Moses. The Pietà.

The Prisoners, or, as they were also called, *The Slaves.*

Those last ones always intrigued him for their unfinishedness—the giant figures, trapped inside the marble. One of the books, titled *Michelangelo: The Master*, went into great detail about those four particular sculptures and where they now lived, in the corridor of the Accademia Gallery in Florence; they led the way to David (although two more had escaped to Paris). In a dome of light stood a prince—a perfection—and flanking him, leading in, were these sad-but-gorgeous inmates, all fighting their way from the marble, unending, for the same:

Each of them pockmarked, white.

Their hands boxed up in stone.

They were elbows, ribs, and tortured limbs, and all were bent in struggle; a claustrophobic wrestle, for life and air, as the tourists flooded past them . . . all focused and fixed on *him:*

The royalty, gleaming, up ahead.

One of them, titled *Atlas* (of whom there were many pictures in that library book, from many angles), still carried the prism of marble on his neck, and battled the width and weight of it: his arms a marble rash, his torso a war on legs.

Like most, the adolescent Michael Dunbar was spellbound by David himself, but he had a soft spot for those beautiful, beaten-up slaves. Sometimes he'd recall a line, or an aspect, to copy out onto paper. Sometimes (and this embarrassed him a little) he actually wished that he could *be* Michelangelo, to become him only for a day or two. Often, he'd lie awake, indulging it, but knowing—he was a few centuries too late, and Featherton was a long way from Italy. Also (and this was the best part, I think), his art results at school had always been fairly poor, and by fourteen, it wasn't even one of his subjects.

That, and his ceiling was flat, and three meters by four.

* * *

Adelle, for her part, encouraged him.

In the years that came before, and the ones that lay ahead, she bought him new calendars, and books: the great natural wonders of the world, and the man-made wonders, too. Other artists—Caravaggio, Rembrandt, Picasso, Van Gogh—and he read the books, he copied the work. He especially loved Van Gogh's portraits of a postman (maybe in homage to old Harty), and he cut out pictures from the calendars as the months passed by, and stuck them to the wall. He enrolled in art again at school when the time came and gradually climbed past the others.

He could never let go of that first calendar, either.

It remained dead center in his bedroom.

When Adelle joked with him about it, he said, "I'd better get going, anyway."

"And where might you be off to?"

It was the closest he ever came to a knowing grin, recalling the monthly dinner date. "To Walt's, of course." He was going out to walk the dog.

"What's he cooking tonight, anyway?"

"Spaghetti."

"Again?"

"I'll bring you some home."

"Don't bother. I'll be asleep here at the table, most likely." She gave the ol' TW a pat.

"Okay, but just don't type too hard, all right?"

"Me?" She rolled a new sheet through the belly of the machine. "No way. A few friends to write to, and that's *it*."

They both laughed, almost for no reason—maybe just happiness.

He left.

At sixteen, his body grew, his hair changed shape.

He was no longer the boy who'd struggled to lift the typewriter, but an aqua-eyed, good-looking kid with dark wavy hair and a fast-looking physique.

Now he showed promise at football, or anything else deemed important, which is pretty much just to say, sport.

Michael Dunbar, however, wasn't interested in sport.

He went onto the school football team, of course, he played fullback, he did well. He stopped people. He'd usually check to see if the kid was okay, and he could also make a break; he could set someone up to score, or score himself.

Off the sports field there was a kindness that set him apart, and also a strange single-mindedness. He would suffer before he'd belong, unable to show himself easily; a preference for greater hope—to find someone who would know him completely.

As was tradition (in the sporting stakes, at least), girls followed, and they were predictable, in their skirts and shoes and matching booze. They chewed gum. They drank drinks.

"Hey, Mikey."

"Oh—hi."

"Hey, Mikey, a couple of us are goin' up to the Astor tonight."

Mikey wasn't interested—for if Michelangelo was the one man he truly loved, he also had his hands full with three girls:

First, the great typist—the counterpuncher in the waiting room.

Then there was the old red cattle dog who sat on the couch with him, watching repeats of *Bewitched* and *Get Smart*, and who lay asleep, chest heaving, as he cleaned the surgery, three nights a week.

And lastly, there was the one who sat in the front right corner of his English class, hunched and lovely, bony as a calf. (And it was she he was hoping might notice.) These days she had smoky grey eyes and wore a green checkered uniform, and hair that fell to her tailbone:

The waiting room spaceship-crusher had also changed.

In the evenings, he walked the town with the red cattle dog called Moon; named for the full moon camped above the house when his mother brought her home.

Moon was ash and ginger, and she slept on the floor of the back shed, while the boy drew at his father's workbench, or painted at the easel—his sixteenth birthday gift from Adelle. She rolled on her back and smiled at the sky when he rubbed her stomach on the lawn. "Come on, girl," and she came. She jogged next to him contently as he walked through months of longing and sketches, longing and portraits, longing and landscapes; the artwork and Abbey Hanley.

Always, in a town that turned slowly toward the dark—he could feel it coming for miles—he saw her up ahead. Her body was a brushstroke. Her long black hair was a trail.

No matter which streets he took through town, boy and dog made it out to the highway. They stood at the strings of a fence line.

Moon waited.

She panted and licked her lips.

Michael placed his fingers down, on the knots of barbed wire fence; he leaned forward, eyeing the corrugated roof, set deep on a distant property.

Only a few of the lights were on.

The TV flashed bright and blue.

Each night, before leaving, Michael stood still, with his hand on the head of the dog. "Come on, girl," and she came.

It wasn't till Moon died that he finally traversed the fence.

Poor Moon.

It was a normal afternoon, after school:

The town was slathered in sun.

She was laid out near the back step with a king brown snake, also dead, in her lap.

For Michael there was "Oh, Jesus" and quickened footsteps. He'd come round the back and heard the scratch of fallen schoolbag, as he kneeled on the ground, beside her. He would never forget the hot concrete, the warm dog-smell, and his head in her ginger fur. "Oh, Jesus, Moonie, no . . ."

He begged her to pant.

She didn't.

He pleaded with her to roll over and smile, or trot toward her bowl. Or dance, foot to foot, waiting for a deluge of dry food.

She didn't.

There was nothing now but body and jaws, open-eyed death, and he kneeled in the backyard sunshine. The boy, the dog and the snake.

Later, not long before Adelle came home, he carried Moon past the clothesline and buried her next to a banksia.

He made a pair of decisions.

First, he dug a separate hole—a few feet to the right—and in it he placed the snake; friend and foe, side by side. Second, he would cross the fence at Abbey Hanley's that night. He'd walk to the tired front door, and the TV's blue-blinking light.

In the evening, on the highway, there was the town behind him and the flies, and the pain of the loss of the dog—that naked, pantless air. The emptiness by his side. But then there was the other feeling. That sweet sickness of making something happen: the newness. And Abbey. The everything-equals-her.

All the way he'd lectured himself not to stand at the barbed wire fence, but now he couldn't resist. His life was reduced to minutes, till he swallowed and walked to the door—and Abbey Hanley opened it.

"You," she said, and the sky was bulging with stars.

An overabundance of cologne.

A boy with burning arms.

His shirt was too big in a country that was too big, and they stood on a front path all swarmed with weeds. The rest of the family ate No Frills ice cream inside, and the tin roof loomed, leaning at him as he searched for words, and wit. Words he found. Wit he didn't.

To her shins, he said, "My dog died today."

"I was wondering why you were alone." She smiled, just short of haughtily. "Am I the replacement?"

She was giving him a hiding!

He fought on.

"She was bitten." He paused. "A snake."

And that pause, somehow, changed it all.

While Michael turned to look at the deepening dark, the girl crossed from cocksure to stoic in a few short seconds; she stepped closer, and now she was next to him, facing the same way. Near enough so their arms touched.

"I'd rip a snake apart before I let it get to you as well."

After that, they were inseparable.

They watched those much-repeated sitcoms of previous years—his *Bewitched* and her *I Dream of Jeannie*. They crouched at the river or walked the highway out of town, watching the world grow seemingly bigger. They cleaned the surgery and listened to each other's heartbeats with Weinrauch's stethoscope. They checked each other's blood pressure till their arms were ready to explode. In the back shed, he sketched her hands, her ankles, her feet. He balked when it came to her face.

"Oh, come on, Michael . . ." She laughed and plunged her hand down into his chest. "Can't you get me right?"

And he could.

He could find the smoke in her eyes.

Her mocking, dauntless smile.

Even on paper she looked ready to speak. "Let's see how good you are—paint with your other hand."

At the highway farmhouse one afternoon, she took him in. She put a box of schoolbooks against her bedroom door, and held his hand and helped him with everything: the buttons, the clips, the descent to the floor. "Come here," she said, and there was the carpet and heat of shoulders and backs and tailbones. There was sun at the window, and books, and half-written essays everywhere. There was breath—her breath—and falling, just like that. And embarrassment. A head turned sideways, and brought back.

"Look at me. Michael, look at me."

And he looked.

This girl, her hair and smoke.

She said, "You know—" The sweat between each breast. "I never even said I was sorry."

Michael looked over.

His arm had gone dead, beneath her.

"For what?"

She smiled. "About the dog, and"—she was almost crying—"for crushing that spaceship thing in the waiting room that morning."

And Michael Dunbar could have left his arm down there forever; he was stunned and stilled, astounded. "You remember that?"

"Of course," she said, and now she spoke upwards, at the ceiling. "Don't you see?" Half of her in shadow, but the sun was on her legs. "I loved you already then."

the murderer's house

Just past the dry riverbed, Clay shook hands with Michael Dunbar in the dark, and their hearts were in their ears. The country was cooling down. For a moment he imagined the river, erupting, just for some noise, a distraction. Something to talk about.

Where was the Goddamn water?!

Earlier, when they'd seen each other, their faces searched, then down. Only when they were meters apart did they look for more than a second.

The ground felt alive.

Final darkness, and still no sound.

"Can I help with your bags?"

"No thanks."

His father's hand had been awfully clammy. His eyes were nervous, badly blinking. His face stooped, his walk was fatigued, and his voice was rarely used; Clay could hear that. He knew that all too well.

When they walked to the house and sat on the front step, the Murderer partly sank. His forearms were splayed; he held his face.

"You came."

Yes, Clay thought. I came.

Had it been anyone else, he'd have reached across and placed a hand on his back, to say it's okay.

But he couldn't.

There was only one thought, and the repetition of that thought.

I came. I came.

Today, that would have to be all.

When the Murderer recovered, it was a good while sitting there before they went in. The closer you got to it, the itchier the house seemed:

Rusty gutters, scales of paint.

It was surrounded by a virulent weed.

In front of them, the moon glowed, onto the worn-out path.

Inside, there were cream walls, and a great blast of hollow; all of it smelt alone.

"Cup of coffee?"

"No thanks."

"Tea?"

"No."

"Something to eat?"

"No."

They sat in the quiet of the lounge room. A coffee table was loaded with books, journals, and bridge plans. A couch ate them up, both father and son.

Jesus.

"Sorry—it's a bit of a shock, isn't it?"

"That's okay."

They were really hitting it off.

Eventually, they stood again, and the boy was given a tour.

It didn't take very long, but it was useful to know where to sleep, and where the bathroom was.

"I'll let you unpack, and have a shower."

In the bedroom there was a wooden desk, where he set up each and every book. He put clothes in the wardrobe, and sat on the bed. All he wanted was to be home again—he could have sobbed just to walk through the door. Or sit on the roof with Henry. Or see Rory staggering up Archer Street, a whole neighborhood of letterboxes on his back . . .

"Clay?"

He lifted his head.

"Come and eat something."

His stomach roared.

He leaned forward, feet glued to the floor.

He held the wooden box, he held the lighter and looked at *Matador*, and the fresh-collected peg.

For a whole range of reasons, Clay couldn't move.

Not yet, but soon.

the coast-long nighttime southerly

Of course, Abbey Hanley hadn't meant to destroy him.

It was just one of those things.

But one of those things turns into other things, which lead to more coincidence, which leads many years later to boys and kitchens, boys and hate—and without that long-lost girl there was none of it:

No Penelope.

No Dunbar boys.

No bridge, and no Clay.

All those years earlier, when it came to Michael and Abbey, everything was open and beautiful.

He loved her with lines and color.

He loved her more than Michelangelo.

He loved her more than the David, and those struggling, statued slaves.

At the end of school, both he and Abbey made good scores, they made city scores, and they were numbers of escape and wonder.

On Main Street, there was the odd pat on the back.

A few congratulationses.

Sometimes, though, there was a mild disdain, a sense of why-the-hell-would-you-want-to-leave? It was the men who did it best, especially the older ones, with their ripe faces, and an eye clenched tight at the sun. The words came out lopsided:

"So you're goin' the city, huh?"

"Yes, sir."

"*Sir?* You're not fuckin' there yet!"

"Shit—sorry."

"Well, just don't let 'em turn you into an arsehole, all right?"

"Say again?"

"You 'eard me. . . . Don't let 'em change y' like they change every other bastard who leaves. Never forget where y' from, right?"

"Right."

"Or *what* y' are."

"Okay."

Clearly, Michael Dunbar was from Featherton, and he was a bastard, but potentially an arsehole. The thing is, no one ever said, "And don't do anything that'll earn you a nickname like *Murderer*."

It was a big world out there, and the possibilities were endless.

The day the results came in, Christmas holidays, Abbey told him she'd stood by the letterbox. He almost could have painted it:

The mass of empty sky.

A hand on her hip.

She'd baked in the sun for twenty minutes before she went back for a lawn chair and a beach umbrella, a thousand miles from the sea. Then for a cooler, and some Icy Poles; God, she had to get out of here.

In town, Michael was hurling bricks up to a guy on a scaffold who was hurling bricks up to another guy. Somewhere, much higher, someone was laying those bricks, and a new pub was going up: for miners, farmers and minors.

At lunch, he walked home and saw his future, folded up, poking out, in the cylinder reserved for the junk mail.

Ignoring the omen, he opened it. He smiled.

When he phoned Abbey, she was panting from running up the path. "I'm still waiting! Bloody town wants to keep me here an extra hour or two, I reckon, just to punish me."

Later, though, at the job, she'd appeared and stood behind him, and he'd glanced back and dropped his bricks, one each side. He faced her fully. "Well?"

She nodded.

She laughed and so did Michael, until the voice flew down, between them.

"Oi, Dunbar, y' useless prick! Where are me Goddamn bricks?!"

Abbey, ever-present, called back.

"Poetry!"

She grinned, and left.

A few weeks later, they *left*.

Yes, they packed and headed for the city, and how do you sum up four years of apparent, idyllic happiness? If Penny Dunbar was good at using a part to tell the whole, these were parts that remained only that—just fragments and drifting moments:

They drove eleven hours, till they saw the rising skyline.

They pulled over and watched the length of it, and Abbey stood up on the hood.

They drove onwards till they were in it, and part of it, and the girl was in her commerce degree, and Michael was painting and sculpting, surviving the surrounding geniuses.

They both worked part-time jobs:

One serving drinks in a nightclub.

The other as a laborer, on construction sites.

At night, they'd fall into bed, and each other.

There were pieces, given and taken.

Season after season.

Year after year.

Now and then, on afternoons, they ate fish-'n'-chips at the beach, and watched the seagulls appear, like magic, like rabbits out of hats. They felt the myriad sea breezes, each one different from the last, and the weight of heat and humidity. Sometimes they'd just sit there, as a giant black cloud floated in, like the mother ship, and then run in its oncoming rain. It was rain that fell like a city itself, with the coast-long nighttime southerly.

It was milestones, too, and birthdays, and one in particular, when she gave him a book—a beautiful hardcover with bronze lettering—called *The Quarryman*, and Michael staying up reading, while she slept against his legs. Always, before he closed it, he'd go again to the front, to the author's short biography, where below, midpage, she'd written:

For Michael Dunbar—the only one
I love, and love
and love.
From Abbey

And of course, not long after, it was going home to get married on a still spring day with the crows *aaring* outside, like inland pirates:

Abbey's mother sobbed happily in the front pew.

Her father traded a worn work singlet for a suit.

Adelle Dunbar sat with the good doctor, eyes glowing behind some brand-new blue-rimmed glasses.

It was Abbey crying herself that day, all wet, white dress and smoky.

It was Michael Dunbar as a younger man, carrying her out into sunshine.

It was driving back, a few days later, and stopping halfway, where the river was awesome, something insane, raging downstream—a river with a strange name, but a name they loved—the Amahnu.

It was lying there, under a tree, her hair itching him, and him not moving it, ever, and Abbey telling him she'd love to come back; and Michael saying, "Of course—we'll make money, and build a house, and come here whenever we want."

It was Abbey and Michael Dunbar:

Two of the happiest bastards who ever had the nerve to leave.

And oblivious of all to come.

the big sleep

THE NIGHT WAS LONG, AND LOUD WITH CLAY'S THOUGHTS.

At one point, he got up to use the bathroom and found the Murderer, half-swallowed, on the couch. Books and diagrams weighed him down.

For a while, he stood over him.

He looked at the books, and the sketches on the Murderer's chest. The bridge, it appeared, was his blanket.

Then the morning—but morning wasn't morning at all, it was two in the afternoon, and Clay woke in bed with a fretful start, the sun on his throat, like Hector. Its presence in the room was huge.

When he got up he was totally mortified; he scrambled. No. No. Where is he? Quickly, he stumbled to the hall, got outside, and stood on the porch in his shorts. How could I have slept so long?

"Hey."

The Murderer watched him.

He'd come round from the side of the house.

He got dressed and they sat in the kitchen, and this time he ate. The old oven with its black-and-white clock had barely clicked over from 2:11 to 2:12, and he'd eaten a few slices of bread, and a fair few murderous eggs.

"Keep going. You're going to need your strength."

"Sorry?"

Now the Murderer chewed and sat, he was opposite.

Did he know something Clay didn't?

Yes.

There'd been calls from the bedroom through the morning.

He'd slept and shouted my name.

One long sleep and now I'm behind.

That was Clay's recurring thought as he continued to eat in spite of himself—and he would fight to scratch himself free.

Bread and words. "It won't happen again."

"Sorry?"

"I never sleep that long. I barely sleep at all."

Michael smiled; yes, he was Michael. Was that a past lifeblood flowing through him again? Or was that just how it appeared?

"Clay, it's okay."

"It's not—ah—God!"

He'd rushed to stand up and collected the table with his knee.

"Clay—please."

For the first time, he studied the face in front of him. It was an older version of me, but the eyes not caught by fire. All the rest of him, though: the black hair, even the tiredness looked the same.

He pulled his chair out properly this time, but the Murderer held up a hand. "Stop."

But Clay was ready to walk, and not just out of the room.

"No," he said, "I—"

Again, the hand. Worn and calloused. Workman's hands. He waved as if at a fly on a birthday cake. "Shh. What do you think's out there?"

Which meant:

What was it that made you come here?

All Clay heard was the insects. The single note.

Then the thought of something great.

He stood, bent-postured against the table. He lied, he said, "There's nothing."

The Murderer wasn't fooled. "No, Clay, it brought you here, but you're afraid, so it's easier to sit here and argue."

Clay straightened. "What are you even talking about?"

"I'm saying it's okay—" He broke off, and slowly studied him. A boy he couldn't touch, or reach. "I don't know how long you stood in those trees yesterday, but you must have come out for a reason. . . ."

Jesus.

The thought came in with the heat.

He saw me. All afternoon.

And "Stay," said the Murderer, "and eat. Because tomorrow I have to show you—there's something you need to see."

zátopek

In terms of Michael and Abbey Dunbar, I guess it's time to ask:

What was the real happiness between them?

What was the truth?

The true one?

Let's start with the artwork.

Sure, he could paint well, often beautifully; he could capture a face, or see things a certain way. He could realize it on canvas or paper, but when it came down to it, he knew: he worked twice as hard as the students around him, who could all produce somehow faster. And he was truly gifted in only one area, which was something he also clung to.

He was good at painting Abbey.

Several times, he'd nearly quit art school altogether.

The only thing that stopped him was the thought of going back to her, admitting failure. So he stayed. He somehow survived on good essays and flashes of brilliance when he so much as inserted her into a background. Someone would always say, "Hey, I like *this* bit." There was patience and revelation only for her.

For his final assignment, he found an abandoned door and painted her, both sides of it. On one panel she was reaching for the handle, on the other she was leaving. She entered as a teenager; the girl in school uniform, that bony-yet-softness, and endless hair. Behind it, she left—high-heeled, in a bob, all business—looking over her shoulder, at everything in between. When he received his result, he knew already what it would say. He was right:

Door idea fairly cliché.
Technique proficient but no more, but I admit I want to know her.
I want to know what happened in between.

Whatever did lie in the world between those images, you knew this woman would be okay on the other side—especially, as it turned out, without him.

When they returned to the city married, they rented a small house on Pepper Street. Number thirty-seven. Abbey had a bank job—the first one she applied for—and Michael worked the construction sites, and painted in the garage.

It was surprising how quickly the cracks appeared.

Not even a year.

Certain things became obvious, like everything was her idea:

That house for rent, those black-edged plates.

They went and saw movies when it was her thought, not his, and while her degree propelled her immediately forward, he was where he'd always been, on those building slabs; it felt like she was a life force, and he was just a life. In the beginning, the end was this:

It was night.

It was bed.

She sighed.

He raised his head to see. "What is it?"

She said, "Not like that."

And from there it went from "Show me" to "I can't teach you anymore" to "What do you mean?" to her sitting up and saying, "I mean I can't show you everything, I can't take you with me. You have to figure it out."

Michael was shocked at how calmly she delivered the blows, with the dark up against the window.

"In all the time we've been together, I don't think you've ever really . . ." She stopped.

"What?"

It was such a small swallow, to prepare. "Initiated."

"Initiated? Initiated what?"

"I don't know—everything—where we live, what we do, what we eat, where and when and how we—"

"Jesus, I—"

She sat up a notch higher. "You never just take me. You never make me feel like you have to *have* me, no matter what. You make me feel like . . ."

He didn't want to know. "Like—what?"

In a mildly slighter tone: "Like the boy I pulled down to the floor, back home . . ."

"I—" But there was nothing else there.

Just I.

I and nothingness.

I and sinking, and the clothes hung over a chair—and Abbey wasn't finished.

"And maybe everything else too, like I said . . ."

"Everything else?"

The room felt sewn together now, there to be pulled apart. "I don't know." She sat straighter, yet again, for the courage. "Maybe without me, you'd still be at home with all the arsehole sayers, blue singlet wearers, and the rest. You might still be cleaning that shit-heap surgery and throwing bricks up to other blokes throwing bricks up."

He ate down his heart, and a fair share of the dark. "I came to you."

"When your dog died."

It hit him hard. "The dog. How long have you been waiting to unleash that?" (There was no pun intended, I'm sure of it.)

"Never. It just came out." Now she crossed her arms, but didn't really cover herself, and she was beautiful and naked and her collarbones so straight. "Maybe it's always been there."

"You were jealous of a dog?"

"No!" Again, he was beside the point. "I'm just—I'm wondering why it took you *months* to walk to my front door after watching and waiting! Hoping I'd do it for you—to chase you down the road."

"You never did that."

"Of course not . . . I couldn't." She didn't quite know where to look now, and settled for directly ahead. "God, you just don't get it, do you?"

That last one was like a death knell—a truth so quiet and brutal. The effort it took had weakened her, if only momentarily, and she slid back down upon him, her cheek like stone on his neck. "I'm sorry," she said, "I'm so sorry."

But for some reason, he went on with it.

Maybe to welcome the nearing defeat.

"Just tell me." The taste of his voice. It was dry and sandy, and those bricks had been thrown up to *him*, and he swallowed them each in turn. "Just tell me how to fix it."

The act of breathing was suddenly an Olympic final, and where was Emil Zátopek when he needed him? Why hadn't he trained like that lunatic Czech? An athlete with that sort of endurance could surely stand up to a night like this.

But could Michael?

Again:

"Just tell me, I'll fix it."

"But that's it."

Abbey's voice was horizontal, put there, dropped on his chest. No anxiety, no labor.

No desire to fix or be fixed:

"Maybe there *is* nothing," she said. "Maybe it's." She full-stopped. She began. "Maybe we're just—not right, the way we thought."

His last gasp now, final breath:

"But I— . . ." He cut off; he trailed. "So much."

"I know you do," and there was such pity in her, but a ruthless kind. "I do too, but maybe it's not enough."

Had she ended it with a pinprick, he'd have bled to death in bed.

the amahnu

The night ahead, having slept so long and hard during the day, was as wretched and restless as the last. He looked through the wooden box, and thought back to the morning porch:

The milk jumping the rail.

The jugular in my neck.

He saw Achilles and Tommy, Henry and Rory.

And Carey.

Of course he thought of Carey, and Saturday, and if she might go to The Surrounds anyway. He'd die to know, but would never ask her, and then he stopped and fully realized—a final forceful acknowledgment.

He got up and leaned forward on the desk.

You're gone, he thought.

You left.

Soon after dawn the Murderer was up, too, and they walked the river like a road; they hiked up from the house.

At first there was a general slant, as the riverbed rose in altitude.

After a few hours, though, they were climbing giant, crestfallen boulders, and holding on to willows and river gums. Whether steep or gradual, one thing never changed; they could always see the power. The banks had a sort of girth. There was an obvious history of debris.

"Look at this," the Murderer said. They were in a heavily wooded section;

there were ladders of sunlight, hung up high in the shade, all in varied directions. His foot on an uprooted tree. A jacket of moss, and foliage.

And this, thought Clay.

He was next to an enormous rock, which appeared to have been dislodged.

They climbed more than half the day like that, and ate lunch on a long, granite overhang. They looked across the ranges.

The Murderer unpacked his bag.

Water. Bread and oranges. Cheese and dark chocolate. All of it passed from hand to hand, but nothing much more was said. Clay was sure there were similar thoughts, though—of the river, its showing of force:

So this is what we're up against.

Through afternoon, they walked back down. Now and then a hand would reach up, to help the other, and when they returned, in darkness, in the riverbed, nothing more yet was spoken.

But surely it was now.

If ever there was a time to begin, it was this.

It wasn't.

Not really:

There were still too many questions, too much memory—but one of them had to make a start, and the Murderer, rightfully, cracked first. If anyone was to attempt a sense of partnership, it should be him. They'd walked many miles together that day, and so he looked at him, and asked:

"You want to build a bridge?"

Clay nodded but looked away.

"Thanks," said Michael.

"For what?"

"For coming."

"I didn't come here for you."

Family bonding, the Clay way.

a gallery of abbeys

In many ways, I guess it's true, that even bad times are full of good times (and great times) and the time of their demise was no different. There were still those Sunday mornings, when she'd ask him to read to her in bed, and she'd kiss him with her morning breath, and Michael could only surrender. He'd gladly read *The Quarryman*. He'd first run a finger on the lettering.

She'd say, "What was the name of that place again, where he learned about marble, and stone?"

Quietly, he'd answer.

The town was Settignano.

Or, "Read what it says about the *Prisoners* again."

Page 265:

"They were wild and twisted—unfashioned, incomplete—but they were colossal, monumental anyway, and would fight, it seemed, for forever."

"*For* forever?" She'd roll onto him and kiss his stomach; she'd always loved his stomach. "Is that a misprint, do you think?"

"No, I think he meant it. He's gambling on us thinking it's a mistake . . . imperfect, like the *Slaves*."

"Huh." She'd kiss and kiss again, across and over, up toward his ribcage. "I love it when you do that."

"Do what?"

"Fight for what you love."

* * *

But he couldn't fight for her.

Or at least, not how she wanted.

To be fair, there was nothing malicious in Abbey Dunbar, but as time widened and the good moments shortened, it became clearer, each day, that their lives were going separate ways. More to the point, she was changing, he stayed the same. Abbey never took aim or attacked him. It just got slippery, the hanging on.

Looking back, Michael remembered movies. He remembered times when the entire Friday-night cinema laughed, when *he* laughed, and Abbey sat watching, unfazed. Then, when the whole brigade of moviegoers was dead silent, Abbey would smile at something private, just her and the screen. If only he could have laughed when she did, maybe they'd have been okay—

But he stopped himself.

That was ridiculous.

Movies and plastic popcorn don't increase the chances of decimation, do they? No, it was more a compilation: a *greatest hits* of two people who'd traveled as far as they could together, to fade away.

Sometimes she had friends over from work.

They had clean fingernails.

Both women and men.

It was a long way from construction zones.

Michael was painting a lot in the garage, too, so his hands were either powdery or stubbed with color. He drank coffee from the kettle, they drank it from machines.

As for Abbey, her hair was increasingly cropped, her smile business-like, and in the end, she was brave enough to leave. She could touch his arm like years gone by, with a comment or a quip. Or joke and wink and smile at him—but each time was less convincing. He knew very well that later on, they'd be in separate states of the bed.

"Good night."

"I love you."

"Love you, too."

Often, he'd get up.

He'd go to the garage and paint, but his hands were so damn heavy, as if caked, cemented in. Often, he took *The Quarryman*, too, and read pages like a kind of prescription; each word to ease the pain. He would read and work till his eyes burned, and a truth beside, then on him.

There was he and Buonarroti.

One artist in the room.

Maybe if they'd argued.

Maybe that's what was missing.

Some volatility.

Or maybe just more cleaning up.

No, it was pure and simple fact:

Life was pointed elsewhere for Abbey Dunbar now, and a boy she once loved, behind her. Where once he painted her and she loved him for it, now it seemed only a lifeline. He could capture her laughing over the dishes. Or standing by the sea, with surfers at her back, post-wave. They were still lovely and rich, those paintings, but where once there was only love in them, now it was love and neediness. It was nostalgia; love and loss.

Then one day, she stopped, midsentence.

She whispered, "It's a shame . . ."

The suburban almost-quiet.

"It's such a shame, because . . ."

"What?"

As was becoming more common, he didn't really want to hear, and he turned his back on the answer. He was at the kitchen sink.

She said, "I think maybe you love the painted version of me more . . . you paint me better than I really am."

The sun glittered. "Don't say that." He died right then, he was sure of it. The water was grey, sort of overcast. "Don't ever say that again."

* * *

When the end came, she told him in the garage.

He stood with paintbrush in hand.

Her bags were packed.

He should keep all the paintings.

Her expression apologetic, as he asked his futile questions. Why? Was there someone else? Did the church, the town, the everything mean nothing?

But even then, when fury should have ruled over sense, it was only threads of sadness that hung from the rafters. They blew and swung like cobwebs, so fragile and, ultimately, weightless.

A gallery of Abbeys stood behind them, watching the whole scene:

She laughed, she danced, she absolved him. She ate and drank and spread herself, naked, on the bed; all while the woman in front of him—the unpainted one—explained. There was nothing he could say or do. A minute's worth of sorries. For all of it.

And his second-last plea was a question.

"Is he waiting out front?"

Abbey closed her eyes.

And the last, like a reflex, was this:

On a stool, by the easel, was *The Quarryman*, lying facedown, and he reached for it, he held the book out; and for some strange reason she took it. Maybe it was purely so that a boy and a girl could go after it, many years later. . . . They would keep and read and obsess over it, lying on a mattress, in an old forgotten field, in a whole city of forgotten fields—and all of that coming from here.

She took it.

She held it in her hand.

She kissed her fingers and placed those fingers on the cover, and she was so sad, and somehow gallant, and she took it away, and the door blew shut behind her.

And Michael?

From the garage, he heard the engine.

Someone else.

He sagged to the paint-spattered stool and said "No" to the girl around him, and the engine grew louder, then ebbed, then disappeared completely.

For a long time, he sat, he kept quiet and shivery, and without a sound he started to cry. He cried his stray silent tears into the passing face of artworks close by—but then he relented, and laid himself down, curled up, on the floor. And Abbey Dunbar, who wasn't Abbey Dunbar anymore, watched over him, all night, in all her many forms.

pont du gard

For the next four or five days, father and son fell into a routine. It was a careful, side-by-side partnership, maybe like two boxers in the opening rounds. Neither was willing to take too big a risk, for fear of being knocked out. Michael, especially, was playing it safe. He didn't want any more of those I-didn't-come-here-for-you moments. They weren't good for anyone—or maybe just not for him.

On Saturday, the day Clay missed home the most, they walked down the river, instead of up, and he was tempted at times to talk.

At first it was only simple things.

Did the Murderer have a job?

Exactly how long had he lived here?

But then more searchingly, or appealing:

What the hell was he waiting for?

When would they start building?

Was this bridge procrastination?

It reminded him of Carey, and old McAndrew—how asking questions would hold her back. In his case, though, there was history.

As a boy who'd once loved stories, he'd been better before at asking.

Most mornings, the Murderer went to the riverbank and stood.

He could do it for hours.

Then he'd come in and read, or write on his loose-leaf papers.

Clay went out on his own.

Sometimes he went upriver; the great blocks of stone. He sat on them, missing everyone.

On Monday, they went to town, for food supplies.

They walked across the riverbed; its dryness.

They took the red box of a car.

Clay sent a letter to Carey and a collective note home, through Henry. Where the first was a detailed account of much that had happened, the second was typical of brothers.

Hi Henry—

Everything okay here.

You?

Tell the others.

Clay

He remembered Henry suggesting a phone to him, and the thought was somehow fitting; his note was more like a text.

He'd agonized over putting a return address on the envelopes, and chose to put one only on Henry's. Telling Carey, though? He didn't know. He didn't want her to feel she had to write back. Or maybe he was scared she wouldn't.

On Thursday, everything changed, or at least just slightly, in the evening; Clay sat with him voluntarily.

It was in the lounge room, and Michael said nothing, he just gave him a careful glance, and Clay on the floor, near the window. At first he'd been reading the last of her books—the generous Claudia Kirkby—but now he was onto a bridge almanac; the one he had read most often. The title wasn't too inspired, but the book itself he loved. *The Greatest Bridges of Them All.*

For a while it was hard to concentrate, but after a good half hour, the first smile came to his face, when he saw his favorite bridge.

Le Pont du Gard.

Great wasn't a great enough word to explain that bridge, which also served as an aqueduct.

Built by the Romans.

Or the devil, if you believed it.

As he looked at its arches—the half dozen huge ones at the bottom, eleven on its midlevel, and thirty-five across the top—he smiled, then felt it broaden.

When he caught himself, he checked.

Close one.

The Murderer nearly saw.

On Sunday evening, Michael found Clay in the riverbed, where the road, each side, was cut off. He stood a way back and spoke. "I have to go, for ten days."

He did have a job.

In the mines.

Another six hours west, out past the old town, Featherton.

As he spoke, the setting sun looked lazy at first, far away. Trees were in lengthening shade.

"You can either go home for those ten days, or you can stay."

Clay stood and faced the horizon.

The sky now hard-fought, leaking blood.

"Clay?"

The boy turned and gave him his first inkling of camaraderie then, or a piece of himself; he told a truth. "I can't go home." It was still far too early to attempt it. "I can't go back—not yet."

Michael's reaction was to pull something from his pocket.

It was a real estate pamphlet, with photos of the land, the house, and a bridge. "Go on," he said. "Take a look."

The bridge had been a handsome one. A simple trestle, of railway sleepers and wooden beams, once spanning the space they were standing in.

"It was here?"

He nodded. "What do you think of it?"

Clay saw no reason to lie. "I like it."

The Murderer ran a hand through his wavy hair. He rubbed at an eye. "The river destroyed it—not long after I moved in. And barely any rain since then. It's been dry like this a good while."

Clay took a step toward him. "Was there anything left?"

Michael pointed to the few embedded planks.

"That's it?"

"That's it."

There was still the red rumbling out there, a silent flood of bleeding.

They walked back to the house.

At the steps, the Murderer asked.

"Is it Matthew?" He'd handed it across more than spoken it. "You say his name a lot, in your sleep," and he hesitated. "You say all of them, to tell you the truth, and others. Ones I've never heard of."

Carey, Clay thought, but Michael said Matador.

He said, "Matador in the fifth?"

But that was enough.

Don't push your luck.

When Clay gave him the look, the Murderer understood. He came back to the original question. "Did Matthew say you couldn't go back?"

"No, not exactly."

There was no need for anything else:

Michael Dunbar knew the alternative.

"You must miss them."

And Clay raged at him, within.

He thought of boys, backyards, and clothesline pegs.

He looked into him and said, "Don't you?"

Early, very early in the morning, close to three o'clock, Clay noticed the shadow of the Murderer, standing next to his bed. He wondered if it recalled in him, as it did in himself, the last time he'd stood just like that, on the terrible night when he'd left us.

At first he'd thought it was an intruder, but soon he was able to see. He knew those hangman's hands anywhere. He heard the fallen voice:

"Pont du Gard?"

Quiet, so quiet.

So he'd seen him after all.

"Is that your favorite?"

Clay swallowed, he nodded in the darkness. "Yes."

"Any others?"

"The Regensburg. The Pilgrim's Bridge."

"That's three arches."

"Yes."

More thoughts, back to back. "Do you like the Coathanger then?"

The Coathanger.

The great bridge of the city.

The great bridge of home:

A different kind of arch, a metal one, who rose above the road.

"I love her."

"It's female?"

"She is to me."

"Why?"

Clay tightened his eyes, then opened them.

Penny, he thought.

Penelope.

"She just is."

Why did it need explaining?

Slowly, the Murderer backed away, into the rest of the house, and told him, "See you soon." But then he added, in a moment of hope and recklessness, "Do you know the legend of Pont du Gard?"

"I need to sleep."

Of course he Goddamn knew.

* * *

In the morning, though, in the empty house, Clay stopped in the kitchen when he saw it—on paper, in thick black charcoal.

He let a finger fall, and he touched them:

Final Bridge Plan: First Sketch

He thought of Carey and thought of arches, and again his voice surprised him:

"The bridge will be made of you."

five years and a piano, and following hand over hand

Five long years he lay in that garage, on the floor, till it happened.

Something made him get up:

The piano.

A muddled address.

The light of afternoon.

Here came a woman with music and two epics on her side, and what else could Michael Dunbar do?

As far as second chances go, he couldn't have been luckier.

But okay, what happened in those five years in between?

He signed the lawyer forms, hands trembling.

He stopped painting altogether.

He was tempted to return to Featherton, but also remembered the voice in the dark, and the head down on his neck:

Maybe you'd still be there.

And then the humiliation.

Returning without the girl.

"Where is she?" people would ask.

"What happened?"

No, he could never go back for good. Word would get around, but that didn't mean he wanted to hear it. It was bad enough listening to the thoughts that lay within.

"*What?*"

It would come to him often, halfway through dinner, or brushing his teeth.

"She just *left* him?"

"Poor guy."

"Well, we can't say we didn't see it coming. . . . She was wild, and he was, well, he was never the quickest of cats, was he?"

No, it was better to stay in the city. Better to stay in the house, and catch the scent of her less each day. After all, there was always work. The city grew. There was always a beer or two, alone at home, or with Bob and Spiro and Phil—just men from work, with wives and kids, or nothing, like him.

It was only to visit his mother that he returned to Featherton every now and then. He was happy to see her involved with the usual array of small-town escapades. Cake stalls. Anzac Day parades. Lawn bowls with Dr. Weinrauch on Sundays. That was the life.

When he told her about Abbey, she didn't say much.

Her hand rested on his.

She was most likely thinking of her own husband, who'd walked into the flames. No one knew why some went in and didn't come out. Did they want to come out that little bit less than the others? If nothing else, Michael Dunbar was never of two minds about Abbey.

Next, the paintings, which he couldn't look at anymore.

Her image would start him wondering.

Where she was.

Who she was with.

The temptation was to imagine her in motion, with another man. A better man. No niceties.

He wanted to be less superficial than that, to say that such things didn't matter, but they did. They reached below, at something deeper, and they were places he didn't want to be.

One night, about three years in, he pulled the paintings to one side of the garage, and covered them end to end, with bedsheets: a life behind a curtain. Even when the job was done, he still couldn't quite resist; he took one last look inside, he ran a palm across the biggest, where she stood, shoes in hand, on the shoreline.

"Go on then," she said, "take them."

But there was nothing left to have.

He pulled the sheets back down.

As the remaining time climbed by, he was swallowed by the city.

He worked, he drove.

He mowed the lawn; a nice boy, a good tenant.

And how could he ever know?

How could he know that two years later again, an immigrant girl's father would be dead on a European park bench? How could he know that she'd go out in a fit of love and despair, and buy a piano, and have it delivered not to her, but to him—and that she'd be standing in the middle of Pepper Street, with a trio of useless piano men?

In many ways he'd never left that garage floor, and so often I can't help seeing it:

He crouches and gets to his feet.

The sound of faraway traffic—so much like the ocean—a long five years behind him, and I think it, again and again:

Do it, do it now.

Go to that woman and piano.

If you don't go now there'll be none of us—no brothers, no Penny, no father or sons—and all that there is is to have it, to make it, and to run with it as long as you can.

part four

cities + waters + criminals
+
arches

the clay stack

On that Monday, after Michael had left in the dark, and Clay saw the sketch in the kitchen, he'd made breakfast and walked to the lounge room. The Murderer's notes, sheets, and workings were in seven separate stacks on the coffee table. Some were taller than others, but all had a title on top. On each stack was a rock, or stapler, or scissors, to keep them from flying off. Slowly, he read each title:

MATERIALS

COUNCIL

SCAFFOLD

THE OLD PLAN (TRESTLE)

THE NEW PLAN (ARCHES)

RIVER

and

CLAY

Clay sat down.

He let the couch devour him.

He spelt Carey's name out in his toast crumbs, then reached for the pile called *SCAFFOLD*.

From there, he read all day.

He didn't eat or go to the bathroom.

He just read and watched and learned everything about the bridge in

Michael Dunbar's mind, and it was a great mess of charcoal and thick-set pencil. Especially *THE OLD PLAN*. That stack was 113 pages (he counted them), full of wood costs, techniques, and pulley systems, and why the previous bridge might have failed.

THE NEW PLAN was six sheets altogether—composed the night before. The first page of that small stack of paper said only one thing, several times.

PONT DU GARD.

The pages that followed were littered with sketches and drawings, and a list of definitions:

Spandrels and *voussoirs*.

Springing and *falsework*.

Crown and *keystone*.

Old favorites like *abutment* and *span*.

In short, the spandrels were standard stone blocks; the voussoirs were contoured for the arching. The springing was the final pressure point, of arches-meeting-pier. His favorite was somehow the falsework, though—the mold the arches were built on; a curvature of wooden construction. It would hold, then be taken from under it: the first test of each arch and survival.

Then *CLAY*.

He kept his eye on that *CLAY* stack, many times, as he read through everything else. The thought of picking it up excited him, but also held him just short. On top, its paperweight was a rusty old key, and below, a single sheet.

When Clay finally read it, it was evening.

He removed the key and held it slackly in his palm, and when he turned the title page, this was written beneath:

Clay—

See page 49 of THE OLD PLAN.

Good luck.

Michael Dunbar

Page forty-nine.

That was where it explained the importance of digging a trench across the forty-meter width of the river—to be working, all times, on the bedrock. As first-time bridge builders, it stated, they should go beyond where experts would, to be sure they weren't taking chances. There was even a sketch: forty by twenty meters.

He read that passage many times, then paused until he thought it:

Forty by twenty.

And God knows how deep.

I should have looked at that pile first.

He'd lost a whole day of digging.

After a brief search, the key opened a shed behind the house, and when Clay went in, he found the shovel, lying benignly on the workbench. He handled it and looked around. A pick was also close by, and a wheelbarrow.

He walked back out, and in the last light of evening-afternoon, he made it to the riverbed. There was now a perimeter marked with bright orange spray. He hadn't noticed from being inside all day.

Forty by twenty.

He thought it as he walked the borders.

Clay crouched, he stood, he watched the rising moon—but soon the toil invited him. He half grinned and thought of Henry, and how he knew he'd count him down.

He was out there all alone, as the past behind him converged—then three more seconds, and, now.

The shovel and splice of the earth.

the lives before they had us

In the tide of Dunbar past, they intersected, Michael and Penelope, and of course it started with the piano. I should also say it's always been a kind of mystery to me, this starting-out time, and the lure of lasting happiness. I guess it's like all our parents' time together—their lives before they had us.

On that sunny afternoon, here in the city, they pushed the instrument down Pepper Street, and watched each other in glimpses, and the piano movers bickered:

"Oi!"

"What?"

"You're not here for your looks, you know."

"What's that s'posed to mean?"

"It means *push*! Move it this way, idiot. Over *here*."

One to the other, secretively: "The pay's nowhere near enough for putting up with him, is it?"

"I know, no way."

"Come *on* then! The girl's putting more into it than you two combined." Now to Penelope, from the upright girth of the piano. "Hey, do you need a job by any chance?"

She smiled, mildly. "Oh, no thanks, I have already a few."

"It shows. Unlike these two useless— Oi! *This* way!"

And there, right there, she looked over, and the man from number thirty-seven gave her the crease of a collegial smile, then tucked it back inside him.

* * *

At the apartment, though, with the piano in place by the window, Michael Dunbar didn't stay. She asked what she might give him as a gift for helping, whether wine or maybe beer, or *wódka* (had she really said that?), but he wouldn't hear a word of it. He said goodbye and left, but when she played she saw him listening; her first experimental notes. The piano still in need of retuning.

He was out by the line-up of garbage bins.

When she stood to look closer he was gone.

In the weeks that followed, there was definitely a sense of *something*.

They'd never seen each other till the day of the piano, but now it was happening everywhere. If he was in line at Woolworths with toilet paper under his arm, she was at the next checkout with a bag of oranges and a packet of Iced VoVos. After work, when she walked onto Pepper Street, he would step from his car, further up.

In Penelope's case (and this embarrassed her) she would often wander around the block a few times, purely for the handful of seconds it took to walk by the front of his house. Would he be on the porch? Would the light be on in the kitchen? Would he come out and ask her inside for coffee or tea, or anything at all? There was a synergy to it, of course, given Michael and Moon, and the walks through long-ago Featherton. Even when she sat at the piano, she often checked; he might be by the bins again.

As for Michael, he resisted.

He didn't want to be *back there* anymore, where all was good but ruinable. In his kitchen he thought of Penelope, and the piano, and his haunted halls of Abbey. He saw this new woman's arms, and the love in her hands, helping the instrument down the road . . . but he could make himself not go to her.

Eventually, months later, in April, Penny put jeans and a shirt on.

She walked up Pepper Street.

It was dark.

She told herself she was ridiculous, that she was a woman, not a girl. She'd traveled thousands of miles to get here. She'd stood ankle-deep on a wine-dark toilet floor, so this was nothing, nothing in comparison. Surely she could breach the gate and knock on a man's front door.

Surely.

She did.

"Hallo?" she said. "But I think . . . I hope you remember me?"

He was quiet and so was the light; the space behind him in the hallway. And there again, that smile. At once surfaced, then lost. "Of course I do . . . the piano."

"Yes." She was getting flustered and it wasn't English forming in her mouth; each sentence was exactly that—its own small punishment. She'd had to plant her own language in the middle and work her way around it. Somehow she managed to ask if he might like to come and visit her. She could play the piano, that is, if he liked the piano, and she had coffee and raisin toast and—

"Iced VoVos?"

"Yes . . ." Why so embarrassed? "Yes. Yes, I have some." He'd remembered. He'd remembered.

He'd remembered, and now, despite all self-warning and discipline, the smile he'd held fell out. It was almost like those army movies—the comedy ones—where the hopeless, hapless recruit struggles over a wall and flops to the other side; stupid and clumsy but grateful.

And Michael Dunbar succumbed:

"I'd love to come and hear you play—I only heard a few notes that first day, when they delivered it." Then, a moment, a long one. "Here. Why don't you come in?"

In his house there was a friendliness, but also something unnerving. Penelope couldn't quite place it, but Michael certainly could. A life once had, now gone.

In the kitchen, they introduced themselves.

He motioned to a chair.

He caught sight of her catching sight of his rough, powdery hands, and just like that, it began. For quite a while, three hours at least, they sat at the table, which was scratched-up, wooden and warm. They drank tea with milk and biscuits, and spoke of Pepper Street and the city. Construction work and cleaning. It actually surprised him how easily it came to her once she'd stopped worrying about her English. After all, there was plenty to tell him:

A new country, and seeing the ocean.

The shock and awe of the southerly.

At one point he asked her more about where she'd come from, and how she got here, and Penelope felt at her face. She moved a blond patch of hair from her eye, and the tide pulled slowly away. She remembered the pale young girl who listened to those books that were read, and read again; she thought about Vienna, and its army of laid-out bunk beds. Mostly, though, she talked of the piano, and the cold barren world at the window. She talked about a man and mustache, and love without emotion.

Very quiet and very calmly, she said:

"I grew up with the statue of Stalin."

As the night wore on, they each told their stories about why and where they were made of. Michael spoke of Featherton—the fires, the mines. The sound of the birds by the river. He didn't mention Abbey, not yet, but she was there at the edge of everything.

Penelope, by comparison, often felt like she should stop, but she suddenly had so much to say. When she mentioned the cockroaches, and the terror they'd inflicted, Michael laughed, but sympathetically; there was the faintest stretch of wonder on his lips for houses made of paper.

When she got up to leave, it was well past midnight, and she apologized for all her talking, and Michael Dunbar said, "No."

They stood at the sink, he washed the cups and plates.

Penelope dried, she stayed.

There was something risen up in her, and so, it seemed, in him. Years of gentle barrenness. Whole towns not had, or lived. Just as each of them knew they were never so game or forward, there was another truth at hand—that this would have to be it:

No waiting, no politeness.

The wilderness out, from in them.

Soon it became too much for him.

The quiet suffering was intolerable for another second, and he stepped, reached over, and gambled—his hands still covered in suds.

He grabbed her wrist, both calm and firmly.

He didn't know how or why but he put the other hand on her hip bone, and without thinking, he held her and kissed her. Her forearm was wet, her clothes were wet, just in that patch of shirt—and he took the cloth hard, and made a fist.

"Jesus, I'm sorry, I—"

And Penelope Lesciuszko, she gave him the fright of his life:

She took his wet hand, put it beneath that shirt—the exact same place, but on skin—and delivered him a phrase from the East.

"*Jeszcze raz.*"

Very quiet, very serious, almost unsmiling, like kitchens were built for this.

"It means," she said, "*again.*"

the boy with bleeding hands

It was Saturday—the halfway point to the Murderer's return—and Clay walked the road from the property, in the dark of just turned night.

His body was part elastic, part hard.

His hands were blistered raw.

Inside he was ready to burst.

He'd been digging alone since Monday.

The depth to the bedrock had been nowhere near as deep as he'd feared—but at times, even inches were hard labor. Sometimes he thought he might never hit it at all—but then, the ache of stone.

By the time he was finished, he couldn't recall anymore which nights he'd slept a few hours inside, and the ones he'd worked till morning; often he'd woken in the riverbed.

It took a while now to work out it was Saturday.

And evening, not dawn.

And in that state of delirium, and those bleeding, burning hands, he'd decided to see the city again, and he packed only very lightly: the box, and the favorite of his bridge books.

Then he'd showered and burned, dressed and burned, and staggered, like that, into town. Only once, he wavered, to turn, to look back at his work, and that was all it took:

In the middle of the road, he sat down, and the country surged around him.

"I made it."

Just three words, and each one had tasted like dirt.

He lay for a while—the pulsing ground, the starry sky. Then forced himself to walk.

like skiers on a mountainside

That first night, at 37 Pepper Street, when she left, it was agreed.

He walked her home and said he'd come down to her apartment, on Saturday at four o'clock.

The road was dark and empty.

Nothing much more was said.

On the return visit, he'd shaved, and brought daisies.

It took a while before she played the piano, and when she did he stood beside her. When she finished, he placed a finger at the far right end.

She nodded for him to let it fall, to press it down.

But a piano's highest note is fickle.

If you don't hit it hard enough, or *right* enough, it makes no noise at all.

"Again," she said, and she grinned—nervously, they both did—and this time he got it to work.

Like a smack to the hand of Mozart.

Or the wrist of Chopin or Bach.

And this time it was her:

There was hesitancy, and awkwardness, but then she kissed the back of his neck, very light, very soft.

And then they ate the Iced VoVos.

Right to the very last.

When I think about it now, I go back through all we were told, and especially all Clay was told, and I wonder what's most important.

Here I think it's this:

For six or seven weeks beyond that, they saw each other, they swapped venues, up and down Pepper Street. Always, for Michael Dunbar, there was a kind of welling up, through the newness and blond of Penelope. When he kissed her he tasted Europe, but also the taste of not-Abbey. When her hands held his fingers as he stood to leave, he felt the feel of a refugee, and it was her but also him.

Eventually, he told her, on the steps of number 37.

It was Sunday morning, grey and mild, and the steps were cool—and he'd been married before, and divorced; her name was Abbey Dunbar. He'd lain on the garage floor.

A car drove by, and a girl on a bike.

He told her he'd been devastated, living, hanging on, on his own. He'd wanted to see her much earlier than the night she came to his front door. He'd wanted to, but wasn't capable. He couldn't risk a fall like that again, not anymore.

It's funny, I guess, how confessions come out:

We admit to almost everything, and the almost is all that counts.

For Michael Dunbar, it was two things he left out.

Firstly, he simply wouldn't admit that he, too, could produce something approximating beautiful—the paintings.

And next (and this was an extension of the first), he didn't confess that somewhere in his murkiest depths, he wasn't so much afraid of being left again as condemning someone else to second best. Such was how he'd felt for Abbey, and the life he'd once had, and lost.

But then again, what choice did he really have?

This was a world where logic was defied by argumentative piano men. It was a world where fate could stand out front, both tanned and pale, simultaneously. God, even *Stalin* was involved, so how could he possibly say no?

Maybe it's true that we don't get to make these decisions.

We think we do, but we don't.

We do laps of all our neighborhoods.

We pass that certain front door.

When we hit a piano key and it makes no sound, we hit it again, because we have to. We need to hear *something*, and we hope it isn't a mistake—

As it was, Penelope was never meant to be here.

Our father should never have been divorced.

But here they were, walking perfectly, and quite fittingly, toward a certain kind of line. They'd been counted down, like skiers on a mountainside, and were hitting it for the *now*.

the traditionalist

At Silver Station, he saw the oncoming glow of the night train.

From far away it looked like a magic, slow-moving torch.

Inside, though, it was heaven.

The air was cool; the seat was warm.

His heart like a broken body part.

His lungs a kind of waxworks.

He lay back lightly, and slept.

The train pulled into the city just after five o'clock, Sunday morning, and a man was shaking him awake.

"Hey, kid, *kid,* we're here."

Clay startled, and managed to stand up, and despite everything—the enormous headache, the searing pain when he picked up his sports bag—the draw was unmistakable.

He felt the glimmer of home.

In his mind he was already there; he was watching the world of Archer Street; he was up on the roof, he saw Carey's place. Or behind, to see The Surrounds. He could even hear the movie in our lounge room—but no. He actually had to remind himself he couldn't go, and especially not like this.

For Archer Street, he'd have to wait.

* * *

Instead, he walked.

He found that the more he moved the less he hurt, and so he trawled the city, to Hickson Road, down to under the bridge; he relented at the slanted wall. The trains came rattling above. The harbor so blue, he almost couldn't look. The rivets in rows, on his shoulders. The great grey arch reached over.

It's a she, he thought, of course she is.

He leaned and struggled to leave.

In the afternoon, he finally managed it, though, and walked the curves of Circular Quay; the clowns, a guitarist. The traditional didgeridoos.

The Manly ferry beckoned him.

The smell of hot chips nearly killed him.

He walked up to the railway, changed at Town Hall, then counted the stops and walked. He'd have crawled if he'd had to, to the racing quarter. There was one place, at least, he could go.

When he got there, way up on that hilltop, for the first time in a long time, he paid proper notice to the gravestone:

PENELOPE DUNBAR
A MANY-NAMED WOMAN:
the Mistake Maker, the Birthday Girl,
the Broken-Nosed Bride, and Penny

MUCH LOVED BY EVERYONE
BUT ESPECIALLY
THE DUNBAR BOYS

When he read it, he dropped to a crouch.

He smiled hardest at the last part, and our brother lay down, cheek-first on the ground, and he stayed there alone a long time. He cried silently, nearly an hour—

And these days, so often, I think of it, and I wish that I just could have been there. As the one who'd be next to beat him up, and bring him down, and punish him hard for his sins, I wish I'd somehow known everything.

I'd have held him, and quietly told him.

I'd have said to him, Clay, come home.

paintwork at the piano

AND SO THEY'D BE MARRIED.

Penelope Lesciuszko and Michael Dunbar.

In terms of time, it took approximately a year and seven months.

In other terms more difficult to measure, it was a garageful of portraits, and paintwork at the piano.

It was a right-hand turn and a car crash.

And a shape—the geometry of blood.

Mostly it comes in glimpses, that period.

Time shrunk down to moments.

Sometimes they're scattered broadly—like winter, and her learning to drive. Or September, and hours of music. There's a whole November of his clumsy attempts at her language, and then December through February to April, and a few visits at least, to the town he grew up in, and its sweat and surging heat.

In between, of course, there were movies (and he didn't check her for laughter), and a love she found for video—likely her greatest teacher. When movies were on TV, she recorded them for practicing English: a 1980s catalogue, from *E.T.* to *Out of Africa*, *Amadeus* to *Fatal Attraction*.

There was continuing *The Iliad* and *The Odyssey*. Cricket games on TV. (Could it really last *five whole days*?) And countless salted ferry rides on that bright, whitecapped water.

There were the slipstreams, too, of doubt, when she'd see him disappearing, to some place, held doggedly, within. The inner terrain of not-Abbey again, a landscape both vast and barren. She'd be calling his name from next to him:

"Michael. *Michael?*"

He'd be startled. "*What?*"

They stood at the borders of anger, or foot holes of small irritation; both sensing how soon they could deepen. But just when she thought he might say to her, "Don't come for me, don't call," he'd place a hand down onto her forearm. Her fears, through the months, were calmed.

Sometimes, though, the moments stretch out.

They stop, and unfold completely.

For Clay, they were the ones Penny told him about in the last few months of her life—when she was high and hot on morphine, and desperate to get everything right. Most memorable was a pair of them, and both occurring in evening; and exactly twelve months between them.

Penelope saw them as titles:

The Night He Finally Showed Me.

And *Paintwork at the Piano.*

The date was December 23, the eve of Christmas Eve.

The first year, they'd eaten together in Michael's kitchen, and just as they'd finished, he'd said to her:

"Here, I'm going to show you."

They walked out into the garage.

It was strange that in all the months they'd known each other, she'd never set foot inside it. Instead of taking the side entrance, he used the roller door out at the front. A noise the sound of a train.

Inside, when he hit the light, and removed the curtain of sheets, Penny was amazed—for amongst the kernels of floating dust there were countless sheets of canvas, all stretched over wooden frames. Some were enormous. Some the size of a sketch pad. On each of them was Abbey, and sometimes she was a woman, sometimes a girl. She could be mischievous, or buttoned-up. Often her hair ran all the way to her waist. In others it was cut to her neckline; she held the streams of it in her arms. Always, though, she was a life force, and she never left you for long. Penelope realized that anyone who looked at these paintings would know that whoever painted them felt even more than the portraits could suggest. It was in every stroke before you, and every one left out. It was the precision of the canvas stretch, and the mistakes kept perfectly intact—like a drip of mauve at her ankle, or an ear that floated next to her, a millimeter from her face.

Its perfection didn't matter:

All of it was right.

In one painting, the biggest one, where her feet sank into the sand, Penny felt like she could ask for the shoes she held out, in her open, generous palm. As she looked, Michael sat by the gaping doorway, his back against the wall, and when Penny had seen enough, she sat herself down beside him. Their knees and elbows touched.

"Abbey Dunbar?" she asked.

Michael nodded. "Formerly Hanley—and now, I have no idea."

She could feel her heart rise then, and quicken in her throat. She forced it slowly back.

"I—" He almost stopped himself. "I'm sorry I didn't show you earlier."

"You can paint?"

"I could. Not anymore."

At first she pondered her next thought, or move—but now she flatly refused it. She didn't ask if he might paint her instead; no, she would never compete with that woman, and now she touched his hair. She ran her hand through, and said, "So just don't ever paint me." She fought to find the nerve. "Do other things instead. . . ."

It was a memory Clay held dear, for it was hard for her to tell him all this (but death was a hell of a motivator); how Michael had come up to meet her, and she'd led him directly over—to the place where Abbey had left him, where he'd lain, undone, on the floor.

"I said to him," she'd said to the boy, and she was in such a withering state. "I said, 'Take me where you were exactly'—and he did it straightaway."

Yes, they'd gone there and they'd held and gave and hurt and fought, and forced everything unwanted away. There was the breath of her, the sound of her, and a flooding of what they'd become; and they did so for as long as it took—and between each turn, they lay and talked; Penelope often spoke first. She'd said she was lonely as a child, and wanted at least five children, and Michael said all right. He even joked and said, "God, I hope we don't get five boys!" He really should have been more careful.

"We'll get married."

It was him—it just came out.

They were grazed by then, and bruised; their arms, their knees and shoulder blades.

He went on. "I'll find a way to ask you. Maybe this time next year."

And she shifted below, holding tightly.

"Of course," she said, "okay," and she kissed him and turned him over. Then a final, near-silent "*Again*."

And the next year came the second title.

Paintwork at the Piano.

December 23.

It was Monday night, with the light turning red outside.

The noise of neighborhood boys came in, playing handball.

Penelope had just walked by them.

On Mondays, she always came home around this time, a little after eight-thirty; she'd finished the last of her cleaning jobs, a lawyer's office, and on this night, she did as always:

She dropped her bag down by the door.

She walked to the piano and sat—but this time something was different. She opened the lid and saw the words, on the keys, and they were lettered there simply, yet beautifully:

P|E|N|E|L|O|P|E L|E|S|C|I|U|S|Z|K|O

P|L|E|A|S|E

M|A|R|R|Y M|E

He'd remembered.

He'd remembered, and how her hand covered her mouth, and how she smiled, and burned in the eyes; all doubt driven far, even gone for now, as she wavered above the letters. She didn't want to disturb them, or smear the paint. Even if it was dry for hours.

But soon she found the resolve.

She allowed her fingers to fall down softly, in the center of the words PLEASE MARRY.

She turned around and called.

"Michael?"

There was no answer, so she walked back out, and the boys were gone, and it was city, red air and Pepper Street.

He was sitting, alone, on his stairs.

Later, much later, when Michael Dunbar slept in the single bed they'd often shared in her apartment, she came back out, in the dark.

She switched on the light.

She turned the knob to a shadowed dimness and sat on the stool at the piano. Slowly, her hands drifted, and gently, she pressed the high-pitched notes. She hit them soft but true and right, where she'd used the paint left over.

She'd played the keys of Y | E | S.

the boy who climbed from the oven

"I CAN'T BELIEVE MY EYES. I THOUGHT YOU'D ONLY MAKE A START."

That's what Michael Dunbar said about the giant trench that was dug by a single boy in less than a week. He should have known better.

"What the hell did you do, dig all night and day?"

Clay looked down. "I slept sometimes."

"Next to the shovel?"

Now he looked up, as the Murderer saw his hands.

"Jesus . . ."

As for Clay, when he told me about that particular little stunt, he spoke more about the aftermath than the exercise itself. He was dying to at least see Archer Street, and The Surrounds, but he couldn't, of course; two reasons.

First, he was in no condition to face me.

And second, coming back and *not* facing me felt like cheating.

No, from the cemetery, he'd caught the train back to Silver, then spent a few days recovering. Not a single part of him wasn't hurting. The blistered hands were the worst, though, and he slept, lay awake, and waited.

When the Murderer came, he'd pulled up on the other side of the river, in the trees.

He walked down and stood, on the floor of the dug-out ditch.

Either side were tidal waves, of rocks and mounds of dirt.

He looked and shook his head, then over, across at the house.

Inside, he sought Clay out, he pulled him apart in the kitchen; he sighed and half slouched, and shook his head once more, between shock and total dismay. He finally had something to say to him:

"I gotta give it to you, kid—you've got heart."

And Clay couldn't stop it.

The words.

They left and returned, several times, and now, in the kitchen, stood Rory; like he'd climbed right out of the oven, directly from Bernborough Park, and the storied 300-meter mark:

Gotta give it to you, kid . . .

The exact same words he'd said to him.

And Clay was unable to stop himself.

He rushed down the hallway and sat on the bathroom floor. In his hurry he'd slammed the door, and—

"Clay? Clay—you okay?"

The interruption was like an echo, like being shouted to, underwater; and he came up gasping for air.

the broken-nosed bride

As far as weddings go, there wasn't much to organize, so it came to them pretty fast. At one point, Michael wondered what to do with the artwork—the Abbey paintings—whether to keep, destroy, or throw them away; Penelope, at first, was certain.

"You should keep them," she said, "or sell them; they don't deserve to be destroyed." She calmly reached out and touched one. "Look at her, she's so beautiful."

It was then, incidentally, she felt it:

A flicker of fire, of jealousy.

Why can't I be like that? she wondered, as she thought once again, of that long and distant terrain in him—where sometimes he vanished from next to her. At times like those she wanted it desperately—to be more and better than Abbey—but the paintings were proof in the making: everything once equaled her.

It was a relief, in the end, when they sold them:

They displayed one of the bigger ones on a roundabout, near Pepper Street, with a sign and date for the art sale—and by nightfall the painting was stolen. In the garage, on the day itself, it took an hour; they went quickly because people liked them; both Abbey and Penny alike.

"You should be painting *this* one," said many of the buyers, and gestured toward Penelope; and Michael could only smile at them.

He said, "This one's much better in person."

* * *

From there, the next hurdle was Penelope's familiar luck:

It wasn't so much what happened—for it was a mistake of her own judgment—but that it had to happen *then:* the morning before they were married. She was making a turn off Lowder Street, onto Parramatta Road, in Michael's old sedan.

She hadn't driven at all in the Eastern Bloc, but her eye was still trained to that side. Here she'd done the exams, she'd passed with reasonable confidence, and often drove Michael's car. There were never any problems, but on this day it counted for nothing. She made the perfect right-hand turn, onto the wrong side of the road.

On the back seat, the wedding dress she'd just picked up lay modest and fluent, and the car was crashed into from the side, like a demon had taken a bite. Penelope's ribs were ruptured. Her nose was slapped, and broken; her face hit the head of the dash.

The man from the other car was swearing, but stopped when he saw the blood.

She said sorry in two different languages.

Next came the police, and competitive men in tow trucks, who negotiated, sweated and smoked. When the ambulance arrived, they tried convincing her to go to the hospital, but said they couldn't force her.

Penny insisted she was fine.

There was a long strange shape down her front:

An oblong mural of blood.

No, she would go to her local doctor, to which all of them agreed: she was tougher than she looked.

The police joked that they were arresting her, and drove her smoothly home. The younger of them, the one chewing spearmint gum, also took care of the dress.

He laid it delicately down in the trunk.

* * *

When she made it home, she knew what had to be done.

Get cleaned up.

Have a cup of tea.

Call Michael, and then the insurance company.

As you might expect, she did none of those things first.

No, with all the strength she could muster, she placed the dress over the couch and sat at the piano, completely dejected, then bereft. She played half of *Moonlight Sonata*, and she couldn't see the notes, not once.

At the doctor, an hour later, she didn't scream.

Michael held her hand while her ribs were gently pushed upon, and her nose yanked back into place.

It was more just a gasp and a swallow.

On the way out, though, she buckled, then lay on the waiting room floor. People craned to see.

As Michael helped her up, he saw, in the corner, the usual fare of children's toys, but he shrugged them quickly away. He carried her out the door.

At home again, on her old used couch, she lay down with her head in his lap. She asked if he would read from *The Iliad*, and for Michael there was great realization—for rather than think the obvious, like, I'm not your long-lost father, he reeled out far beyond it; he knew and got used to a truth. He loved her more than Michelangelo and Abbey Hanley combined.

He wiped at the tear on her cheek.

There was blood cracked into her lips.

He picked up the book and read to her, and she cried, then slept, still bleeding. . . .

There was the *fast-running Achilles*, the *resourceful Odysseus*, and all the other gods and warriors. He especially liked *Hector the panic maker*—also named *tamer of horses*—and *Diomedes, true son of Tydeus*.

He sat like that all night with her.

He read, turned pages, and read.

* * *

Then the wedding, which went ahead as planned, the following day.

February 17.

The gathering was small:

A few tradesman friends on Michael's side.

That clump of cleaners for Penny.

Adelle Dunbar was there, and so was old Weinrauch, who offered her anti-inflammatories. Thankfully, the swelling was down; she still bled now and then, and a black eye shone through her makeup, no matter how hard they tried.

The church, too, was small, but seemingly cavernous. It was dark with leadlight windows; a tortured, colorful Christ. The preacher was tall and balding. He'd laughed when Michael leaned toward her and said, "See? Not even a car crash could get you out of this." Then again, he'd looked so sad when the first drop of blood slipped to the dress and grew like a science litmus test.

A rush of help arrived, from all quarters of the audience, and Penny sobbed back a smile. She took the hanky offered by Michael, and said, "You're marrying a broken-nosed bride."

"Good boy," said the preacher, when the blood was quelled, and tentatively, he proceeded—and the colorful Christ looked on, till they were Michael and Penelope Dunbar.

They turned, as most couples do, and smiled at the congregation.

They signed the appropriate papers.

They walked down the center of the church, where the doors were held open, to a white-hot sunlight in front of them—and when I think of it I see that lure again; they're holding that hard-to-catch happiness. They've brought it to life in their hands.

In those lives before they had us, there were still two chapters left.

war of the roses

Again, time passed.

Weeks passed, closer to a month, and it was spent in various ways.

They started, as they had to, with the hardest:

The shifting of earth from the river.

They worked from sunrise to sunset, and prayed for no rain, which would have made everything meaningless. If the Amahnu flowed, and flowed hard, it would bring with it silt and soil.

At night, they sat in the kitchen, or on the edge of the couch at the coffee table; they properly designed the falsework. Between them they made two models—of the mold and the bridge itself. Michael Dunbar was mathematical, and methodical in angles of stone. He talked to the boy of trajectory, and how each block would need to be perfect. Clay was sick at the thought of *voussoirs;* he didn't even know how to say it.

Exhausted both physically and mentally, he'd walk sleepily to the bedroom and read. He held each item from the box. He lit the flame just once.

He missed everyone, more as the weeks went on, when an envelope arrived in the letterbox. Inside, two handwritten letters.

One from Henry.

One from Carey.

In all his time at the Amahnu, this was the event he'd waited for, but he didn't read them right away. He walked upwards to the stones and river gums, and sat in the dappled sun.

He read in the order he found them.

Hi Clay,

Thanks for your letter the other week. I kept it a while before showing the others—don't ask me why. We miss you, you know. You say practically nothing, but we miss you. The roof tiles probably miss you the most, I'd say. Well, that, and me on Saturdays . . . When I hit the garage sales I get Tommy to help, but that kid's useless as tits on a bull. You know that.

The least you could do is visit. You just have to get it over with first—you know. Goddamn it, how long does it take to build a bridge anyway?

Sincerely,
Henry Dunbar esq.

PS. Can you do me a favor? When you do come back, call and tell me what time you think you'll get home. We all have to be here for that. Just in case.

As he read the letter, Clay was nothing but grateful, for the *Henryness* of the writing. His crap really *was* endless, but Clay couldn't help but pine for it. That, and he was nothing if not gallant; people often forgot that about Henry, seeing only self-interest and money. You did better with Henry beside you.

Next was Tommy, and it was clear both he and Rory had been asked to contribute. Or, more likely, they were coerced. Tommy had gone first:

Hi Clay,

I don't have much to say except that Achilles misses you. I got Henry to help me check his hooves—THAT'S what I call USELESS!!!!!!

(And I miss you, too.)

Then Rory:

Oi Clay—come home, for Christ's sake. I miss our little hart-to-harts. Ha!

You thought I couldn't spell heart then, didn't you?

Hey—do me a favor. Give the old man a hug for me.

Just kidding—give him a kick in the coins okay? A good one.

Say THAT'S FROM FUCKING RORY!

Come home.

It was funny. Tommy set things up perfectly, but it was Rory who always got to him—who made him feel things with greatest gravity. Maybe it was because Rory was the sort of person who didn't really want to love anyone or anything, but he loved Clay, and he showed it in the oddest ways.

Dear Clay,

How can I tell you in one note how much I miss you, and how it is to sit at The Surrounds on Saturdays and imagine you there beside me? I don't lie down. I don't do anything. I just go and hope you'll come, but you don't, and I know why. It has to be that way, I guess.

It's funny, because this has been the best few weeks ever, and I can't even tell you.

Last week I got my first mount. Can you believe it??? It was on Wednesday and it was a horse called War of the Roses—an old journeyman only there to make up the numbers, and I never whipped him once, I just talked to him and got him to the line on hands-and-heels, and he came in third. Third!!! Holy shit! It's the first time my mum's been to the track in years. The silks were black, white, and blue. I'll tell you everything when you come home, even if it isn't for long. I've got another ride coming next week. . . .

God, in all that, I haven't even asked. How are you? I miss seeing you up on the roof.

Lastly, I finished The Quarryman again. I know why you love it so much. He did all those great things. I hope you get to do something great out there too. You will. You have to. You will.

See you soon, I hope. See you at The Surrounds.

I'll show you my tips.

I promise.

Love,
Carey

Well, what would you do?

What would you say?

He read it way upriver, many times, and he knew.

After a long time working it out, he calculated seventy-six days now he'd been away, and the Amahnu would be his future—but it was time to come home and face me.

the house at eighteen archer street

When Michael Dunbar married the Broken-Nosed Bride, the first thing they did was drag the piano back up Pepper Street, to number thirty-seven. It took six extra men from the neighborhood, and this time a carton of beer. (And not unlike the Bernborough boys—if there was beer it had to be cold.) They worked their way round the back of the house, where there weren't any steps to get in.

"We should actually call those other guys," said Michael, later on. He leaned an arm on top of the walnut, like he and the piano were friends. "They got the address right after all."

Penny Dunbar could only smile.

She had one hand on the instrument.

The other hand on him.

A few years later, they moved out of that place, too; they bought a house they fell in love with. It was relatively close, in the racing quarter, with track-and-stables behind it.

They looked on a Saturday morning:

The house at 18 Archer Street.

An agent waited inside, and asked them for their names. Seemingly, there'd been no other expressions of interest that day.

To the house itself, there was hallway, there was kitchen. There were three bedrooms, a small bathroom, a long backyard with an old Hills Hoist, and both of them immediately imagined; they saw kids with lawn and garden, and the outbreaks of childhood chaos. It was paradise as far as they were concerned, and they were soon to fall even harder:

With an arm on the pole of the clothesline, and an eye in the clouds above her, Penny heard the sound. She turned back to the agent.

She said, "Excuse me, but what is that noise?"

"Sorry?"

He'd been dreading this moment, for it was possibly the cause of losing every other couple he'd taken through the property—all of whom had most likely had similar dreams, and thoughts of how they'd live there. They'd probably even seen the same laughing children getting in fights over unfair football tactics, or dragging dolls through the grass and dirt.

"You don't hear it?" she persisted.

The agent adjusted his tie. "Oh, *that?*"

The night before, when they'd looked in the *Gregory's* street directory, they'd seen the field behind the house, and all it said was *The Surrounds*. Now Penny was sure she heard hooves coming down the back, and deciphered the adjacent smell—of animal, of hay, and horses.

The agent tried to hurry them back in.

It didn't work.

Penny was drawn closer, to the clopping she heard at the fence line.

"Hey, Michael?" she said. "Could you please lift me up?"

He walked the yard toward her.

His arms and her stick-thin thighs.

On the other side, Penny saw the stables, she saw the track.

There was the laneway behind the fence line, which turned by the edge of the house; Mrs. Chilman was the only neighbor. Then the grass and slanted building work, and the white obligatory sports fence; from there it looked made of toothpicks.

In the laneway there were grooms leading horses, track to stables, and most of them didn't see her; some of them nodded on their way. A minute or two later, an old groom came leading the final horse by, and when its head leaned down, he shrugged it gruffly away. Just before he saw Penny he gave its mouth a gentle slap. "Go on," he said, "get out." Penny, of course, smiled, at all of it.

"Hallo?" She cleared her throat. ". . . Hello?"

The horse saw her instantly, but the groom was oblivious.

"What? Who's there?"

"Up here."

"Jesus, love, give a man a bloody heart attack!" He was a stocky build and curly hair, with moistened face and eyes, and the horse was tugging him over. It had a flash of white from ears to nose, but the rest was mahogany brown. The groom saw it was useless stopping him. "All right, here we go. Come on, love."

"Really?"

"Yeah, give 'im a pat, he's the biggest bloody sook here anyway."

Before she did it, Penny checked that Michael was okay, and truth be told, she was light but not weightless, and his arms were starting to shake. She placed her hand on the horse's blaze, the great white texture, and couldn't hold back her delight. She looked in the prying eyes. *Any sugar? You got some sugar?*

"What's his name?"

"Well, his race name's City Special." He gave the horse a pat himself now, on the chest. "Stable name's Greedy, though, I wonder bloody why."

"Is he fast?"

He scoffed. "You really *are* new around here, aren't you? The horses in these stables are all bloody useless."

But still, Penelope was charmed. When the horse bobbed upwards for a rougher pat, she laughed. "Hi, Greedy."

"Here, give him these." He passed her a few grubby sugar cubes. "Might as well. He's a lost bloody cause, anyway."

Beneath her, Michael Dunbar was thinking about his arms, and how long they could possibly hold her.

The agent was thinking SOLD.

the violence of brothers

Now it was Clay's turn, to leave his father with the house and the Amahnu.

He stood above him by the couch, the morning still dark.

His hands were healed, from blisters to scars.

"I'll be away awhile."

The Murderer woke.

"I'll be back, though."

It was fortunate Silver was on a main line; trains came through twice a day in each direction. He caught the 8:07.

At the station, he remembered:

That first afternoon, when he came.

He listened.

The land beside him still sang.

On the train he read for a while, but in his stomach the nerves had begun. Like a kid with a windup toy.

Eventually, he put the book down.

There was really no point.

In everything he read, all he saw was my face, and my fists, and the jugular in my neck.

When he reached the city, late afternoon, he stood at the station and made the call. A phone booth near Platform Four.

"Hello, Henry here." Clay could hear he was on a street somewhere; the close-up sound of traffic. *"Hello?"*

"I'm here, too."

"Clay?" The voice came through tighter, faster, from the grip at the other end. "Are you home?"

"Not yet. Tonight."

"When? What time?"

"I don't know. Maybe seven. Maybe later."

That would give him a few more hours.

"Hey—Clay?"

He waited.

"Good luck, okay?"

"Thanks. I'll see you."

He wished he was back in the eucalypts.

For a while he considered going most of the way on foot, but he caught the train and bus. On Poseidon Road, he got out one stop before he normally would, and the city was well into evening.

There was nothing now but cloud cover.

Sort of copper, mostly dark.

He walked and stopped, he leaned at the air, as if waiting for it to finish him off, only it wouldn't—and quicker than he'd hoped, he stood at the mouth of Archer Street:

Relieved to have finally made it.

Terrified to be there.

In every house, the lights were on, people were home.

As if sensing the oncoming theater, the pigeons arrived from nowhere, and dug in close on the power lines. They were perched on TV aerials, and God forbid, on the trees. There was also a single crow, fat-feathered and plump, like a pigeon disguised in a trench coat.

But he wasn't fooling anyone.

* * *

To our front yard—one of the few with no fence, no gate, just lawn—it was leafless, freshly mowed.

The porch, the roof, the blink of one of my movies.

Strangely, Henry's car wasn't there, but Clay couldn't be distracted. He walked slowly on, then, "Matthew."

He only said it at first, as if careful to be casual and calm.

Matthew.

Just my name.

That was all.

Just above quiet.

And again, a few steps more, he felt the cushion of grass, and now, in the middle, facing the door, he expected me to come—but I didn't. He had to shout or stand and wait, and he chose, as it was, the first one. His voice so much not-his, as "MATTHEW!" he screamed, and put down his bag, and the books inside—his reading.

Within seconds, he heard movement, and then Rosy let loose a bark.

I was the first to appear out front.

I stood on the porch in almost exactly what Clay was wearing, only my T-shirt was dark blue and not white. The same faded jeans. The same thin-soled sports shoes. I'd been watching *Rain Man*, three-quarters through.

Clay—it was so damn good to see him . . . but no.

My shoulders fell, but barely; I couldn't show how much I didn't want to. I had to look willing and sure.

"Clay."

It was the voice of that long-lost morning.

The killer in his pocket.

Even when Rory and Tommy came out, I kept them back, almost benignly. When they argued, I held up my hand. "No."

They stayed, and Rory said something Clay couldn't hear.

"Go too far and I'm coming in, okay?"

Had it all been whispered?

Or was it spoken normally and Clay just couldn't hear it for the noise inside his ears?

I closed my eyes a moment, and walked to the right, and down; and I don't know how it is with other brothers, but with us there would be no circling. It wasn't Clay and the Murderer, like boxers—this was me, and I walked at him just short of a run, and it was soon that he hit the ground.

Oh, he fought, all right, he fought hard, and he searched and flailed and falled—for there was no grammar to this, no beauty to it at all. He could train and suffer all he wanted, but this wasn't training the Clay way, it was living *my* way, and I found him from the first; no more words but those inside me:

He killed us.

He killed us, Clay, don't you remember?

We had no one.

He left us.

What we were is dead—

But now those thoughts weren't thoughts at all, they were clouds of landed punches, and every one fell true.

Don't you remember?

Don't you see?

And Clay.

The smiler.

As I watch us now, after all he later told me, I see him clearly thinking:

You don't know everything, Matthew.

You don't know.

I should have told you—

About the clothesline.

About the pegs—

But he couldn't say anything, and he couldn't even remember going down the first time, except that he'd fallen so hard he left a gash there, a scar in the grass—and the world was incoherent. It struck him that it was raining, but truth be told, it was blood. It was blood and hurt and getting up, and going down, till Rory called out enough.

And me—chest heaving, calling in air.

And Clay on the grass, all curled up, then rolling toward the sky. How many skies were there, really? The one he'd focused on was breaking, and with it came the birds. The pigeons. And one crow. They flocked into his lungs. That papery sound of flapping wings, all fast, and gorgeous, at once.

The next person he saw was a girl.

She said nothing. Nothing to me, nothing to Clay.

She only crouched and took his hand.

She could hardly say *welcome back*, and actually—shockingly—it was Clay who moved to speak.

I stood a few meters to the left.

My hands were all quivered and bloody.

I was breathing, trying not to.

My arms were awash with sweat.

Rory and Tommy kept a short distance, and Clay looked up at the girl. The good-green eyes. He said and slowly smiled it:

"War of the Roses?"

He saw her change from abject worry, to a smile all long and hopeful, like horses entering the straight.

"He okay?"

"I think so."

"Just give me a minute and we'll take him in."

The small exchange was hard for him to hear, but he knew it was me and Carey, and soon the others were near. Rosy licked his face.

"Rosy!" I said. "Get out of there!"

Still no sign of Henry.

Finally, there was Rory:

He had to step in at some point.

He told everyone to get the hell out of his way, and picked Clay up and carried him. In his arms Clay hung like an arch.

"Oi, Matthew," Rory called, "check this out—it's all that letterbox practice!" Then to Clay, down at face and blood. "How's *this* for a heart-to-heart?" And finally his happiest afterthought. "Hey—did you kick him in the coins, like I asked?"

"Twice. The first one wasn't that good."

And Rory laughed, right there on the steps, and it hurt the boy he was holding.

As promised and planned, I *had* killed him.

But true to his word as ever—Clay just wasn't dead.

It felt good to be a Dunbar boy again.

the tw,
the snake,
and moon

THEY BOUGHT THE PLACE, OF COURSE THEY DID, AND THINGS BEGAN TO BEGIN.

Job-wise, Michael still did his construction work, with his always-powdery hands, and Penny did her cleaning, and studied English till the time was near. She started wondering about a different career, and was pulled between two teaching strands: the first could only be music. Then English as a Second Language.

Maybe it was memory that did it:

The indoor tarmac.

The floor-to-ceiling heat.

"Passport?"

"*Przepraszam?*"

"Oh, Jesus . . ."

She chose the ESL.

She applied to university, resolved to still going cleaning at night—an accounting firm, the lawyer's office—and the acceptance letter arrived. Michael found her at the kitchen table. He stood, not far from the exact same place where, many years later, he'd be watched and interrogated by a mule.

"Well?"

He sat down closely next to her.

He watched the insignia, and letterhead.

Some people celebrate things with champagne, or a night out somewhere nice, but in this case, Penelope sat; she put her head against Michael's side, and read the letter again.

And like that, the time flowed by:

They planted things in the garden.

Half of it lived. Half died.

They watched the Wall come down in November of '89.

Through the slits in the back fence, they often saw the horseflesh, and loved the racing quarter's other eccentricities—like a man or woman walking out on the road, midafternoon, with a stop sign to hold up traffic. Behind them, a groom would lead a horse across, likely 10-1 next day, at Hennessey.

The last and most important quirk of the place, though, already back then, was the number of forgotten fields; you only had to know where to look. In some cases, as we're well aware, such places could hold great meaning—and one was near the train line. Sure, there would be The Surrounds, and the dying track at Bernborough—but this one, too, was crucial.

So I'm begging you please to remember.

It had everything to do with the mule.

Three years into Penny's university course, the phone rang at 18 Archer Street; Dr. Weinrauch.

Adelle.

She'd died at the dining room table, most likely late at night, having just typed a letter to a friend.

"Looks like she finished up, took her glasses off and laid her head down next to the Remington," he'd said, and it was sad and aching, but beautiful:

One last, lethal combination.

A hard-hit final full stop.

Of course, they drove straight out to Featherton, and Michael knew he was lucky, compared to Penelope. Here at least they could stand in the church and sweat beside the box. He could turn to the retired old doctor, and stare at his tie, which hung like a long-stopped clock.

"Sorry, son."

"Sorry, Doc."

Later, they sat in the old house, at the table, with her blue-rimmed glasses and the typewriter. For a while he contemplated putting a new sheet in and punching out a few lines. He didn't, though, he just looked at it, and Penelope brought tea, and they drank it and walked the town, and finished out back, by the banksia.

When she asked if he'd take the typewriter home, he said it was home already.

"You're sure now?"

"I'm sure." He realized. "Actually, I think I know what to do."

For whatever reason, it just felt right, he went out to the shed; he found the same old shovel and dug one more hole, to the left of the dog and the snake.

In the house, he sat a last while with the Remington.

He found three rounds of plastic, strong and smooth, and wrapped it up, so clear you could see the keys—first the Q and the W, then the midsection of F and G, H and J—and in the old backyard of an old-backyard-of-a-town, he took it there, he placed it there, and buried it in the ground:

The TW, the snake, and Moon.

You didn't put that in ads for real estate.

At home again, life had to go on, and it did, with Michael staying up with her, as she wrote her assignments, and checked them. When she did the practical work, she was sent to Hyperno High. The toughest high school in town.

On her first day, she came back beaten:

"They've eaten me alive."

On the second, it was worse:

"Today they spat me out."

There were times when she would shout at them, in total loss of control—of them and of herself—and kids moving in for the kill. When once she near exploded, screaming, "QUIET!" then a mutter of "Little shits," the class erupted with laughter. The mirth, the mockery of teenagers.

The fact of Penny Dunbar, though, as we know, is that she might have been slight, and perennially fragile, but she was an expert at somehow surviving. She spent lunchtimes with whole classes—the queen of detention and boredom. She bludgeoned them with organized silence.

As it turned out, she was the first candidate in years to last the student-teacher period, and they offered her a job, full-time.

She left the cleaning completely.

Her workmates took her out drinking.

Michael sat with her next day, by the toilet. He rubbed her back and spoke to her soothingly:

"Are these the spoils of freedom?"

She threw up and sobbed but laughed.

Early the next year, when Michael picked her up from work one afternoon, there were three giant boys surrounding her, with their sweat, their haircuts and arms. For a moment, he nearly got out, but then he saw it—she was holding a copy of Homer; she was reading aloud, and it must have been one of the gruesome bits, for the boys all grimaced and crowed.

She wore a dress the shade of peppermint.

When she realized Michael had pulled up, she clapped the book shut and the boys all cleared a path. They said, "Bye Miss, bye Miss, bye Miss," and she got into the car.

But that's not to say it was easy—it wasn't.

When he was heading out to work sometimes, he heard her talk herself into it, in the bathroom; it was hard to face the day. He'd say, "Which kid is it this time?"—for the job became working with the toughest ones, one on one; and sometimes it took an hour, sometimes several months, but always she wore them down. Some would even protect her. If other kids mucked up, they'd be taken to the toilets, and shoved amongst the troughs. Don't mess with Penny Dunbar.

In many ways, the title of ESL was ironic, because a good percentage of her students were kids whose first language was actually English, but could barely read a paragraph—and those were always the angriest.

She'd sit with them by the window.

She brought a metronome in from home.

The kid would stare, incredulous, saying, "What the fuck is that?"

To which Penny would answer flatly:

"Read in time with this."

But then, it had to happen.

After four years of teaching, she came home one evening with a pregnancy kit, and this time they *did* go out to celebrate, but would wait out the week for Saturday.

In the meantime, next day, they were at work again:

Michael was pouring concrete.

He told a few of his friends there—they stopped and shook his hand.

Penelope was at Hyperno, with a belligerent yet beautiful boy.

She read with him at the window.

The metronome went click.

On Saturday, they ate in that fancy place in the Opera House, they stood at the top, on the steps. The great old bridge, it hung there, and the ferries pulled in at the Quay. By midafternoon, when they came back out, a ship had arrived to dock. There were crowds of people on the esplanade, and cameras and smilers in flocks. At the building and glasswork were *them*—Michael and Penny Dunbar—and at the bottom of the Opera House stairway, five boys had appeared, and stood standing . . . and soon they came down to meet us.

And we walked back out together—through the crowds and words of people, and a city all swollen with sun.

And death came walking with us.

part five

cities + waters + criminals + arches + stories

the grand entrance

Of course, Henry had to make an entrance that night of fists and feathers and brothers.

When I think of it now, I see it as the last wave of our collective adolescence. Just like Clay, individually, when he walked out the Bernborough Park tunnel that last time, so it was tonight for this, and Henry, and us. In the next few days, on and off, there'd be a kind of holding-on; a final nod to the last vestiges of youngness and dumbness.

We'd never see it or be it again.

It wasn't long after. The TV was on.

There'd been much arguing, and *Rain Man* was replaced by a movie I got from Rory one year for Christmas. *Bachelor Party*. In Rory's words, if we had to watch bullshit from the '80s, it might as well be the good stuff. In Henry's, it was Tom Hanks in his heyday, before he started getting crap and winning Golden Globes and shit; he'd researched it.

All four of us, we sat there:

I was icing my hands.

Rory and Tommy were laughing.

Hector was sprawled like a steel-striped blanket, purring on Tommy's lap.

Clay was on the couch, quietly watching; quietly bleeding away.

It was right at Rory's favorite part—when the ex-boyfriend of the female lead falls naked through the sunroof of a car—when Henry finally arrived.

First there were footsteps.

Then keys getting dropped.

Then in.

Then a bloodied, grinning face, in the light of the lounge room doorway.

"What?" he shouted. "Are you bastards kidding? You're watching *Bachelor Party* without me?"

At first none of us looked.

Actually, Clay did, but couldn't move.

The rest of us were too engrossed in the mayhem on screen.

It was only when the scene was over that Rory saw the state of him, and then came all the swearing, stunned silence, and blasphemy. I finished it off with a good long "Je-sus *Christ* . . ."

Henry, unfazed, plonked himself on the couch and looked at Clay. "Sorry I'm late, kid."

"That's okay."

This had been Henry's plan; to come in looking something like this, just before Clay had made it home himself, so I might get all distracted. The trouble was, the two boys from the 200-meter mark had taken much longer than he'd thought—and it took a lot more drinking—and of course he'd left his car behind, and walked from Bernborough Park. By then he was so drunk and beaten up he'd almost crawled, and really, looking back, it's one of Henry's dumbest greatest moments. He'd planned it all, and invited it all, and all of it for Clay.

He studied him, with a kind of satisfaction. "Good to see you, though. Is it good to be home? I see Matthew rolled out the welcome mat, the big muscly prick."

"That's all right, I had it coming." Clay turned to him now, and was shocked by the extent of the damage. His lips, especially, were hard to look at; his cheekbones cooked and charred. "I'm not too sure about you, though."

"Oh," said Henry cheerfully, "I did, old boy, I did."

"*And?*" That was me now, standing in the middle of the lounge room. "You want to tell us what the hell's going on?"

"Matthew," Henry sighed, "you're *innerrupting* the movie," but he knew. If he'd enlisted Schwartz and Starkey (and Starkey's girl, as it turned out) for the job of making a mess of him, here was my chance to finish it. "You see, gentlemen"—he grinned, and his teeth were more a butcher's bone, all thickly red and mess—"if you ever want to look like this, all it takes is one blond Boy Scout with iron fists, one thug with disgusting breath, and lastly, the thug's girlfriend, who hits harder than the pair of 'em put together. . . ."

He tried to talk on, but didn't get any further, for in the next few seconds, the living room swayed, and the *Bachelor Party* high jinks got funnier and funnier. At last he clattered forward, straight past me, and crash-tackled the TV to the floor.

"Shit!" shrieked Rory. "That's one of the greatest movies of *all time* he's wrecking—" but he was there and close for catching him, though he couldn't save the board games. Or the birdcage, which tumbled down, like raucous, stadium-sized applause.

Soon we all crouched around him, with the carpet, blood, and cat hair. And dog hair. And Jesus—was that *mule* hair?

Henry was out cold.

When he came to, he recognized Tommy first: "Young Tommy, ay? The pet collector—and Rory, the human ball and chain, and ahh, you're Matthew, aren't you? Mr. Reliable." Then lastly, fondly: "Clayton. The smiler. You've been gone for years, *years*, I tell you!"

It registered.

The movie was still playing, sideways on the floor, the birdcage was sloped and doorless—and further left, near the window, the fish tank had capsized amongst the chaos. We'd only noticed now that the water had reached our feet.

Henry looked at the movie, maneuvering his head, but the rest of us were watching T, the pigeon, as he climbed out of his cage, onto the floor, past the goldfish, headed straight for the open front door. Clearly, the bird knew what was what—this was no place to be for the next few hours. Well, that, and he was totally pissed off. He walked and half-flapped, walked and half-flapped. All he needed was a suitcase. Once he even looked back:

"Right, that's *it*." He honestly seemed to say it, seething in grey and purple. "I'm outta here, you lot—good Goddamn luck."

As for the goldfish, Agamemnon, he flipped, he flopped, he gulped the air for liquid; he leapt across the carpet. There had to be more water out there somewhere, and he'd be damned if he wouldn't find it.

growing up the dunbar way

So there they were, way up in the far-flung future:

A cantankerous bird.

An acrobatic goldfish.

Two bloodied boys.

And look here at Clay, in the backstory.

What can we say about him?

How did life begin, as a boy and a son and a Dunbar?

It was pretty simple, really, with a multitude lying within:

Once, in the tide of Dunbar past, there were five brothers, but the fourth of us was the best of us, and a boy of many traits.

How *did* Clay become Clay, anyway?

In the beginning there was all of us—each our own small part to tell the whole—and our father had helped, every birth; he was first to be handed to hold us. As Penelope liked to tell it, he'd be standing there, acutely aware, and he'd cry at the bedside, beaming. He never flinched at the slop or the burnt-looking bits, as the room began to spin. For Penelope, that was everything.

When it was over, she'd succumb to dizziness.

Her heartbeat leapt in her lips.

It was funny, they liked to tell us, how when we were born, we all had something they loved:

Me, it was my feet. The newborn crinkly feet.

Rory, it was his punched-up nose when he first came out, and the noises he made in his sleep; something like a world title fight, but at least they knew he was alive.

Henry had ears like paper.

Tommy was always sneezing.

And of course, there was Clay, between us:

The boy who came out smiling.

As the story went, when Penny was in labor with Clay, they left Henry, Rory, and me with Mrs. Chilman. On the drive to the hospital they nearly pulled over; Clay was coming quickly. As Penny would later tell him: the world had wanted him badly, but what she didn't do was ask why.

Was it to hurt, to humiliate?

Or to love and make great?

Even now it's hard to decide.

It was morning, summer and humid, and when they made it to the maternity ward, Penny was shouting, still walking, and his head was starting to crown. He was very nearly torn rather than born, as if the air had reefed him out.

In the delivery room, there was a lot of blood.

It was splayed on the floor like murder.

As for the boy, he lay in the muggy atmosphere, and was strangely, quietly, smiling; his bloodcurdled face dead silent. When an unsuspecting nurse came in, she stood openmouthed and blaspheming. She stopped and said, "Jesus Christ."

It was our mother, all dizzy, who replied.

"I hope not," she said, and our father still grinned. "We know what we did to *Him*."

As a boy, as I said, he was the best of us.

To our parents, in particular, he was the special one, I'm sure of it, for he rarely fought, hardly cried, and loved everything they spoke of and told him.

Night for night, while the rest of us made excuses, Clay would help with the dishes, as a trade for one more story. To Penny he'd say, "Can you tell me about Vienna again, and all those bunk beds? Or what about *this* one?" His face was in the dinner plates, the suds across his thumbs. "Can you tell me about the statue of Stalin? And who *was* Stalin anyway?"

To Michael he'd say, "Can you tell me all about Moon, Dad, and the snake?"

He was always in the kitchen, while the rest of us watched TV, or fought in the lounge or the hallway.

Of course, as things go, though, our parents were also editors:

The stories were almost-everythings.

Penny didn't tell him yet how long they spent on a garage floor, to beat, to blow and burn themselves, to exorcise past lives. Michael didn't talk of Abbey Hanley, who became Abbey Dunbar, then Abbey Someone-Else. He didn't tell him about burying the old TW, or of *The Quarryman*, or how once he'd loved to paint. He'd said nothing yet about heartbreak, or how lucky heartbreak could be.

No, for now, most-of-truths were enough.

It was enough for Michael to say he was on the porch one day and met a woman out front with a piano. "If it wasn't for that," he'd solemnly explain, "I wouldn't have you or your brothers—"

"Or Penelope."

Michael smiled and said, "Damn right."

What neither of them could know was that Clay *would* hear the stories in their entireties, not long before it was too late.

Her smile would be hoisted up by then.

Her face would be in decay.

As you might imagine, his first memories were only vague, of two particular things:

Our parents, his brothers.

The shapes of us, our voices.

He remembered our mother's piano hands as they sailed across the keys. They had a magical sense of direction—hitting the M, hitting the E, and every other part of PLEASE MARRY ME.

To the boy her hair was sunny.

Her body was warm and slim.

He would remember himself as a four-year-old, being frightened of that upright brown thing. While each of us had our own dealings with it, Clay saw it as something not-his.

When she played he put his head there.

The stick-thin thighs belonged to him.

As for Michael Dunbar, our father, Clay recalled the sound of his car—the engine on winter mornings. The return in the half dark. He smelt like strain, long days, and brickwork.

In what would later go down as the Shirtless Eating Days (as you'll soon see), he remembered the sight of his muscles; for apart from all the construction labor, he would sometimes—and this was how he put it—*go out to the torture chamber*, which was push-ups and sit-ups in the garage. Sometimes it was a barbell as well, but not even heavily weighted. It was the number of lifts, overhead.

Sometimes we went out with him:

A man and five boys doing push-ups.

The five of us falling away.

And yes—in those years of growing up in that place, our dad was a sight to see. He was average height, slight in weight, but fit and tight-looking; lean. His arms weren't big or bulging, they were athletic and charged with meaning. You could see each move, each twitch.

And all those Goddamn sit-ups.

Our dad had a concrete stomach.

In those days, too, I remind myself, our parents were something else.

Sure, they fought sometimes, they argued.

There was the odd suburban thunderbolt, but they were mostly those people who'd found each other; they were golden and bright-lit and funny. Often they seemed in cahoots somehow, like jailbirds who wouldn't leave; they loved us, they *liked* us, and that was a pretty good trick. After all, take five boys, put them in one small house, and see what it looks and sounds like: it's a porridge of mess and fighting.

I remember things like mealtimes, and how sometimes it got too much: the forks dropping, the knives pointing, and all those boys' mouths eating. There'd be arguing, elbowing, food all over the floor, food all over our clothes, and "How did that piece of cereal end up *there*—on the wall?" until a night came when Rory sealed it; he spilt half his soup down his shirt.

Our mother didn't panic.

She stood, cleaned up, and he would eat the rest of it shirtless—and our father got the idea. We were all still celebrating when he said it:

"You lot, too."

Henry and I nearly choked. "Sorry?"

"You didn't hear me?"

"Ohhh, *shit*," said Henry.

"Should I make you take your pants off, too?"

For a whole summer, we ate like that, our T-shirts heaped near the toaster. To be fair, though, and to Michael Dunbar's credit, from the second time onwards, he took his own shirt off with us. Tommy, who was still in that beautiful phase when kids speak totally unfiltered, shouted, "Hey! Hey, Dad! What are you doing here in just your nipples?"

The rest of us roared with laughter, especially Penny Dunbar, but Michael was up to the task. A slight flickering in one of his triceps.

"And what about your mum, you blokes? Should *she* go shirtless, too?"

She never needed rescuing, but it was Clay who'd often be willing.

"No," he said, but she did it:

Her bra was old and scruffy-looking.

It was faded, strapped to each breast.

She ate and smiled regardless.

She said, "Now don't go burning your chests."

We knew what to get her for Christmas.

In that sense there was always a bulkiness to us.

A bursting at the seams.

Whatever we did, there was more:

More washing, more cleaning, more eating, more dishes, more arguing, more fighting and throwing and hitting and farting, and "Hey, Rory, I think you better go to the toilet!" and of course, a lot more denying. *It wasn't me* should have been printed on all our T-shirts; we said it dozens of times each day.

It didn't matter how in control or on-top-of-things things were, there was chaos a heartbeat away. We could be skinny and constantly agile, but there was never quite room for all of it—so everything was done at once.

One part I remember clearly is how they used to cut our hair; a barber would have cost too much. It was set up in the kitchen—an assembly line, and two chairs—and we'd sit, first Rory and me, then Henry and Clay. Then, when it came to Tommy's turn, Michael would cut Tommy's, to give Penny a small reprieve, and then she'd resume and cut his.

"Hold *still*!" said our father to Tommy.

"Hold still," said Penny to Michael.

Our hair lay in lumps in the kitchen.

Sometimes, and this one comes so happily it hurts, I remember when we all got into one car, the entire lot of us, piled in. In so many ways I can't help but love the idea of it—how Penny and Michael, they were both completely law-abiding, but then they did things like this. It's one of those perfect things, really, a car with too many people. Whenever you see a group squashed in like that—an accident waiting to happen—they're always shouting and laughing.

In our case, in the front, through the gaps, you could see their hand-held hands.

It was Penelope's fragile, piano-playing hand.

Our father's powdery work hand.

And a scrum of boys around them, of blended arms and legs.

In the ashtray there were lollies, usually Anticols, sometimes Tic Tacs. The windshield was never clean in that car, but the air was always fresh; it was boys all sucking on cough drops, or a festival of mint.

Some of Clay's fondest memories of our dad, though, were the nights, just before bed, when Michael wouldn't believe him. He'd crouch and speak to him quietly: "Do you need to go to the toilet, kid?" and Clay would shake his head. Even as the boy was refusing, he'd be led to the small bathroom, and cracked tiling, and proceed to piss like a racehorse.

"Hey, Penny!" Michael would call. "We've got bloody Phar Lap here!" And he'd wash the boy's hands and crouch again, not saying another thing—and Clay knew what it meant. Every night, for a long, long time, he was piggybacked into bed:

"Can you tell me about old Moon again, Dad?"

Then to us, his brothers, we were bruises, we were beatings, in the house at 18 Archer Street. As older siblings do, we marauded all that was his. We'd pick him up by his T-shirt, right in the middle of his back, and deposit him somewhere else. When Tommy arrived, three years later, we did the same to him. All through Tommy's childhood, we craned him behind the TV, or dropped him out the back. If he cried he was dragged to the bathroom, a horsey bite at the ready; Rory was stretching his hands.

"Boys?" would come the call. "Boys, have you seen Tommy?"

Henry did the whispering, by the long blond hairs in the sink.

"Not one word, y' little prick."

Nodding. Fast nodding.

That was the way to live.

At five years old, like all of us, Clay began the piano.

We hated it but did it.

The MARRY ME keys and Penny.

When we were very young, she'd spoken her old language to us, but only as we went to sleep. Now and then she'd stop and explain something of it, but it left us year by year. Music, on the other hand, was nonnegotiable, and there'd been varying degrees of success:

I was close to competent.

Rory was downright violent.

Henry might have been brilliant, if only he could have cared.

Clay was quite slow to get things, but once he did he would never forget.

Later, Tommy had only done a few years when Penny fell sick, and maybe she was already broken by then, mostly, I think, by Rory.

"All right!" she'd call from next to him, through the barrage of battered music. "Time's up!"

"What?" He was desecrating that marriage proposal, which was fading by then, and fast, but would never fade completely. "What was that?"

"I said time's *up*!"

Often she wondered what Waldek Lesciuszko would have made of him, or more to the point, of her. Where was her patience? Where was the branch of a spruce tree? Or in this place, a bottlebrush or eucalypt? She knew there was a big difference between five boyish boys and a father's studious girl, but there was still a disappointment, as she watched him swagger away.

For Clay, sitting in the corner of the lounge room was a duty, but one he was willing to endure; he tried at least to try. When he was finished, he'd trail her to the kitchen, and ask his two-word question:

"Hey, Mum?"

Penny would stop at the sink. She'd hand him a checkered tea towel. "I think," she'd say, "I'll tell you about the houses today, and how I thought they were made of paper. . . ."

"And the cockroaches?"

She couldn't help herself. "So big!"

But sometimes I think they wondered, our parents, about why they'd chosen to live like this. Most often they would snap over minor things, as the mess and frustration mounted.

I remember how once it rained a whole fortnight, in summer, and we came home deep-fried in mud. Penny had duly lost it with us, and resorted to the wooden spoon. She gave it to us on the arms, on the legs—everywhere she could (and the dirt, like crossfire, like shrapnel)—till finally she'd splintered two of those spoons, and threw a boot down the hall instead. As it tumbled, end over end, it somehow gathered momentum, and elevation, hitting Henry, a thud in the face. His mouth was bleeding, and he'd swallowed a loose tooth, and Penny sat down near the bathroom. When a few of us went to console her, she sprang up and said, "Go to *hell*!"

It was hours till finally she'd checked on him, and Henry was still deciding. Was he ridden with guilt, or furious? After all, losing teeth was good for business. He said, "I won't even get paid by the Tooth Fairy!" and showed her the gap within.

"The Tooth Fairy," she said, "will know."

"Do you think you get more if you swallow it?"

"Not when you're covered in mud."

For me, the most memorable arguments our parents had were linked often to Hyperno High. The endless marking. Abusive parents. Or injuries from breaking up fights.

"Jesus, why don't you just let 'em kill each other?" our dad said once. "How could you be so—" and Penny was starting to seethe.

"So—*what?*"

"I don't know—naïve, and just, stupid—to think you can make a difference." He was tired, and sore, from building work, and putting up with the rest of us. He waved a hand back out through the house. "You spend all that extra time marking, and trying to help them, and look here—look at this place." He was right; there was Lego everywhere, and a scattergun of clothes and dust. Our toilet recalled those public ones, in the time of her spoils of freedom; not one of us aware of the brush.

"And what? So I should stay home and do the cleaning?"

"Well, no, that's not what I—"

"Should I get the bloody vacuum?"

"Oh, shit, that's not what I meant."

"WELL, WHAT *DID* YOU MEAN?" she roared. "HUH?"

It was the sound that makes a boy look up, when anger spills over to rage. *This time they really mean it*.

And still it wasn't quite over.

"YOU'RE SUPPOSED TO BE ON MY SIDE, MICHAEL!"

"I am!" he said. ". . . I am."

And the quieted voice, even worse. "Then how about actually showing it."

Then after-storm, and silence.

As I said, though, such moments were isolated, and they would soon reconvene at the piano:

Our symbol of boyhood misery.

But their island of calm in the maelstrom.

Once, he'd stood beside her, as she recovered by playing some Mozart; then he placed his hands on the instrument, in the sun on the lid by the window.

"I'd write the words *I'm sorry*," he'd said, "but I've forgotten where all the paint is—" and Penelope stopped, momentarily. An inkling of smile at the memory.

"Well, that and there's really no room," she said, and played on, on the handwritten keys.

Yes, she played on, that one-woman band, and while sometimes the chaos spilled over, there were also what we'd call *normal* arguments—normal fights—mostly between us boys.

In that regard, at six years old, Clay had started football, both the organized kind, and the one we played at home, front to back, around the house. As time went by it was our father, Tommy, and Rory versus Henry, Clay, and me. On the last tackle, you could kick the ball over the roof, but only if Penny wasn't reading on a lawn chair, or marking that flow of assignments.

"Hey, Rory," Henry would say, "run at me so I can smash you," and Rory would do it, and run straight over the top of him, or be driven back into the ground. Every game, without fail, they would need to be prized apart—

"Right."

Our father looked at both of them, back and forth:

Henry all blond and bloody.

Rory the color of a cyclone.

"Right what?"

"You *know* what." He'd be breathing hoarse and heavily, with scratch marks on his arms. "Shake hands. Now."

And they would.

They'd shake hands, say sorry, and then, "Yeah, sorry I had to shake your hand, *dick*head!" and it was on again, and this time they'd be dragged out back where Penelope sat, the assignments littered around her.

"Now what have you two been up to *this* time?" she'd ask, in a dress, and barefoot in the sun. "Rory?"

"Yeah?"

She gave him a look.

"I mean, *yes?*"

"Take my chair." She started walking inside. "Henry?"

"I know, I know."

He was already on hands and knees, collating the fallen sheets.

She lengthened a look at Michael, and a collegial, cahootsful wink.

"Goddamn bloody boys."

No wonder I got a taste for blasphemy.

And what else?

What else was there, as we skip the years like stones?

Did I mention how sometimes we'd sit on the back fence, for end-of-morning trackwork? Did I say how we'd watched as it all got packed up, to be another forgotten field?

Did I mention the Connect Four war when Clay was seven?

Or the game of Trouble that lasted four hours, maybe more?

Did I mention how it was Penny and Tommy who won that battle at long last, with our dad and Clay second, me third, and Henry and Rory (who were forced to play together) last? Did I mention that they both blamed each other for being crap at hitting the bubble?

As for what happened with Connect Four, let's just say we were still finding the pieces months later.

"Hey, look!" we'd call, from the hallway or kitchen. "There's even one in here!"

"Go pick it up, Rory."

"*You* go pick it up."

"*I'm* not pickin' it up—that's one of yours."

And on. And on.

And on.

Clay remembered summer, and Tommy asking who Rosy was, when Penny read from *The Iliad*. We were up late, in the lounge room, and Tommy's head was in her lap, his feet across my legs, and Clay was down on the floor.

Penny tilted and stroked Tommy's hair.

I told him, "It's not a person, stupid, it's the sky."

"What do you mean?"

This time it was Clay, and Penelope explained.

"It's because," she said, "you know how at sunrise and sunset the sky goes orange and yellow, and sometimes red?"

He nodded from under the window.

"Well, when it's red, it's rosy, and that's all he meant. It's great, isn't it?" and Clay smiled then, and so did Penny.

Tommy, again, was concentrating. "Is Hector a word for the sky, too?"

That was it, I got up. "Did there really need to be five of us?"

Penny Dunbar only laughed.

The next winter there was all the organized football again, and the winning and training and losing. Clay didn't especially love the game, but did it because the rest of us did, and I guess that's what younger siblings do for a time—they photocopy their elders. In that respect, I should say that although he was set apart from us, he could also be just the same. Sometimes, mid-household-football-game, when a player was secretly punched or elbowed, Henry and Rory would go at it—"It wasn't me!" and "Oh, bullshit!"—but me, I'd seen it was Clay. Already then his elbows were ferocious, and deliverable in many ways; it was hard to see them coming.

A few times he'd admit it.

He'd say, "Hey, Rory, it was me."

You don't know what I'm capable of.

But Rory wouldn't have it; it was easier fighting with Henry.

To that end (and *this* one), it was proper, really, that Henry was publicly infamous back then, when it came to sport and leisure—sent off for pushing the ref. Then ostracized by his teammates, for the greatest of footballing sins; at halftime the manager asked them:

"Hey, where's the oranges?"

"What oranges?"

"Don't get smart—you know, the quarters."

But then someone noticed.

"Look, there's a big pile a peels there! It was Henry, it was bloody Henry!"

Boys, men and women, they all glared.

It was great suburban chagrin.

"Is that true?"

There was no point denying it; his hands spoke for themselves. "I got hungry."

The ground was six or seven kilometers away, and we'd caught the train, and Henry was made to go home on foot, and the rest of us as well. When one of us did something like that, we all seemed to suffer, and we walked the Princes Highway.

"Why'd you push the ref like that, anyway?" I asked.

"He kept treading on my foot—he was wearing steel studs."

Now Rory: "Why'd you have to eat all the oranges, then?"

"Because I knew you'd have to walk home, too, shithead."

Michael: "Oi!"

"Oh, yeah—sorry."

But this time there was no retraction of the sorry, and I think we were all somehow happy that day, though we were soon to start coming undone; even Henry throwing up in the gutter. Penny was kneeling next to him, our father's voice beside her:

"I guess these *are* the spoils of freedom."

And how could we ever know?

We were just a bunch of Dunbars, oblivious of all to come.

peter pan

"Clay? You awake?"

At first there was no answer, but Henry knew he was. One thing with Clay was that he was pretty much always awake. What surprised him was the reading light coming on, and Clay having something to say:

"How you feeling?"

Henry smiled. "Burning. You?"

"I smell like hospital."

"Good old Mrs. Chilman. That was pretty hurtful, that stuff she put on, wasn't it?"

Clay felt a hot streak on the side of his face. "Still better than metho spirits," he said, "or Matthew's Listerine."

Earlier, a fair few things had happened:

The lounge room was cleaned up.

We convinced both the fish and bird to stay.

The story of Henry's exploits came out in the kitchen, and Mrs. Chilman dropped in from next door. She'd come to patch up Clay, but Henry needed it more.

First to the kitchen, though, and before anything else, Henry had to explain himself, and this time he mentioned more than said it; he talked about Schwartz and Starkey, and the girl, and he was a lot less jovial now, and so was I. Actually, I was ready to throw the kettle, or smack him in the head with the toaster.

"You did *what*?" I couldn't believe what I was hearing. "I thought you were one of the smarter ones here—this I'd expect from Rory."

"Hey!"

"Yeah," agreed Henry, "show a bit of respect—"

"I wouldn't start any shit like that right now if I were you." I had my eye on the frying pan, too, lounging around on the stove. It wouldn't be hard giving it something to do. "What the hell happened, anyway? Did they beat you up, or run you over with a truck?"

Henry touched a cut, almost fondly. "Okay, look—Schwartz and Starkey are good guys. I asked them, we got drinking, and then"—he took a breath—"neither of them would do it, so I sort of started in on the girl." He looked at Clay and Rory. "You know—the one with the lips."

You mean the bra strap, thought Clay.

"You mean the tits," said Rory.

"That's her." Henry nodded happily.

"And?" I asked. "What did you do?"

Rory again. "She's got tits like bread rolls, that chick."

Henry: "You think? Bread rolls? I've never heard such a thing."

"Are you two quite bloody finished?"

Henry ignored me completely. "Better than pizzas," he said. It was a private conversation between him and Rory, for Christ's sake. "Or doughnuts."

Rory laughed, then serious. "Hamburgers."

"You want fries with that?"

"And a Coke." Rory giggled; he *giggled*.

"Calzones."

"What's a calzone?"

"Je-sus C*hrist*!"

Still they both grinned, and blood ran to Henry's chin, but at least I'd gotten their attention.

"Are you right, Matthew?" said Rory. "That's the best bloody talk Henry and I have had in years!"

"Probably ever."

Rory looked at Clay. "That was quality heart-to-heart."

"Well"—I pointed between them—"I'm sorry to interrupt the pizzas, burgers and calzones debate, and you two bonding over a floury pair of—"

"See?! Floury! Even Matthew can't resist 'em!"

"—but I wouldn't mind knowing what the hell happened out there."

Now Henry looked dreamily in the general direction of the sink.

"And?"

He blinked himself back. "And what?"

"What *happened?*"

"Oh—yeah . . ." He conjured up the energy. "Well, anyway, you know, they wouldn't hit me, so I just went over to her—I was pretty drunk by then—and I thought I might press the flesh, so to speak. . . ."

"And?" Rory asked. "How was it?"

"I don't know—I hesitated." He had a good think about it.

"Then what?"

Henry, half-grin, half-grim. "Well, she'd seen I was coming in." He swallowed and felt it all over again. "So she punched me four times in the balls, and three times in the face."

There was a genuine outcry of "Jesus!"

"I know—she threw the whole bloody display at me."

Rory, especially, got excited. "See that, Clay? Four! That's commitment! None of this two-times-in-the-coins shit."

Clay actually laughed; out loud.

"And then," Henry finally went on, "old Starkers and Schwartz, they finished me off—they had to."

I was perplexed. "Why?"

"Isn't it obvious?" Henry was matter-of-fact. "They were worried they were next."

* * *

In the bedroom again, it was well past midnight, and Henry sat up, abruptly.

"Bugger this," he said, "I'm sober enough, I'm going out to get the car."

Clay sighed and rolled from bed.

There was rain like a ghost you could walk through.

Almost dry when it hit the ground.

Earlier, not long after the enigma of Henry's head, and the talk of well-baked chests, there was scratching at the back door, and knocking at the front.

At the back were both Rosy and Achilles, standing and thoroughly expectant.

To the dog: "You—in."

To the mule: "You—get it through your thick head. Kitchen's closed."

As to the front, the knocking came with calling out:

"Matthew, it's Mrs. Chilman!"

I opened up to the small squat woman with her ever-present wrinkles and shining eyes, and no incrimination. She was too aware that a whole other world existed in this house, and who was she to judge? Even when she'd first realized we were down to just us Dunbar boys, she'd never questioned me on how we lived. Mrs. Chilman wore the wisdom of *old school*—she'd seen boys the age of Rory and me sent off to be shot at overseas. Early on she'd brought us soup sometimes (tremendously chunky and hot) and would call us for help with opening jars until her dying day.

On this night, she was ready for business.

She spoke at me economically:

"Hi, Matthew, how are you, I thought I might get a look at Clay, he's a bit banged up, is he? Then I'll look at your hands."

That was when the voice arrived from the couch, and attached to it, happily, was Henry.

"Me first, Mrs. Chilman!"

"Jesus!"

What was it about our house?

It brought the blasphemy out in everyone.

* * *

The car was in the Bernborough Park car park, and they walked to it through the moisture.

"Feel like doing a few laps?" Clay asked.

Henry tripped on a laugh.

"Only if we can drive 'em."

In the car they traveled in silence, they took each street and laneway, and Clay catalogued the names. There was Empire, Carbine, Chatham Street, and onto Gloaming Road: the site of Hennessey and the Naked Arms. He remembered all the times he'd walked these streets with the just-arrived Carey Novac.

Still they drove meanderingly on, and Clay looked over between them.

"Hey," he said, "hey, Henry," when they stopped at the Flight Street traffic lights, but he spoke toward the dash. "Thanks for what you did."

And you had to give it to Henry, especially at times like these; he gave him a black-eyed wink. "Good old Starkey's girl, ay?"

Their last stop before heading home was the edge of Peter Pan Square, where they sat and watched the windshield, and the statue out in the middle. Through the sheath of rain, Clay could just make out the cobblestones, and the horse the square was named for. On the mounting block it said this:

PETER PAN
A VERY GALLANT HORSE
TWICE WINNER OF THE RACE
THAT STOPS THE NATION
1932, 1934

It felt like he was watching them, too, his head turned sideways, but Clay knew—the horse was after attention, or a bite of one of his rivals. Especially Rogilla. Peter Pan hated Rogilla.

Up top, Darby Munro, the jockey, seemed to be watching the car as well, and Henry turned the key. When the engine ran, the wipers clocked over maybe every four seconds, and horse and rider, they cleared and obscured, cleared and obscured, till Henry finally spoke.

"Hey, Clay," he said, and shook his head, and smiled just slight and slightedly. "Tell me what he's like these days."

piano wars

In later years, it was understandable.

People got it wrong.

They thought it was Penny's death and our father leaving that made us what we were—and sure, it definitely made us rowdier and harder and hardier, and gave us a sense of fight—but it isn't what made us tough. No, in the beginning it was something more.

It was the wooden, the upright.

The piano.

As it was, it started with me, in sixth grade, and now, as I type, I'm guilty; I apologize. This, after all, is Clay's story, and now I write for myself—but it somehow feels important. It leads us somewhere else.

At school till then it was easy. Class was fine, I was in on every football game. I'd barely had an argument, till someone cared to notice: I was ribbed for learning the piano.

Never mind that we were forced to, or that the piano, as an instrument, had a long history of rebellion—Ray Charles was coolness personified; Jerry Lee Lewis set the thing on fire. As a kid growing up in the racing quarter, only one type of boy played the piano; it didn't matter how much the world had advanced. It didn't matter if you were the school football captain or a juvenile amateur boxer—the piano made you one thing, and that thing, of course, was this:

You were clearly a homosexual.

* * *

It had actually been known for years that we'd learned, even if we weren't much good. None of that really mattered, though, given that childhoods latch on to things at different times. You can be left alone for a decade, only to be hung out to dry in your teens. You could collect stamps and have it labeled *interesting* in first grade, and have it haunt you in ninth.

For me, as I said, it was sixth grade.

All it took was a kid a few inches shorter, but a lot more powerful, who actually *was* a juvenile boxer—a kid named Jimmy Hartnell. His father, Jimmy Hartnell Sr., owned the Tri-Colors Boxing Gym, over on Poseidon Road.

And Jimmy, what a kid.

He was built like a very small supermarket:

Compact; expensive if you crossed him.

His hair was a ginger fringe.

In terms of how it started, there were boys and girls in the corridor, and angles of dust and sun. There were uniforms and callings-out, and countless moving bodies. It was beautiful in that off-putting way, how the light came streaking in; those perfect, long-lit beams.

Jimmy Hartnell strode the hallway, freckly, confident, toward me. White-shirted, grey-shorted. The look he wore was pleased. He was perfect schoolish thuggery; his smell the smell of breakfast, his arms all blood and meat.

"Hey," he said, "isn't that that Dunbar kid? The one who plays the piano?" He rolled a shoulder, givingly, into me. "What a fucking *poofter*!"

That kid was made for italics.

It went on like that for weeks, maybe a month, and always a little bit further. The shoulder became an elbow, the elbow a punch in the balls (although not nearly as lethal as old Bread Rolls), which soon became standard favorites—nipple cripples in the boys' toilets, here and there a headlock; choker holds in the hall.

In so many ways, looking back, it was just the spoils of childhood, to be twisted and rightfully ruled. It's not unlike that dust in the sun, being tumbled through the room.

But that didn't mean I enjoyed it.

Or even more, that I wouldn't react.

For me, like so many in that situation, I didn't face the problem directly, or at least I didn't yet. No, that would have been pure stupidity, so I fought back where I could.

In short I blamed Penelope.

I railed against the piano.

Of course, there are problems and there are problems, and my problem now was this:

Next to Penelope, Jimmy Hartnell was a Goddamn softy.

Even if she could never quite tame us at the piano, she always made us practice. She clung to an edge of Europe, or a city, at least, in the East. By then there was even a mantra she had (and by God we had it too):

"You can quit if you want by high school."

But that didn't help me now.

We were halfway through first term, which meant most of the year to survive.

My attempts had started lamely:

Going to the toilet midpractice.

Arriving late.

Playing poorly on purpose.

Soon I was outright defying her; not playing certain pieces, and then not playing at all. She had all the patience in the world for those troubled and troublesome Hyperno kids, but they hadn't prepared her for this.

At first she tried talking to me; she'd say, "What's gotten into you lately?" and "Come on, Matthew, you're better than *that*."

Of course I told her nothing.

I had a bruise in the middle of my back.

For a good week or so, we sat, me on the right, Penny on the left, and I'd look at the language of music; the quavers, the rhythm of crotchets. I remember the look on my dad's face, too, when he came in from the torture chamber, and found us both at war.

"Again?" he'd say.

"Again," she'd say, and looked not at him, but ahead.

"You want a coffee?"

"No thanks."

"Some tea?"

"No."

She sat with a face like a statue.

There were words now and then, in clenches, and most of them coming from me. When Penelope spoke, it was calmly.

"You don't want to play?" she'd say. "Okay. We'll sit here." Her stillness became infuriating. "We'll sit here each day till you break."

"But I won't break."

"You will."

Now I look back and see me there, at the written-on keys of the piano. Messy dark hair and gangly, eyes gleaming—and they were definitely a sort of color back then, they were blue and pale like his. I see me taut and miserable, as I assure her again, "I won't."

"The boredom," she countered, "will beat you—it'll be easier to play than not."

"That's what you think."

"Sorry?" She hadn't heard me. "What did you say?"

"I said," I said, and turned to her, "that's what *you* fucking think."

And she stood.

She wanted to explode beside me, but she'd channeled him so well by then, and gave nothing, not a spark, away. She sat back down and watched me. "Okay," she said, "we'll stay then. We'll stay here and we'll wait."

"I hate the piano," I whispered. "I hate the piano and I hate *you*."

It was Michael Dunbar who heard me.

He was over on the couch, and now he became America, he entered the war with force; he leapt across the lounge room, and dragged me out the back, and he could have been Jimmy Hartnell, pushing me past the clothesline, and hauling me under its pegs. There were great big shrugs of breaths of him; my hands against the fence.

"Don't you—*ever*—talk to your mum like that," as he pushed me, harder, again.

Do it, I thought. Hit me.

But Penny was near at arms.

She looked at me, she studied me.

"Hey," she said, "hey, Matthew?"

I looked back, I couldn't help myself.

The weapon of unexpectedness:

"Get up and get back in there—we've got ten fucking minutes left."

Inside again, I was wrong.

I knew it was wrong to admit it—to buckle—but I did.

"I'm sorry," I said.

"For what?"

She was staring straight ahead.

"You know. *Fucking*."

Still, she stared forward, that music-language, unblinking. "And?"

"Saying I hate you."

She made the slightest of moves toward me.

A move with no movement at all.

"You can swear all day, and hate me all day, if only you would play."

But I didn't play, not that night, or the next.

I didn't play the piano for weeks, then months, and if only Jimmy Hartnell could have seen. If only he knew the pains I was going to, to free myself from him:

Damn her in those slim-cut jeans, and the smoothness of her feet; and damn the sound of her breathing. Damn those murmurs in the kitchen—with Michael, my father, who backed her to the hilt—and while we're at it, damn him too, that groveler, and his sticking up for Penelope. About the only thing he did right in that period was giving Rory and Henry a clip on the ear when they refused it, too. It was my war, not theirs, not yet. And they could come up with their own shit, of which, believe me, they were capable.

No, for me, those months were endless.

The days shortened into winter, then lengthened into spring, and still Jimmy Hartnell went for me; he never got bored or impatient. He nippled me in those toilets, and his punches bruised my groin; he was good at boxing's low blows, all right, as both he and Penelope waited; I was there to be pushed, and broken.

How I wanted her to erupt!

How I wanted her to slap her thigh, or tear at her shampooed hair.

But no, oh no, she did him justice this time, that monument of communist silence. She'd even changed the rules on me—the practice hours were extended. She would wait in the chair beside me, and my father would bring her coffee, and toast with jam, and tea. He'd bring her biscuits, and fruit, and chocolates. The lessons were journeys of backache.

One night, we sat till midnight, and this was the night it came. My brothers were all in bed, and as always, she waited me out; Penelope was still upright when I stood and staggered to the couch.

"Hey," she said, "that's cheating—it's piano or off to bed," and it was then I made myself known; I crumbled and felt the mistake.

Disgruntled, I got up; I walked past her, into the hall, unbuttoning my shirt, and she saw what lay within—for there, on the right side of my chest, were the marks and signature fingerprints of a ginger-fringed schoolboy nemesis.

Quickly, she slung out an arm.

Her slender and delicate fingers.

She'd stopped me beside the instrument.

"What," said Penelope, "is that?"

As I've told you before, our parents back then, they were certainly something else.

Did I hate them for the piano?

Of course I did.

Did I love them for what they did next?

Bet your house, your car, and your hands on it.

Because next came moments like this.

I remember sitting in the kitchen, in the river mouth of light.

I sat and spoke down all of it, and they listened intently, in silence. Even Jimmy Hartnell's boxing prowess, there was first only taking it in.

"Poofters," said Penelope, eventually. "Don't you know that's bloody stupid—and wrong, and . . ." She was searching, it seemed, for more—its greatest crime of all. *"Unimaginative?"*

Me, I had to be honest. "It's the nipple cripples that *really* hurt. . . ."

She looked down into her tea. "Why didn't you ever tell us?"

But my dad was a clear-eyed genius.

"He's a boy," he said, and he winked at me, and everything would be okay. "Am I right, or am I right?"

And Penelope understood.

She admonished herself, and quickly.

"Of course," she whispered, "like them . . ."

The boys from Hyperno High.

In the end, it was decided in the time she drank her tea. There was the abject knowledge of only one way to help me, and it wasn't them going to the school. It wasn't seeking protection.

Michael said okay.

A quiet declaration.

He went on to say there was nothing that could be done but to mix it up with Jimmy Hartnell, and put the matter to rest. It was mostly just a monologue, and Penelope agreed. At one point she almost laughed.

Was she proud of him and his speech?

Was she happy for what I would go through?

No.

Looking back, I think it was more just a sign of life—to picture fronting the scary bits, which, of course, was the easiest part:

Imagining was one thing.

Actually doing it felt almost impossible.

Even when Michael finished, and asked, "What do *you* think?" she'd sighed, but was mostly relieved. There was nothing here to be joking about, but joking was what she did.

"Well, if fighting that kid will get him to the piano again, I guess that's all there is." She was embarrassed, but also impressed; I was completely, utterly dismayed.

My parents, who were there to protect me, and raise me the right way, were sending me, without a moment's more hesitation, into imminent schoolyard defeat. I was torn between love and hatred for them, but now I just see it was training.

After all, Penelope would die.

Michael would leave.

And I, of course, would stay.

Before any of that could happen, though, he would teach me and train me for Hartnell.

This was going to be great.

the warm-armed claudia kirkby

Next morning, both Henry and Clay woke up swollen.

One of them would go to school, all bashed and quiet and bruised, and one would work with me, all bashed and quiet and bruised. He'd start the wait for Saturday.

This time, though, it was different:

The wait to see her race.

There was much to come that initial day, due mostly to Claudia Kirkby. But first Clay met with Achilles.

I was working close to home, so we could leave a little later, and Clay went out to the yard. The sunshine bathed the animals, but beat Clay up in the face. Soon it would soothe the soreness.

First he patted Rosy, until she lapped the grass.

The mule smiled below the clothesline.

He watched him, he said, You're back.

Clay stroked him on the mane.

I'm back . . . but not for long.

He bent down, he checked the mule's feet, and Henry came calling out to him.

"Hooves all good?"

"All good."

"He speaks! I should get myself down to the newsagent's!"

Clay even gave him more, looking up from the front right hoof. "Hey, Henry—one to six."

Henry grinned. "You bet."

As for Claudia Kirkby, at lunch, Clay and I were sitting in a house, amongst the delivery of flooring. When I stood to wash my hands, my phone rang and I got Clay to answer; it was the teacher who doubled as counselor. To her surprise at Clay being home, he told her it was only temporary. As for the point of the phone call, she'd seen Henry, she said, and wondered if all was okay.

"At home?" Clay asked.

"Well . . . yes."

Clay looked over and half smiled. "No, no one roughed Henry up at home. No one here would ever do anything like that."

I had to walk across. "Give me the Goddamn phone."

He did it.

"Ms. Kirkby? . . . Okay, Claudia, no, it's all okay, he just had a small problem in the neighborhood. You know how stupid boys can be."

"Oh, yes."

For a few minutes, we talked, and her voice was calm—quiet but sure—and I imagined her through the phone. Was she wearing her dark skirt and cream shirt? And why did I imagine her calves? When I was about to hang up, Clay made me wait, to tell her he'd brought back the books she'd lent him.

"Does he want new ones?"

He'd heard her, and thought, then nodded.

"Which one did he like the most?"

He said, "*The Battle of East Fifteenth Street*."

"That's a good one."

"I liked the old chess player in it." A touch louder this time. "Billy Wintergreen."

"Oh, he's *so* good," said Claudia Kirkby; I was standing, caught in the middle.

"Are you two quite all right?" I asked (not unlike between Henry and Rory, the night when Clay had come home), and she smiled inside the phone line.

"Come and get the books tomorrow," she said. "I'll be here for a while, after work." On Fridays the staff stayed for drinks.

When I hung up, he was weirdly smiling.

"Stop that stupid grin."

"What?" he asked.

"Don't *what* me—just grab that Goddamn end."

We carried floorboards up the stairs.

Next afternoon, I sat in the car when Clay went into the schoolyard.

"You're not coming?"

She was down by the side of the car park.

She held her hand up, high in the light, and they made the exchange of books; she said, "God, what happened to *you*?"

"It's okay, Ms. Kirkby, it had to be done."

"You Dunbars, you surprise me every time." Now she noticed the car. "Hi, Matthew!" Damn it, I had to get out. This time I took note of the titles:

The Hay-Maker.

The See-Sawer.

(Both by the same author.)

Sonnyboy and Chief.

As for Claudia Kirkby, she shook my hand and her arms looked warm, as evening flooded the trees. She asked how everything was, and was it good having Clay back home again, and of course I said of course, but he wouldn't be home for long.

Just before we left, she lasted Clay a look.

She thought, decided, and reached.

"Here," she said, "give me one of those books."

On a slip of paper, she wrote her phone number and a message, then placed it in *Sonnyboy and Chief*:

In case of an emergency
(like you keep running out of books)
ck

And she *had* been wearing that suit, just like I'd hoped, and there was that sunspot center-cheek.

Her hair was brown and shoulder-length.

I died as we drove away.

On Saturday the moment came, and all five of us went to Royal Hennessey, because word had gotten around; McAndrew had a gun new apprentice, and she was the girl from 11 Archer Street.

The track had two different grandstands:

The members and the muck.

In the members there was class, or at least pretend-class, and stale champagne. There were men in suits, women in hats, and some that weren't even hats at all. As Tommy had stopped and asked: what *were* those strange things, anyway?

Together, we walked to the muck—the paint-flaked public grandstand—with its punters and grinners, winners and losers, and most of them fat and fashionless. They were beer and clouds and five-dollar notes, and mouthfuls of meat and smoke.

In between, of course, was the mounting yard, where horses were led by grooms, doing slow, deliberate laps. Jockeys stood with trainers. Trainers stood with owners. There was color and chestnut. Saddles and black. Stirrups. Instructions. Much nodding.

At one point, Clay saw Carey's father (known for a time as Trackwork Ted), and he was tall for an ex-jockey, short for a man, as Carey once had told him. He was wearing a suit, he leaned on the fence, with the heft of his infamous hands.

After a minute or so, his wife appeared too, in a pale green dress, and ginger-blond hair that flowed but was cut with control: the formidable Catherine Novac. She bounced a matching purse at her side, uneasy, part angry and quiet. At one point she put the purse in her mouth, and it was something a bit like a sandwich bite. You could tell she hated race days.

* * *

We walked up and sat at the back of the grandstand, on broken seats with water stains. The sky was dark, but no rain. We pooled our money, Rory put it on, and we watched her in the mounting yard. She was standing with old McAndrew, who said nothing at first, just staring. A broomstick of a man, his arms and legs were like clock hands. When he turned away, and Clay caught his eyes, and they were crisp and clean, blue-grey.

He recalled something McAndrew had said once, not only in Clay's earshot, but by his face. Something about time and work and cutting out the dead wood. He'd somehow come to like it.

Of course, Clay smiled when he saw her.

McAndrew called her closer.

When he gave her the orders, it was seven or eight short syllables, no less than that, and no more.

Carey Novac nodded.

In one movement she strode at the horse and climbed aboard.

She trotted him out the gate.

hartnell

IN THE PAST, WE COULDN'T KNOW.

An oncoming world was coming.

While I began the task of taking on Jimmy Hartnell, our mother would soon start dying.

For Penelope, it was so innocuous.

We traced it back to this:

I was twelve, and in training, and Rory was ten, Henry nine, Clay was eight, and Tommy five, and our mother's time had shown itself.

It was Sunday morning, late September.

Michael Dunbar woke to the sound of TV. Clay was watching cartoons: *Rocky Reuben—Space Dog*. It was just past six-fifteen.

"Clay?"

Nothing. His eyes were wide with screen.

This time he whispered more harshly—"*Clay!*"—and now the boy looked over. "Could you turn that thing down a bit?"

"Oh—sorry. Okay."

By the time he'd adjusted it, Michael had woken up an extra notch, so he went there and sat with him, and when Clay asked for a story, he spoke of Moon and snake and Featherton, and didn't even contemplate skipping bits. Clay always knew if he missed something, and fixing it would only take longer.

When he was done they sat and watched, his arm slung round Clay's shoulders. Clay stared at the bright-blond dog; Michael dozed but soon awoke.

"Here," he said, "it's the end." He pointed at the TV. "They're shooting him back to Mars."

A voice came quietly between them. "It's Neptune, idiot."

Clay and Michael Dunbar, they grinned and turned, to the woman behind, in the hallway. She was in her oldest pajamas. She said, "Don't you remember anything?"

On that particular morning, the milk was off, so Penny made pancakes, and when the rest of us came in, we argued, spilt orange juice and laid blame. Penny cleaned up and called over: "You spilt the bloody orange *chooce* again!" and we laughed and none of us knew:

So she dropped an egg between Rory's toes.

So she lost control of a plate.

What could that mean, if anything?

But looking back now, it meant plenty.

She'd started leaving us that morning, and death was moving in:

He was perched there on a curtain rod.

Dangling in the sun.

Later, he was leaning, close but casual, an arm draped over the fridge; if he was minding the beer he was doing a bloody good job.

On the other side, on the incoming fight with Hartnell, it was just as I'd thought, it was great. In the lead-up to that seemingly ordinary Sunday, we'd bought two pairs of boxing gloves.

We punched, we circled.

We weaved.

I lived in those giant red gloves back then, like cabins strapped to my wrists.

"He's gonna kill me," I said, but my dad, he wouldn't allow it. He was truly just my dad back then, and maybe that's all I can say; it's the best thing I can tell you.

It was moments like those he'd stop.

He put his boxing-gloved hand on my neck.

"Well." He thought, and talked to me quietly. "Then you've gotta start thinking like this. You have to make up your mind." The encouragement came so easily to him, as he touched the back of my head. It was all so very tender, very sweet. A lot of love beside me. "He can kill you all he wants to—but you're not going to die."

He was good at before-the-beginnings.

For Penny, it kept coming on, and for us it was vaguely noticeable. The woman we'd known our whole short lives—who had barely had a cold—was sometimes looking shaky. But as fast, she'd ward it off.

There were moments of apparent wooziness.

Or sometimes a distant cough.

There was a sleepiness midmorning, but she worked so long and hard—and that, we'd thought, explained it. Who were we to say that it wasn't the working at Hyperno—the proximity of germs and kids. She was always up late with her marking.

She was only in need of rest.

At the same time, you can imagine how gloriously we trained:

We fought in the yard, we fought on the porch.

We fought beneath the clothesline, sometimes in the house—everywhere we could—and first it was Dad and me, but then everyone had a crack. Even Tommy. Even Penelope. Her blond was slightly greying.

"Watch out for her," said our dad one day, "she's got a frightening overhand left."

As for Rory and Henry, they'd never gotten on so well, as they rounded, fought, and clapped each other, clashing arms and forearms. Rory even apologized once, and willingly, too—a miracle—when he'd hit him that little too low.

In the meantime, at school, I took it best I could—and at home we did defense work ("Keep your hands up, watch your footwork") and attack ("Make that jab all day") till it was close to now-or-never.

On the night before it happened, when I was finally to face Jimmy Hartnell, my dad came into my bedroom, which I shared with Clay and Tommy. The other two were asleep at the bottom two slots of the triple bunk, and I lay awake on top. As most kids do, I closed my eyes when he came in, and he gently shook me and spoke:

"Hey, Matthew, a bit more training?"

I didn't need any talking into it.

The difference was, when I reached for the gloves, he told me I wouldn't need them.

"What?" I whispered. "Bare fists?"

"They'll be bare when the moment comes," he said, but now he spoke quite slowly. "I've been for a visit to the library."

I followed him to the lounge room, where he pointed to an old video cassette, *and* an old video machine (a black-and-silver ancient thing), and told me to get it working. As it turned out, he actually bought the machine with some scratched-together pay; the start of Christmas savings. Even as I looked down at the video's name, *The Last Great Famous Pugilists*, I could feel my father smiling.

"Pretty good, huh?"

I watched it swallow the tape. "Pretty good."

"Now just press *play*," and soon we sat in silence as boxers paraded the screen; they arrived like presidents of men. Some were in black-and-white, from Joe Louis to Johnny Famechon, Lionel Rose to Sugar Ray. Then color and Smokin' Joe. Jeff Harding, Dennis Andries. Technicolor Roberto Durán. The ropes flexed under their weight. In so many of the fights, the boxers went down, but climbed back up to their feet. Such brave and desperate weaving.

Near the end I looked at *him*.

The glint in my father's eye.

He'd turned the sound right down.

He held my face, but calmly.

He held my jaws in his hands.

For a moment I thought he might echo the screen, saying something like the commentary. But all he did was hold me like that, my face in his hands in the darkness.

"I gotta give it to you, kid—you've got heart."

The before-the-beginning of that one.

Leading up to that moment, there was a day for Penny Dunbar, a morning, with a sweetheart named Jodie Etchells. She was one of her favorite kids, held back because of dyslexia, and she worked with her twice a week. She had hurt eyes, tall bones, and a big long braid down her back.

That morning, they were reading with the metronome—the old familiar trick—when Penny got up for a thesaurus. Next, she was shaken awake.

"Miss," said Jodie Etchells, "Miss," and "*Miss!*"

Penny came to, she looked in her face, and the book a few meters away. Poor young Jodie Etchells. She seemed near to collapsing herself.

"Are you okay, Miss, are you okay?"

Her teeth were perfectly paved.

Penelope tried reaching over, but her arm was somehow confused.

"I'm fine, Jodie," and she should have sent her out, for help, or a drink of water, or anything to at least distract her. Instead, though—and talk about typical Penny—she said, "Open up that book, okay, and look up, let's see, how about *cheerful*? Or *gloomy*? Which would you prefer?"

The girl, her mouth and symmetry.

"Maybe *cheerful*," she said, and read the alternatives aloud. "*Happy . . . joyful . . . merry.*"

"That's good, very good."

Her arm still wasn't moving.

Then school, it came, a Friday.

I was taunted, by Hartnell and his mates:

There was *piano* and *playing* and *poofter*.

They were virtuosos of alliteration and didn't know it.

Jimmy Hartnell had that fringe a little longer then—he was a few days shy of a haircut—and he'd leaned and muscled down. His mouth was small and slit-like, like a can just partly opened. It widened soon into a smile. I walked my way toward him, and found the courage to speak.

"I'll fight you in the nets at lunch," I said.

Best news he'd ever had.

Then to an afternoon:

As she often did, she read to those kids, as they waited for sight of the buses. This time it was *The Odyssey*. The chapter about the Cyclops.

There were boys and girls in green and white.

The usual foray of hairstyles.

As she read about Odysseus, and his trickery of the monster in his lair, the print swam over the page; her throat became the cave.

When she coughed she saw the blood.

It splashed down onto the paper.

She was strangely shocked by its redness; it was just so bright and brutal. Her next thought was back to the train, the first time she'd ever seen it; those titles typed in English.

And what was my blood to *that* blood?

It was nothing, nothing at all.

It was windy that day, I remember, when clouds move fast through the sky. One minute white, one minute blue; a lot of shifting light. There was one cloud like a coal mine, as I walked down to the cricket nets, in the darkest patch of shade.

At first I didn't see Jimmy Hartnell, but he was there on the concrete pitch. He was grinning the width of his fringe.

"He's here!" called one of his friends. "The poofter's fucking *here*!"

I walked and raised my fists.

Mostly it comes in circles now, in half turns right and left. I remember how terribly fast he was, and how soon I'd come to taste it. I remember the roar of schoolkids, too, like waves all down the beach. At one point, I saw Rory, and he was just a little kid. He was standing next to Henry, who was Labrador-blond and skinny. Through the diamonds of wire in the netting, I could see them mouthing *hit him,* while Clay watched numbly on.

But Jimmy was hard to hit.

First I was caught in the mouth (like chewing on a piece of iron), then up, and into the ribs. I remember thinking they were broken, as those waves came crashing in.

"Come on, fucking Piano Man," the kid whispered, and again he came skipping in. Each time he did that, he somehow came around me, and caught me with a left, then a right and another right. After three like that I went down.

There were cheers and checking for teaching staff, but no one had yet found out, as I crawled and stood up quickly. Possibly a standing eight-count.

"Come on," I said, and the light kept interchanging. The wind howled through our ears, and again he came in and around.

This time, as previously, he caught me with the left, and then that punishing follow-up—but the success of that tactic changed, as I blocked the third punch outright, and clobbered him on the chin. Hartnell went reeling backwards, and he stammered, adjusting, and swept. He took a shocked and hurried backstep, which I followed to the front and left; I committed myself with a pair of jabs, hard above that slit there, above and into the cheek.

It became what commentators of every sport everywhere—probably even marbles—would call a battle of attrition, as we traded knuckles and hands. At one point, I went down on a knee, and he'd clipped me and quickly apologized, and I'd nodded; a silent integrity. The crowd had grown and climbed, their fingers all clenched in the wire.

Eventually, I knocked him down twice, but he always came punching back. By the end I'd gone down four times myself, and on the fourth I couldn't get up. Vaguely, I could sense the authorities then, for those beaches and waves had flocked; the lot of them were like seagulls now, except for my brothers, who'd stayed. Beautifully—and looking back, not surprisingly—Henry held out his hand, to some fleeing kid or other, who gave him the rest of his lunch. Already he'd had a bet on, and already he'd gone and won.

In the corner, over near the cricket stumps, Jimmy Hartnell stood side-on. He was something like an injured wild dog, both pitiable and grounds for caution. The teacher, a man, went and grabbed him, but Hartnell had shrugged him off; he almost tripped on his way toward me, and his slit was now just a mouth. He crouched and called down next to me.

"You must be good at piano," he said, "if it's anything like you fight."

I searched my mouth with my fingers; the victory of relief.

I lay back, I bled and smiled.

I still had all my teeth.

And so it was.

She went to the doctor.

A cavalcade of tests.

To us, for now, she said nothing, and all went on like always.

Once, though, there was a crack of it, and it becomes so cruel and clean, the more I sit and type it. The kitchen is crisp, clear water.

Because once, in Rory and Henry's room, the two of them were wheeling and fighting. They'd abandoned the gloves and were back to normal, and Penelope ran toward it.

She grabbed both scruffs-of-the-school-shirt.

She held them out and away.

Like boys hung up to dry.

A week later, she was in the hospital; the first of many visits.

But back then, way back then, that handful of days and nights earlier, she'd stood with them in their bedroom, in that sock-and-Lego pigsty. The sun was setting behind her.

Christ, I'm gonna miss this.

She'd cried and smiled and cried.

the triumvirate

EARLY ON SATURDAY NIGHT, CLAY SAT WITH HENRY, UP ON THE ROOF.

Close to eight o'clock.

"Like old times," Henry said, and they were happy in the moment, if feeling their various bruisings. He also said, "That was a great run." He'd been referring to Carey.

Clay stared, diagonally. Number 11.

"It was."

"She should have won. A protest, bloody hell."

Later, he waited.

The Surrounds, and the steady sound of her; the quiet rustle of feet.

When she arrived, they didn't lie down till they'd been there a long time.

They'd sat on the edge of the mattress.

They talked and he wanted to kiss her.

He wanted to touch her hair.

Even if just two fingers, in the falling of it by her face.

In the light that night it looked sometimes gold, sometimes red, and there was no telling where it ended.

He didn't, though.

Of course he didn't:

They'd made rules, somehow, and followed them, to not break or risk what they had. It was enough that they were here, alone, together, and there were plenty more ways to be grateful.

He took out the small heavy lighter, and *Matador in the fifth*.

"It's the best thing anyone's ever given me," he said, and he lit it a moment, then closed it. "You rode so well today."

She gave him back *The Quarryman*.

She smiled, she said, "I did."

Earlier, it was one of those good nights, too, because Mrs. Chilman opened her window. She called out to them, and up.

"Hey, Dunbar boys."

Henry had called back first. "Mrs. Chilman! Thanks for patching us up the other night." Then he went to work. "Hey, I like your curlers there."

"Shut up, Henry," but she was smiling, those wrinkles at work as well.

Both boys now stood and walked closer.

They crouched at the side of the house.

"Hey, Henry?" Mrs. Chilman asked, and it was all a bit of fun. Henry knew what was coming. Whenever Mrs. Chilman looked up like this, it was to ask for a book, from his collections every weekend. She loved romance, crime, and horror—the lower the brow, the better. "You got something for me?"

He mocked. "Do I *have* something for you? What-a-y' *think*? How does *The Corpse of Jack the Ripper* sound?"

"Got it already."

"*The Man She Hid Downstairs*?"

"That was my husband—they never found the body."

(Both boys laughed—she'd been a widow since before they knew her; she joked about it now.)

"All right, Mrs. Chilman, shit, you're a tough customer! How about *The Soul Snatcher*? That one's a bloody beauty."

"Done." She smiled. "How much?"

"Oh, come on, Mrs. Chilman, let's not play that game. How about we do the usual?" He gave Clay a quick flick of the eyes. "Let's just say I give it to you *gratis*."

"Gratis?" She was peering up now, contemplating. "What's that, German, is it?"

Henry roared.

When they did lie down, she recalled the race.

"But I lost," she said, "I blew it."

Race Three.

The Lantern Winery Stakes.

1,200-meters and her mount was called The Gunslinger, and they missed the start terribly, and Carey brought him back. She weaved her way through the traffic and took him home—and Clay watched in perfect silence when the field had hit the straight; a riot of passing hoofbeats, and the eyes and the color and the blood. And thc thought of Carey amongst it.

The only problem came in the last furlong when she veered too close to the second-placegetter, Pump Up the Jam—seriously, what a name—and the win was taken off her.

"My first time in front of the stewards," she said.

Her voice against his neck.

On the roof, when the transaction was approved (Mrs. Chilman insisted on paying ten dollars), she said, "And how are you, Mr. Clay? You looking after yourself these days?"

"Mostly."

"*Mostly?*" She came out a little further. "Try to make it always."

"Okay."

"Okay, lovely boy."

She was about to close the window again, when Henry tried for more. "Hey, how come *he* gets to be lovely?"

Mrs. Chilman returned. "You've got a lovely *mouth*, Henry, but he's the lovely boy," and she gave them a final wave.

Henry turned to Clay.

"You're not lovely," he said. "Actually, you're pretty ugly."

"Ugly?"

"Yeah, ugly as Starkey's arse."

"You've looked at it lately, have you?"

This time he gave Clay a shove, and a friendly slap to the ear.

It's a mystery, even to me sometimes, how boys and brothers love.

Near the end he started telling her.

"It's pretty quiet out there."

"I bet."

"The river's completely dry, though."

"And your dad?"

"He's pretty dry, too."

She laughed and he felt her breath, and he thought about that warmness, how people were warm like that, from inside to out; how it could hit you and disappear, then back again, and nothing was ever permanent—

Yes, she'd laughed and said, "Don't be an idiot."

Clay said only "Okay," and his heart was beating too big for him; he was sure the world could hear it. He looked at the girl beside him, and the leg slung loosely over. He looked at her highest buttonhole, the fabric of her shirt:

The checks there.

The blue turned sky blue.

The red all faded to pink.

The long ridges of collarbone, and the pool of shadow beneath.

The faintest scent of her sweat.

How could he love someone this hard and be so disciplined, and stay silent and still so long?

Maybe if he'd done it then: if he'd found the nerve earlier, it wouldn't have gone the way it did. But how could he ever predict such things? How could he know that Carey—this girl who lay across him, and whose breath drew in and out on him, who'd had a life, who *was* a life—would make up his trifecta, or triumvirate, of love and loss?

He couldn't, of course.

He couldn't.

It was all in what was to come.

the single cigarette

BACK THEN, FOR PENNY DUNBAR, SHE PACKED HER BAGS FOR THE HOSPITAL, and the world that waited within it.

They would push, they'd prod and cut bits.

They would poison her with kindness.

When they first talked radiation, I saw her standing alone in the desert, then *boom*—a little bit like the Hulk.

We'd become our own cartoon.

From the outset there was the hospital building, and all the infernal whiteness, and the spotless shopping mall doors; I hated how they parted.

It felt like we were browsing.

Heart disease to the left.

Orthopedics to the right.

I also remember how the six of us walked the corridors, through the pleasant terror inside. I remember our dad and his hard-clean hands, and Henry and Rory not fighting; these places were clearly unnatural. There was Tommy, who looked so tiny, and always in short Hawaiian shorts—and me still bruised-but-healing.

At the very back, though, long behind us, was Clay, who was scaredest, it seemed, to see her. Her voice fought out from the nose cord:

"Where's my boy, where's my boy? I've got a story, it's a good one."

Only then did he come between us.

It took all of everything in him.

"Hey, Mum—can you tell me about the houses?"

Her hand stretched out to touch him.

She came in and out of the hospital twice more that year.

She was opened, closed up, and pinkened.

She was sewn and raw-and-shiny.

Sometimes, even when she was tired, we'd ask if we could see them:

"Can you show us that longest scar again, Mum? That one's a bloody beauty."

"Hey!"

"What—*bloody?* That's not even proper swearing!"

She was usually home by then, back in her own bed, being read to, or lying with our dad. There was something about their angles; her knees curled up and sideways, at forty-five degrees. Her face lay down on his chest.

In many ways, that was a happy time, to be honest, and I see things through that frame. I see the weeks go by in a shoulder blade, and months disappear in pages. He read out loud for hours. There was wearing round his eyes by then, but the aqua always as strange. It was one of those comforting things.

Sure, there were frightening times, like her vomiting in the sink, and that God-awful smell in the bathroom. She was bonier, too, which was hard to believe, but then back at the lounge room window. She read to us from *The Iliad*, and Tommy's body, in pieces, asleep.

In the meantime, there was progress.

We made music all of our own:

The piano wars went on.

There were many outcomes that could have arisen from my bout with Jimmy Hartnell, and many of them did. He and I became newborn friends. We became those boys who fought each other to find our common standing.

After Jimmy, there were many more lined up, and I was up to fending them off. They only need mention the piano. But there were never the heights of Hartnell again. It was Jimmy I fought for the title.

In the end, it wasn't me who was famed for fighting, though; it could only ever be Rory.

In terms of age, the year had clicked over, and I was well now into high school (free of the piano at last) and Rory was in grade five, and Henry the year below him. Clay had hit year three, and Tommy was down in kindergarten. Old stories soon washed to shore. There were memories of the cricket nets, and boys who were more than willing.

The problem with that was Rory.

His force was true and terrible.

But the aftermath was worse.

He dragged them through the playground, like the brutalist end of *The Iliad*—like Achilles with Hector's corpse.

There was one time, in the hospital, when there were kids from Hyperno High.

Penny sat, punctured, in bed.

God, there must have been more than a dozen of them, crowded and noisy around her, both boys and girls alike. Henry said, "They're all so . . . *furry*." He was pointing at the boys' legs.

I remember we'd watched from the corridor, and their uniforms green and white; those overgrown boys, the perfumed girls, and covered-up cigarette. Just before they left, it was the girl I mentioned earlier, the lovely Jodie Etchells, who pulled out a strange-looking present.

"Here, Miss," she said, but she unwrapped it herself; Penny's hands were inside the blankets.

And soon, our mother's lips.

They cracked, so dry and smiley:

They'd brought her in the metronome, and it was one of the boys who said it. I think his name was Carlos.

"Breathe in time with this, Miss."

* * *

It was evenings at home were the best, though.

They were blond and black hair greying.

If they weren't asleep on the couch, they were in the kitchen playing Scrabble, or punishing each other at Monopoly. Or sometimes they'd actually be awake on the couch, watching movies into the night.

For Clay, there were clearer standout moments, and they came on Friday nights. One was the end of a movie they'd watched, as the credits rolled up the screen; I think it was *Good Bye, Lenin!*

Both Clay and I were in the hallway, after hearing the rise in volume.

We saw the lounge room, then we saw them:

Hard-held in front of the TV.

They were standing, they were dancing, but slowly—barely—and her hair hung on to its yellowness. She looked so weak and brittle; a woman all arms and shins. Their bodies were pressed together, and soon our father saw us. He signaled a silent hello.

He even mouthed the words—

Have a look at this gorgeous girl!

And I guess I have to admit it:

Through the tired and ache, in the joy of that look, Michael Dunbar was truly handsome back then, and not too bad a dancer.

Then the next, it was out front, on the steps, and the mist of coolest winter.

At Hyperno a few days earlier, Penelope was back as a substitute, and had confiscated cigarettes. To be honest she didn't really think it her place—to tell these kids not to smoke. Whenever she took such things from them, she said to come back later. Was that plain irresponsible? Or showing them proper respect? No wonder they all came to love her.

In any case, whether the student had been embarrassed, or ashamed, no one came back for those Winfield Blues, and Penny found them in the evening. They were crushed at the bottom of her handbag. As she took out her wallet and keys before bed, she held the cigarettes.

"And what the hell is *this?*"

Michael had promptly caught her.

And call them impulsive, or ridiculous, but I love them so much for this one. The sickness was gone away in that time, and they went out front to the porch. They smoked, they coughed and woke him.

On the way in, a few minutes later, Penny went to throw them out, but for some reason Michael stopped her. He said, "How about we just hide them?" A conspiratorial wink. "You never know when we might need one again—it can be our little secret."

But a boy was in on it, too.

See, even when they lifted the piano lid, and deposited the packet beneath, they still had no idea; he watched them from the hallway, and one thing, at that point, was clear:

Our parents might have danced well.

But their smoking was amateur at best.

central

Clay was tempted to stay longer, but couldn't.

The hardest was knowing he'd miss Carey's next race meeting, out at Warwick Farm, but again, she expected him to go. When she left him at The Surrounds that Saturday night, she'd said, "See you when you're here, Clay. I'll be here, too, I promise."

He watched her down the laneway.

Leaving us was the same as last time.

We knew without saying anything.

But also totally different.

This time there was obviously a lot less gravity, for what needed to be done was done. We could go on.

It was Monday night when we finally got around to finishing *Bachelor Party*, and Clay got up to leave. His things were in the hallway. Rory looked over, appalled.

"You're not leaving *now*, are you? They haven't even put the mule in the lift yet!"

(It's actually quite scary how similar our lives were to that movie.)

"It's a donkey," said Tommy.

Rory again: "I don't care if it's a quarter horse crossed with a Shetland bloody pony!"

Both he and Tommy laughed.

Then Henry:

"Here, Clay—put your feet up," and as he faked his way to the kitchen, he threw him to the couch, twice—once as he'd tried to get up again. Even when he did manage to break free, Henry got him in a headlock and ran him round. "How does *that* feel, y' little shit? We're not in Crapper's building now, are we?"

Behind them, the *Bachelor Party* high jinks got dumber and dumber, and as Hector streaked away, Tommy jumped on Clay's back, and Rory called over to me.

"Oi, give us a bloody hand, huh?"

I stood in the lounge room doorway.

I leaned against the frame.

"Come on, Matthew, help us pin him down!"

Given Clay's form as an opponent, their breath came deep from within, and finally I walked toward them.

"All right, Clay, let's beat these bastards up."

Eventually, when the struggle was over, and the movie, too, we'd driven him to Central; the one and only time.

It was Henry's car.

He and I in the front.

The other three in back, with Rosy.

"Shit, Tommy, does that dog have to pant so bloody loud?"

At the station, all was how you'd imagine:

The coffee smell of brakes.

The overnight train.

The orange globes of light.

Clay had his sports bag, and there were no clothes in it; only the wooden box, the books of Claudia Kirkby and *The Quarryman*.

The train was ready to leave.

We shook hands—all of us and him.

Halfway to the last carriage, it was Rory who called out.

"Oi, Clay!"

He turned back.

"The coins, remember?"

And happily, he boarded the train.

And again, again, the mystery—how the four of us all stood watch there, with the smell of the brakes and a dog.

the woman who became a dunbar boy

By the end of my first year of high school, it was apparent we were in serious trouble. There was so much air in her clothes by then; she'd be better less and less. There were times, it seemed, that were normal, or something we kind of mimicked. Pretend-normal, or normal-pretend, I'm not sure how we did it.

Maybe it was just that we all had lives, we had to get by, and that included Penelope; us boys kept being kids. We kept it all together:

There was the haircut, there was Beethoven.

There was for all of us something personal.

You know your mother's dying when she takes you out individually.

We skip the moments like stones.

The others were all still in primary school (Rory, his last year), and expected still to piano, even when she was in the hospital. In later years, Henry swore she'd stayed alive just to torture them with practice, or even just to ask about it, no matter which bed she lay in—the faded sheets of home, or the other ones, the bitter ones, so perfect, bleached and white.

The problem was (and Penelope finally resigned herself to it) that she had to face the reality:

They were so much better at fighting.

Their piano playing was shithouse.

As for all the questioning, it was pretty much reduced to ritual.

Mostly in the hospital, she'd ask if they'd practiced, and they lied and said they had. Often they showed up and their lips were cut and their knuckles split, and Penny was damp and jaundiced-looking, but also rightly suspicious. "What on earth is going on?"

"Nothing, Mum. Really."

"Are you practicing?"

"Practicing what?"

"You know."

"Of course." Henry did the talking. He motioned to his bruises. "What do you think all this is?" That smile, it swerved already.

"What do you mean?"

"Beethoven," he said. "You know how tough that guy is."

Her nose bled when she grinned.

Still, when she made it back home, she had them sit there again to prove themselves, while she frayed in the chair beside them.

"*You* never practiced," she said to Rory, with half-amused disdain.

He looked down and admitted it. "You're absolutely right."

Once, Clay stopped, midsong.

He was butchering it anyway.

He, too, had a light shadow of navy blue below his eye, after a fight—roped in with Henry.

"Why'd you stop?" But quickly then, she softened. "A story?"

"No, not that." He gulped and looked at the keys. "I thought—maybe you could play."

And she did.

Minuet in G.

Perfect.

Note for note.

It had been a long time, but he kneeled and laid his head there.

Her thighs were paper-thin.

* * *

In that period there'd been one last memorable fight, on the way back home from school. Rory, Henry and Clay. Four other guys against them. Tommy was off to the side. A woman sprayed them with her garden hose; a good one, a good nozzle. Good pressure. "Go on!" she shouted. "Git out of it."

"*Git out of it*," repeated Henry, and he got another blast. "Hey! What the hell was that for?"

She was in a nightgown and worn-out flip-flops, at three-thirty in the afternoon. "Being smart," and again she blasted him. "And that one's for the blasphemy."

"That's a good hose you got there."

"Thanks—now piss off."

Clay helped him up.

Rory was out ahead, feeling at his jawline, and at home there was a note. She was back in. The dreaded white sheets. At the bottom was a smiley face, with long hair either side of it. Beneath, it said:

> *OKAY! YOU CAN QUIT THE PIANO!*
> *BUT YOU'LL REGRET IT, YOU LITTLE BASTARDS!*

In a way it was kind of poetry, but not in the nicest sense.

She'd taught us Mozart and Beethoven.

We'd steadily improved her swearing.

Soon after, she made a decision:

She would do something once with each of us. Maybe it was to give us one memory that was ours, and ours alone, but I hope she did it for herself.

In my case, it was a movie.

There was an old cinema further in the city.

They called it the Halfway Twin.

Every Wednesday night there was an older film shown there, usually from another country. On the night we went, it was Swedish. It was called *My Life as a Dog*.

We sat with a dozen people.

I finished the popcorn before it started.

Penny struggled hard with a Choc-Top.

I fell in love with the tomboy girl named Saga in that movie, and struggled with the pace of the subtitles.

At the end, in the dark, we stayed.

To this day, I stay for the credits.

"And?" Penelope said. "What did you make of it?"

"It was great," I said, because it was.

"Did you fall in love with Saga?" The ice cream was dead in its plastic.

My mouth fell silent, my face felt red.

My mother was a kind of miracle, of long but breakable hair.

She took my hand and whispered.

"That's good, I loved her, too."

For Rory it was a football game, high up in the stands.

For Henry it was out to a garage sale, where he bargained and talked them down:

"A buck for that lousy yo-yo? Look at the state of my *mum*."

"Henry," she mocked him, "come on. That's low, even for you."

"Shit, Penny, you're no fun," but there was laughter, cahoots, between them. And he got it for thirty-five cents.

If I had to choose, though, I'd say it was what she did for Tommy that had the most influence on things, apart from her time with Clay. See, for Tommy, she took him to the museum; and his favorite was the hall named Wild Planet.

For hours, they walked the corridors:

An assembly line of animals.

A journey of fur and taxidermy.

There were too many to list as a favorite, but the dingo and lions ranked highly, and the weird and wonderful thylacine. In bed that night, he kept talking; he gave us facts on Tasmanian tigers. He said *thylacine* over and over. He said they looked more like a dog.

"A *dog*!" he almost shouted.

Our room was dark and quiet.

He fell asleep midsentence—and the love for those animals would lead to them; to Rosy and Hector, Telemachus, Agamemnon, and of course, to the great but mulish one. It could only all end with Achilles.

As for Clay, she took him many places and nowhere.

The rest of us all went out.

Michael took us to the beach.

Once we were gone, Penelope invited him; she said, "Hey, Clay, make me some tea and come out front." But it was more a kind of warm-up.

When he got there, she was already on the porch floor, her back against the wall, and the sun was out all over her. There were pigeons on the power lines. The city was open-ended; they could hear its distant singing.

When she drank, she swallowed a reservoir, but it helped her tell the stories, and Clay had listened hard. When she asked him how old he was, he'd answered he was nine. She said, "I guess that's old enough—to at least start knowing there's more—" and from there, she did what she always did, she went on with paper houses, and at the end she reminded him this:

"One day I'm going to tell you, Clay, a few things no one knows, but only if you want to hear them. . . ."

In short, the *almost-everythings*.

How privileged he really was.

She swept her hand through his boyish hair, and the sun was now much lower. Her tea had fallen over, and the boy had solemnly nodded.

By evening we were all back home, beach and sandy tired, and Penny and Clay were asleep. They looked knotted together on the couch.

A few days later, he'd almost approached her, about when the last stories might come, but was disciplined enough not to ask. Maybe in some way he knew—they would come at the near-to-the-end.

No, instead, there was our regular overrunness, as weeks were made into months, and again she was leaving for treatments.

Those singular moments were gone now.

We were used to uncomfortable news.

"Well," she said, quite bluntly, "they're going to take my hair—so now I think it's your turn. We might as well beat them to it."

Between us we formed a queue; it was the opposite of the world, as the barbers lined up to cut. You could see us all waiting in the toaster.

There are a few things I remember of that night—how Tommy went first, unwillingly. She got him to laugh at a joke, though, of a dog and a sheep in a bar. He was still in those damn Hawaiian shorts, and he cut so crooked it hurt.

Next went Clay, then Henry; then Rory said, "Going to the army?"

"Sure," said Penny, "why not?"

She said, "Rory, let me see," and she peered inside his eyes. "You've got the strangest eyes of all of you." They were heavy but soft, like silver. Her hair was short and vanishing.

When it was my turn, she reached for the toaster, to look at her mirrored image. She begged me to show some mercy. "Make it neat and make it quick."

To finish, it was our father, and he stood and didn't shirk it; he positioned her head, nice and straight, and when he was done he slowly rubbed her; he massaged the boyish haircut, and Penny leaned forward, she enjoyed it. She couldn't see the man behind her, and the chop-and-change of his face, or the dead blond hair at his shoes. She couldn't ever see how broken he was, while the rest of us stood and watched them. She was in jeans, bare feet and T-shirt, and maybe that's what finished us off.

She looked just like a Dunbar boy.

With that haircut she was one of us.

return to river

This time he didn't wait in the trees but walked the corridor of eucalypts, and burst quietly into the light.

The ditch was still there, clean-cut and clear, but now more had been dug out, both up and down the Amahnu, to give them more room in the riverbed. The remaining debris—the dirt and sticks, the branches and rocks—had been removed or leveled out. In one place he brushed a hand across, on smoothened-over land. To his right he saw the tire tracks.

In the riverbed, he stopped again, he crouched in all its colors. He hadn't realized before what a multitude it was; a history lesson of rocks. He smiled and said, "Hi, river."

As for our father, he was in the house, asleep on the couch, with half a mug of coffee. Clay watched him a moment and put his bag down in the bedroom. He took out the books and the old wooden box, but left *The Quarryman* in the bag, well hidden.

Later, they sat together, on the steps, and despite the cooling weather, the mosquitoes were out, and heinous. They crouched, light-footed, on their arms.

"God, they're monsters, aren't they?"

The black mountains stood tall in the distance.

A panel of red behind them.

Again, the Murderer spoke, or tried to.

"How was—"

Clay cut him off. "You hired equipment."

A friendly sigh. Had he been caught cheating? Had he severed the bridge's ethos? "I know—it's not very Pont du Gard, is it?"

"No," said Clay, but gave him a break. "More than two people built that one, though."

"Or the devil, if—"

He nodded. "I know."

He couldn't tell him just how relieved he was that the job was already done.

Now Michael tried again.

He finished his bitten-off question.

"Home?"

"Not bad."

Clay could feel him looking, then—at the almost-heal of bruising.

He finished his coffee.

Our dad bit his mug, but gently.

When he stopped, he looked at the steps, and nowhere near the boy. "Matthew?"

Clay nodded. "Everything's good, though." He thought a moment. "Rory ended up carrying me," and there was the slightest smile in front of him.

"They were good with you coming back—here, I mean?"

"Of course," Clay said, "I had to."

Slowly he got up and there was so much more, so many things to say, so much at the inner edges; there was Henry and Schwartz and Starkey (and let's not forget Starkey's girl), and Henry and Peter Pan. There was Claudia Kirkby, and me. There was all of us at the station, still standing as the train was leaving.

And, of course.

Of course, there was Carey.

There was Carey and Royal Hennessey, and weaving through the traffic . . . and losing to Pump Up the Jam—

But there again, the quietness.

The unsaidness.

To break it, Clay said, "I'm going inside . . . while I've still got some blood left in me—"

But then—what was this?

A surprise.

As halfway in, he came back; he was suddenly, expansively talkative, which for Clay was eight extra words.

Coffee cup in hand, he said, "I like it here, I like being here," and he wondered why he'd done it. Maybe it was to acknowledge a new existence—of both Archer Street and the river—or even a kind of acceptance:

He belonged as much to each of them.

The distance between us was him.

when boys
were still boys

In the end, it had to end.

The fistfights were coming to a close.

A cigarette had been found and smoked.

Even the piano-mongering was over.

In hindsight, they were worthy distractions, but could never quite turn the tide of her.

The world inside her escalated.

She emptied, she overflowed.

If anything, in the months to come, there were a few last stands of reliable life—as our mother was punished with those treatments. She'd been opened up and shut back tight, like a car on the side of the highway. You know that sound, when you slam the front down, when you've just got the bloody thing running again, and pray for a few more miles?

Each day was like that ignition.

We ran till we stalled again.

One of the best examples of living that way was made quite early in January; the middle of the Christmas holidays:

The gift and glory of lust.

Yes, lust.

In later years there might have been the naked excitement and pure idiocy of *Bachelor Party*, but in that early period of Penny's decline were the beginnings of boyhood depravity.

Perversions or living completely?

It depends which way you look at it.

Regardless, it was the hottest day of summer so far, like a harbinger of things to come. (Clay liked the word *harbinger*, from his formidable teacher at school, who was full to the brim with vocab. While other teachers kept strictly to the curriculum, this one—the brilliant Mr. Berwick—would no sooner walk into class than test them on words they *simply had an obligation* to know:

Harbinger.

Abominable.

Excruciating. Luggage.

Luggage was a great word, for being so perfect for what you did with it; you lugged.)

But yes, anyway, not long into January, the sun was high, and achingly hot. The racing quarter was searing. The distant traffic hummed to them. It turned casually the other way.

Henry was in the newsagent's, up on Poseidon Road, just down from Tippler Lane, and when he came back out triumphantly, he dragged Clay into the alley. He looked left and right, and said it.

"Here." A giant whisper. He pulled the *Playboy* from under his T-shirt. "Get a load of *this*."

He handed him the magazine, and opened it to the middle, where the fold went across her body—and she was hard and soft, and pointed and amazing, in all the perfect places. She looked positively thrilled with her hips.

"Pretty great, huh?"

Clay looked down, of course he did, and he knew all this—he was ten years old, with three older brothers; he'd seen naked women on a computer screen—but here was totally different. It was stealing and nudity combined, on glossy printed paper. (As Henry said, "This is the life!") Clay trembled amongst the glee of it, and weirdly, he read her name. He smiled, looked closer, and asked:

"Is her last name really *January*?"

Inside, his heart beat big, and Henry Dunbar grinned.

"Of course," he said, "you bet."

Later, though, when they made it home (after several stops to ogle), our parents were caught in the kitchen. They were down on the worn-out floor, and sitting just barely upright.

Our father was against the cupboards.

His eyes were a wasted blue.

Our mother had thrown up—it was a horrible mess—and now she slept back against him; Michael Dunbar sat only staring.

The two boys, they stood.

Their erections suddenly deserted them; dismantled, deep in their pants.

Henry called out, he reacted, and he was suddenly quite responsible. "Tommy? You home? Don't come in here!" as they watched our mother's fragility—and Miss January, rolled up, between them.

That smile, her perfect furniture.

It hurt now to even think of her.

Miss January was just so . . . *healthy*.

Early autumn it had to happen; there was a destined afternoon.

Rory was a month into high school.

Clay was ten years old.

Her hair had grown back, a strange and brighter yellow, but the rest of her was going-and-gone.

Our parents went out without us knowing.

It was a small cream building near a shopping mall.

The smell of doughnuts from the window.

A cavalry of medical machines, and they were cold and grey but burning, and the cancerous face of the surgeon.

"Please," he said, "sit down."

He said *aggressive* at least eight times.

So ruthless in the delivery.

* * *

It was evening when they returned, and we all came out to meet them. We always helped bring shopping in, but that night there was nothing more. There were pigeons on the power lines. They were coo-less, watching on.

Michael Dunbar stayed at the car, leaning down, his hands on the warmth of the hood, while Penny stood behind him, her palm against his spine. In the smoothing, darkening light, her hair was like straw, all tied and tidied back.

As we watched them, none of us asked.

Maybe they'd had an argument.

But of course, looking back, death was out there too that night, perched high up with the pigeons, hanging casually from the power lines.

He was watching them, side to side.

The next night Penny told us, in the kitchen; cracked and sadly broken. Our father in several fragments.

I remember it all too clearly—how Rory refused to believe it, and how soon he'd gone berserk, saying, "What?" and "*What?*" and "*WHAT?*" He was wiry-hard and rusty. His silver eyes were darkening.

And Penny, so slim and stoic:

She steadied toward matter-of-fact.

Her own eyes green and wild.

Her hair was out and open, and she repeated herself, she said it:

"Boys, I'm going to die."

The second time was what did it for Rory, I think:

He clenched his hands, and opened them.

There was a sound inside of all of us then—a sound of quiet-loud, a vibration unexplainable—as he tried to beat the cupboards up, he shook them and bucked me off. I could see it, but couldn't hear.

Soon he grabbed the person nearest him, who happened to be Clay, and roared right through his shirt; and it was then when Penny came at him, she finished across them both, and Rory couldn't stop. I could hear it far away now, but in a moment it blew me back—a voice in our house like a street fight. He roared into Clay's chest, straight through the buttons; he shouted right into his heart. He struck him over and over—till the fire was lit in Clay's eyes, and his own turned flat and hard.

God, I can still hear it.

I try so much to keep my distance from that moment.

Thousands of miles if I can.

But even now, that depth of scream.

I see Henry near the toaster, speechless when it counted.

I see Tommy all numb beside him, looking down at the blurry crumbs.

I see our father, Michael Dunbar, unfixable, at the sink; then going down for Penny—hands on shaking shoulders.

And me, I'm in the middle, collecting a fire up all of my own; paralyzed, folded-armed.

And lastly, of course, I see Clay.

I see the fourth Dunbar boy—dark-haired and thrown to the floor—his face staring up from below. I see the boys and tangled arms. I see our mother cloaked around them—and the more I think about it, maybe *that* was the true hurricane in that kitchen, when boys were only that, just boys, and murderers still just men.

And our mother, Penny Dunbar, with six months left to live.

part six

cities + waters + criminals + arches + stories + survivors

the girl who climbed from the radio

On Wednesday morning, Clay ran to town in the dark, got there in the light, and bought a paper from the Silver Corner Shop.

Halfway back he stopped; he studied the form guide.

He looked for a certain name.

In the day, as they talked and worked, wrote and planned, the Murderer was curious about the newspaper, but he didn't yet dare to ask. He busied himself with other things. There were sheets of sketches and measurements. There were wood costs for the falsework and scaffolding. There were stone plans for the arching—for which Clay said he had some money, but was quickly told he should keep it.

"Trust me," said the Murderer, "there are holes out here all over the place. I know where to find the stone."

"Like that village," said Clay, almost absently. "Settignano."

Michael Dunbar stopped. "What did you just say?"

"Settignano."

And there, caught in the moment, from absence to realization—of what he'd said, and more importantly, what he'd *referred* to—Clay had managed to both bring the Murderer closer, and also push him away. He'd erased, in an instant, the previous night's generosity—of "I like it here, I like being here"—but let it show he knew so much more.

There, he thought, think that one over.

But he left it alone at that.

* * *

At just past twelve-thirty, the sun was blazing in the riverbed, and Clay said, "Hey, do you mind if I borrow your car keys?"

The Murderer was streaming sweat.

What for?

But he said, "Sure, you know where they are?"

It was the same just before two, and then once more, at four.

Clay jogged across to the eucalypts and sat inside at the steering wheel, listening to the radio. The horses that day were Spectacular, then Heat, and Chocolate Cake. The best she placed was fifth.

After the last race, when he got back to the river, he said, "Thanks—I won't ever do that again, that was bad discipline," and Michael Dunbar was amused.

"You better do some overtime."

"Okay."

"I'm kidding." But then he found the nerve. "I don't know what you're doing over there"—the aqua eyes brightened, momentarily, in the depth inside his cheekbones—"but it's gotta be pretty important. When boys start walking away from things, it usually means a girl."

Clay was appropriately stunned.

"Oh—and Settignano," the Murderer went on (given he had him on the ropes), "is where Michelangelo learned about marble, and carved slabs out for his sculptures."

Which meant:

I don't know when.

I don't know how.

But you found it, you found *The Quarryman*.

Did you find the woman, too—Abbey Hanley, Abbey Dunbar? Is that how you got it?

Yes.

Penny told you about her, didn't she?

Before she died.

She told you, you found her, and she even gave you the book—and the Murderer looked at Clay, and the boy was sculpted himself now, as if made of blood and stone.

I'm here, said Michael Dunbar.

I left you, I know, but I'm here.

Think *that* over, Clay.

And he did.

the hangman's hands

In the tide of Dunbar past, three and a half years passed, and Clay lay in bed, awake. He was thirteen years old. He was dark-haired, boyish and skinny, and his heartbeat stung in the stillness. There was fire in each of his eyes.

In a moment he slid from bed, he was dressed.

He was in shorts and a T-shirt, barefoot.

He escaped out to the racing quarter, and he ran the streets and screamed. He did all of it without speaking:

Dad!

DAD!

WHERE ARE YOU, DAD?!

It was spring, just before first light, and he ran at the bodies of buildings; the rumored placement of houses. The lights of cars would shine at him, twin ghosts, then by, then gone.

Dad, he called.

Dad.

His footsteps slowed, then stopped.

Where were you, Michael Dunbar?

Earlier that year, it happened:

Penelope was dead.

She'd died in March.

The dying took three years; it was supposed to last six months. She was the ultimate in Jimmy Hartnelling—it could kill her all it wanted, but Penelope wouldn't die. When finally she'd succumbed, though, the tyranny started immediately.

From our father we hoped for hope, I think—for courage, and close proximity—like hugging us one by one, or to carry us up from our lowest.

But nothing like that had come:

The police-car pair had left us.

The ambulance swam down the street.

Michael Dunbar came to all of us; toward us, then out, and away. He got to the lawn, and walked on.

There were five of us stranded on the porch.

The funeral was one of those bright-lit things.

The sunny hilltop cemetery.

Our father read a passage from *The Iliad:*

They dragged their ships to the friendly sea.

He wore the suit he'd worn on his wedding day, and the one he'd wear years later, when he'd return and be faced with Achilles. His aqua eyes were lightless.

Henry had made a speech.

He imitated her put-on accent from the kitchen and people laughed, but he had tears in his eyes, and there were at least two hundred kids there, all from Hyperno High, and all in perfect uniform; heavy, and neat, dark green. Boys and girls alike. They talked about the metronome. A few she'd taught to read. The toughest took it hardest, I think. "Bye Miss, bye Miss, bye Miss." Some of them touched the box as they walked and passed in the light.

The ceremony was outside.

They would take her back in to burn her.

The coffin-slide into the fire.

It was sort of like the piano, really, but the instrument's homely cousin. You could dress it up all you wanted; it was still just a piece of hardwood, with daisies thrown on top. She'd chosen not to be scattered, or kept like sand in an urn. But we paid for a small memorial—a stone for us to stand and remember by, to watch her above the city.

From the service we carried her away.

On one side was Henry, Clay and me. On the other, Michael, Tommy and Rory—same as our Archer Street football teams—and the woman inside was weightless. The coffin weighed a ton.

She was a feather wrapped up in a chopping block.

At the end of the wake, and its assortment of teas and coffee cakes, we stood outside the building.

All of us in black pants.

All of us in white shirts.

We looked like a bunch of Mormons, but without the generous thoughts:

Rory was angry and quiet.

Me, like one more tombstone, but my eyes agleam and burning.

Henry looking outwards.

Tommy still wet with streaks.

And then, of course, there was Clay, who stood, then eased to a crouch. On the day of her death he'd found a peg in his hand, and he clenched it now till it hurt; then returned it soon to his pocket. Not one of us had seen it. It was bright and new—a yellow one—and he flipped it compulsively over. Like all of us he waited for our father, but our father had disappeared. We kicked our hearts around at our feet; like flesh, all soft and bloody. The city lay glittering below us.

"Where the hell is he?"

It was me who'd finally asked, when the wait became two hours.

When he arrived, it was hard to look at us, and us to look at him.

He was bent and broken-postured.

He was a wasteland in a suit.

It's funny, the time beyond a funeral.

There are bodies and the injured everywhere.

Our lounge room was more like a hospital ward, but one like you'd see in a movie. There were boys all torrid, diagonal. We were molded to whatever we lay on.

The sun not right, but shining.

As for Michael Dunbar, it surprised us how fast the cracks appeared, even given the state of him.

Our father became a half father.

The other half dead with Penny.

One evening, a few days after the funeral, he left again, and the five of us went out looking, and first we tried the cemetery, and then the Naked Arms (our reasoning still to come).

When we did find him, it was a shock to open the garage, and he lay beside an oil stain, since the police had taken her car. The only thing missing was a gallery of Penny Dunbars, but then, he never did paint her, did he?

For a while he still went to work.

The others went back to school.

I'd already been working a long time by then, for a company of floorboards and carpet. I'd even bought the old station wagon, from a guy I sometimes worked with.

Early on, our father was called to the schools, and he was the perfect post-war charlatan: well-dressed, clean-shaven. In control. We're coping, he'd said, and principals nodded, teachers were fooled; they could never quite see the abyss in him. It was hidden beneath his clothes.

He wasn't like so many men, who set themselves free with drink, or outbursts and abuse. No, for him it was easier to withdraw; he was there but never there. He sat in the empty garage, with a glass he never drank from. We called him in for dinner, and even Houdini would have been impressed. It was a slow and steady vanishing act.

He left us like that, in increments.

* * *

As for us Dunbar boys those first six months, we looked a lot like this:

Tommy's primary school teacher kept an eye on him.

She reported he was doing okay.

For the three of them in high school, they each had to see a teacher, who doubled as a kind of psychologist. There'd also been one previous to this, but that guy had since moved on, replaced by a total sweetheart; the warm-armed Claudia Kirkby. Back then, she was still just twenty-one. She was brown-haired, and quite tall. Not too much makeup, but always wore high heels. In her classroom there were the posters—Jane Austen and her barbell, and *MINERVA McGONAGALL IS GOD*. On her desk there were books and projects, in various stages of marking.

Often, at home, after they'd seen her, they had the sort of talks boys seem to have: talks but not talks at all.

Henry: "Good old Claudia, ay?"

Rory: "She's got a good pair of legs."

Boxing gloves, legs and breasts.

That's all they ever bonded with.

Me: "Shut up, for Christ's sake."

But I imagined those legs, I had to.

As for Claudia herself, up closer: She had an endearing sunspot on her cheek, right in the middle. Her eyes were kind and brown. She taught a hell of an English unit on *Island of the Blue Dolphins* and *Romeo and Juliet*. As a counselor, she smiled a lot, but didn't have much idea; at university, she'd done one small unit of psychology, which made her qualified for disasters like these. Most likely, she was the newest teacher at the school, and handed the extra work—and probably more out of hope than anything else, if the boys said they were fine, she wanted quite badly to believe them; and two of them actually *were* fine, given the circumstance, and one was nowhere near it.

And maybe it's the little things that kill you in the end—as the months dropped down to winter. It was seeing him arrive home from work.

Sitting in his car, sometimes for hours.

His powdery hands at the wheel:

No more Anticols.

Not a single Tic Tac left.

It was me paying the water bill, instead of him.

Then the electricity.

It was the sideline at weekend football games:

He watched but didn't see, then didn't show up at all.

His arms became uncharged; they were limp and starved of meaning. His concrete stomach mortared. It was death by becoming *not him*.

He forgot our birthdays; even my eighteenth.

The gateway into adulthood.

He ate with us sometimes, he always did the dishes, but then he'd go outside, back to the garage, or stand below the clothesline, and Clay would go there with him—because Clay knew something we didn't. It was Clay our father feared.

On one of the rare nights he was home, the boy found him at the piano, staring at the handwritten keys, and he stood there, close behind him. His fingers were stalled, mid-MARRY.

"Dad?"

Nothing.

He wanted to tell him—Dad, it's okay, it's okay what happened, it's okay, it's okay, I won't tell anyone. Anything. Ever. I won't tell them.

Again, the peg was there.

He slept with it, it never left him.

Some mornings, after lying on it through the night, he examined his leg in the bathroom—like a drawing, stenciled to his thigh. Sometimes he wished he would come to him in the dark, and reef him, awake, from his bed. If only our dad would have hauled him through the house, out the back; he wouldn't care if he was only in underpants, with the peg tucked in at the elastic.

Maybe then he could be just a kid again.

He could be skinny arms and boyish legs; he'd hit the clothesline pole so hard. His body would catch the handle. The metal in his ribs. He'd look up and inside those lines up there—the silent ranks of pegs. The darkness wouldn't matter; he'd see only shape and color. For hours he could let it happen, beaten gladly through till morning, when the pegs could eclipse the city—till they took on the sun, and won.

But that was exactly the thing.

Our father never came and took him like that.

There was nothing but the measure of increments.

Michael Dunbar was soon to leave us.

But first he left us alone.

By the end it was almost six months to the day since her death:

Autumn was winter, then spring, and he left us barely saying anything.

It was a Saturday.

It was in that crossover between very late, and very early.

We still had the triple bunk at that stage, and Clay was asleep in the middle. Around quarter to four, he awoke. He saw him beside the bedsides; he spoke to the shirt and torso.

"Dad?"

"Go back to sleep."

The moon was in the curtains. The man stood motionless, and Clay knew, he closed his eyes, he did what he was told, but talked on. "You're leaving, Dad, aren't you?"

"Be quiet."

For the first time in months, he touched him.

Our father leaned in and touched him, both hands—and they were hangman's hands, sure enough—on his head and over his back. They were powdery and hard. Warm but worn-out. Loving but cruel, and loveless.

For a long time, he stayed, but when Clay opened his eyes again, he was gone; the job was officially done. Somehow he still felt the hands, though, who had held and touched his head.

There were five of us in that house then.

We dreamed in our rooms and slept.
We were boys but also miraculous:
We lay there, living and breathing—
For that was the night he'd killed us.
He'd murdered us all in our beds.

arkansas

AT SILVER, IN THE DRY RIVERBED, THEY BUILT DAYS INTO WEEKS, WEEKS TO A month. For Clay there became a compromise—he went home for The Surrounds on Saturdays, but only when Michael was at the mines.

Other than that, they were up every day before sunrise.

They came in long after dark.

When winter set in, they built fires down there, and worked hours into the night. The insects had long since quieted. There were cool red sunsets, and the smell of smoke through the morning; and very slowly, very surely, a bridge was forming—but you wouldn't know to see it. The riverbed was more like a bedroom, a teenager's; but instead of socks and clothes, it was scattered with shifted earth, and crossworks and angles of wood.

Each dawn they arrived and stood with it.

It was a boy, a man, and two coffee mugs.

"That's pretty much all you need," he said, but they knew the Murderer was lying.

They also needed a radio.

On a Friday, they drove into town.

He found it in St. Vincent de Paul:

It was long, black, and crusty-looking—a broken tape deck that somehow worked, but only if you forced it with Blu-Tack. There was even a tape still in it: a homemade best of the Rolling Stones.

Every Wednesday and Saturday, though, the antenna was always outwards, at forty-five degrees. The Murderer soon came to know; he knew which races had meaning.

In the intervals, when Clay came home to Archer Street, he was shockingly alive and worn; he was powdery. His pockets were full of dust. He took clothes, he bought boots, and they were brown, then tan, then faded. He always brought the radio, and if she raced at Hennessey he'd go there. If it was somewhere else—Rosehill, Warwick Farm, or Randwick—he'd listen, inside, in the kitchen, or alone out back, on the porch. Then wait for her at The Surrounds.

She'd go there and she'd lie with him.

She told him about the horses.

He'd look at the sky and not mention it; that none of her mounts were winning. He could see how it weighed her down, but saying it would make it worse.

It was cold but they never complained; they lay in jeans and heavy jackets. Her puzzle of blood-lit freckles. Sometimes she had a hood on, and lengths of hair climbed out. They itched against his neck. She always found a way.

It was typical Carey Novac.

In July, on a night he'd gone to the mines, Michael Dunbar left new notes, to add to his plans for the scaffold, and dimensions for the molds and arches. Clay smiled at the drawing of falsework. But sadly, he had to start digging again—this time to build a ramp, for delivery of blocks of stone.

He cut into the walls of the riverbed, and gently fashioned a road; it wasn't just the bridge, it was everything around it—and he'd work at these things, even harder, when he was left in the river alone. He worked and listened, and staggered inside. He collapsed to the sunken couch.

Since Settignano, there'd been an unspoken understanding.

The Murderer wouldn't mention it.

He wouldn't ask what Clay had learned:

How much of *The Quarryman*, and Michelangelo? And Abbey Hanley, Abbey Dunbar? And painting? *His* paintings.

In Michael's absence, Clay read his favorite chapters, and the favorite chapters of Carey.

For her it was still the earlier ones:

The city and his upbringing.

The teenage broken nose.

The carving of the *Pietà*, the Christ—like liquid—in Mary's arms.

For Clay, it was still the *David*.

The *David* and the *Slaves*.

He loved them like his father did.

He loved another of the book's descriptions, too, of where those statues stood today—in Florence, in the Accademia:

> *Today, the David remains, at the end of the gallery's corridor, in a dome of light and space. Still in the grip of decision: forever fearing, forever defiant and deciding. Can he take on the might of Goliath? He stares over us, far away, and the Prisoners wait in the distance. They've struggled and waited for centuries—for the sculptor to return and finish them—and must wait a few centuries longer. . . .*

At home, when he was here, in the evenings, sometimes he went to the roof. Sometimes he read on one side of the couch, while I read on the other.

Often we all watched movies together.

Sometimes a double feature:

Misery and *Mad Max 2*.

City of God. ("What?" called Henry from the kitchen. "Not something made this *century* for a change!") And later, for balance, *Weird Science*. ("That's a bit bloody better—1985!") That last one had been a gift again, this time for a birthday, from Rory and Henry combined.

The night of the second double feature was a great one.

We all sat, we gaped and watched.

We were floored by the slums of Rio.

Then marveled at Kelly LeBrock.

"Hey," said Rory, "take that bit back!" and "This shit shoulda won Oscars!"

At the river, by the radio, out of handfuls, then dozens of races, her first win would remain elusive. That first afternoon at Hennessey—when she'd veered and lost to the protest—felt suddenly, seemingly years ago, yet near enough to still burn.

Once, when she came storming through the field, on a mare by the name of Stun Gun, a jockey lost his whip in front of her, and it struck her below the chin. It caused her a moment's distraction, and loss of the horse's momentum.

She finished fourth, but alive, and pissed off.

At last, it came, though, it had to.

A Wednesday afternoon.

The meeting was at Rosehill, and the horse was a miler named Arkansas.

Clay was alone in the riverbed.

It had rained in the city for days, and she'd kept him on the inside run. While the other jockeys took their horses, quite rightly, out to firmer ground, Carey had listened to McAndrew. He'd told her wise and drily:

"Just take him right through the slop, kid. Keep him on the rail—I almost want paint marks on him when you bring him in, got it?"

"Got it."

But McAndrew could see the doubt in her. "Look—no one's run there all day, it might hold up, and you'll be racing him a few strides shorter."

"Peter Pan once won the Cup like that."

"No," he corrected her, "he didn't—he did the opposite, he ran out wide, but the whole *track* was slopped to bits."

For Carey this was a rare mistake; it must have been nerves, and

McAndrew smiled, halfway—as much as he ever did on race day. A lot of his jockeys didn't even know who Peter Pan was. The horse *or* the fictional character.

"Just win the bloody thing."

And she did.

In the riverbed, Clay rejoiced:

He laid a hand on a plank of the scaffold. He'd heard drinking men say things like "Just give me four beers and you'll never get the smile off me," and that was how this was for him.

She'd won one.

He imagined her bringing him in, and the gleam and the clock hands, McAndrew. On the radio, they would soon cross to Flemington, down south, and the commentator finished with laughter. He said, "Look at her, the jockey, she's hugging the tough old trainer—and *take a look at McAndrew!* Did you ever see someone look so *uncomfortable?*"

The radio laughed, and Clay laughed, too.

A pause, then back to work.

The next time he came home, he thought and dreamed on the train. He concocted a great many moments, for celebrating the win of Arkansas, but should have known it would always be different.

He went straight to the stands of Hennessey.

He watched her race for two fourths and a third. And then her second first. It was a sprinter called Blood on the Brain, owned by a wealthy undertaker. Apparently, all the horses he owned were named for fatal conditions: Embolism, Heart Attack, Aneurysm. His favorite was Influenza. "Very underrated," he'd say, "but a killer."

For Blood on the Brain, she'd kept him nice and relaxed, and brought him through on the turn. When she came in, Clay watched McAndrew.

He was tight but thrilled in his navy blue suit.

He could almost read his lips.

"Don't even think of hugging me."

"Don't worry," she'd said, "not this time."

Afterwards, Clay walked home.

He crossed the Hennessey floodgates, out through the smoke of the car park, and the bright red rows of taillights. He turned onto Gloaming Road, which was suitably noisy and choked.

Hands in pockets.

The city folding in, at evening, then—

"Hey!"

He turned.

"Clay!"

She appeared from around the gate.

She'd changed from out of her racing silks, in jeans and shirt, but barefoot. Her smile, again, like the straight.

"Wait up, Clay! Wait up—" And he could feel the heat and blood in her, as she caught him and stood five meters away, and he said to her, "Blood on the Brain." Then smiled, and told her, "Arkansas."

She stepped through the dark, and half leapt at him.

She almost tackled him down.

Her heartbeat like a storm front—but warm, inside his jacket—and that traffic still trapped, still standstill.

She hugged him terribly hard.

People walked past and saw, but neither of them cared to notice.

Her feet were on his shoes.

What she said in the pool of his collarbone.

He felt the beams of her bony ribcage, a scaffolding all of its own, as she hugged him fierce and friendless:

"I missed you, do you know that?"

He squeezed her and it hurt but they liked it; and the soft of her chest hardened flat.

He said, "I missed you, too."

When they lessened, she asked him, "Later?"

And, "Of course," he said. "I'll go there."

They would go there and they'd be disciplined—their rules and regulations; unsaid but always sensed. She would itch but nothing-more him. Nothing more but tell him everything, and not saying that this was the best of it—her feet on top of his.

the searchers

In the past there were hardening facts.

Our mother was dead.

Our father had fled.

Clay searched for him after a week.

In its lead-up, with every passing hour, something in him was building, but he didn't quite know what it was; like nerves before a football game, but it never seemed able to dissolve. Maybe the difference was that football games were played. You ran out onto the field; it began, it ended. But not this. This was constant beginning.

Like all of us, Clay missed him in a strangely worn-out way.

It was hard enough missing Penny.

At least with her you knew what to do with it; the beauty of death—it's definite. With our dad there were too many questions, and thoughts were much more dangerous:

How could he leave us?

Where did he go?

Was he okay?

That morning a week later, when Clay found himself awake, he stood and dressed in the bedroom. Soon, he made his way out; he had to fill that space. His reaction was sudden and simple.

He got to the street and ran.

* * *

As I said, he went Dad! DAD! WHERE ARE YOU, DAD?!

But he wasn't quite able to shout.

The morning was cool with spring.

He'd run hard when he first slipped out, then walked the early darkness. In a rush of fear and excitement, he didn't know where he was going. When he'd started the internal calling, he'd soon discovered he was lost. He got lucky and wandered home.

Upon arrival, I was on the porch.

I walked down and took his collar.

I held him, one-armed, against me.

Like I said, I'd turned eighteen.

I thought I should try to act it.

"You okay?" I asked, and he'd nodded.

The stomach-feeling had eased.

The second time he did it, the very next day, I wasn't quite as forgiving; there was still a reach for his collar, but I dragged him across the lawn.

"What the hell are you thinking?" I asked. "What the hell are you doing?"

But Clay was happy, he couldn't help it; he'd quelled it again, momentarily.

"Are you even listening?"

We stopped at the fly-screen door.

The boy was barefoot-dirty.

I said, "You have to promise me."

"Promise what?"

It was the first time he noticed the blood down there, like rust between his toes; he liked it and he smiled at it, he liked that blood a lot.

"Take a Goddamn guess! Stop bloody disappearing!"

It's bad enough *he's* disappeared.

I thought it but couldn't yet say it.

"Okay," he said, "I won't."

Clay promised.

Clay lied.

He did it every morning for weeks.

Sometimes we went out, we searched for him.

Looking back, I wonder why.

He wasn't in abject peril—the worst would be losing his way again—but it somehow felt important; another holding-on. We'd lost our mother and then our father, so we couldn't lose any more. We simply wouldn't allow it. That said, we wouldn't be nice to him, either; he got dead-legged upon return, at the mercy of Rory and Henry.

The problem, already back then, though, was that it didn't matter how much we hurt him; we couldn't hurt him. Or how much we held him; we couldn't hold him. He'd be gone next day again.

Once, we actually found him out there.

It was a Tuesday, seven a.m.

I was going to be late for work.

The city was cool and cloudy, and it was Rory who caught a glimpse. We were several blocks east, where Rogilla met Hydrogen Avenue.

"There!" he said.

We chased him to Ajax Lane, with its backstreet line of milk crates, and tackled him into the fence; I got a thumbful of cold grey splinters.

"Shit!" cried Henry.

"What?"

"I think he just bit me!"

"That was my belt buckle."

"Pin that knee!"

He didn't know it, but somewhere, deep inside, Clay had made a vow; he'd never be pinned like that again, or at least not quite so easily.

That particular morning, though, when we pushed him back through the streets, he'd also made a mistake:

He thought it was over.

It wasn't.

If Michael Dunbar couldn't haul him through the house in the months that came beforehand, I could help him out; I shoved him down the hallway, slung him out the back, and banged a ladder against the gutter.

"There," I said to him. "Climb."

"What—the roof?"

"Just do it, or I'll break your legs. See how you go running then—" And his heart sank even deeper; because when Clay made it up to the ridge, he saw exactly what I meant.

"You get the idea? Do you see how big that city is?"

It reminded him of something five years earlier, when he'd wanted to do a project on every sport in the world, and asked Penelope for a new exercise book. He'd been under the impression that all he had to do was list every sport he knew, and halfway down the first page, he'd listed eight measly things, and realized it was hopeless—and so, he now realized, was this:

Up here, the city multiplied.

He could see it every side.

It was huge and massive and humongous. It was every expression he'd ever heard used, to describe something undefeatable.

For a moment or two, I was almost sorry, but I had to hammer it home. "You can go as far as you want, kid, but you're never going to find him." I looked out over the houses; the countless slants of rooves. "He's gone, Clay, he killed us. He murdered us." I forced myself to say it. I forced myself to like it. "What we were—there's nothing left."

The sky was blanket grey.

Around us, nothing but city.

Beside me, a boy and his feet.

He killed us hung between us, and we knew, somehow, it was real.

The birth that day of a nickname.

the horse from the riverina

From the moment in the Hennessey car park, something new was set in motion. On the surface, all felt normal, as winter continued in full—the dark mornings, the clean sunlight—and bridge and tireless building.

In a steady stream of races, Carey won four, which took the total to six. As always she climbed from the radio; he loved to sit and imagine her. There were also three third placings, but never any seconds. The girl was incapable of finishing second.

On Wednesdays, when Michael was away, and Clay missed things more than usual, he took his radio and box to the trees. He held the lighter and held the peg. He smiled at the iron and feather. He sat amongst the shedded bark skins, like models or casts of body parts, like arms and fallen elbows. Sometimes he stood, the last furlong:

Come on, Carey, take him home.

A cavalcade of horses:

Kiama, Narwee, and Engadine.

(She had a knack, it seemed, for place names.)

The Lawnmower. The Kingsman.

Sometimes War of the Roses again.

She rode him hands-and-heels.

Then a day arrived, a horse arrived, when a jockey pulled out of a race; a dislocated shoulder. It was Carey who got the mount. The horse was named for a country town, out in the Riverina—and things were about to change for her, and change the course of here.

A horse called Cootamundra.

It was August by then, and the mornings close to frozen. There was wood and woodwork everywhere. There were masses of blocks and stone. They worked silently with only their hands, and it was like they were building a grandstand, and maybe they kind of were.

He held giant planks in place for him.

"Not there," said Michael Dunbar. "*There*."

He realigned.

Many nights, when his father turned in, Clay stayed out in the river. He planed wood where it needed planing, and rubbed stone against stone for exactness. Sometimes Michael brought tea out, and they sat on the stones and watched, surrounded by wooden monoliths.

Sometimes he climbed the falsework, which grew each day, each arch. The first was almost a testing mold (falsework for the falsework), and the second built faster and stronger; they learned their trade on the job. More than once he thought of a photo; the famous one of Bradfield—the man who planned the Coathanger. The great arch was coming together, and he'd stood one foot either side of it. The gap, like death, below.

As always, he listened to the radio, they played both sides of the tape. There were so many iconic tracks, but his favorite was "Beast of Burden"—maybe in tribute to Achilles, but more likely, a plea to Carey. She was buried inside the songs.

Then came Saturday, late in the month, and the radio on for the racing; there'd been a problem, in the sixth, in the barriers. A horse called Now You're Dreaming. The jockey was Frank Eltham, and the horse was spooked by a seagull, and caused them a hell of a mess. Eltham did well to hang on, but just when he thought he'd recovered, he was bucked a final time, and that was it, the shoulder.

The horse was scratched, but survived.

The jockey was sent to the hospital.

He was riding a real prospect—the up-and-coming Cootamundra—in the last race of the day, and the owner was at the trainer, for the best McAndrew could get.

"There *is* no one to get. This is all I have."

Every seasoned jockey was already booked; they'd have to go with the apprentice.

The old man called behind him:

"Hey, Carey."

She was bursting for the ride.

When she was handed the colors of red-green-white, she walked straight back to the Shit Can—the name for the female jockey room, for that's exactly what it was, an old toilet—and she walked out ready to run.

And she knew.

The horse was going to win.

Sometimes, she said, you just feel it.

McAndrew felt it, too.

He was quiet but witheringly forceful:

"Take him straight to the front, and don't stop till you hit Gloaming Road," and Carey Novac nodded.

He smacked her on the back as she went.

In Silver, at the Amahnu, they heard the late inclusion, and when Clay stopped work on the molding, Michael Dunbar fully realized.

It's her.

Carey Novac.

That's the name.

For the race they sat and listened, and it was just as McAndrew had said; she took him to the front. The horse was never headed. He was big, deep brown—a bay. He was courageous and full of running. He won by four good lengths.

* * *

From there, this is what happened:

Through September, at the river, whenever Michael returned from the mines, they shook hands, and worked like madmen.

They cut and measured and sawed.

They sliced off edges of stones; they worked in perfect rhythm.

When they finished up work on the pulley system, they tested the weight of a spandrel. There were half nods—then nods—of happiness; the ropes were as tough as the Trojans, the wheels were discounted steel.

"Sometimes the mines are good for us," said Michael, and Clay could only agree.

There were moments when they noticed the light change; of sun being swallowed in the sky. Dark clouds would meet at the mountains, then seemingly trudge away. No business yet to be here, but their day was surely coming.

In time, they planned the deck—what to lay on top:

"Wood?" said Michael Dunbar.

"No."

"Concrete?"

Nothing but sandstone would do.

And from there, this is what happened:

The owner loved the jockey.

His name was Harris Sinclair.

He said she was fearless, and lucky.

He liked her garrulous hair (you'd think it was hair that talked, he said), and she was skinny and country-real.

In the lead-up to spring carnival, Cootamundra won twice more, against better, more experienced fields. She told Clay she loved this kind of front-running horse, how they were the bravest ones. It was a howling Saturday night. The pair of them at The Surrounds. "He just gets out and runs," she'd said, and the wind flung up the words.

Even when he ran second (the first time ever for Carey), the owner presented her with a gift: a fresh-bought consolation beer.

"Really?" said old McAndrew. "Give that bloody thing here."

"Oh, shit—sorry, kid."

He was one of those hard-boiled businessmen, a lawyer—deep-voiced and commanding—and always like he'd just had lunch; and you could bet it had been a good one.

By October, the bridge was slowly forming, and the prestigious spring races started.

It was partly here at home, but mostly south at Flemington, and other fabled tracks down there; like Caulfield, Moonee Valley.

McAndrew was taking three horses.

One was Cootamundra.

There was discussion now with Sinclair. Where before he'd seen Carey's promise—and self-glory through association—that second-placing had got him wondering. Till now they could often claim; that is, they could race him at lighter weight, because the jockey was only an apprentice. In the big ones that wasn't the case. One afternoon, she heard them; it was in McAndrew's office, of schedules and unwashed breakfast plates. Carey was outside, eavesdropping, her ear against the fly screen.

"Look, I'm just exploring the options, okay?" said the thick-voiced Harris Sinclair. "I *know* she's good, Ennis, but this is Group One."

"It's a horse race."

"It's the Sunline-Northerly Stakes!"

"Yes, but—"

"Ennis, listen—"

"No, *you* listen." The scarecrow voice cut through her. "This isn't emotional, it's because she's the rider of the horse—that's *it*. If she's injured, suspended, or turns into a cake shop in the next three weeks, fair enough, we'll change her, but as it is? The thing isn't broken so I'm not gonna fix it. You have to trust me on this one, okay?"

There was a chasm of doubtful silence, before McAndrew spoke again.

"Who's the bloody trainer, anyway?"

"Okay . . . ," said Harris Sinclair—and the girl tripped back and ran.

She forgot all about her bike chained up at the fence line, and ran home to Ted and Catherine. Even in the night, the thrill of it was too much, she couldn't sleep, so she escaped, she went out, she lay down on her own at The Surrounds.

Unfortunately, what she hadn't heard were the words that were spoken next.

"But, Ennis," said Harris Sinclair, "I'm the owner."

She was close, so close, then replaced.

survival of
the dunbar boys

HERE, AT 18 ARCHER STREET, THERE WERE FIVE OF US WHO REMAINED.

We were the Dunbar boys, we lived on.

Each in ways of our own.

Clay, of course, was the quiet one, but not before he was the strange one—the one who ran the racing quarter, and the boy you'd find on the roof. What a mistake to take him up there that day—he turned it forcefully straight into habit. As for his running the suburbs, we knew he would always come back now, to sit with the tiles and the view.

When I asked if I might run with him, he'd shrugged and we soon became:

It was training, it was escaping.

It was perfect pain and happiness.

First, in between, there was Rory.

His goal was expulsion from school; he'd wanted to leave since kindergarten, and would take the opportunity. He made it clear I wasn't his guardian, or parent by hostile takeover. He was frank and undeniable:

Vandalism. Constant truancy.

Telling teachers where to stick their assignments.

Alcohol on school grounds.

("It's just a beer, I don't see what you're all so upset about!")

Of course, the only good thing to come of it was my meeting Claudia Kirkby; the first time he was suspended.

I remember knocking on her door, and going in, and the essays strewn on the desk. It was something on *Great Expectations*, and the top one got four out of twenty.

"Jesus, that isn't Rory's, is it?"

She made an attempt to tidy them. "No, Rory actually got *one* out of twenty—and that was for handing in paper. What he wrote was totally worthless."

But we weren't here for the essay.

"Suspended?" I asked.

"Suspended."

She was candid but very friendly; it amazed me that she spoke with humor. Suspension was no laughing matter, but there was something in the tone of her. I think she was reassuring me. There were twelfth graders in this place who looked older than her, which made me strangely happy; if I'd stayed till the end myself, I'd have finished the previous year. Somehow that felt important.

Soon she got down to business, though.

"So, you're okay with the suspension?"

I nodded.

"And your—"

I could tell she was about to say *father*. I hadn't notified the school yet that he'd left us; they would find that out in due course.

"He's away at the moment—and besides, I think I can cover it."

"You're—"

"I'm eighteen."

It didn't need to be justified, given I looked a little older, or maybe that's just my perception. To me, Clay and Tommy always looked younger than they were. Even now, all these years later, I remind myself Tommy's not six.

In her classroom, we talked on.

She told me it was only two days.

But then, of course, the *other* business:

They were certainly something to see—her calves, her shins—but not what I'd first imagined. They were just, I don't know, hers. There's no other way to say it.

"So you've seen the principal?" she interrupted, for I was lost in my glance down floorwards. When I looked up, I saw the writing on the board. It was neat and looped, in cursive. Something about Ralph and Piggy; the theme of Christianity. "You've spoken to Mrs. Holland?"

Again, I nodded.

"And, you know—I have to ask. Is it . . . do you think it's because—"

I was caught in the warmth of her eyes.

She was like your morning coffee.

I recovered.

"Our mother dying?"

She didn't say anything else then, but she didn't look away from me, either. I spoke to the desk and its pages:

"No." I even went to touch one, to read it, but stopped myself in time. "He's always been like this; it's just now I think he's decided."

Twice more he would be suspended; more visits for me to the school—and to be honest, I wasn't complaining.

It was Rory at his most romantic.

He was Puck with a pair of fists.

Next Henry, and Henry was on his way.

He was stick-skinny. A sinewy mind.

His first touch of genius was making money at the Naked Arms. It was all the middle-aged drinkers there, standing out the front. He noticed they all had dogs with them, and the dogs were overweight; as diabetic as their owners.

When he, Clay and Rory came back from the shops one night, he put his shopping bags down on the ground.

"What the hell are you doin'?" said Rory. "Pick those bloody bags up."

Henry looked over. "Check that bunch of blokes out." He was fourteen years old, and a mouth. "Look—they've all told the missus they're walking the dog."

"What?"

"Look there, are your eyes painted on? They go out for a walk, but come to the pub and drink. Look at the state of those retrievers!" Now he walked over. He gave them a turn of his smile, for the first but not the last time. "Any of you lazy bastards want me to walk your dogs?"

Of course, they loved him, they fell for him.

They were amused by the sheer audacity.

He made twenty a night for months.

Then Tommy, and what was to come:

Tommy got lost in the city; he was trying to find the museum.

He was only ten then, and it was bad enough we'd had Clay disappearing, though at least Tommy actually called. He was in a phone booth many miles away, and we drove there to pick him up.

"Hey, Tommy!" Henry called. "I didn't know you knew what a phone booth *was*," and it was great, that afternoon. We drove for a few good hours, through the city and by the coast. We promised we'd take him another day.

As for Clay, and for me, the training started one morning.

I'd caught him, midescape.

It was first light, and he came out front, and if he was surprised to see me by the letterbox, he was able not to show it; he only walked casually on. At least, by then, he wore shoes.

"You want some company?" I asked.

He shrugged, looked away, and we ran.

We ran together each morning, and me, I came back to the kitchen, I drank coffee, and Clay came back to the roof—and honestly, I saw the attraction:

First, the legs, they lit with pain.

Then the throat and lungs.

You knew you were running hard when you felt it in your arms.

We ran up to the cemetery. We ran Poseidon Road. On Carbine we ran the middle; a car once blew its horn at us, and we parted, we veered, each side. We pounded the rotten frangipanis. From the cemetery, we watched the city.

Then there were the other great mornings, seeing boxers from up at the Tri-Colors, as they ran their early roadwork.

"Hey, boys," they'd say, "hey, boys."

Hunched backs and healing cheekbones.

The steps of broken-nosed boxers.

Of course, one of them was Jimmy Hartnell, and once he ran backwards and called to me. Like most of them he wore a lake there, of sweat round the rim of his T-shirt. "Hey, Piano!" he called. "Hey, Dunbar!" Then waved, and carried on. Other times when we crossed, we tapped hands like replacement footballers; one of us on, one off. We ran through all our problems.

Sometimes there were extras, too—young jockeys apprenticed to McAndrew. That was one of his requirements: in the first year of your jockey trade, you ran with the Tri-Colors boys, alternate days of the week. There wouldn't be any exceptions.

I remember when we first ran to Bernborough, too:

It was a Sunday, an arsonist sunrise.

The grandstand burned like a tenement—like the criminals had lit the place up—and the track was already awash: with weeds, and bedsores and eczema. The infield not quite a jungle, but certainly well on its way.

We did eight 400 meters.

Thirty seconds of rest.

"Again?" I asked.

Clay nodded.

That world in his stomach was gone from him, and the suffering a perfect beauty. At Bernborough, he switched back to barefoot, too, with the peg in the pocket of his shorts . . . and sometimes I think he planned it. Sometimes I think he knew:

We would run through the streets of the racing quarter.

He would search for him up from on the roof.

In the guise of looking for our father, I think Clay knew something was out there, and now I know it, too—because in there, out in the suburbs-world, we trained our way toward him:

We ran and we searched to a mule.

the photo

On the weekend that Cootamundra ran in the racing capital down south, Ennis McAndrew made a decision, a shrewd one:

Carey wouldn't ride at all.

She'd been robbed of a ride in the Sunline-Northerly Stakes—her first Group One—and she was still just seventeen. He wouldn't be here in the city for her, and he wouldn't be taking her along. That surely would have killed her; watching the big bay horse hit the turn.

No, instead he told her simply.

"I think you've earned a weekend off."

He wasn't your average trainer.

Clay made a special point of coming back that Saturday, and there'd been talk in the week on the radio, of the horse and replacement rider.

On Friday night, when he left, Michael Dunbar surprised him.

He drove him into town, and they were their usual silent selves, but when they made it to the railway, he pulled an envelope from out of the glove box; he placed it on Clay's lap. On top it said *Carey Novac*.

"What's—"

"Just give it to her, okay? She'll like it. I promise."

There was no thought of *think that one over*, just a nod, just barely, across. The lights of the station felt miles away, and the town was mostly quiet. Only murmurs from a distant pub. He looked something like he once had, and Clay gave something back.

In plain sight, he pulled out *The Quarryman*.

He slid the envelope gently inside.

On Archer Street, next day, Ted and Catherine were both out working, so it was Carey and Clay in her kitchen.

They'd set up the scrappy black radio.

There was a nice small stereo in the lounge room, with digital and all the rest, but they chose to hear it on his. As he sat he realized quickly—this kitchen was amazingly clean.

Between them they exchanged short glances.

Neither of them wanted to speak.

The rider was a consummate professional, Jack Bird, and when the race was run, close to three o'clock, he didn't let the horse out early, and the lead wasn't quite enough; he was pocketed on the turn. When he asked him to give there was nothing left, and Clay listened but mostly watched her. He watched her distance of mile-long hair, the forearms above the table, and her face cupped tight in her palms; she was caught between wistful and miserable, but all she said was "Damn."

They went to a movie not long after.

She reached over, she held his hand.

When he looked at her, she was watching the screen, but a tear was down her face.

It was such a strange thing that happened.

He leaned over and kissed her cheek.

It wasn't a breach of the rules, though, and both of them somehow knew. He could taste its hurt and saltiness, then looked at her hand in his.

Later, they went to The Surrounds, and she lay down close beside him. She was ready to say some more now, a number she spoke like a grievance:

"Seventh."

Seventh, an abject failure.

At one point he counted her freckles, and there were fifteen on her face, but so tiny you had to search. There was a sixteenth down on her neck. They were so much redder than her hair, that blood against bronzy sunshine.

"I know," she said, "there are worse things," and there were, there definitely were.

For a while she lay with her head on him.

As always, Clay felt her breathing; the warmth of it, the gait.

It seems silly to talk about breath that way—like stride, like length in a race—but that was how he described it.

For a moment he looked down.

Again, that sixteenth blood spot—he wanted to touch it, to let his hand fall, but found himself suddenly speaking. What only she could understand.

"Bonecrusher," he told her, "Our Waverley Star," and expected the girl to stir. "That was a two-horse war." Then, "Saintly," he said, "and Carbine . . ." He was talking about a certain race, and horses who had won it. She'd told him only once of it—the first time they'd walked the racing quarter. "And Phar Lap, the greatest of them all." Then he swallowed and said, "The Spaniard," and that one almost hurt; The Spaniard, the bloodline of Matador—but still, he had to go further. "Hey," he said, and he held her; he brought her closer, briefly. He clenched her flannelette arm. "But your favorite's never changed, I think—it's always Kingston Town."

And finally, a last beat longer.

He felt the checkered squares.

"God," she said, "you remember."

With her he remembered everything. And he would always know how she'd quickened, when she answered about the Cox Plate, in 1982. How fitting to be in that period, when Penelope came to live here—and Carey now said what the commentary said, which was "Kingston Town can't win."

He held her, parceled up there.

His voice, part-voice, part-whisper:

"I always hear the crowd," he said, "going crazy as he came from nowhere."

* * *

Soon he got up, and he got her up, too, and they made the mattress bed; they shoved the heavy plastic down and tucked it into the ground.

"Come on," he said as they hit the lane, and the book was in beside him, the envelope still within.

They walked to the bottom of Archer Street, onto Poseidon Road.

During the movie she held his hand, but now she did what she used to do, when first they'd come to be friends; she linked her arm through his. He smiled and didn't worry. There was no thought of looking like an old couple, or any such misunderstanding. She did such unusual things.

And there were streets so known, and storied—like Empire, Chatham, and Tulloch—and places they'd gone the first time, up further, like Bobby's Lane. At one point they passed a barber's shop, with a name they knew and loved; but all of it led to Bernborough, where the moon hung into the grass.

On the straight he opened the book.

She was up a few meters ahead.

It was somewhere close to the finish line, when he called to her, "Hey, Carey."

She swiveled, but did it slowly.

He caught up and gave her the envelope.

She studied it down in her palm.

She read her name out, out loud, and on the red rubber track at Bernborough, she'd somehow made her comeback:

He caught the glint of sea glass.

"Is this your father's writing?"

Clay nodded but didn't speak, and she opened the thin white package, and looked at the photo within. I imagine what she must have thought, too—thoughts like *beautiful* or *magnificent* or *I wish I could be there to see you like that*—but for now all she did was hold it, then pass it slowly to him.

Her hand, it slightly wavered.

"You," she whispered, and "the bridge."

love in the time of chaos

As spring turned into summer, it was life in tracks of two.

There was running, there was living.

There was discipline, perfect idiots.

At home we were almost rudderless; there was always something to argue for, or laugh about, and sometimes both, parallel.

In the racing quarter it was different:

When we ran, we knew where we were.

It was really the perfect blend, I guess, of love in the time of chaos, love in the time of control; we were pulled each way, between them.

In the running, we ran at October, when Clay enrolled in athletics—not remotely excited, nor reticent. The club wasn't down at Bernborough (far too rundown), but at Chisholm, near the airport.

Everyone over there hated him:

He ran only in the 400, and hardly spoke.

He knew a kid, an animal-boy named Starkey:

He was the mountainous shot put, discus guy.

The gun 400-meter runner was a kid called Spencer.

Clay took off with 300 to go.

"Shit," they said, the whole clubful of them.

He won by half the straight.

* * *

At home it was afternoon.

Just one in a series of many:

Fight 278.

Rory and Henry were having it out.

There was a ruckus coming from their bedroom, which was well and truly a *boys' bedroom* bedroom—of beached and forgotten clothing, lost socks and fumes and headlocks. The words like strangulation:

"I told you to keep your shit with the rest of your shit and it keeps encroaching onto *my side*," and "Like I'd want my shit *encroaching* (have a listen to you!) on your stupid side anyway—the state of it," and "You got a problem with my stupid side, you'd think you'd keep your shit away from it!"

And so on.

After ten minutes, I went in, to separate them, and there was blond and rusty argument. Their hair was pointing outwards—north and south, east and west—and Tommy, so small, in the doorway.

"Can we go to the museum or what?"

It was Henry who'd heard and answered, but spoke across to Rory.

"Sure," he said, "but wait a minute, okay? Just give us a sec to beat Matthew up," and like that, they were both of them friends again.

They buried me fast and furiously.

My face in the taste of socks.

On the streets, it was almost business.

Clay ran.

I struggled to stay with him.

Him and his burning left pocket.

"Up, up."

That's all the talk was reduced to by then, if he ever said anything at all.

At Bernborough, always the same.

Eight 400 sprints.

Thirty seconds of rest.

We ran to the point of collapse.

* * *

At the museum, we all went in, and we complained about the cost of things, but it was worth it, every cent; it was worth it just to see the kid, as he met the thylacine's eye. The other thing, too, was that he'd been right, it was true, it did look more like a dog, with a peculiar oval stomach; we loved the Tasmanian tiger.

But Tommy loved all of everything:

Above us, the blue whale skeleton, sprawled out like a laid-down office block. The nimble neck of the dingo again, and the parade of various penguins. He even loved the most frightening of it, especially the red-bellied black snake, and the shine and grace of the taipan.

For me, though, there was an eeriness; a confederate for all the taxidermy—something dead and unwilling to leave. Or to be fair, unwilling in me:

Of course, the thought of Penelope.

I imagined her here with Tommy.

I saw her crouching slowly down, and so, I think, did Clay.

Sometimes I'd see him watching, but it was often just left of the specimen—especially when shown behind glass. I'm sure he'd caught her reflection then, of blond and stick-thinned, smiling.

We leaned outside at closing.

All of us tired but Tommy.

The city fast-moving around us.

On one of our runs, it happened.

It came to us, early morning.

The worlds infused together.

We really should have thought of it sooner.

We were running at first light, on Darriwell Road, a few kilometers from home. Clay saw it strapped to a telegraph pole, and propped, and mindfully backtracked. He stared at the wrapped-round advertisement:

A cat had just had kittens.

Why take Tommy to dead animals, when live ones could come to him?

I memorized the first half of the phone number, and Clay the second, but when we called, we were loudly told. The notice was three months old; the last kitten was sold six weeks ago. But the woman who'd answered knew exactly where to go. Her voice was like a man's voice, both close and not-for-nonsense. "There are dozens of internet animal sites, but your best bet's the *RQT*."

She meant the *Racing Quarter Tribune*, and she was pinpoint, she was astute; the first time we looked in that paper—our local suburban news—there was a collie for sale, and a kelpie, and a pair of cockatiels. A guinea pig, a king parrot, and three cats of different breeds.

At the bottom, though, he was waiting, and he'd be there a little while yet. Already I should have known, from the fire inside Clay's eyes; they were each both suddenly smiling, as his finger pointed downwards:

ONE STUBBORN BUT FRENDLY MULE
NEVER BUCKS, NEVER BRAYS
****
$200 (negotiable)
YOU WON'T BE SORRY
Call Malcolm

I said, "Don't show Tommy, whatever you do," but Clay wasn't close to caring. He'd gently thrown a finger again, at the mistake on the very first line.

"*Stubborn*," he said, "but *frendly*."

We settled for one of the cats—a family moving overseas. Too expensive to carry the tabby. They told us his name was Stripey, but we knew for a fact we would change it. He was a big and purring heap of a thing—black lips and tarmac paws—and a tail like a shaggy sword.

We drove to the place in Wetherill, two suburbs west, and the cat came home in Clay's lap; he never moved an inch, he just purred with the engine, in tune. He happy-pawed him with his claws.

God, you should have seen Tommy.

I wish you could have seen him.

At home, we hit the porch.

"Hey, Tommy!" I called, and he came, and his eyes were young and permanent. He nearly cried when he brought the cat close, the stripes against his chest. He patted him, he stroked him, he spoke to him without speaking.

When Rory and Henry both came out, they were both of them gorgeously right; they complained with jinx-like timing.

"Hey—how come Tommy gets a bloody cat?"

Clay looked away. I answered.

"Because we like him."

"And you don't like *us*?"

Soon we heard Tommy's announcement, and Clay's instantly blunt response:

"I'm gonna call him Achilles."

Abruptly, "No, not this one."

Immediately, I looked at him.

I was stubborn and certainly *unfrendly*:

No, Clay, God*damn* it, I said, if only with my eyes—but who did I think I was kidding? After all, Tommy held the cat like a newborn.

"Okay then," he said, "Agamemnon," and now it was Rory who stopped him.

"How about a name we can fucking *pronounce*?"

And still he paid homage to Penelope.

"What about Hector then?"

The champion of all the Trojans.

There were nods and murmured approvals.

Next morning, out in the racing quarter, there were turns I'd never known of, and we came to Epsom Road. Not far from the Lonhro Tunnel. The train line rattled above. It was one of those forgotten streets here, with a single forgotten field. The fences were mostly wayward. The trees were molting stringy barks; they towered and stood their ground.

At the bottom was the patch of land; and grass, like fists, in the dust. There was a barbed wire fence, corroded. A shack had faded to greyness. And a caravan, old and weary; a drunk at three a.m.

I remember the sound of his footsteps then, how they slowed on the pot-holed road. Clay never slowed down at this point of a run; it was up and only up—and soon I understood. Once I'd seen the caravan, and the unkempt segment of land, I saw that logic didn't live here, but mules most definitely did. I walked and spoke with disgust.

"You called the number from the *Tribune*, didn't you?"

Clay walked purposefully on.

His breath was so quick to normalize, from running to everyday life.

"I don't know what you're talking about."

And then we saw the sign.

Looking back, there was something right about it.

I can see it and say that now.

At the time, though, I was suspicious—highly annoyed, as we walked to the fence line—and the sign had once been white. Musty and dirty, it hung diagonally, from the middle of the highest wire—probably the greatest sign in the racing quarter, if not racing quarters worldwide.

In faded thick black marker pen, it said:

ENYONE CAUGHT
FEEDING THESE HORSES
WILL BE PROSECUTED!

"God," I said, "look at that."

How could a person spell *anyone* wrong and get *prosecuted* right? But that, I guess, was the racing quarter. That, and there weren't any horses there, and for a while, it seemed, nothing else—

But then he came rounding the shack.

Quite suddenly there was a mule's head, and the expression that often defined him:

He watched, he gleaned.

He communicated.

Like a supreme-yet-derelict being.

Already he had that what-the-hell-you-lookin'-at look on his long, lop-sided face—till he'd watched a moment longer, and seemed to say, Oh, *okay* then.

In the pieces of dappled sunrise, he slowly gangled over.

Up close he was almost charming; he was talkative, though mute, and personable. His head was a texture, a scrubbing brush—and he ranged in careless colors, from sandy to rust throughout; his body, a dug-up farmland. His hooves were the shade of charcoal—and what were we supposed to do? How do you talk to a mule?

But Clay would take him on.

He looked in the eyes of the animal, which seemed so much like calves' eyes, like babies sent for the slaughterhouse, pure sadness but so alive. He went to his pocket and reached for it; and it wasn't the bright yellow peg.

No, it was Clay Dunbar at his best:

A hand, a sandful of sugar.

It was raw and sweet in his palm—and the mule was eternally blessed—and to hell with the sign and its spelling; his nostrils began to spin. His eyes were undone as he grinned at him:

I knew you'd one day come.

the slaves

YOU HAD TO GIVE IT TO THE OLDER MICHAEL DUNBAR.

This time he got it right:

The photo was a work of art.

When Clay came back to Silver, he stood in the kitchen near the oven.

"So you gave it to her?"

His sunken eyes were hopeful.

His hands looked vague; distracted.

Clay nodded.

"She loved it."

"So do I; I've got another one I took earlier," and reading Clay's thoughts, he said, "It's pretty easy to sneak up on you out there—you're lost in another world."

And Clay, the right response; and something else, first time since coming.

"It helps me to forget," he said, and he looked from the floor to face him. "But I'm not sure I really want to." By the sink was a certain Mistake Maker; the blond-haired Penny Dunbar. "Hey—Dad?" It was such a shock, to both of them, and then came a second, a follow-up. "You know . . . I really miss her. I miss her so much, Dad, I miss her so much," and it was then, a few footsteps, the world altered:

He went over and brought the boy closer.

He grabbed his neck in his arm and hugged him.

Our dad became his father.

* * *

But then they went back to the bridge.

Like nothing had ever happened.

They worked the scaffold and prayed for arches, or better, arches that lasted forever.

It's funny, though, really, when you think of it, the air between fathers and sons—and especially this one and *this* one. There are hundreds of thoughts per every word spoken, and that's if they're spoken at all. Clay felt it especially hard that day, and in the days that stacked up after it. Again, there was so much to tell him. There were nights he'd come out to talk, then retreat, heart beating, to the bedroom. He remembered so vividly the boy he'd been, who'd ask for the stories from Featherton. He'd been piggybacked, back then, into bed.

He'd practice at the barren old desk; the box and his books beside him. The feather of T in his hand.

"Dad?"

How many times could he rehearse?

Once, he almost arrived, in the heavier light of the kitchen, but again, he returned to the hallway. The next time he actually made it, *The Quarryman* tight in his grip—and Michael Dunbar caught him:

"Come in, Clay, what have you got there?"

And Clay stood snared in the light.

He brought the book up from his side.

He said, "Just."

"Just," then held up higher. The book, so white and weathered, with its creased and crippled spine. He held Italy out before him, and the frescoes on the ceiling, and all those broken noses—one for each time she'd read it.

"Clay?"

Michael in jeans and a T-shirt; his hands were weathered concrete. They might have had similar eyes, but then, for Clay, all the constant burning.

He'd had a concrete stomach once, too.

Do you remember?

You had wavy hair; you still do, but more grey in it now as well—because you died and got a bit older, and—

"Clay?"

He finally did it.

Blood flowed through the stone.

The book, in hand, held out to him:

"Can you tell me about the Slaves and David?"

the hand between the sandhills

In many ways, you could argue the cat was our biggest mistake; he had a string of disgraceful habits:

He drooled almost uncontrollably.

He had a nasty stench of breath.

He had a God-awful shedding problem, dandruff, and a tendency to throw his food overboard when he ate.

He vomited.

("Look at *this*!" shouted Henry one morning. "Right next to my shoes!"

"Just be grateful it wasn't *in* 'em."

"Shut up, Rory. . . . Tommy! Come clean this shit up!")

He meowed all hours of the night—such pathetic and high-pitched meowing! And then all the ball-tearing happy-pawing, on anyone's lap he could find. Sometimes, when we watched TV, he'd move from boy to boy, sleeping and purring the house down. It was Rory who despised him most, though, and summed up all of us best:

"If that cat starts slicing up my balls again, Tommy, I'm gonna kill the bastard, I swear it—and trust me, you'll be next."

But Tommy was looking much happier; and Henry had taught him to reply:

"He's only trying to *find* 'em, Rory," and even Rory couldn't resist—he laughed—and actually gave the big tabby a pat there, as he clawed through the shorts on his lap. There was the fish and the bird and Achilles to come, but next in line was the dog. It was Hector who paved the way home.

* * *

By then we'd hit December, and there was a single, immutable fact:

Clay was a 400 specialist.

He took the distance apart.

There was no one at Chisholm who could go with him, but challengers would soon be coming. The new year would bring Zone and Regionals, and if good enough, he'd make it to State. I looked for new ways of training him, and harked back to old motivations. I started, where *he* had, the library:

I looked at books and articles.

I scoured the DVDs.

All I could find on athletics, till a woman was standing behind me.

"Hello?" she said. "Young man? It's nine o'clock. It's time to close."

In the lead-up to Christmas, he did it.

Hector went out and went missing.

All of us took to searching, and it was something like looking for Clay, except Clay, this time, was with us. We all went out in the mornings, and the others went out after school; I joined them when I came home. We even drove back to Wetherill, but the cat had up and vanished. Even jokes were falling flat.

"Hey, Rory," Henry said, as we wandered the streets. "At least your balls have had a chance to recover."

"I know, good bloody riddance."

Tommy was out on the outskirts of us, and mad and sad as hell. As they spoke he'd come running over, and tried tackling them down to the ground.

"You bastards!" He spat the hurt out. He flailed and punched away. He swung his boyish arms. "You bastards, you fucking *pricks*!"

At first they just made light of it, in the darkened street around us.

"Shit! I didn't know Tommy could swear so well!"

"I know—that's pretty good work!"

But then they felt the eyes of him, and the pain in his ten-year-old soul. Much as Clay had broken that night, in the future, in the kitchen, in Silver,

Tommy was breaking now. As he fell to the road on hands and knees, it was Henry who bent and reached for him; then Rory who held his shoulders.

"We'll find him, Tommy, we'll find him."

"I miss them," he said.

We all fell on him.

We walked home that night in silence.

When the others all went to bed, Clay and I watched the movies I'd borrowed, we read the small crowd of books. We watched films about the Olympics, and endless documentaries. Anything to do with running.

My favorite was *Gallipoli*, recommended by the librarian. World War I and athletics. I loved Archy Hamilton's uncle—the tough-faced, stopwatched trainer.

"What are your legs?" he'd say to Archy.

Archy would say, *"Steel springs."*

We watched it many times over.

For Clay it was *Chariots of Fire*.

1924.

Eric Liddell, Harold Abrahams.

He loved two particular things:

The first was when Abrahams first saw Liddell run, and said, *"Liddell? I've never seen such drive, such commitment in a runner. . . . He runs like a wild animal."*

Then his favorite Eric Liddell:

"So where does the power come from, to see the race to its end?

From within."

Or as the actor Ian Charleson delivered it, with the amazing Scottish accent:

From wethun.

As time went by, we wondered.

Should we place an ad in the *RQT*, for a lost but annoying tabby?

No—we would never do anything so logical.

Instead there was Clay and me.

We'd look at what remained in that classifieds section, which culminated, always, in the mule. When we ran he'd be steering us over there, and I'd stop and call to him, "NO!"

He'd look at me, disappointedly.

He'd shrug, he'd go, come *on*.

To ward him off, I softened when something else arrived, in an ad that was placed by the pound:

A female, three-year-old border collie.

I drove there myself and picked her up, and came home to the shock of my life—for there, right in front of me, on the porch, they were all out laughing and celebrating, and between them, the Goddamn cat. The bastard had come back!

I got out of the car.

I watched the beaten-up, collarless tabby.

He looked at me; he knew all along.

He was a cat with particular schadenfreude.

For a moment I expected a salute.

"I s'pose I'll just take the dog back," I said, and Rory threw Hector sideways; he went flying a good five meters—and there was high-pitched, bloodcurdled meowing. (I bet he was glad to be home.) Then Rory came stalking over.

"You got the little bastard a *dog* now?" But he was also partly congratulatory.

And Tommy?

Well, Tommy picked up Hector, and shielded him from the rest of us, and came over and opened the car. He hugged the cat and the dog simultaneously, and said, "God, I can't believe it." He looked over at Clay and asked; it's so strange how he knew what to do:

"Achilles?"

Again, a shake of the head.

I said, "This one's actually a girl."

"Okay then, I'm calling her Rosy."

"You know that isn't—"

"I know, I know, it's the sky," and we were back for a moment together:

His head in her lap in the lounge.

Mid-December, a Sunday, early morning, we drove to a beach in the south, in the depths of the national park. Its official name was Prospector, but the locals called it Anzacs.

I remember the car and the drive there:

That sick and unslept feeling.

The outline of trees in the dark.

Already the traditional smell inside, of carpeting, woodwork and varnish.

I remember how we ran the sand dunes, and they were cool in the sunrise, but punishing; by the top we were both on our knees.

At one point, Clay beat me to the peak, and he didn't just lie there, or capsize, which was more than appealing, believe me. No, instead, he turned and reached for me, and the backdrop of shore and ocean; his hand came down, and he pulled me up, and we lay at the top with the suffering.

When he talked to me about that later—when he spoke and told me of everything—he'd said, "It was one of our greatest moments, I think. Both you and the sea were burning."

By that point, Hector wasn't just back.

It was clear he'd never leave us, ever.

There seemed to be fourteen different versions of that bloody cat, because wherever you went, he appeared. If you walked toward the toaster, he was sitting just left or right of it, amongst the surrounding crumbs. If you went to sit on the couch, he was purring on top of the remote. Even once, I went to the toilet, and he watched from up on the cistern.

Then Rosy was running the clothesline, rounding its stenciled shadows up. We could walk that dog for miles on end: black legs, white paws, and flecks of eyes and gold. But still she'd come back and run. Only now do I see the significance. She was likely corralling memory—or at the very least, the scent of it—or worse, the restless spirits.

In that sense, there was always something stirring by then, at the house at 18 Archer Street. To me it was death and goneness, and a compulsory sense of mischief. It would lead to the madness of Christmas, and specifically Christmas Eve—when they brought home the bird and the fish.

Me, I arrived from work.

Henry was beaming, delirious.

I said my maiden "Je-sus *Christ*!"

Apparently, they'd gone to the pet shop, to buy the goldfish to add to the list—but Tommy loved the resident pigeon. It had hopped down onto his finger as he listened to the story—how a mob of hoodlum mynah birds had been picking on him over on Chatham Street, so the pet shop owner went in.

"Did you think he might have deserved it?" said Rory, but Tommy was following instinct. He was over, examining the fish. The pigeon clung sideways to his arm.

"Here," he told them, "this one."

The goldfish had scales like plumage.

He had a tail like a golden rake.

Which left only bringing them home, and me standing in the doorway; and where could I turn but to blasphemy, while Tommy provided the names.

By then he'd made sense of everything:

They were neither of them close to an Achilles.

"The *goldfish* is Agamemnon," he informed me, "and the pigeon, I'm calling Telemachus."

The king of men, and the boy from Ithaca:

The son of Penelope and Odysseus.

The sky was hit by sunset, and Rory was looking at Henry.

"I'm gonna kill that little shit."

carey novac in the eighth

After the spectacular failure of seventh placing in Group One company, Cootamundra was spelled for summer. On return he was ridden by Carey—four times, for three wins and a third.

And now she was becoming sought-after.

For Clay, there was radio and riverbed, city and Surrounds.

There was the silence of the Amahnu, and the stories he'd heard in the kitchen—for they'd stayed up the entire night that night, when he'd asked about the Slaves and David; they drank coffee. Michael told him of finding the calendar. Emil Zátopek. Einstein. All the rest of them. There was a girl who once broke a boy's spaceship, and sat down the front in English; she had hair down to her waist.

He didn't do details like Penelope did—he wasn't dying, so wouldn't go as far—but the effort was true, and truthful. He said, "I don't know why I never told you these things."

"You would have," said Clay, "if you'd stayed."

But he wasn't intending to puncture him; he'd meant they were stories for when he was older.

And you're telling them to me now.

He was sure he'd understood.

It was dawn when they talked of the David, and the Slaves imprisoned in the marble. "Those twisted, struggling bodies," said Michael, "fighting from out of the stone." He said he hadn't thought of them for decades, but they were somehow always there. "I'd die to find greatness, like the David someday—even for just a moment." He watched the boy's eyes, in front of him. "But I know—I know . . ."

Clay answered.

It hit them both hard, but he had to.

"We live the lives of the Slaves."

The bridge was all they had.

There was the week in mid-January, when it rained up in the mountains, and the Amahnu started to flow. They saw the great sky coming. They stood out on the scaffold, and the heavy wooden falsework, with the splinters of rain around them.

"It could all be washed away."

Clay was quiet but certain. "It won't be."

He was right.

The water rose only to shin-height.

It was the river in sort-of-training.

Warming up the Amahnu way.

In the city, through March, there was the buildup to the autumn carnival, and this time the Group One was hers.

Cootamundra.

Race Eight on Easter Monday, at Royal Hennessey.

The race was the Jim Pike Plate.

Of course, Clay came home that long weekend, but had done something else, a while earlier:

He'd walked up Poseidon Road, to a key-cutting, shoe-fix, engraving place. It was an old man inside, with a snow-white beard, like Santa Claus wearing overalls. When he looked at the Zippo, he said, "Oh, I remember this." He shook his head. "Yeah, that's it—*Matador in the fifth*. A girl . . .

Strange thing to write on a lighter," and the headshake turned to a nod. "Real likeable, though." He gave Clay pen and paper. "Write it clearly. Where do you want it?"

"There are two."

"Here, give us a look." He snatched the translucent paper. "Ha!" He'd returned from nod to vigorous headshake. "You kids are bloody mad. You know about Kingston Town?"

Did they know about Kingston Town.

"Maybe," said Clay, "put *Carey Novac in the eighth* under the first one, and the other on the other side."

Santa Claus smiled, then laughed. "Good choice." But it wasn't a ho-ho-ho; more of a heh-heh-heh. "*Kingston Town can't win,* ay? What's that s'posed to mean?"

"She'll know," said Clay.

"Well, that's the most important thing."

The old man got to engraving.

As he left the shop, the thought struck him.

Since leaving home that first time, for the river, he'd thought the money—the roll of it from Henry—would be only for building the bridge. But it was always meant for this. He'd used all of twenty-two dollars.

At 18 Archer Street, he put the remainder of the big thick roll onto the bed lying opposite his.

"Thanks, Henry," he whispered, "you keep the rest," and he thought of Bernborough Park then—back to boys and never quite men—and turned and left for Silver.

Early on Easter Saturday, two days before the race, he got up and sat in the dark; he looked for the Amahnu. He sat on the edge of his bed, and the box was in his hands. He took everything out but the lighter, then included a folded-up letter.

He'd written it the previous night.

* * *

In the evening that Saturday, they lay there and she told him.

The same instructions.

Go out hard.

Let him run.

Then pray and take him home.

She was nervous, but they were good nerves.

Near the end, she said, "Are you coming?"

He smiled at the bulging stars.

"Of course."

"Your brothers?"

"Of course."

"Do they know about this?" she said, and she was talking about The Surrounds. "And us?"

She'd never asked about that before, and Clay was pretty certain. "No—they just know we've always been close."

The girl nodded.

"And, hey, I have to tell you . . ." He paused. "There's also something else—" and now he stopped completely.

"What?"

He retreated, still as he was. "No. Nothing."

It was too late, though, because now she was up on an elbow. "Come on, Clay, what is it?" She reached across and poked him.

"Ow!"

"Tell me." She was poised for another strike, right between the ribs; and there was once when this happened before, in waters still to come, when things had turned out badly.

But this was the beauty of Carey, the real beauty; because forget the auburn hair, and the sea glass—she would take the risk a second time. She would gamble and do it for him.

"Tell me or I'll hit you again," she said. "I'll tickle you half to death."

"Okay! Okay . . ."

He said it.

He told her that he loved her:

"You've got fifteen freckles on your face, but you have to look hard to find them . . . and there's a sixteenth one down here." He touched that piece of her neck. When he attempted to take his hand away, she reached up and trapped his fingers. The answer was how she looked at him.

"No," she said, "don't move it."

Later, much later, it was Clay who got up first.

It was Clay who rolled over and took something, and placed it against her, on the mattress.

He'd wrapped it in the racing section.

The lighter was in the box.

A gift within a gift.

And a letter.

TO BE OPENED ON MONDAY NIGHT.

On Easter Monday she was on the back page of the paper: the auburn-haired girl, the broomstick trainer, and the horse, deep brown, between them.

The headline said *MASTER'S APPRENTICE*.

On the radio, they played an interview with McAndrew, from earlier in the week, in which they queried the choice of jockey. Any professional in the country would have ridden that horse, given the chance, to which McAndrew said simply and stiffly, "I'm sticking with my apprentice."

"Yes, she's a prospect, but—"

"I'm not in the business of answering that kind of question." The voice, pure dryness. "We swapped her last spring in the Sunline-Northerly, and look what happened there. She knows the horse and that's it."

Monday afternoon.

The race was at four-fifty and we got there for three, and I paid the admission. When we pooled our money near the bookies, Henry took the roll out. He gave Clay a certain wink. "Don't worry, boys, I've got this."

When it was done, we made our way over, and up, past the members, to the muck. Both stands were close to packed. We found seats in the very top row.

By four the sun was dropping, but still white.

By four-thirty, with Carey stock-still in the mounting yard, it was starting to yellow, behind us.

In the color and noise and movement, McAndrew was in his suit. He said not a single word to her, just a hand down onto her shoulder. Petey Simms, his best groom, was there, too, but McAndrew lifted her upwards, to the breadth of Cootamundra.

She trotted him lightly away.

At the jump, the crowd all stood.

Clay's heart was out of its gate.

The deep-brown horse, and rider on top, went straight out to the front. The colors, red-green-white. "As *expected*," the course caller informed them, *"but this is no ordinary field, let's see what* Cootamundra's *got for us. . . . Let's see what the young apprentice has—Red Centre three lengths second."*

In the grandstand shade we watched.

The horses ran in the light.

"Jesus," said the man standing next to me. "Five lengths bloody ahead."

"Come on, Coota, you big brown bastard!"

That, I think, was Rory.

At the turn, they all closed in.

In the straight, she asked him for more.

Two horses—Red Centre and Diamond Game—climbed forward, and the crowd called all of them home. Even me. Even Tommy. The shouts of Henry and Rory. We roared for Cootamundra.

And Clay.

Clay was in the middle of us, he was standing on his seat.

He didn't move.

He didn't make a sound.

Hands-and-heels and she brought him home.

Two lengths and girl and sea glass.

Carey Novac in the eighth.

It had been a long time since he'd sat on the roof, but he did that Monday night; he was camouflaged amongst the tiles.

But Carey Novac saw him.

When she'd pulled up with Catherine and Trackwork Ted, she'd stood on the porch, alone. She held her hand up, fleetingly.

We won, we won.

Then, in.

Dear Carey,

If you've done the right thing (and I know you have), you're reading this when you get home, and Cootamundra has won. You took it away from them in the first furlong. I know you like that style of racing. You always liked the great front-runners. You said they were the bravest ones.

See? I remember everything.

I remember what you said when you first saw me:

There's a boy up there on that roof.

I eat toast sometimes just to write your name in the crumbs.

I remember everything you've told me, about the town you grew up in, and your mum and dad, your brothers—everything. I remember how you said, "And? You don't want to know my name?" It was the first time we spoke on Archer Street.

There are so many times I wish Penny Dunbar was still around, just so you could talk to her, and she'd have told you a few of her stories. You'd have been in our kitchen for hours. . . . She'd have tried to teach you the piano.

Anyway—I want you to keep the lighter.

I never really had many friends.

I have my brothers and you and that's all.

But okay, I'll stop talking now, except to say that if Cootamundra didn't win by some chance, I know there'll be other days. My brothers and I, we'll have put some money on, but we didn't bet on the horse.

Love,

Clay

And sometimes, you know, I imagine it.

I like to think she hugged her parents for the last time that night, and that Catherine Novac was happy, and that her father couldn't have been prouder. I see her in her room; her flannel shirt, jeans, and forearms. I see her holding the lighter, and reading the letter, and thinking Clay was something else.

How many times *did* she read it? I wonder.

I don't know.

We'll never know.

No, all I know is that she left the house that night and the Saturday rule was broken:

Saturday night at The Surrounds.

Not Monday.

Never Monday.

And Clay?

Clay should have gone back.

He should have been on a train that night—back to Silver, to the Amahnu, on his way to finish a bridge, to shake our father's hand—but he, too, was at The Surrounds, and she came with a rustle of feet.

And us?

We can't do anything.

One of us writes, and one of us reads.

We can't do anything but me tell it, and you see it.

We hit it, like this, for the now.

state and anniversary

As we watch them both walk toward it—The Surrounds, the very last time—the past tucks close inside me. So much of that time would lead them there: to each approaching footsteps.

There was Zone and then the Regionals.

Anniversary and State.

There was Tommy's quadruple animals.

As New Year passed into February, there was Clay and the nuisance of injury (a boy with broken-glass feet), and the promise, or more like a warning:

"I win State and we'll go and get him, okay?"

He was referring, of course, to Achilles.

I could go in all sorts of orders here, in many kinds of ways, but it just feels right to start there, and thread the rest toward it:

How it was on the anniversary.

A year since Penelope's death.

In the morning that day in March, all of us woke up early. No work that day, and no school, and by seven we'd been to the cemetery; we'd climbed up over the graves. We put daisies down in front of her, and Tommy looked out for our dad. I told him he should forget it.

By eight we started cleaning; the house was filthy, we had to be ruthless. We threw out clothes and sheets. We stamped out knickknacks and *other crap*, but preserved her books and bookshelves. The books, we knew, were sacred.

There was a moment when all of us stopped, though, and sat on the bed, on the edges. I was holding *The Odyssey* and *The Iliad*.

"Go on," said Henry, "read some."

The Odyssey, book twelve:

"From the flowing waters of the River of Ocean my ship hit the open sea . . . where ever-fresh Dawn has her dancing lawns, and the sun would soon be rising. . . ."

Even Rory was silent, and stayed.

The words plowed on and the pages turned; and us, in the house, and drifting.

That bedroom went floating down Archer Street.

In the meantime, Clay stopped competing barefoot, but hadn't been wearing shoes.

In the training, we'd kept it simple.

We ran the early mornings.

400s down at Bernborough.

In the evenings, we watched the movies.

The beginning and end of *Gallipoli*—Jesus, what an ending!

The entire *Chariots of Fire*.

Rory and Henry claimed that both were boring as bat shit, but they always came around; I caught their captured faces.

On the Thursday before Zone there was a problem, just two days out from racing, because kids had got drunk at Bernborough; there was glass all over the track. Clay hadn't even seen it, and he didn't notice the blood. Later, it took us hours to pick the pieces out. In the process I remembered what I had to—a moment from a documentary (and one that we still had at home): *Olympic Highs and Lows*.

Again, all of us were in the lounge room, and I pulled out the old footage, of the amazing but tragic race, in Los Angeles. You might know the one I mean. Those women. The 3,000 meters.

As it is, the athlete who won the event (the awesomely upright Romanian, Maricica Puică) wasn't as famous for that race, but two of the others were: Mary Decker and Zola Budd. We all stared on in the darkness—and Clay, especially, in horror—as the so-called controversial Budd was accused of deliberately tripping Decker in the jostle, on the straight of the Olympic stadium. (Of course she did no such thing.)

But also, and most importantly:

Clay saw.

He saw what I hoped he would see.

He said, "Pause it—quick," and looked closer, at the legs of Zola Budd's running. "Is that . . . *tape* there, under her feet?"

The scars were healing nicely by anniversary day, but since we'd started taping his feet up, it was something he'd loved and maintained. As I finished up the reading, in Penny and Michael's bedroom, he was rubbing them, in and away. The soles were calloused but cared-for.

At last, our parents' clothing was gone; there was only one garment we kept. I walked it through the hallway; we found its rightful resting place.

"Here," I said to Rory, who opened the lid to the strings.

"Hey, look!" said Henry to all of us. "A packet of cigarettes!"

And first I laid the two books down, and then the blue woolen dress. They belonged for now to the piano.

"*Quick*," said Rory, "shove Hector in!" but even he couldn't summon the strength. He placed a hand down gently, on the pocket and button within; she'd never had the heart to mend it.

In the lead-up—in January and February that year—I realize there were hardships. But there were good times, there were great times, like Tommy and each of his pets.

We loved Agamemnon's antics, the so-called king of men; and sometimes we sat and watched him, headbutting the glass of his tank.

"One . . . two . . . three," we'd count, and by forty only Rory was left.

"Don't you have anything better to do?" I'd ask.

"No," he'd say, "I don't."

He was still on the road to expulsion, but I gave it a shot, nonetheless. "Homework?"

"We all know homework's useless, Matthew." He marveled at the goldfish's toughness. "This fish is the bloody best."

Of course, Hector went on being Hector, purring and ball-tearing through summer, and watching bathroom-work from the cistern.

"Oi, Tommy!" I'd often call to him. "I'm trying to have a shower!"

The cat sat like an apparition, in the steam room haze around him. He'd stare and somehow smirk at me:

And *I'm* tryin' to get a *schwitz*!

He'd lick those tarmac paws of his, he'd smack his tire-black lips.

Telemachus (whom we'd already reduced to T) marched inside and out of his cage. Only once did the Trojan strike at him, and Tommy had told him *no*, and Hector went back to sleep. He likely dreamed of the steam.

Then Rosy, and Rosy still ran, but when Henry brought her a beanbag, which he'd found in a council cleanup (he always had his eye out), we loved how she'd cast it around. In the moments when she actually did lie down, she preferred the open sunshine; she would pick it up and drag it along, following the path of the light. Then she'd dig to make herself comfortable, which could only have one result:

"Hey, Tommy! Tommy! Come have a look at this!"

The backyard was covered in snowfall, from the beanbag's Styrofoam balls. The most humid day of the summer so far—and Rory looked over at Henry.

"I swear you're a Goddamn genius."

"What?"

"Are you kidding me? Bringing that bloody beanbag home."

"I didn't know the dog would *destroy* it—that's Tommy's fault—and anyway . . ." He disappeared and came back with the vacuum.

"Oi, you can't use the vacuum for this!"

"Why not?"

"I don't know—you'll wreck it."

"You're worried about the vacuum, Rory?" This time it was me. "You wouldn't even know where to switch the bloody thing on."

"Yeah."

"Shut up, Henry."

"Or how to use it."

"Shut up, Matthew."

All of us stood and watched, though, as Henry finished the job. Rosy leapt forward and sideways, barking and carrying on, and Mrs. Chilman, grinning, at the fence. She stood on her toes on a paint tin.

"You Dunbar boys," she said.

One of the best parts of the anniversary was the great bedroom swap, which we did after moving her books, and the dress inside the piano.

First we dismantled the bunk beds.

They could each be made into singles, and although I wasn't overly keen, it was me who moved to the main bedroom (no one else wanted anything to do with it), but I took my old bed there with me. No way would I sleep on theirs. Before any of that was dealt with, though, we decided it was time for a change—for Henry and Rory to disband.

Henry: "Finally! I've been waiting for this my whole life!"

Rory: "*You've* been waiting, bloody hell, good riddance! Pack up your shit and leave."

"Pack *my* shit up? What are *you* on about?" He gave him a generous shove. "I'm not going!"

"Well *I'm* not going!"

"Oh, just shut up," I said. "I wish I could get rid of the pair of you, but I can't, so here's what we'll do—I'll toss this coin. *Twice*. The first one's for who moves out."

"Yeah, but he's got more—"

"Not interested. Winner stays, loser moves. Rory, you call."

The coin went up, it hit the bedroom ceiling.

"Heads."

It bounced over the carpet; it landed on a sock.

Tails.

"Shit!"

"Ha ha, bad luck, buddy boy!"

"It hit the ceiling, it doesn't count!"

I turned now to Henry.

Rory persisted. "It hit the fucking ceiling!"

"Rory," I said, "shut up. Now, Henry—I'm throwing again. Heads you get Tommy, tails you get Clay."

It was tails again, and the first thing Henry said when Clay moved in was "Here, get a look at this." He threw him the old *Playboy*—Miss January—and Rory made friends with Tommy:

"Get the cat off my Goddamn bed, shithead."

Your bed?

Typical Hector.

Again, in the lead-up, mid-February, when he hit the Regional Championships, at E. S. Marks—where the grandstand was a concrete gargantuan—we had the tape network down to an art. We'd made it a kind of ritual; it was our version of *what are your legs*, or *the power that came from within*.

First, I'd crouch below him.

Slowly I'd roll out the strapping tape.

A line straight down the middle.

A cross before his toes.

It started like a crucifix, but the result was something different, like a long-lost letter of the alphabet; a few edges would curl to the top.

When the 400 was called, I walked with him near the marshal zone, and the day was muggy and motionless. As he left he thought of Abrahams, and the bible-man, Eric Liddell. He thought of a skinny, diminutive South African, whose taped feet inspired his.

I said, "I'll see you after the end," and Clay had actually answered me, his peg in his shorts, in the pocket:

"Hey, Matthew," and then just, "Thanks."

He ran like a Goddamn warrior.

He was truly the lightning Achilles.

In the end, it was close to evening that day, on that first anniversary, when Rory came to his senses; he said, "Let's burn the bed."

Together, we made the decision.

We sat at the kitchen table.

But there was no decision to make.

Maybe it's a universal truth of boys and fire; the same way we'll often throw stones. We pick them up and aim for anything. Even me, edging close to nineteen:

I was supposed to be the adult.

If moving into the main bedroom was the grown-up thing to do, then burning the bed was the *young* one, and that's how I bit the bullet; I took a bet each way.

Initially, not much was said:

Clay and Henry were assigned the mattress.

Rory and I took the base.

Tommy, the matches and turpentine.

We took it out through the kitchen, into the backyard, and launched it all over the fence. It was roughly the same place, all those years earlier, where Penelope met City Special.

We got to the other side. I said, "Right."

It was warm and a breeze had picked up.

Hands for a while in our pockets.

Clay had a handful of peg—but then the mattress went back on the base, and we walked out to The Surrounds. The stables were tired and leaning. The grass was patchy-uneven.

Soon we saw a distant old washing machine.

Then a shattered, lifeless TV.

"There," I said.

I pointed—close to the middle, but nearer our place—and we carried our parents' bed there. Two of us stood, and three crouched. Clay was off to the side; he was standing, facing our house.

"Is it a bit windy, Matthew?" Henry asked.

"Probably."

"Is that a westerly?" It grew gradually stronger each minute. "We might set the whole field on fire."

"Even better!" shouted Rory, and just as I started to admonish him, it was Clay who cut through everything—the field, the grass, the TV. The lonesome carcass of washing machine. His voice directed away:

"No."

"What?"

We all said it at once, and the wind blew even harder.

"What'd you say, Clay?"

He looked cold in the warmth of the field. His short dark hair was flat on his head, and that fire inside him was lit; he said it, quietly, again.

A firm and final "No."

And we knew.

We would leave things exactly like this. We'd let the thing die its own death here—or at least that's what we believed—for how could we ever foresee it?

That Clay would come back and he'd lie here.

He'd squeeze the peg till it bit through his hand.

The first time was the night before State, once we'd sat for a while in the kitchen; him and me. He laid the truth down in between us:

He'd win State, then go for Achilles.

He had the two hundred dollars—probably his whole life savings.

He didn't even wait for an answer.

What he *did* do was go out the front, run a light run through the racing quarter, feed a few of our carrots to the mule—and end up back on the roof.

Then, later, much later, while the rest of us slept, he got out of bed and wandered there; he picked out a brand-new peg. He climbed up onto the fence, then walked the width of the laneway. It was dark and there wasn't a moon out, but he found his way easily through.

He wandered and climbed over onto it.

The bed lay down in the gloom.

He curled himself up like a boy.

He lay down in the dark and he dreamed there, and cared nothing for winning or State. No, he spoke only to another boy, from a small country town, and a woman who'd crossed the oceans.

"I'm sorry," he whispered to both of them, "I'm so sorry, I'm sorry, I'm *sorry*!" The peg was clenched tight in his hand, and he addressed them, lastly, again. "I promise, I'll tell you the story," he said, "how I brought you both home Achilles."

That mule was never for Tommy.

part seven

cities + waters + criminals + arches + stories + survivors
+
bridges

the girl at gallery road

ONCE, IN THE TIDE OF DUNBAR PAST, THERE WAS A GIRL WHO KNEW A DUNBAR boy, and what a girl she was.

She had auburn hair and good-green eyes.

She had a puzzle of blood-colored freckles.

She was famous for winning a Group One race, and dying the very next day—and Clay was the one to blame.

He lived and breathed and became it.

He eventually told them everything.

In the beginning, though, and quite fittingly, when Carey first had seen him, she'd seen him up on the roof.

She grew up in a town called Calamia.

Her father was a jockey.

Her father's father, too.

Before that, she didn't know.

She loved horses, trackwork, and trackwork riding, and records and stories of Thoroughbreds.

Calamia was seven hours away, and her first memories were of her dad. He'd come home from trackwork in the mornings, and she'd ask him how it had been. Sometimes she'd wake up when he left the house, at 3:45 a.m. She'd rub her eyes and say to him, "Hey, Ted, can I come, too?"

For some reason, whenever she woke in darkness, she called her mother

Catherine, she called her father Ted. In the daytime it disappeared; they were simply Mum and Dad. That was one of many things not written or spoken about, years later, when they found her fallen, and dead.

As I said, she loved horses, but not in the way most girls did.

It was atmosphere, not ribbons.

It was stables more than shows.

As she grew older, in school holidays, she and her brothers begged to go to trackwork, and she loved those full dark mornings, of hoofbeats through mist and fog. She loved the way the sun came up, so distantly huge and warm-looking, and the air so close and cold.

Back then they ate toast on the fence line—all white, all rail and no palings—and they loved the trainers, how they swore beneath various breaths, and old jockeys hanging around, like toughened, deep-voiced children. It was funny seeing them in trackwork clothes, in jeans and vests and old skullcaps.

Her brothers were four and five years older, and when they hit the age, they'd also joined the racing game; it was obviously in the blood.

In racing they always talk about blood.

Or more, they talk of bloodlines:

Just as with Clay and the rest of us, there's much to discover in the past.

According to Carey, her mother, Catherine Novac, was the only member of her family to both mistrust and despise the racing world, subject to her mood. She could be cold and pale-blue water-color; or gingery-blond and fuming. Sure, she loved horses, she enjoyed racing, but she abhorred the racing *business*; its wastage, its overbreeding. Its greedy girth of underbelly. It was something like a beautiful whore, and she'd seen it void of makeup.

Carey's brothers had called her Catherine the Great, for she was formidably strict and serious; she was never fooling around. On race days, when she said to come back in one piece, they knew what she really meant:

Don't count on sympathy if you fall.

Life was hard for jockeys.

It was much, much harder for the horse.

* * *

Then Ted.

Trackwork Ted.

Carey knew the story.

Early on in his career, he was likely the most promising apprentice in the country, like a Pike, or a Breasley, or a Demon Darb Munro. At five-foot-seven, he was tall for a jockey and short for a man, but he had the perfect physique for riding, and a metabolism people would die for; he seemed unable to put on weight. The downside was that his face looked hastily assembled, like the manufacturers were in a rush. But that depended who you asked. A girl named Catherine Jamison thought he wasn't half too bad. She loved his cluttered face and good-green eyes, and that she could carry him in her arms—till tragedy struck, one morning.

He was twenty-three years old.

Overnight, there was a sudden, metabolic change.

Where once he could eat a whole packet of Tim Tams on race day, now he could eat only the wrapper.

They'd been in the city for a while by then; they'd moved to make a real go of it. Catherine had a nursing job, at the Prince of Wales, near Randwick.

There came a week, a good few years into the stint, when Ted started feeling different. Then, a few hours before first light that day, he'd made the ritual trip to the bathroom, and the scales there didn't lie; and neither did the mirror. He was simultaneously stretched out and filled in, and his face had lost its tardiness. But what was the good of that? Did he want to be handsome, or ride the perfect miler in the Doncaster? The world stopped making sense.

The worst part was his hands.

In their small apartment kitchen, he didn't even contemplate his breakfast; he sat at the kitchen table, looking at those hands, and they were the meatiest things he'd ever seen.

For five long years, he worked and fasted.

He steam-roomed.

He lettuce-leaved.

When he read the paper he sat in the car in the heat of day, the windows all up, in his newest, warmest tracksuit. He mowed lawns in jacket and jeans, with a wetsuit underneath. He cramped up, he was irritable. He ran with garbage bags strapped to his legs, under winter woolen pants. These were the spoils of the racing game, and a thousand pent-up dreams—of Crunchie bars and chocolate cake, and impure thoughts of cheese.

There was the usual fare of injuries, too—he was thrown, he broke both wrists. He was kicked in the face in the stables. Trampled twice at trackwork. Once, in Race Three at Warwick Farm, a horse in front threw a shoe; it clipped him over the ear. It could have been many times worse.

By the twilight of his career he was like a soldier, or an ancient charioteer; each race was like going into battle. Through the purgatory in his stomach, and the toothaches, headaches, and dizzy spells, the final insult was a raging case of athlete's foot, caught from the floor of the jockey room—

"And that," he often joked to Carey, age seven, in the car on their way to trackwork, "is what got me in the end."

The thing is, though, Ted Novac was lying, because what got him in the end wasn't athlete's foot, or hunger pains, or dehydration and deprivation. It was, of course, a horse:

A chestnut giant, The Spaniard.

The Spaniard was just a sensational horse, bighearted, like Kingston Town, or Phar Lap. On top of that, he was entire, which meant his bloodline could carry on.

He was worked by Ennis McAndrew, the noted broomstick trainer.

When the horse came to his stable, McAndrew made a phone call.

"How much do you weigh these days?"

He'd dialed Ted Novac's number.

The Spaniard raced in almost all the big ones a mile or over.

He could sprint, he could stay, he did everything you could ask.

Running second or third was a failure.

Fourth was a disaster.

Up top, every time, was Ted Novac, his name in the paper, and his smile caught napping on his face—or was it a grimace to scratch the itch? No. On The Spaniard he never felt it; he'd put him to sleep for half the race, stoke him slowly for a furlong, and then he'd bring him home.

By the end of the horse's career, Ted was looking to get out, too.

Only one race had eluded them, and no, it wasn't the Race That Stops the Nation. Neither McAndrew nor Ted nor the owners cared about that one; it was the Cox Plate that they coveted. In the minds of the true experts, that was the greatest race.

For Ted it was a travesty.

He couldn't make the weight.

Even at weight-for-age, where he knew the mark well in advance, Ted was too far gone. He'd done everything he'd always done. He'd mowed a hundred lawns. At home he collapsed in the shower. The decision was made a week in advance, a scarecrow hand on his shoulder—and, of course, The Spaniard won.

In later years, it was still hard for him when he told her. Another jockey—the ever-affable, mustachioed Max McKeon—brought the horse round the lot of them, on the vanishing Moonee Valley straight, and The Spaniard won by a length.

As for Ted Novac, he listened in the car, on his driveway.

They lived in a different racing quarter by then—at number eleven, here on Archer Street, years before Penny and Michael—and he'd smiled and cried, cried and smiled.

He itched but didn't scratch it.

He was a man with burning feet.

For a time, after retirement, he still rode trackwork, and was one of the most popular morning riders in the city. But they soon moved back to the land.

Catherine liked the country, and the worst and wisest decision they made was to keep the old house on Archer Street. The game, at least, gave them that.

As the years climbed by, they had kids out there. Ted grew to his natural weight—or a few kilos heavier, if he went too hard on the cake. He felt by then he'd earned it.

He worked many jobs, from shoe salesman to video shop assistant to cattle hand on farmland, and some of them he did well. It was mornings were his favorite, though; he rode trackwork at the track out there. They called it Gallery Road.

By then he got the nickname: Trackwork Ted.

Two incidents defined him.

The first was when the trainer, McAndrew, brought two promising jockeys out to watch. It was a Tuesday. The sky was blond and beaming.

"See that?"

The trainer had barely changed.

Just the whitening of his hair.

He pointed to the rider rifling past them.

"See his heels? And those hands? He's on that horse like he's not even riding him."

The two kids were standard arrogance.

"He's fat," said one, and the other one laughed, and McAndrew slapped them hard. Twice to the chin and cheeks.

"Here," he said, "he's coming again." He spoke like all trainers everywhere. Looking outwards. "And for the record, that guy's ridden more winners than you two bastards'll ride your whole life. He'll have more wins at *trackwork*."

Just then, Ted arrived on foot.

"McAndrew!"

And McAndrew grinned, quite broadly. "Hey, Ted."

"How do I look?"

"I thought, what's Pavarotti doin' all the way out here bein' a jockey?"

They hugged each other warmly, a few good hits, each back.

They thought about The Spaniard.

* * *

The second moment came a few years later, when the Novac boys were thirteen and twelve, and Carey, the girl, still eight. It would be Trackwork Ted's last trackwork.

It was spring, school holidays, there'd been rain, and the grass was green and long (it's always surprising how long the grass gets grown for Thoroughbreds), and the horse bucked, Ted was thrown, and everyone saw him fall. The trainers kept the boys away, but Carey somehow got there; she weaved her way through, she parted the legs—and first she saw the sweat, and the blood mixed up with skin, then his collarbone, snapped and bent.

When he saw her, he forced a grin.

"Hey, kid."

That bone, so bony-white.

So raw and pure, like sunlight.

He was flat on his back, and men in overalls, men in boots, men of cigarettes, agreed that they shouldn't move him. They formed a scrum and showed respect. At first he wondered if he'd broken his neck, for he couldn't feel his legs.

"Carey," he said.

The sweat.

A rising, wobbling sun.

It rolled down through the straight.

And still, she couldn't stop looking, as she kneeled there, closely, next to him. She watched the blood and dirt, merged like traffic on his lips. It caked his jeans and flannel shirt. It caught the zipper down his vest. There was a wildness clawing out of him.

"Carey," he said again, but this time he followed with something else. "Can you go down and scratch my toes?"

Yes, of course.

The delirium.

He thought he was back there, in the halcyon athlete's foot days, and hoped he might distract her. "Never mind the collarbone . . . that itch is Goddamn killing me!"

When he smiled, though, he couldn't hold it.

She went to his boots to loosen them, and now he screamed in pain.

The sun flopped down and swallowed him.

In the hospital, a few days later, a doctor came in on his rounds.

He shook the boys' hands.

He ruffled Carey's hair:

A tangled, boyish auburn thing.

The light was collarbone-white.

After he'd checked on Ted's progress, the doctor looked amiably at the children.

"And what are you three going to be when you grow up?" he asked, but the boys didn't even get a word in—for it was Carey who looked, it was Carey who grinned, as she squinted through the glare in the window. She pointed, casually over, at her roughed-up trampled-down dad, and already she was on her way:

To here and Clay, and Archer Street.

She said, "I'm gonna be just like him."

the figures in the river

So this is where I washed up—in the trees—on the day beyond Cootamundra.

I stood there, alone in the eucalypts, my feet amongst the bark.

The long belt of sun in front of me.

I heard that single note, and for now I couldn't move. There was music from out of his radio, which meant he didn't know.

I watched them in the riverbed.

I can't even tell you how long—and the bridge, even in pieces, was more beautiful than I could believe.

The arches were going to be glorious.

The curvature of stone.

Just like Pont du Gard, there wouldn't be any mortar; it was fit to exactness and form. It glowed in the open like a church.

I could tell by the way he leaned on it, too, and ran his hand across.

How he spoke to it and fastened it; and fashioned and stood alongside it:

That bridge was made of him.

But by then I had to commit to it.

My station wagon, behind me.

Slowly, I left the trees, I walked out all the way. I stood in the afternoon, and the figures in the river, they stopped. I'll always remember their arms; they were tired but hardened with life.

They looked up, and Clay said, "Matthew?"

And nothing could ever prepare me, as I made my way down toward them. I was nothing but a shell of what I needed to be, for I wasn't expecting this—such buoyancy and life in the tilt of his face—or such a wondrous bridge.

And it was me, not him, who fell down first, my knees in the earth of the riverbed.

"It's Carey," I said. "She's dead."

achilles at four a.m.

What if they hadn't kept the place?

The house at 11 Archer Street.

If only they hadn't come back.

Why didn't they just sell it and move on, instead of prudence, collecting the rent?

But no—I can't go thinking like that.

Once again, I can only tell it.

She arrived at nearly sixteen—to a street of boys and animals, who now included a mule.

In the beginning, it was the night of the day in March, when Clay had run and won State.

It was back at E. S. Marks.

I'd lovingly taped his feet.

The closest kid was a farm boy from Bega.

It took a while to convince Clay to stay.

He didn't want the dais, or the medal; he only wanted Achilles.

He'd broken the state record by just over a second, which they said, at that level, was ludicrous. Officials had shaken his hand. Clay was thinking of Epsom Road.

As we pulled out of the car park, and joined the late-afternoon traffic, he watched me in the rearview, and I looked, briefly, at him. Fair's fair, he seemed to be intimating, the gold medal round Goddamn Rosy. She was panting in Tommy's lap. I glanced back and silently said it:

You're lucky you're refusing to wear it—I'd use it to wring your neck.

Back home we dropped Rory and Henry off.

We also dropped off the dog.

As Tommy got out of the car, Clay put a hand on his arm.

"Tommy, you're coming with us."

When we got there, in the evening, he was waiting at the fence, and he called and cried at the sky. I remembered the ad from the classifieds: *"Doesn't buck,"* I said, *"doesn't bray,"* but Clay had flatly ignored me, and Tommy had fallen in love. The fifth of the undangerous bunch.

This time when we'd stood for a while, the caravan shifted and shook, and a man came pouring outwards. He wore tired old pants and a shirt, and a smile of camaraderie. He walked over as fast as he could, like pushing a lorry with a limp, uphill.

"Are you the bastards who've been feeding *this* miserable old bastard?" he asked, but he was grinning the grin of a kid. Was he the groom Penelope had met that first time, over the fence at 18 Archer Street? We'll never know.

By then the evening was fading.

The man was Malcolm Sweeney.

He had the physique of a dressed-up doughnut.

He'd been a jockey once, then a groom, then a certified stable shit-shoveler. His nose was alcoholic. Despite the boyish outlook, you could swim in the sorrows of his face. He was moving up north, to his sister's.

"Can we let the kid in, to give him a pat?" I asked, and Malcolm Sweeney was happy to oblige. He reminded me of a character in a book I'd once read, called *The Sad Glad Mad Bad Glad Man*—full of kindness but also regret.

"You've seen the *Tribune*?" he said. "And the ad?"

Clay and I nodded, and Tommy was already over there; over and patting his head.

Malcolm spoke again.

"His name's—"

"We don't need to know the name," Clay informed him, but he was watching only Tommy.

I smiled at Malcolm Sweeney, as encouragingly as I could, then motioned across to Clay. "He'll give you two hundred dollars to change it," and I felt myself almost scowling. "But feel free to charge him three."

There was a laugh like something-once-had-been.

"Two hundred," he said, "it is."

At the fence were Clay and Tommy.

"Achilles?" said one to the other.

"Achilles."

At last, they thought, at last.

With Achilles we had to think ahead, though, and there was beauty and stupidity, common sense and pure outlandishness; it's hard to know where to begin.

I looked up council regulations, and there was definitely some sort of bylaw—written in 1946—explaining that livestock could be kept on premises, as long as they were aptly maintained. *The said animals*, it stated, *can in no way infringe upon the health, safety, and well-being of any residents on the property itself, or those bordering the property*—which, reading between the lines, meant keeping whatever you wanted, unless someone else complained. Which brought us to Mrs. Chilman: the only real neighbor we had.

When I went over she invited me in, but we stayed on the afternoon porch. She asked if I could open a jam jar, and when I mentioned the mule, she creaked inwards at first; her wrinkles into her cheeks. Then she laughed from deep in her lungs. "You Dunbar boys are terrific." There were three or four good *marvelouses*, too, and a thrill to her final statement. "Life was always once like this."

And then there was Henry and Rory.

Henry we told from the outset, but with Rory we kept it a secret; his reaction was going to be priceless (and likely the reason I agreed to it). He was already in a constant bad mood because of Hector sleeping on his bed, and sometimes even Rosy, or at least she'd just rest her snout there:

"Oi, Tommy," he'd call across the bedroom, "get this bloody cat off me," and "Tommy, stop Rosy's bloody breathing."

Tommy would try his best. "She's a dog, Rory, she has to breathe."

"Not near *me* she doesn't!"

And so on.

We waited the rest of the week, so we could bring the mule home on Saturday. We could all be there to supervise that way, in case anything went wrong (which it might).

On Thursday we got the supplies. Malcolm Sweeney no longer had a horse trailer, so we'd have to walk him home. The best, we agreed, was early morning (trackwork hour), on Saturday, at four a.m.

The previous Thursday night, though, it was beautiful, it was four of us there with Sweeney, and Rory most likely out drinking. The sky and the clouds were pink, and Malcolm looked lovingly into it.

Tommy was brushing the mane, while Henry appraised the tools. He carried stirrups and bridles toward us, and held them approvingly up. "This shit," he said, "we can do something with . . . but that thing's bloody useless."

He'd jerked his head with a grin at the mule.

And so it was—we brought him home.

On a still morning in late March, four Dunbar boys walked the racing quarter, and between us a Greek-named mule.

He'd stop sometimes by a letterbox.

He'd gangle and crap on the grass.

Henry said, "Got any dog bags?"

All of us laughed on the footpath.

What always gets me hardest is the memory of Malcolm Sweeney, crying silently by his fence line, as we walked the mule slowly away. He'd wiped at the yeast of his cheeks, and ran a hand through his frosted hair. He was moist and the color of khaki; a sad old fat man, and beautiful.

And then just simply the sound of it:

The hooves clopping over the streets.

Everything around us was urban—the road, the streetlights, the traffic; the shouts that flew right past us, from revelers out all night—and between it the rhythm of mules' feet, as we walked him over pedestrian crossings, and crossed the empty Kingsway. We negotiated one long footbridge, and the patches of dark and streetlights:

Henry and me on one side.

Tommy and Clay on the other.

And you could set your watch to those hoofbeats, too, and your life to the hand of Tommy—as he led the mule fondly home, to the months and the girl to come.

two treasure chests

So this is what happened:

They'd broken the unwritten rules.

There was the feel of her naked legs.

He remembered the laid-down length of her, and the plastic mound beside them; and how she moved and gently bit him. And the way she'd pulled him down.

"Come here, Clay."

He remembered.

"Use your teeth. Don't be scared. It won't hurt me."

He remembered how at just past three a.m. they left, and at home, Clay lay awake, then headed for Central Station.

Back to the bridge and Silver.

Carey, of course, went to trackwork, where in the dawn, the old stager, War of the Roses, returned from the inside training track—but returned without his rider.

She'd fallen on the back straight.

The sun was cold and pallid.

The sky of the city was quiet.

The girl lay face turned sideways, and everyone started running.

At the Amahnu, in Silver, when I told him, Clay broke wildly away. He ran raggedly up the river.

God, the light here was so long, and I watched him clear to the tree line, till he vanished into the stones.

My father looked at me numbly; so sad but also lovingly.

When he attempted to follow, I touched him.

I touched and I held his arm.

"No," I said, "we should trust him."

The Murderer became the Murdered. "What if—"

"No."

I didn't know all I needed to know, but with Clay I was sure of his choices; right now he would choose to suffer.

We agreed we should wait an hour.

In the trees up high in the riverbed, he kneeled against its steepness—his lungs two treasure chests of death.

He wept there, uncontrollably.

That thing he heard outside himself, at last, he could tell, was his voice.

The trees, those stones, the insects:

Everything slowed, then stopped.

He thought of McAndrew, and Catherine. Trackwork Ted. He knew he would have to tell them. He'd confess it was all his fault—because girls just didn't disappear like this, they didn't fail without someone making them. Carey Novacs didn't just die, it was boys like him who made them.

He thought of the fifteen freckles.

The shapes and glimpse of sea glass.

A sixteenth one on her neck.

She'd talked to him; she knew him. She'd linked her arm through his. And sometimes she'd called him an idiot . . . and he remembered that slight smell of sweat, and the itch of her hair on his throat—her taste was still in his mouth. He knew that if he searched himself, down near the bone of his hip, her imprint was bitten, and visible; it remained as a hidden reminder, of someone, and something, outlived.

The clear-eyed Carey was dead.

* * *

As the air grew cool, and Clay felt cold, he prayed for rain and violence.

The drowning of the steep Amahnu.

But the dry and its quietness held him, and he kneeled like just more debris; like a boy washed up, upstream.

the arguments

You had to give it to the young Carey Novac.

She had a healthy sense of resolve.

Despite her mum and dad resigning themselves to the fact that their sons would be jockeys, they denied the ambition in her. When she talked about it, they only said, "No." In no uncertain terms.

In spite of this, when she was eleven years old, she started writing letters to a particular horse trainer, in the city, at least two or three times a month. At first she was asking for information, on how best to become a jockey, even if she already knew. How could she start training up early? How could she better prepare? She signed the letters as *Kelly from the Country*, and waited patiently for answers, using the house of a friend in Carradale (a neighboring town) as the sender.

Soon enough, the phone rang, at Harvey Street, in Calamia.

About halfway through the call, Ted stopped and simply said, "*What?*" A moment later, he went on. "Yeah, it's the next town over." Then, "Really? *Kelly from the Country*? You've gotta be joking. Oh, it's bloody her all right, I'm sure of it. . . ."

Shit, thought the girl in the lounge room, listening in.

She was halfway down the hall, making her escape, when the voice came calling through her.

"Oi, Kelly," he said, "not so fast."

But she could tell her dad was smiling.

That meant she had a chance.

* * *

In the meantime, weeks became months and years.

She was a kid who knew what she wanted.

She was hopeful and perennial.

She ate work up at Gallery Road—a skinny-armed talented shit-shoveler—but she also looked good in the saddle.

"Good as any kid I've ever seen," admitted Ted.

Catherine wasn't overly impressed.

Neither was Ennis McAndrew.

Yes, Ennis.

Mr. McAndrew.

Ennis McAndrew had rules.

First, he made apprentices wait; you never rode your first year, ever, and that was if he took you in the first place. He naturally cared about riding ability, but he also read your school reports, and especially all the comments. If *easily distracted* was written just once, you could forget it. Even when he accepted your application, he'd have you come to the stables early morning, three out of six days a week. You could shovel, and lead rope. You could watch. But never, under any circumstance, could you talk. You could write your questions down, or remember them and ask on Sundays. On Saturdays you could come to race meetings. Again, no talking. He knew you were there if he *wanted* to know you were there. Very factually, it was stated you should stay with your family, go with your friends—because from second year on you'd hardly see them.

On the alternate days of the week, you could sleep in—that was, you could report to the Tri-Colors Boxing Gym at five-thirty, to run roadwork with all the boxers. If you missed one, the old man would know—he'd know.

But still.

He'd never been set upon like this.

At fourteen she started up the letters again, this time from Carey Novac. *Kelly from the Country* was gone. She apologized for the error of judgment, and hoped it hadn't blighted thoughts on her character. She was aware of everything—his laws of an apprenticeship—and she would do whatever it took; she'd muck the stables out nonstop if she had to.

Finally, a letter came back.

In Ennis McAndrew's tight-scrawled hand was the inevitable, identical phrasing:

Permission from your mother.

Permission from your father.

And that was her biggest problem.

Her parents were resolved as well:

The answer was still firmly no.

She would never become a jockey.

As far as Carey was concerned, it was a disgrace.

Sure, fine, it was perfectly acceptable for her miscreant brothers to be jockeys—and average, lazy ones at that—but not for her. Once she even pulled a framed photo of The Spaniard off the lounge room wall, and threw herself into her argument:

"McAndrew's even got a horse from the bloodline of *this* one."

"What?"

"Don't you read the paper?"

And then:

"How could you have had this yourself and not let me? Look at him!" Her freckles were blazing. Her hair, tangled. "Don't you remember what it was like? Hitting the turn? Taking the straight?"

Rather than hang it on the wall again, she slammed it to the coffee table, and the impact cracked the glass.

"You can pay for that," he said, and it was lucky the frame was a cheap one.

But never as lucky (or *unlucky*, as some would argue) as this—

As they both kneeled down and cleaned up the glass, he spoke absently into the floorboards.

"Of course I read the paper—the horse's name is Matador."

* * *

Eventually, Catherine slapped her.

It's funny what a slap can do:

Her water-color eyes were that little bit brighter—unmanaged, alive with anger. Her hair was lifted, just a few strands, and Ted was alone in the doorway.

"You really shouldn't have done that."

He was talking and pointing at Carey.

But then the fact of something else.

Catherine only slapped you when you'd won.

This is what Carey had done:

One of the best old childhood chestnuts.

School holidays.

She'd left in the morning and was supposedly staying the night at Kelly Entwistle's house, but caught a train to the city instead. Late afternoon, she stood for close to an hour, outside the McAndrew Stables; the small office in need of a paint job. When finally she could loiter no longer, she walked in and faced the desk. McAndrew's wife was behind it. She was in the midst of a mathematical working-out, and chewing a ball of gum.

"Excuse me?" Carey asked, outrageously jittery and quiet. "I'm after Mr. Ennis?"

The woman looked at her; she was permed and Stimoroled, then curious. "I think you might mean McAndrew."

"Oh yeah, sorry." She half smiled. "I'm a bit nervous," and now the woman noticed; she'd reached up and lowered her glasses. In one motion she'd gone from clueless to all summed up.

"You wouldn't be old Trackwork Ted's daughter, would you?"

Shit!

"Yes, Miss."

"Your mum and dad know you're here?"

Carey's hair was in a braid, wired tautly down her head. "No, Miss."

There was almost remorse, almost regret. “Good lord, girl, did you get here on your own?”

“Yes, I got the train. And the bus.” She almost started babbling. “Well, I got the wrong bus the first time.” She controlled it. “Mrs. McAndrew, I’m looking for a job.”

And there, right there, she had her.

She’d stuck a pen in the curls of her hair.

“How old are you again?”

“Fourteen.”

The woman laughed and sniffed.

Sometimes she heard them talking at night, in the confines of the kitchen.

Ted and Catherine.

Catherine the Great and Belligerent.

“Look,” said Ted. “If she’s going to do it, Ennis is the best. He’ll look after her. He doesn’t even let ’em live in the stables—they have to have proper homes.”

“What a guy.”

“Hey—be careful.”

“Okay,” but she was hardly softening. “You know it’s not him, it’s the game.”

Carey stood in the hallway.

Pajamas of shorts and singlet.

Warm and sticky feet.

Her toes in the streak of light.

“Oh, you and the bloody game,” said Ted. He got up and walked to the sink. “The game gave me everything.”

“Yeah.” Sincere damnation. “Ulcers, collapsing. How many broken bones?”

“Don’t forget the athlete’s foot.”

He was trying to lighten the mood.

It didn’t work.

She went on, the damnation went on, it darkened the girl in the hall.

"That's our *daughter* in there, and I want her to live—not go through the hell that you did, or what the boys will. . . ."

Sometimes they rumble through me, those words, and they're hot, like the hooves of Thoroughbreds:

I want her to live.

I want her to live.

Carey had told Clay that once; she'd told him one night at The Surrounds.

And Catherine the Great was right.

She was right about all of everything.

the bike combination

We found him upstream where the river gums start.

What could we possibly say?

Michael mostly stood with him; he put his hand on him very gently, till we quietly made our way down.

I stayed the night, I had to.

Clay made me sleep in his bed, while he sat propped against the wall. Six times I woke in the night, and Clay had remained quite upright.

By the seventh he'd finally fallen.

He was sideways, asleep on the floor.

Next morning, he took only the contents of his pocket:

The feel of a fading peg.

On the drive home, he sat beside me very straightly. He kept looking into the rearview, expecting to almost see her.

At one point he said, "Pull over."

He thought he might throw up, but he was just cold, so cold, and he thought she might catch up, but he sat by the roadside alone.

"Clay?"

I said it close to a dozen times.

We walked back to the car and drove on.

* * *

The newspapers talked about one of the best young jockey prospects in decades. They talked of old Mr. McAndrew, who, in the pictures, was a broken broomstick. They talked about a family of jockeys, and how her mother had wanted to stop her—to forbid her from joining the game. Her brothers would come from the country, to make it in time for the funeral.

They spoke of ninety percent:

Ninety percent of jockeys are injured every year.

They talked about a tough business, predominantly flimsy pay, and one of the most dangerous jobs in the world.

But what about what they *didn't* say in the papers?

The papers didn't talk about the sun when first they'd spoken—so near, and huge, beside her. Or its glowing of light on her forearms. They didn't mention the sound of her footsteps, when she came to The Surrounds, and the way she rustled closer. They didn't mention *The Quarryman*, and how she would read and always return it. Or how she'd loved his broken nose. What good were newspapers anyway?

On top of everything else, they didn't mention if there was an autopsy, or if the previous night was upon her; they were certain it was instant. Taken, like that, so quickly.

McAndrew was retiring.

They claimed it wasn't his fault, and they were right; it was the game and these things happened, and his care for his jockeys was exemplary.

They all said it, but he needed a rest.

Much like Catherine Novac, way back from the start, the horse protectionists called it tragic, but so was the death of horses—overrun and overbred. The game was killing all of them, they said.

But Clay knew the answer was him.

At home, when we arrived, we sat in the car a long time.

We turned into our father, after Penny died.

Just sitting. Just staring.

Even if there *had* been Tic Tacs or Anticols, I'm sure we wouldn't have eaten them.

Clay thought it, over and again:

It wasn't the game, it was me, it was me.

And credit to the rest of them, they came.

They came and sat in the car with us, and at first all they said was "Hi, Clay." Tommy, as the youngest and greenest, tried to talk about the good things, like the day she came and met us—in waters still to come—and how she'd walked right through the house.

"Remember that, Clay?"

Clay said nothing.

"Remember when she met Achilles?"

This time he didn't run anymore, he only walked the maze of suburbs; the streets and fields of the racing quarter.

He didn't eat, and didn't sleep, and couldn't shake that feeling of seeing her. She was a girl at the edge of everything.

As for the rest of us, it was so clear how hard it had hit him, but we barely knew the half of it—and how could we understand? We didn't know that they met at The Surrounds. We didn't know about the night before, or the lighter, or *Kingston Town* or *Matador*, or *Carey Novac in the eighth*. Or the bed we'd failed to burn.

When our father called us up, a few nights in a row, Clay just shook his head at me. I said we'd take good care of him.

And the funeral?

It could only be one of those bright-lit things, even if they held it indoors.

The church was totally packed.

People came out of the woodwork, from racing identities to radio hosts. Everyone wanted to know her. So many knew her best.

No one even saw us.

They didn't hear his countless confessions.

We were buried down deep in the back.

For a long time, he couldn't face it.

He would never go back to the bridge.

What he did was feign alrightness:

He came to work with me.

When our father called, he talked to him.

He was the perfect teenage charlatan.

In the night, he watched the house diagonally across the street, and the shadows moving within. He wondered where the lighter was. Had she left it under her bed? Was it still in the old wooden box down there, with the letter folded within?

There was no sitting on the roof, not anymore—only the front porch, and not sitting, but standing, leaning forward.

One evening he walked to Hennessey, the grandstands gaping casually.

A small crowd was by the stables.

They gathered at the fence.

Grooms and apprentice jockeys all bent down, and for twenty minutes, he watched them, and when they'd dispersed he came to realize; they were trying to free her bike.

Despite every internal talking-to, and the desolate void in his stomach, he found himself gently crouching, and touching the four-digit gauge—and he knew the number instantly. She'd have gone right back to the start of things, and the horse and the Cox Plate without him:

Out of thirty-five races, The Spaniard won twenty-seven.

It was 3527.

The lock came out so easily.

He pushed it back in and muddled it.

The grandstands felt much closer then; both open in the darkness.

the breakup artist

In many ways it feels ridiculous, almost trivial—to come back to 18 Archer Street, in the time before her arrival. If there's one thing I've come to learn, though, it's that if life goes on in our aftermaths, it goes on in our worlds before it.

It was a period when all was changing.

A kind of preparation.

His before the beginning of Carey.

It starts, as it must, with Achilles.

To be honest, I might not have been too impressed with that dubious two hundred bucks we spent, but there was one part I'll always cherish; it was Rory at the kitchen window, the morning we'd brought him home.

As was common for a Saturday, he staggered through the hallway around eleven, then thought he was still drunk, and dreaming.

Is that?

(He shook his head.)

What the hell?

(He wrung his eyes out.)

Until finally he shouted behind him:

"Oi, Tommy, what's goin' on 'ere?"

"What?"

"What-a-y' mean *what*, are you shitting me? There's a donkey in the backyard!"

"He's not a donkey, he's a mule."

The query was stuck to his beer breath. "What's the difference?"

"A donkey's a donkey, a mule's a cross between—"

"I don't care if it's a quarter horse crossed with a Shetland bloody pony! . . ."

Behind them, we were in stitches, till Henry eventually settled it. "Rory," he said, "meet Achilles."

By the end of the day he'd forgiven us—or at least enough to stay in. Or at least to stay in and complain.

In the evening we were all out back together, even Mrs. Chilman, and Tommy was going, "Hey, boy, hey, boy," in the most loving voice you can imagine, and patting the scruff of his coat. The mule stood calmly eyeing him, while Rory was grumbling to Henry.

"Next he's gonna take the bastard out to dinner, for Christ's sake."

In the night he lay smothered by Hector, and Rosy lay lightly snoring. From the left-hand bed you could hear it—an anguished but quiet muttering. "These animals are Goddamn killing me."

In his running, I thought Clay might have lessened, or loosened, now that State was over, and the mule was in our keeping. I couldn't have been more mistaken. If anything he was running harder, which somehow seemed to bother me.

"Why don't you take a break?" I said. "You just won State, for God's sake."

He stared down the rest of Archer Street.

All that time and I'd never noticed it.

That morning was no exception:

It burned inside his pocket.

"Hey, Matthew," he said, "you coming?"

By April, the problems started.

The mule was enigmatic.

Or more so, purely stubborn.

He did love Tommy, I'm sure of it; he just happened to love Clay more. It was Clay he let check his feet. No one else could budge them. It was Clay, alone, who could quiet him.

A few nights in particular, very late, early morning, Achilles would bray up a storm. Even now I hear those sad-but-terrifying *eey-ores*—a mule-and-hinge-like crying—and between them, the other voices. There was Henry shouting "Shit, Tommy!" and me saying "Shut that mule up!" There was Rory calling "Get this fucking cat off me!" and Clay, just lying, silent.

"Clay! Wake *up*!"

Tommy was frantically pushing him, pulling him, till soon he got to his feet; he made his way to the kitchen. Through the window he saw Achilles, and the mule was under the clothesline; he cried like a rusty gate. He stood and reached his head up, his mouth thrown into the sky.

Clay watched, he couldn't move; for a while he remained transfixed. But then Tommy had waited enough. As the rest of us surfaced, and the mule howled out and onwards, it was Clay who handled the sugar. He took the lid off, and the stuck-in spoon, and walked out back with Tommy.

"Here," he said firmly, "cup them," as they stood on the porch by the couch. It was dark but for mule and moonlight, and Tommy produced both palms.

"Okay," he said, "I'm ready," and Clay poured all of it out, a handful, a sandful, I'd seen it once before; and Achilles, he'd seen it, too. For a moment, he stopped, he looked at them, and he ambled his way across. Pigheaded and clearly delighted.

Hey, Achilles.

Hi, Clay.

That's quite a noise you're making there.

I know.

When Tommy met him, he held out his hands, and Achilles got in and sucked them—he hoovered into every corner.

The last time it happened was in May, and Tommy was finally resigned. He'd looked after every animal, all of them the same, and for Achilles we'd bought more grain, more hay, and cleaned the racing quarter out of carrots. When Rory asked who'd eaten the last apple, he knew it had gone to the mule.

On this occasion, a midnight southerly; it blew through the streets and suburbs. It brought with it sound from the trains. I'm sure that's what set him going, actually, and the mule just couldn't be quieted. Even when Tommy ran out to him, Achilles only shook him off; he brayed onwards at forty-five degrees, and above them, the clothesline spun.

"The sugar bowl?" Tommy asked Clay.

But that night he'd told him no.

Not yet.

No, this time, Clay walked down, and a peg was against his thigh, and all he did first was stand with him, then stretched, very slowly, upwards; he halted the turning clothesline. With his other hand, he reached even slower, and placed it on the face of the mule, on that dry and crackly brushland.

"It's okay," he told him, "it's over—" but Clay knew better than anyone; there are some things that never stop. Even when Tommy ignored him, and came back out with the sugar bowl, and Achilles hoovered it up—the crystals around his nostrils—the mule was watching Clay.

Could he see the outline of his pocket?

Maybe, probably not.

One thing I know for certain, though, is that the mule was nowhere near stupid—Achilles always knew.

He knew that this was the Dunbar boy.

This was the one he needed.

We ran a lot in that time to the cemetery, up, and in, at winter.

The mornings were getting much darker.

The sun climbed onto our backs.

Once, we ran to Epsom, and Sweeney was a man of his word:

The caravan was gone, but the shack went dying on.

We smiled and Clay said, "Enyone."

Then June, and seriously, I think Achilles was more intelligent than Rory, because Rory was again suspended. He edged his way closer to expulsion; his ambitions were being rewarded.

I met again with Claudia Kirkby.

This time her hair was shorter, just noticeably, and she wore a beautiful pair of earrings, formed into lightweight arrows. They were silver, slightly hanging. There were papers all strewn on her desk, and the posters remained intact.

The trouble, this time, was that a new teacher had arrived—another young woman—and Rory had made an example of her.

"Well, apparently," explained Ms. Kirkby, "he was swiping grapes from Joe Leonello's lunch, and lobbing them at the whiteboard. She was hit when she stopped and turned. It went down the front of her shirt."

Already, her grasp of poetry.

I stood, I closed my eyes.

"Look, honestly," she went on, "I think the teacher may have overreacted a little, but we just can't keep putting up with it."

"She had a right to be upset," I said, but soon I started to flounder. I was lost in the cream of *her* shirt, and the way it had waves and ripples. "I mean, what are the odds?" Could a shirt be somehow tidal? "Turning around at that exact moment—" It jumped from my mouth and I knew it. What a mistake!

"Are you saying it was *her* fault?"

"No! I—"

She was giving me a hiding!

She was holding those papers now. She smiled gently, reassuringly. "Matthew, it's okay. I know you didn't mean it that way—"

I sat on a graffitied desk.

The usual teenage subtlety:

A deskful of Goddamn penises.

How could I possibly resist?

It was then she stopped talking and took a silent, brazen risk—and it was *that* that I first fell in love with.

She laid her palm down on my arm.

Her hand was warm and slim.

"To tell you the truth," she said, "so much worse happens here every day, but with Rory, it's one more thing." She was on our side, she was showing me. "It's not an excuse, but he's hurting—and he's a boy," and she killed me, like this, in an instant. "Am I right, or am I right?"

All she'd had to do was wink at me then, but she didn't, for which I was grateful—for she'd quoted something word for word, and soon she'd stepped away. She sat now herself, on a desk.

I had to give something back.

I said, "You know," and it hurt to swallow. The waters now still in her shirt. "The last person who ever told me that was our dad."

In the running, something was coming.

Something sad, but mainly for me.

Through winter, we stayed consistent; we ran Bernborough, we ran the streets, and me then to coffee and kitchen, and Clay gone up to the roof.

When I timed him, the problem was awkward.

The runner's most dreaded dilemma:

He ran harder, but wasn't getting faster.

We thought it was lack of adrenaline; motivation was suddenly thin. What else could he do but win State? The athletics season was still months away; no wonder he was feeling lethargic.

Clay, though, wasn't buying it.

At his side, I talked him on.

"Up," I said, "up. Come on, Clay. What would Liddell do, or Budd?"

I should have known I was being too nice to him.

When Rory was suspended that last time, I had him come to the job with me; I fixed it with the boss. Three days' worth of carpet and floorboards, and one thing was certainly clear—he wasn't allergic to work. He seemed disappointed when each day ended; and then he left school, it was final. I ended up almost begging them.

We sat in the principal's office.

He'd snuck in and stolen the sandwich press from the science staff room. "They eat too much in there, anyway!" he'd explained. "I was doing 'em a bloody favor!"

Rory and I were on one side of the desk.

Claudia Kirkby, Mrs. Holland, the other.

Ms. Kirkby was in a dark suit and light blue shirt, Mrs. Holland, I can't remember. What I do remember is her silver, sort of slicked-back hair, the softness of her crow's feet, and the brooch on the pocket, on her left; it was a flannel flower, the school's emblem.

"Well?" I said.

"Well, um, what?" she asked.

(Not the answer I was expecting.)

"Is he getting kicked out for good this time?"

"Well, I'm, um, not sure if that's—"

I cut her off. "Let's face it, he bloody deserves it."

Rory ignited, almost with joy. "I'm sitting right here!"

"Look at him," I said. They looked. "Shirt out, sneer on. Does he look like he cares even remotely about this? Does he look repentant—"

"Remotely?" Now it was Rory who interjected. "Repentant? Shit, Matthew, give us the dictionary, why don't you?"

Holland knew. She knew I wasn't stupid. "To be honest, um, we could have used you last year in our, um, year twelve cohort, Matthew. You never looked that interested, but you were, weren't you?"

"Hey, I thought we were talking about me."

"Shut up, Rory." That was Claudia Kirkby.

"There, that's better," replied Rory. "Firm." He was looking firmly somewhere else. She hugged her suit jacket a little tighter.

"Stop that," I said.

"*What?*"

"You know." But now I was back onto Holland. It was afternoon and I'd come home from work early to be well-dressed and clean-shaven, but that didn't mean I wasn't tired. "If you don't expel him this time, I'm going to jump over this desk, rip off that principal's badge, pin it on me, and expel the bastard myself!"

Rory was so excited he almost clapped.

Claudia Kirkby somberly nodded.

The principal felt for the badge. "Well, I'm, um, not so sure—"

"Do it!" cried Rory.

And to everyone's surprise, she did.

She methodically did the paperwork, and suggested surrounding schools, but I said we didn't need them, he was going to work, and we shook hands and that was it; we left them both behind us.

Halfway to the car park, I ran back. Was it for us, or Claudia Kirkby? I knocked on the door, I reentered the room, and they were both inside, still talking.

I said, "Ms. Kirkby, Mrs. Holland, I apologize. I'm sorry for your trouble, and just—thanks." It was crazy, but I started sweating. It was the truly sympathetic look on her face, I think, and the suit, and the gold-colored earrings. The small hoops that circled a glint there. "And also—and sorry to ask this now, but I've always been caught up with Rory—so I've never asked how Henry and Clay are doing."

Mrs. Holland deferred to Ms. Kirkby.

"They're doing fine, Matthew." She'd stood up. "They're good kids," and she smiled and didn't wink.

"Believe it or not," and I nodded to the doorway, "so's that one out there."

"I know."

I know.

She said I know, and it stayed with me a long time, but it started outside at the wall. For a while I hoped she'd come out, as I leaned, half bruising my shoulder blades, but there was only the voice of Rory.

"Oi," he said, "you coming?"

At the car he asked, "Can I drive?"

I said, "Don't even Goddamn think about it."

He got a job by the end of the week.

* * *

And so winter turned into spring.

Clay's times were still much slower, and it happened, a Sunday morning.

Since Rory got his job as a panel beater, he worked hard at the trade of drinking. He started taking up and breaking up with girls. There were names and observations; one I remember was Pam, and Pam was blond hair and bad breath.

"Shit," said Henry, "did you tell her that?"

"Yeah," said Rory, "she slapped me. Then dumped me and asked for a mint. Not necessarily in that order."

He would stumble back home in the mornings—and the Sunday was mid-October. As Clay and I headed for Bernborough, Rory was staggering in.

"Jesus, look at the state of *you*."

"Yeah, good one, Matthew, thanks. Where are you two bastards going?"

Typical Rory:

In jeans and a beer-soaked jacket, he had no problems staying with us—and Bernborough was typical, too.

The sunrise looted the grandstand.

We did the first 400 together.

I told Clay, "Eric Liddell."

Rory grinned.

It was more like a dirty smirk.

On the second lap he entered the jungle.

He had to take a leak.

By the fourth he'd gone to sleep.

Before the last 400, though, Rory seemed nearer to sober. He looked at Clay, he looked at me. He shook his head in contempt.

On the fiery hue of the track, I said, "What's the matter with you?"

Again, that smirky smile.

"You're wrong," he said, and he glanced at Clay, but the assault was aimed at me. "Matthew," he said, "you're kidding, aren't you? You *must* know why it's not happening." He looked ready to come and shake me. "Come on,

Matthew, *think*. All that nice romantic shit. He won State—so fucking what? He couldn't care any less."

But how could this be happening?

How could Rory be knowing such perfect things, and altering Dunbar history?

"Look at him!" he said.

I looked.

"He doesn't want *this*—this . . . *goodness*." To Clay now. "Do you want it, kid?"

And Clay had shaken his head.

And Rory didn't relent.

He shoved a hand right into my heart. "He needs to feel it *here*." There was suddenly such gravity, such pain in him, and it came like the force of a piano. The quietest words were the worst. "He needs to hurt nearly enough to kill him," he said, "because that's how we Goddamn *live*."

I worked to make an argument.

Not a single thought came out.

"If you can't do it, I'll do it for you." He breathed stiffly, strugglingly, inwards. "You don't need to be running *with* him, Matthew," and he looked at the boy crouched by me, at the fire inside his eyes. "You have to try and stop him."

That evening Clay had told me.

I was watching *Alien* in the lounge room.

(Talk about suitably grim!)

He said he was grateful and sorry—and I spoke toward the TV. A smile to keep it together.

"At least I can have a rest now—my legs and my back are killing me."

He placed a look down onto my shoulder.

I'd lied; we pretended to believe it.

To the training itself, it was genius:

There were three boys at the 100 mark.

Two at the 200.

Then Rory, the final stretch.

It wasn't hard to find boys who would hurt him, either; he'd come home with groups of bruises, or a burn down the side of his face. They punished him till he was smiling—and that was when training finished.

One night we were in the kitchen.

Clay washed and I dried the plates.

"Hey, Matthew," he said quite quietly. "I'm running tomorrow, at Bernborough—no one stopping me. I'm trying for the time I won State."

And me, I didn't look at him, but I couldn't look somehow away.

"I'm wondering," he said, "if you don't mind," and the look on his face said everything. "I thought maybe you'd tape my feet."

At Bernborough, next morning, I watched.

I sat in the flames of the grandstand.

I'd taped him my very best.

I was somewhere between knowing it was the last time I'd ever do it, and the truth it was also one extra. I could watch in a different way now, too; I saw him run just to see him run. Like Liddell and Budd put together.

As for the time, he broke his best by more than a second, on a track that lay sick and dying. When he crossed the line, Rory was smiling, hands in pockets; Henry shouted the numbers. Tommy ran over with Rosy. All of them hugged and carried him.

"Hey, Matthew!" Henry called. "New State record!"

Rory's hair was wild and rusty.

His eyes the best metal for years.

And me, I walked out of the grandstand, and shook Clay's, then Rory's hand. I said, "Look at the state of *you*," and I meant it, every word. "Best run I've ever seen."

After that he'd crouched and waited, on the track just before the line—so close he could smell the paint. In well past twelve months' time, he'd be back here training with Henry, and the boys and chalk and bets.

For a while there was an eerie quiet, as dawn broke down into day.

On the Tartan, he remained, he felt for it:

The peg, intact, within.

Soon he would stand, soon he would walk, to a clear-eyed sky in front of him.

two front doors

Beyond the bike combination, there were two front doors to negotiate, and the first was Ennis McAndrew's, just outside the racing quarter.

The house was one of the bigger ones.

It was old and beautiful, tin-roofed.

A giant wooden veranda.

Clay did laps around the block.

There were camellias in all the front yards around there, a few enormous magnolias. Many old-fashioned letterboxes. Rory would certainly have approved.

He didn't count how many times he walked that block—walking just like Penny had once, like Michael had—to a certain front door in the night.

This door was a heavy red one.

At times he could see the brushstrokes.

Those other front doors got glorious.

Clay knew that his one wouldn't.

Then the second front door:

Diagonally down on Archer Street.

Ted and Catherine Novac.

He watched it from the porch, and weeks were molded from days, as Clay came to work with me. There was no return to Bernborough yet, no cemetery, no roof. Certainly not The Surrounds. He dragged the guilt behind him.

At one point I buckled; I asked if he'd return to the bridge, and Clay could only shrug.

I know—I'd beaten him up once, for leaving.

But it was clear he had to finish.

No one could live like this.

Finally, he did it, he traversed the McAndrew steps.

An old lady answered the door.

She had permed and colored hair—and me, I disagree with him, for this door, it *did* get glorious, and it was all in the showing up for it.

"Can I help you?"

And Clay, at his very worst, and very best, said, "I'm sorry to bother you, Mrs. McAndrew, but if you don't mind, is there a chance I could talk to your husband? My name's Clay Dunbar."

The old man in the house knew the name.

At the Novacs' place, they knew him, too, but as the boy they'd seen on the roof.

"Come in," they said, and they were both so maddeningly sweet to him; so kind to him it hurt. They made tea, and Ted shook his hand, and asked how he was. And Catherine Novac smiled, and it was a smile to keep from dying, or crying, or maybe both; he couldn't quite decide.

Either way, when he told them, he made sure not to look where she'd sat that day, when they'd listened to the race down south—when the big bay horse had failed. His tea was cold and untouched.

He told them what Saturday night meant.

The mattress, the plastic sheet.

He told them of *Matador in the fifth*.

He said he loved her from the very first time she'd talked to him, and it was his fault, it was all his fault. Clay cracked, but didn't break, because he deserved no tears or sympathy. "The night before she fell," he said, "we met there, we were naked there, and—"

He stopped because Catherine Novac—in a shift of ginger-blondness—

had stood and she'd walked toward him. She lifted him gently out of his chair and hugged him hard, so hard, and she patted his short flat hair, and it was so damn nice it hurt.

She said, "You came to us, you came."

See, for Ted and Catherine Novac, there was no incrimination, at least not for this poor boy.

It was they who brought her to the city.

It was they who knew the risk.

Then there was McAndrew.

Picture frames with horses.

Picture frames with jockeys.

The light inside was orange.

"I know you," he said, and the man himself looked smaller now, like a broken twig in a lounge chair. In the very next chapter you'll see it back there—what Ennis McAndrew once explained. "You're the dead wood I told her to cut out." His hair was yellow-white. He wore glasses. A pen in his pocket. The eyes gleamed, but not very happily. "I guess you've come to blame me, have you?"

Clay sat on the lounge chair opposite.

He watched him, stiffly straight.

"No, sir, I came to tell you you were right," and McAndrew was caught by surprise.

He looked keenly across, and said, "What?"

"Sir, I—"

"Call me Ennis, for Christ's sake, and speak up."

"Okay, well . . ."

"I said speak *up*."

Clay swallowed. "It wasn't your fault, it was mine."

He didn't tell him what he told the Novacs, but made sure McAndrew saw. "She never could quite get rid of me, you know, and that was how it happened. She must have been overtired, or couldn't concentrate—"

McAndrew slowly nodded. "She lost herself, in the saddle."

"Yes. I think she did."

"You were out with her the previous night."

"Yes," Clay said, and he left.

He left, but at the bottom of the steps, both Ennis and his wife came out, and the old man shouted down to him.

"Hey! Clay Dunbar!"

Clay turned.

"You have no idea what I've seen jockeys get up to over the years, and they did it"—he was suddenly so empathetic—"for things worth much less than you." He even came down the steps; he met him at the gate. He said, "Listen to me, son." For the first time, Clay noticed a silver tooth in McAndrew's mouth, deep and leaning on the right. "I can't imagine what it took to come and tell me that."

"Thank you, sir."

"Come back in, won't you?"

"I'd better get home."

"Okay, but if there's ever anything—anything—I can do for you, let me know."

"Mr. McAndrew?"

Now the old man stopped, and the paper was under his arm. He raised his head just a touch.

Clay nearly asked just how good Carey was, or might have been, but knew that neither of them could bear it—so he tried for something else. "Could you carry on training?" he asked. "It wouldn't be right if you didn't. It wasn't your—"

And Ennis McAndrew propped, readjusted the paper, and walked back up the path. He said to himself, "Clay Dunbar," but I wish he'd been more obvious.

He should have said something of Phar Lap.

(In waters so soon to come.)

At Ted and Catherine Novac's house, the last could only be finding them:

The lighter, the box and Clay's letter.

They didn't know because they hadn't touched her bed yet, and it lay on the floor, beneath.

Matador in the fifth.

Carey Novac in the eighth.

Kingston Town can't win.

Ted touched the words.

For Clay, though, what puzzled him most, and ultimately gave him *something*, was the second of two more items now that lay inside the box. The first was the photo his father had sent, of the boy on top of the bridge—but the second he'd never given her; it was something she'd actually stolen, and he would never know exactly when.

It was pale but green and elongated.

She'd been here, 18 Archer Street.

She'd stolen a Goddamn peg.

six hanleys

For Ted and Catherine Novac, the choice would make itself. If she wasn't apprenticed to McAndrew, it would only be someone else; it might as well be the best.

When they told her, there was kitchen and coffee cups.

The clock ticked loudly behind them.

The girl stared down and smiled.

She was pretty much sixteen, early December, when she stood on a lawn in the city, in the racing quarter, with the toaster plug at her feet. She stopped, looked harder, and spoke.

"Look," she said, "up there. . . ."

The next time, of course, was evening, when she came across the road.

"And? You don't want to know *my* name?"

The third was a Tuesday, at dawn.

Her apprenticeship didn't start till the beginning of next year, but she was already running with the Tri-Colors boys, weeks earlier than instructed by McAndrew.

"Jockeys and boxers," he was known to say, "they're almost the bloody same." Both had obsessions with weight. Both had to fight to survive; and there was danger, and death, close at hand.

That Tuesday, mid-December, she was running with those lake-necked boxers. Her hair was out—she almost always wore it out—and she fought to hold ground behind them. They came down Poseidon Road. There were the usual fumes, of baking bread and metalworks, and at the corner of Nightmarch Avenue, it was Clay who first saw her. At that time he trained alone. He'd quit the athletics club altogether. She was in shorts and a sleeveless T-shirt. When she looked up, she saw him see her.

Her T-shirt was faded blue.

Her shorts were cut from jeans.

For a moment she turned and watched him.

"Hey, boy!" called one of the boxers.

"Hey, boys," but quiet, to Carey.

The next time he was on the roof, it was warm and close to darkness, and he climbed back down to meet her; she was standing alone on the footpath.

"Hey, Carey."

"Hi, Clay Dunbar."

The air twitched.

"You know my last name?"

Again, he noted the teeth of her; the not-quite-straight and sea glass.

"Oh yeah, people know you Dunbar boys, you know." She almost laughed. "Is it true you're harboring a mule?"

"Harboring?"

"You're not deaf, are you?"

She was giving him a hiding!

But a small one, a happy one, and one he was willing to answer.

"No."

"You're *not* harboring a mule?"

"No," he said, "I'm not deaf—we've had the mule for a while. We've also got a border collie, a cat, a pigeon, and a goldfish."

"A pigeon?"

He struck back. "You're not deaf, are you? He's called Telemachus—our animals have got the worst names you ever heard, except maybe Rosy, or Achilles. Achilles is a beautiful name."

"Is Achilles the name of the mule?"

He nodded; the girl was closer.

She'd turned outwards, toward the suburbs.

Without thought, they both started walking.

When they got to the mouth of Archer Street, Clay looked at her legs in her jeans; he was a boy, after all, he noticed. He also saw the tapering at her ankles, the worn-out sandshoes—the Volleys. He was aware when she moved, of the singlet she wore, and materials he glimpsed beneath.

"It's pretty great," she said at the corner, "to end up living on Archer Street." She was lit by the glow of the streetlight. "First horse who ever won it: the Race That Stops the Nation."

Clay then tried to impress her. "Twice. The first and the second."

It worked, but only to a degree.

"Do you also know who trained him?"

On that one he was no chance.

"De Mestre," she said. "He won five and no one knows it."

From there they walked the racing quarter, down streets all named for Thoroughbreds. Poseidon, the horse, was a champion, and there were shops with names they loved, like the Saddle and Trident Café, the Horse Head Haberdashery, and a clear and present winner—the barbershop: the Racing Quarter Shorter.

Near the end, close to Entreaty Avenue, which led up to the cemetery, there was a small right turn beside them; an alley called Bobby's Lane, where Carey stopped and waited.

"It's perfect," she said, and she leaned on the fence, into its sheet of palings. "They called it Bobby's Lane."

Clay leaned a few meters next to her.

The girl looked into the sky.

"Phar Lap," she said, and when he thought she might be teary, her eyes were giving and green. "And look, it's an alley, not even a street; and they called it after his stable name. How can you not like that?"

For a while there was close to silence, just the air of urban decay. Clay knew, of course, what most of us know, about the iconic horse of our country. He knew about Phar Lap's winning streaks, how the racing board almost crippled him, from the force of too much weight. He knew about America, how he went there, won a race, and died seemingly the very next day. (It was actually just over two weeks.) He loved, like most of us, what people say, for courage, or trying with everything:

You've got a heart as big as Phar Lap.

What he didn't know was what Carey told him that night, as they leaned, in that nondescript laneway.

"You know, when Phar Lap died, the prime minister was Joseph Lyons, and that same day he'd won a high court decision—no one cares anymore about what—and when he came down the court steps and someone asked him about it, he said, 'What good is winning a high court decision when Phar Lap is dead?'" She looked from the ground to Clay. Then the sky. "It's a story I really love," and Clay, he had to ask.

"Do you think he got murdered up there, like people say?"

Carey could only scoff.

"Nah."

Happy but sad as hell, and adamant.

"He was a great horse," she went on, "and the perfect story—we wouldn't love him so much if he'd lived."

From there, they pushed off from the fence, and walked a long way through the racing quarter, from Tulloch, to Carbine, to Bernborough—"They even named the athletics track after a horse!"—and Carey knew every one of them. She could recite each horse's record; she could tell you how many hands they were, or what they weighed, or if they led from the front, or waited. At Peter Pan Square she told him how, at the time, Peter Pan was loved every bit as much as Phar Lap, and he was blond and outrageously bragful. In the empty-cobbled square, she put a hand on the statue's nose, and looked at Darby Munro. She told Clay how this horse had lost a race once, by biting poor old Rogilla, one of his great rivals, as they tussled their way down the straight.

Her favorite race, inevitably, was the Cox Plate (for it was the race that racing purists loved) and she talked of the greats who'd won it: Bonecrusher, Saintly, and colossal Might and Power. The mighty Kingston Town: three years in a row.

Then at last she told him the story, of Ted and the horse, The Spaniard—how he'd smiled and cried, cried and smiled, and they were in the Lonhro Tunnel.

Sometimes I imagine Clay waiting back for a while, as she crossed to the other side. I see the orange lights, I hear the passing trains. There's even a part of me that has him watch her, and sees her body as a brushstroke, her hair an auburn trail.

But then, I stop, I gather myself, and he catches her easily up.

After that, you can probably guess, they were inseparable.

The first time she climbed the roof was also the first time they went to The Surrounds, and the day she'd met the rest of us, and touched the great Achilles.

It was early new year, and her work routine was established.

Ennis McAndrew did it his way, and some trainers called him abnormal. Others said many things worse—they accused him of being *human*. You had to love racing people, you really did; as many of them said themselves: "Us racing crowd, we're different."

She was at Hennessey by four a.m. each day, or the Tri-Colors by five-thirty.

There was horse schooling, and exams, but she couldn't yet contemplate trackwork. The way Ennis put it, in his usual broomstick manner, you couldn't mistake patience for softness, or protection for waiting too long. He had his own theories on training, and when to promote the jockey. Those stables, he said, needed shoveling.

Often, in the evening, they made their way through the racing quarter; they walked to Epsom Road. He said, "This is where we found him. How great was Sweeney's spelling?"

She met Achilles when they got back; he'd brought her quietly through the house. He'd cleared it much earlier with Tommy.

"Was that," said Henry, "a girl?"

They were laid out watching *The Goonies*.

Even Rory was taken aback. "Did a *woman* just walk through our house? What the hell's going on here?"

We all went bounding out back, and the girl, she looked up from the scrubbing brush; she came over, part solemn, part nervous. "I'm sorry I walked straight past you just now." She looked us each in our faces. "It's good to finally meet you," and the mule came hustling between. He arrived like an unwanted relative, and when she stroked him he in-and-awayed. He eyed us with great severity:

Don't any of you bastards interrupt, okay?

This is bloody brilliant.

At The Surrounds there'd been a few changes:

The bed had been broken apart.

The base was stolen and burned; just kids who'd wanted a fire, I guess, which more than suited Clay. The mattress was harder to find. When he got there and stood and stayed silent, the girl asked if she might sit, on the edge.

"Sure," he told her, "of course."

"Do you mean to say," she asked, "that sometimes you come and you sleep here?"

He could have been defensive, but decided with her it was pointless.

"Yeah," he said, "I do," and Carey, she put her hand down, like she could rip a piece off if she wanted. Also, had anyone else said what she was about to say next, it would never have come out correctly:

She looked down at her feet.

She spoke directly into the ground.

"It's the strangest, most beautiful thing I ever heard of," and then, maybe a few minutes later, "Hey—Clay?" He looked over. "What were their names?"

And it felt like such a long time then, both quiet and calm at the mattress edge, and the dark not too far away.

He said, "Penny and Michael Dunbar."

On the roof he showed her where he liked to sit down, part hidden amongst the tiles, and Carey listened and looked at the city. She saw those pinpricks of light.

"Look there," she said, "Bernborough Park."

"And there," he said, he couldn't stop himself, "the cemetery. We can go—if you don't mind, that is. I'll show you the way to the gravestone."

Pulling her into the sadness made him guilty—more guilty than he already was—but Carey was open, oblivious. She'd treated knowing him like some kind of privilege—and she was right to, I'm glad that she did.

There were moments when Clay was torn open—so much he'd kept from the surface. But now it was all flooding outwards; she could see in him what others couldn't.

It happened that night on the roof.

"Hey, Clay?" She looked out at the city. "What have you got there, in your pocket?"

In months ahead, she would push too soon.

At Bernborough, late March, she raced him.

She ran like a girl who could run the 400, and didn't mind suffering for doing it.

He chased her freckly outline.

He watched her bony calves.

Only when they passed the discus net did he come round her, and she said, "Don't you dare take it easy on me," and he didn't. He took the turn and accelerated; at the end they were bent and hurting. Their lungs were sore and hopeful, and did what they were there for:

Two pairs of burning breath.

She looked over and said, "Again?"

"No, I think that one'll do us."

It was the first time she would reach for him, and link her arm through his. If only she'd known how right she was:

"Thank God," she said, "I'm dying."

And then to April, and a race day, which was something she'd been saving.

"Wait'll you see this horse," she said, and she spoke, of course, of Matador.

She loved to watch the bookies and the punters, and those spendthrift men in their fifties: all of them unshaven arse-scratchers, their odor of drunken westerlies. Whole ecosystems in their armpits. She watched them with sadness and affection. . . . The sun was setting around them, in many more ways than one.

Her favorite was standing at the fence, the grandstand at her back, while the horses entered the straight:

The turn was the sound of a landslide.

The calls of desperate men.

"Come on, Gobstopper, you bastard!"

It was always a long wide wave—of cheer and jeer, love and loss, and many open mouthfuls. Weight gain was pumped to its limits, of the shirts and jackets that dammed it. Cigarettes at many angles.

"Move your Goddamn arse, Shenanigans! Go, son!"

The wins were won and worshipped.

The losses were all sat down with.

"C'mon," she said that first time, "there's someone you should meet."

Behind the two grandstands were the stables; a length and breadth of shed rows, and horses all within them—either waiting for their races, or recovering.

At number thirty-eight, he stood enormously, unblinking. A digital sign said *Matador*, but Carey called him Wally. A groom, Petey Simms, wore jeans and a tattered polo shirt, cross-sectioned by a belt. A smoke was erected upwards, at the platform of his lip. He grinned when he saw the girl.

"Hey, Carey kid."

"Hey, Pete."

Clay got a better look now, and the horse was bright chestnut; a white blaze, like a crack, down his face. He flicked the flies off his ears, and he was smooth but rich with veins. His legs, like branches, were locked. The mane was cut back, a little shorter than most, for he somehow attracted more filth than any other horse in the stable. "Even the dirt loves him!" That's what Petey used to say.

Finally, the horse blinked, when Clay came closer, his eyes so big and deep; an equine kind of kind.

"Go on," said Petey, "give the big bugger a pat."

Clay looked at Carey, for permission.

"Go on," she said, "it's okay."

She did it herself first, to show him to be unafraid; even touching him was a front-on tackle.

"Bloody 'orse bloody loves her," said Petey.

It was different from patting Achilles.

"How's the big fella?"

The voice from behind was desert-like.

McAndrew.

Dark suit, pale shirt.

A tie he'd been wearing since the Bronze Age.

Petey didn't answer, though, because he knew the old man didn't want one; he was talking only to himself. He wandered in and ran his hands along the horse, he went lower for a look at the hooves.

"Spot-on."

He stood and watched Carey, then Clay.

"Who the hell is this?"

The girl was sweet but defiant.

"Mr. McAndrew, this is Clay Dunbar."

McAndrew smiled, a scarecrow smile, but something nonetheless. "Well," he said, "enjoy yourselves, kids, because this right here is it. Next year—" and he spoke more gravely now, and motioned to Carey, about Clay. "Next year he gets the chop. You have to cut the dead wood out."

Clay would never forget.

The race that day was a Group Two called the Plymouth. For most horses, a Group Two race was massive; for Matador it was only a warm-up. His odds were 2-1.

His colors were black and gold.

Black silks. Gold arms.

Carey and Clay sat in the stand, the first time all day she'd been nervous. When the jockey was aboard, she looked down into the mounting yard, and saw Petey waving her toward him—he was standing with McAndrew, at the fence—and they made their way through the crowd. When the gates opened, Clay watched, and McAndrew wrung his hands. He looked at his shoes and spoke.

"Where?" he said, and Petey answered.

"Third last."

"Good." Next question. "Leader?"

"Kansas City."

"Shit! That plodder. That means it's slow."

Now the announcer confirmed it:

"Kansas City from Glass Half Full and a length to Woodwork Blue . . ."

Now McAndrew again. "How's he look?"

"He's fighting him."

"That fucking pilot!"

"He's handling him, though."

"Bloody better."

At the turn there was no need to worry.

"Here. Comes. Matador!"

(The announcer knew his punctuation.)

And just like that, the horse hit the front. He opened up, and extended the lead. The jockey, Errol Barnaby, glowed up high in the saddle:

The relief of old McAndrew.

Next was something Petey said, more ember than cigarette:

"He ready for the Queen, you think?" and McAndrew grimaced and left.

The last note, though, belonged to Carey.

She'd somehow put a dollar on, and given the winnings to Clay—well spent on the way back home:

Two dollars and change put together.

Hot chips and a mound of salt.

As it turned out, it would be Matador's last year of racing, and he won everything he ran in, except the ones that counted.

The Group Ones.

In each Group One he was up against one of the greatest horses of this or any era, and she was big and dark and stately, and all of the country loved her. They called her every *everything*, and compared her to the lot of them:

Kingston Town to Lonhro.

Black Caviar to Phar Lap.

Her stable name was Jackie.

At the track she was Queen of Hearts.

Sure, Matador was an exceptional horse, but he was likened to another one: a powerhouse bay called Hay List, who lost all the time to Black Caviar.

For Ennis McAndrew and the owner, they had no choice but to run him. There were only so many Group Ones at the right distance, and Queen of Hearts would always be in them. She, too, was unbeaten, and unbeatable. She'd conquer other horses by six or seven lengths—two if she was eased to the line. Matador she would beat by a single length, or once, by half a head.

Her colors were like a card game:

White with red and black hearts.

Up close, she made Matador look boy-like, or at best, an ungainly young adult; she was the darkest brown you could imagine, you could be fooled she was actually black.

On TV there were close-ups in the barriers.

She towered over other horses.

She was ever-alert and wakeful.

Then the jump, and she was gone.

The second time they raced that autumn, in the T. J. Smith, it looked like he might have had her. The jockey let him out well before the turn, and the lead looked insurmountable. But Queen of Hearts had eaten him up. In five or six gigantic strides, she hit the front and kept it.

Back at the stables, a giant crowd surrounded slot fourteen.

Somewhere, inside, was Jackie, Queen of Hearts.

In slot forty-two, there were only a few stray enthusiasts, and Petey Simms and Carey. And Clay.

The girl ran her hand down his blaze.

"Great run, boy."

Petey agreed. "I thought he had her—but that's some horse."

Halfway between them, around stall slot twenty-eight, the two trainers stood and shook hands. They spoke while looking away.

Clay, for some reason, liked that part.

He liked it more than the race.

Midwinter, the horse was spelled, after losing again to his nemesis, this time a total slaughter; this time four good lengths. He was barely ahead of the rest of them. They'd watched that one on TV, in the lounge at the Naked Arms, where it was showing live on Sky. It was a race run up in Queensland.

"Poor old Wally," she said, then called out to the barman—a guy named Scotty Bils. "Hey, how 'bout a beer or two to commiserate?"

"Commiserate?" He grinned. "She won! That, and you're underage."

Carey was disgusted. At the first comment, not the second.

"C'mon, Clay, let's go."

The barman looked at the girl, though, and then he looked at Clay; both Scotty Bils and the boy were older, and Scott just couldn't place him; but there was something, he knew, between them.

When finally he did, they were almost out the door.

"Hey," he called, "it's you; you're one of 'em—a fair few years ago—aren't you?"

It was Carey who first did the talking.

"One of who?"

"Seven beers!" shouted Scotty Bils, and his hair was almost gone, and Clay came back and spoke to him:

"She said those beers were good."

And what have I told you before?

Carey Novac could make you tell her things, although Clay was her hardest case. Outside, when he'd leaned on the Naked Arms tiles, she leaned against them with him. They were close, their arms were touching.

"Seven beers? What was that guy talking about?"

Clay's hand went into his pocket.

"Why is it," she asked, "that every time you're uneasy, you reach for whatever you've got there?" She was facing him, applying pressure.

"It's nothing."

"No," she said, "it's not."

She shook her head and decided to risk it; she reached down.

"Stop."

"Oh, come on, Clay!"

She laughed, and her fingers touched the pocket; her other hand went for his ribs—and it's always something awful and anxious, when a face ignites, then changes; he'd taken her and shoved her away.

"STOP!"

His shout like a frightened animal.

The girl fell back, she stammered; a single hand kept her up off the ground, but she refused to be helped to her feet. She slumped back against the tiles, her knees curled up at throat-height. He started to speak. "I'm sorry—"

"No—don't." She looked fiercely at the boy beside her. "Don't, Clay." She was hurt and wanted to hurt him. "What the hell's wrong with you, anyway? Why are you such a . . ."

"A what? *What?*"

Such a Goddamn freak.

The vernacular of young people everywhere.

The words like a wound, between them.

They must have sat there a good hour after that, and Clay wondered how best to fix it; or if it was fixable at all—the swollen taste of conflict.

He took the peg out softly and held it.

He laid it slowly down onto her thigh.

"I'll tell you everything," he said, but quietly. "Everything I can but this." They looked at it, perched amongst them. "The seven beers, all her nick-names . . . how her dad had Stalin's mustache. She said it was camped on his mouth."

She cracked, just slightly; she smiled.

"That's how she once described it," and his voice now more like a whis-per. "But not about the peg. Not yet." The only way he could live with him-self was knowing he'd tell her at the end—when she'd need to leave him behind.

"Okay, Clay, I'll wait." She stood and she pulled him upwards; she forgave by being relentless. "So for now, just tell me the rest of it." She said it like not many said such things. "Tell me all of everything."

And that was what he did.

He told her everything I've told you so far, and so much more to come—

just short of a backyard clothesline—and Carey did what no one could, she saw exactly what somehow he couldn't.

The next time they stood at the cemetery, with their fingers each clenched in the fence, she reached over with a small piece of paper.

"I was thinking," she said, and the sun backed away, "of that woman who left your father . . . and the book she'd taken with her."

Her freckles were fifteen coordinates, with a last one down on her neck—because there, on that small crumpled paper, was a name and several numbers, and the name she had written was *HANLEY*.

"There are six of them," she said, "in the phone book."

the rip

He woke up.

He was sweating.

He swam up through the sheets.

Since the telling of truth to McAndrew, and Ted and Catherine Novac, he was left with a lasting question.

Did he confess for only himself?

But not even in his darkest moments did he believe that; he did it because he'd had to. They deserved to know how it happened.

Now, many nights later, he woke and felt her upon him:

The girl was on his chest.

It's a dream, I know it's a dream.

She came at his will of imagining.

There was the smell of horses and death, but also alive and life-like; he knew because she was warm. She was still, but he felt her breath.

"Carey?" he said, and she moved then. She got up sleepily and sat beside him. Her jeans and glowing forearms, like the day she'd first walked over.

"It's you," he said.

"It's me . . ." But now she turned away from him. He'd have touched her auburn hair. "I'm here because you killed me."

He sank in a channel of sheets.

In bed, but caught in a rip.

* * *

After that, he returned to running, in mornings before work with me. His theory was perfect logic; the harder he ran, the less he ate, the more chance he might see her again.

The problem was only he didn't.

"She's dead."

He quietly said it.

Some nights he walked to the cemetery.

His fingers would cling to the fence.

He would ache to see that woman again, from the start, from way back when—the one who'd asked for a tulip.

Where are you? he almost asked her.

Where are you now that I need you?

He'd have looked inside that streak she had, that wrinkle above her eyebrows.

Instead he ran to Bernborough.

He did this night for night.

In the end, a good few months went by, till he stood on the track at midnight. The wind was up and howling. There was no moon. Only streetlights. And Clay stood close to the finish line, then turned to the height of the grass.

For a moment he slid his arm in; it was cold and unfriendly to the hand. For a moment he heard a voice. Quite clearly, it called out *Clay*. For a moment he wanted to believe, and so "Carey?" he called in after it—but he knew there was no going in.

He just stood and he said her name—for hours, until the sunrise, and felt sure this would never recede. He would live like this and die like this, no sun would rise in him.

"Carey," he whispered, "Carey," and the wind slung all around him, till finally dying down.

"Carey," he whispered, more desperately, then his final act of futility.

"Carey," he whispered—"Penny."

And someone out there heard it.

the game show girl

In the past, in the year they had for their friendship, there were times it was easy being Carey and Clay, and they lived upwardly, closely together. But still, there were so many moments. He would sometimes stop and remind himself:

He shouldn't be falling in love like this.

How could he feel deserving?

Yes, it's safe to say they loved each other, on rooves, in parks, even cemeteries. They walked through the streets of the racing quarter, and were fifteen and sixteen years old; they touched but never kissed.

The girl was good and green-lit:

The clear-eyed Carey Novac.

The boy was the boy with the fire in his eyes.

They loved each other almost like brothers.

On the day of the phone book, they called each name from the top.

There was no initial starting with A, so they decided on calling all of them, and hoped for the chance of a relative.

The fourth one was the one.

His name was Patrick Hanley.

He said, "What? Who? *Abbey?*"

It was Carey, that time, who spoke, because they'd alternated the calling, name for name, and she'd been second and fourth. She'd forced Clay to go first. They both listened up close to the earpiece, and could tell by the suspicion in his voice—this was definitely it. The others had all been clueless. Carey said they were looking for a woman, and she'd come from a place called Featherton. The other end, however, hung up.

"Looks like we're going out there," she said, and searched, again, for the address. "Ernst Place, Edensor Park."

It was July by then, and she had a day off, a Sunday.

They caught the train and bus.

There was a field and a bike track footpath.

The house was in a corner, the right-hand side of a cul-de-sac.

At the door, he knew them right away.

They stared at him next to the brickwork.

He had dark hair, a black T-shirt, and an archway masquerading as a mustache.

"Wow!" said Carey Novac; she'd spoken before she'd realized. "Look at the size of that handlebar!"

Patrick Hanley wasn't swayed.

When Clay found the courage to talk to him, his questions were met with a question:

"What the hell would you want with my sister?"

But then he'd had a good look at him; and he looked a lot like *him*—Clay could see the moment it changed. Was Patrick remembering Michael, not only as a man Abbey married, but as the boy she'd walked the town with?

Regardless, things became friendlier, and introductions were made.

"This is Carey," Clay said, "and I'm Clay—" and Patrick Hanley now stepped closer.

"Clay Dunbar," he said quite casually; but he'd split them right down the middle. He'd said it, he didn't ask.

She lived in a gorgeous apartment block:

She was several bright windows in a concrete Goliath—the capitalist type—and they went there a few weeks later (Carey's next day free), on an August afternoon. They stood in its frightening shade.

"It goes all the way up to heaven," said Carey, and as usual, her hair was out. Her blood-spot freckles were jittery. "You ready?"

"No."

"Come on, look at you!"

She slid a hand through so they linked arms, and they could have been Michael and Abbey.

Yet still, he didn't move.

"Look at what?"

"You!"

As always she wore her jeans, and worn-out ones at that. Her flannel shirt was faded. A black jacket was loosely open.

She hugged him by the buzzers.

"I wouldn't be listed, either," she said, "if I lived in a place like this."

"I think it's the first time you've ever seen me in a shirt," he said.

"Exactly!" She tightened their linking arms. "See? I told you. You're ready."

He typed in 182.

In the lift, he shifted his feet, he was so nervous he might throw up, but in the corridor he was better. It was rendered white, with dark blue trimmings. At its end was the greatest view of the city you could imagine. There was water everywhere—the salty kind—and a skyline that felt within reach.

On the right you could see the Opera House.

To its left was its constant running mate:

They looked from the sails to the Coathanger.

A voice stood up behind them.

"Goodness."

Her eyes were sweet and smoky.

"You look exactly like him."

Inside, the apartment was a woman's.

There was no man there, no children.

It was somehow immediately obvious.

When they looked at the former Abbey Dunbar, they knew she was, and had been, beautiful. They knew she had great hair, good clothes, attractive in every way—but even so, there was love and loyalty; this was no Penelope. Nowhere even close.

"Would you like a drink?" she asked.

They spoke together. "No thanks."

"Tea? Coffee?"

Yes, her eyes were grey and glorious.

Her hair was as good as television—she had a bob to knock your socks off—and you needn't look hard to see the girl again, as bony as a calf.

"What about milk and cookies?" said Carey, an attempt to lighten the mood. She played Abbey; she felt she had to.

"Hey, kid." The woman smiled—this older version—and even her pants were perfect. That, and a priceless shirt. "I like you, but best be quiet."

When Clay told me about all this, he said the funniest thing.

He said the TV was on, and there was the background noise of game shows. Where once she'd loved *I Dream of Jeannie*, now it seemed to be this. He couldn't tell which show it was, but they were introducing the contestants, one of whom was Steve, and Steve was a computer programmer, whose hobbies were paragliding and tennis. He loved the outdoors and reading.

When they all sat down, and Carey had *settled* down, they talked for a while of small things—of school and work and how Carey was an apprentice jockey, but it was Clay who did the talking. Abbey spoke of his father, and what a beautiful boy he'd been, and how he'd walked that dog through Featherton.

"Moon," said Carey Novac, but quietly, almost to herself.

Both Clay and Abbey smiled.

When Carey did actually come to speak louder again, it was to ask a burning question. "Did you ever get remarried?"

Abbey said, "That's better," and then, "Oh yes. I did."

As Clay looked at Carey, thinking, Thank God you're here, he also felt blind in the light. This place was so well lit! The sun came in so directly, and hit the modern couch, the mile-long oven, and even the coffee machine as if they were holy—but he could tell there wasn't a piano. Again, she was all but nothing. He was staunch and would quietly fight it.

As for Abbey, she looked out, she nursed her cup of coffee.

"Oh yes, I got remarried—I did it twice," and abruptly, like she couldn't wait any longer, she said, "Come here, I want to show you something," and "Come on, I won't bite," when he hesitated, for she was leading him into the bedroom. "Here—"

And yes, *here* all right—because there, across from the bed, on a snippet of a piece of wall, was something to beat his heart down, then lift it slowly out of him:

It was something so soft and simple, in a scratchy silver frame.

A picture of Abbey's hands.

A sketch like sticks, but gentle.

Like sticks, but soft; you could lie in them.

She said, "He was seventeen, I'd say, when he drew that," and Clay, for the first time, looked at her: beneath, to other beauty.

"Thank you for showing me," he said, and Abbey would use the momentum. She could have no idea of Clay and Penny, and five brothers and noise and chaos, and fights about the piano; and dying. There was only the boy in front of her, and she intended to make it count.

She said, "How can I ever tell you, Clay?" She was between the boy and the girl. "I'd tell you how sorry I am, what a fool I was—but you're here, and I can see it." For a moment she looked at Carey. "Is this boy a beautiful boy?"

And Carey, of course, looked back at her, then kept her focus on Clay. The freckles no longer anxious. A smile recalling the sea. And of course, she'd said, "Of course."

"I thought so," said Abbey Hanley, and there was regret but no self-pity. "I guess my leaving your dad," she explained, "was really my best mistake."

After that, they did have tea, they couldn't refuse, and Abbey had more coffee, and told them some of her history; she worked at one of the banks.

"It's all as boring as bat shit," she said, and Clay, he felt the pang.

He said, "That's what two of my brothers say—they say it about Matthew's movies."

Her smokiness slightly widened.

"How many brothers do you *have*?"

"There are five of us," he said to her, "and five animals, including Achilles."

"Achilles?"

"The mule."

"The *mule*?"

He was actually starting to relax now, and Carey answered bluntly. "You've never seen a family like this," and maybe Abbey could have been hurt by such things—by a life she'd never live—and maybe it could have gone wrong then, and so none of them tried their luck. They didn't talk about Penny or Michael, and it was Abbey who put her cup down.

With genuine affection, she said, "Look at you two kids."

She shook her head and laughed, at herself:

You remind me of me and him.

She thought it—he could tell—but didn't say it.

She said, "I think I know why you came here, Clay."

She left and came back with *The Quarryman*.

It was pale and bronze, and the spine was cracked, but the age of it only enhanced it. At the window it was growing darker; she turned the light on in the kitchen, and took a knife from the wall by the kettle.

Very gently, at the table, she made an incision, inside—precisely against the spine—to extract the very first page: the one with the author's biography. Then she closed it, and gave it to Clay.

As to the page itself—she showed them. She said, "I'll keep this one if you don't mind," and "*Love and love and love*, huh?" but she was wistful rather than flippant. "I think I always knew, you know—it was never mine to have."

When they left, she saw them out, and they stood together, out by the lifts. Clay approached to shake her hand, but she refused, and said, "Here, just give me a hug."

It was strange how it felt to be held by her.

She was softer than she looked, and warm.

He could never explain how grateful he was, for the book and the flesh of her arms. He knew he would never see her again, that this was all there was. In the very last crack, before the lift went down, she smiled through the closing doors.

the last letter

He would never see Abbey again:

Clay, of course, was wrong.

Once, in the tide—

Oh, fuck it—

See, at Carey Novac's funeral, when we'd sat at the back of the church, he was wrong to think no one saw him—for between the genuine mourners, and the racing people and identities, a woman had also been there. She had sweet-smoke eyes and beautiful clothes, and a bob to knock your socks off.

Dear Clay—

I'm sorry for so many reasons.

I should have written to you much earlier.

I'm sorry for what happened to Carey.

One minute I was telling her to stop being such a smart mouth, and the next she was telling me his dog's name . . . and next minute (even though more than a year had passed) there were all those people in the church. I was standing in the crowd in the doorway, and saw you at the back with your brothers.

For a moment I nearly came to you. I regret now that I didn't.

When I met you both, I should have told you—that you reminded me of Michael and me. I could see by the way you were near each other, you were only an arm's length away. You would save each other from me, or from anything else that might harm her. You looked so devastated in that church. I hope you're doing okay.

I won't ask where your mother was, or your father, because I know what we keep to ourselves, especially withheld from our parents.

Don't feel like you need to reply.

I won't tell you to live how she'd want you to, but maybe to live how you have to.

But you do, I think, have to live.

I'm sorry if I've spoken out of turn here, so please forgive me if I have.

Sincerely,
Abbey Hanley

It came a few days after Bernborough, when he'd stood on the track till sunrise. The letter was hand-delivered. No stamp and no address. Just *Clay Dunbar* and left in the letterbox.

A week later, he walked through the racing quarter, and the city, until he reached her. He refused to use the buzzer. He waited for another resident; he slipped through the entrance behind him, and took the lift to the eighteenth floor.

He balked when he reached her door, and took several minutes to knock, and even then he'd done it benignly. He was shocked when she came to open it.

Like before she was kind and immaculate, but quickly overrun with concern. Her hair, and this light, they were lethal.

"Clay?" she said, and stepped closer. She was beautiful even when sad. "God, Clay, you look so thin."

It took all of his will not to hug her again, to be held in the warmth of her doorway—but he didn't, he couldn't allow himself. He could talk to her and that was all.

"I'll do what you said in your letter," he said. "I'll live the way I have to—I'll go out and finish the bridge."

His voice was as dry as the riverbed, and Abbey had done things well. She didn't ask what he meant by the bridge, or for anything else he might tell her.

He'd opened his mouth to speak again, but then wavered, and welled in the eyes. In fury, he wiped the tears away—and Abbey Hanley took a risk, and a gamble; she bet double and to hell with the worry, or her place in this whole mess, or what was right. She did what she'd done once before:

She kissed a pair of her fingers, but placed them across, on his cheek.

He wanted to tell her about Penny then, and Michael, and all that had happened to all of us—and all that had happened to *him*. Yes, he wanted to tell her everything, but this time he just shook her hand; then caught the lift and ran.

matador vs. queen of hearts

And so, once again, it was.

After he'd met Abbey Hanley with Carey, and she'd torn the first page of *The Quarryman* out, they could never know what it would mean. At first it was one more yardstick; the start of another beginning, as months flowed in and by them.

In spring, they both came back:

Matador and Queen of Hearts.

In summer, the ache of waiting, given Carey had been forewarned:

She would have to cut the dead wood out, and Clay would make her commit. Clay would make a plan.

In between, as you might guess, the one constant—the thing they loved most—was the book of Michelangelo, whom she lovingly called the sculptor, or the artist, or his favorite: the fourth Buonarroti.

They lay down at The Surrounds.

They read there, chapter for chapter.

They brought flashlights, and batteries for backup.

To protect the fading mattress, she brought a giant sheet of plastic, and when they left they made the bed with it, they tucked the whole thing in. Walking home, she'd link her arm through. Their hips would touch between them.

* * *

By November, history was repeated.

Queen of Hearts was just too good.

Matador tried his heart out, when they'd raced twice more and he'd faded. But there was one chance still to come; a final Group One was to be run in the city, early December, and Ennis McAndrew was building him. He'd said he'd faded because he still wasn't ready; this was the one he wanted. It had a strange name—not a plate or guineas, a cup or a stakes—but a race called the Saint Anne's Parade. It would be Matador's last ever run. Race Five at Royal Hennessey. December 11.

On the day, they did what she liked to do.

They put a dollar on Matador in the fifth.

She asked an arse-scratcher to put the money on.

He did it but told them, laughingly: "You know he's got bloody no hope, don'tcha? He's up against Queen of Hearts."

"So?"

"So he's never going to win."

"They said that about Kingston Town."

"Matador's no Kingston Town."

But now she beat him up a bit. "What am I even talkin' to *you* for? How many wins have you had lately?"

He laughed again. "Not many." He ran a hand down his cheekfuls of whiskers.

"That's what I thought. You're not even sharp enough to lie about it. But, hey"—she grinned—"thanks for putting the bet on, okay?"

"Sure," and when they went their separate ways, he called out to them one more time. "Hey, I think you might have convinced me!"

The crowd that afternoon was the biggest they'd ever seen, for Queen of Hearts was also leaving, for a stint running overseas.

There was almost no room in the grandstand, but they found two seats, and watched Petey Simms, doing laps with the horse in the mounting yard. McAndrew, of course, looked pissed off. But that meant business as usual.

Before the jump, she held his hand.

He looked outwards, he said, "Good luck."

She gave him a squeeze, then released it—for when the horses left the barriers that day, the crowd was on its feet; people screamed, and something changed.

The horses hit the turn, it was wrong.

When Queen of Hearts surged forward, Matador, black and gold, went stride for stride, beside her—which was really saying something, because her strides were so much bigger. When she accelerated, he somehow went with her.

The grandstand shade became desperate.

They called raucously, near-terror, for the Queen—for it couldn't be, it couldn't.

But it was.

When they hit the line, it came down to their bobbing heads.

It looked like Matador got it, and it sounded that way, too—for a hush blew over the crowd.

She looked at him.

She held him, single-handed.

Her freckles nearly exploded.

He won.

She thought it but didn't speak, and it was lucky she didn't, too, because it was the greatest run they'd ever seen, or been part of in the stands, and there was a poetry, they knew, to the thought of it.

So close, so close, then gone.

The photo somehow proved it:

Queen of Hearts won by her nostrils.

"Her nostrils, her fucking nostrils!" called Petey afterwards, in the confines of the stalls—but this time McAndrew was smiling.

When he saw Carey so hurt and dejected, he came over and took a look at her. Almost an examination. She thought he might check her feet.

"And what the hell happened to you? The horse is still alive, isn't he?"

"He should have won."

"Should've nothing—it was something we've never seen, a run like that," and now he made her look at him, in the hard blue eyes of a scarecrow. "That, and you'll get that Group One for him one day, okay?"

The beginnings of a kind of happiness.

"Okay, Mr. McAndrew."

From there, Carey Novac, the girl from Gallery Road, would start her apprenticeship in earnest. She started on January 1.

She'd be essentially working round the clock now.

There was no time for anything, or anyone else.

She'd be riding now, more trackwork and into barrier trials, and start begging, internally, for races. From the outset she was told by McAndrew:

"If you pester me, you'll never get anything."

She would gladly put her head down, keep her mouth shut, and do the work.

As for Clay, he was determined.

He knew she had to leave him.

He could make her stay away.

He'd already planned to start training again, as hard as he could, and Henry was ready, too. They'd sat together up on the roof one night, and Miss January was in on everything. They'd get a key for Crapper's apartment block, and make a comeback at Bernborough Park. There'd be money, and plenty of gambling.

"Done?" said Henry.

"Done."

They shook hands and it was appropriate, really, for Henry was letting go, too—of that woman of great anatomy. For whatever reason, he decided:

He folded her up and laid her down, on the slanted slab of roof tiles.

The evening of December 31, Carey and Clay went down to Bernborough.

They ran a lap of the decimated track.

The stand gone to hell in the sunset; but a hell you'd gladly enter.

They stood and he clenched the peg.

He held it slowly out.

He said, "Now I need to tell you," and he told her all of everything, of those waters always to come. They were ten meters short of the finish line, and Carey, she listened in silence; she squeezed the peg through his hand.

When he'd told her the story entirely, he said, "Do you see now? Do you see? I took a year and I never deserved it. A year with *you*. You can never, ever stay with me." He looked at the infield, that jungleland, and thought there was no disputing it, but Carey Novac could never be beaten. No—horses could lose, but not Carey; and damn her for this, but we can love her, because this is what she did next.

She turned his face and she held it.

She took and she handled the peg.

She held it up slow to her lips.

She said, "God, Clay, you poor kid, you poor boy, you poor kid . . ." The grandstand lit her hair. "She was right, you know, Abbey Hanley—she said *beautiful*—can't you see it?" Up close she was light but visceral, she could keep you alive with her pleading; the pain in her good-green eyes. "Can't you see I'll never leave you, Clay? Can't you see I'll never leave?"

Clay looked like he might fall then.

Carey wrapped him tightly.

She just held him and hugged him and whispered to him, and he felt all her bones within her. She smiled and cried and smiled. She said, "Go to The Surrounds. Go on Saturday night." She kissed him on the neck there, and pressed the words all down. "I'll never leave you, ever—" and that's how I like to remember them:

I see her holding him, hard at Bernborough.

They're a boy, a girl and a peg.

I see the track, and that fire, behind them.

the burning bed

At 18 Archer Street, I was elated, but tempered by sadness.

Clay was packing his bag.

For a while, we stood together, out on the old back porch, and Rosy was down on the couch. She slept on the ball-less beanbag, which we'd thrown, all worn, on top of it.

Achilles was under the clothesline.

He chewed his way into mourning.

We stood till the sky had paled into view, and soon the perfection of brothers, who said nothing but knew he was going.

See, when Clay told us there was one more thing to do, and that Tommy should get the turpentine, but no matches, we all walked silently out. We walked to The Surrounds.

We stood with the household monuments:

Their distance and downtroddenness.

We walked to the mattress and stayed with him, and said nothing of the plastic sheet; no, all we did was stand, as the lighter came out of his pocket. In the other he still had the peg.

We stood till Tommy doused it, and the flame stood straightly upwards. Clay crouched down with the lighter, and first the bed resisted, but soon came roaring on. That sound, the sound of surf.

The field lit up.

The five of us stood.

Five boys and a burning mattress.

When we went back inside, The Surrounds remained.

There hadn't been close to a westerly.

He'd go alone to Central Station.

He hugged each of us warmly, and separate.

After Tommy he finished with me—and both of us told him to wait, at different moments—and me, I lifted the piano lid, and reached through the dress for its button. The books, I could tell, should wait.

He held it, the button from Vienna.

She was back in the grip of decision.

It was worn but pristine in his palm.

As for Tommy, it was close to ten minutes after, when the rest of us stood on the porch, and watched Clay walk away, and he did something utterly crazy:

He trusted Rory to look after Hector.

"Here," he said quickly, "hold him."

For both Rory and Hector there was shock, and not a small amount of distrust. As they eyed each other closely, Tommy raced in through the house, and soon came running back round.

We stood and we looked at Clay.

And Tommy was running down after him.

"Clay!" he screamed. "Hey, Clay!"

And of course he was taking Achilles—and the mule, amazingly, was running. He was running! You could hear the hollowing hoofbeats, as the boy ran him down the street; and Clay had turned to meet them, and looked at the boy and the beast.

There wasn't even a moment.

Not a second of hesitation.

It was how it was meant to be, and his hand came out for the reins.

"Thanks, Tommy."

It was quiet but all of us heard, and he turned and he walked and took him, as full morning had come to hit Archer Street—and we all went downwards to Tommy. We watched as they left us behind.

In there, out in the suburbs-world, a boy walked the streets with a mule. They set out for a bridge in Silver, and took the darkest waters with them.

part eight

cities + waters + criminals +
arches + stories + survivors + bridges
+
fire

joker in the hallway

ONCE—AND I WRITE THIS AT LEAST ALMOST FOR THE LAST FEW TIMES—IN THE tide of Dunbar past, there was a woman who told us she would die, and the world ended that night, in that kitchen. There were boys on the floor, they were burning; and the sun came up the next morning.

All of us woke up early.

Our dreams were like flight, like turbulence.

By six o'clock, even Henry and Rory were mostly awake; our notorious sleeper-inners.

It was March, and awash with leftovers from summer, and we stood together, in the hallway—skinny arms and anchored shoulders. We stood but we were stuck there. We wondered what to do.

Our dad came out and tried; a hand on each of our necks.

An attempt at some sort of comfort.

The problem was, when he walked away, we saw him take hold of the curtains, and one hand on the piano; he hung on, his body was shaking. The sun was warm and wavy, and we were quiet in the hall, behind him.

He assured us he was okay.

When he turned and came to face us, though, his aqua eyes were lightless.

As for us:

Henry, Clay, and I were in singlets and old shorts.

Rory and Tommy wore just underwear.

It was what they'd gone to sleep in.

All of us tightened our jaws.

The hallway was full of tiredness, of boyish legs and shins. All outside their bedroom—strung toward the kitchen.

When she came out, she was dressed for work, in jeans and a dark blue shirt. The buttons were slits of metal. Her hair was braided down the back; she looked ready to go out riding or something, and cautiously, we watched her—and Penelope couldn't help it.

She was blond and braidwork, beaming.

"What's got into you lot?" she asked. "No one died, did they?"

And that was what eventually did it:

She laughed but Tommy cried, and she crouched down close and held him—and then came all the rest of us, in singlets, shorts and falling.

"Too much?" she asked, and she knew it was, from being smeared by all those bodies.

She felt the clench of boys' arms.

Our dad looked helplessly on.

the silver mule

So THERE SHE WAS.

Our mother.

All those years ago:

In the hallway, in the morning.

And here was Clay, in afternoon, in a hallway of his own, or as he preferred it himself, a corridor.

The corridor of strapping eucalypts.

It was Ennis McAndrew who drove him there, in a truck and horse trailer combined. At least three months had passed them by since Clay had gone and faced him.

The great thing was that McAndrew was training again, and when he saw him with Achilles at Hennessey, he shook his head and came over, and dropped everything.

He said, "Well, look what the bloody cat dragged in."

They'd driven much of the way in silence, and when they spoke, they spoke looking outwards; the world beyond the windshield.

Clay asked him about The Spaniard.

And the opera singer, Pavarotti.

"Pava-*what?*"

His knuckles were white on the steering wheel.

"You called Trackwork Ted that once—when you saw him at Gallery Road. You took two young jockeys to see him, remember? To watch him, and learn to ride?" But now Clay looked away from the windshield, and out the window instead. Those reams of empty space. "Once, she told me the story."

"Oh, yeah," said Ennis McAndrew, and he drove on very thoughtfully. "Those jockeys were effing worthless."

"Effing?"

"Worthless."

But then they returned to hurting again.

There was guilt for enjoying anything.

Especially the joy of forgetting.

When they made it to the turnoff, Clay said he could take it from there, but Ennis wouldn't have a bar of it. "I want to meet your father," he said. "I want to see this bridge. Might as bloody well . . . We've come too far for me not to."

They drove the open hill, then turned down into the corridor, and the eucalypts were always the same. They were gathered, and waited around down there, like muscled-up thighs in the shade. A football team of trees.

When McAndrew saw them, he noticed.

"Jesus," he said, "look at them."

On the other side, in the light, they saw him in the riverbed, and the bridge remained the same. No work had been done for several months, since I'd sunk to my knees in the dirt:

The curvature, the wood and stone.

The pieces stood waiting for this.

They climbed from out of the truck.

When they stood by the riverbed and looked, it was Ennis who'd spoken first. "When it's finished, it's going to be magnificent, isn't it?" and Clay was matter-of-fact.

He answered only "Yes."

* * *

When they opened the trailer, and brought the animal out, they walked him down to the bedrock, and the mule looked dutifully around. He studied the dry of the river. It was Clay with a pair of questions.

"What?" he asked the animal.

"What's so unusual about this?"

Well, where's the bloody water?

But Clay knew it was coming, and at some point, so would the mule.

In the meantime, Ennis shook hands with Michael.

They spoke drily, like friends, as equals.

McAndrew had quoted Henry.

He pointed to the bridles and hay.

He said, "That stuff you can probably do something with, but the animal's totally useless."

Michael Dunbar knew how to answer, though, and almost absently, he looked at Clay, and the knowingness embodied in the mule. He said, "You know, I wouldn't be totally sure of that—he's pretty good at breaking and entering."

But again there was guilt and embarrassment, and if McAndrew and Clay knew to quell it, the Murderer knew he should, too.

For a while they watched the mule—the slow and meandering Achilles—as he steadily climbed from the riverbed and began his work in the field; he stooped and mildly chewed.

Without thinking, McAndrew spoke; he motioned slightly but surely at the boy.

"Mr. Dunbar, take it easy on him, okay—" and this time, finally, he said it. "He's got a heart like Goddamn Phar Lap."

And Michael Dunbar agreed.

"You don't even know the half of it."

* * *

Ten minutes later, once coffee and tea had been offered, and declined, McAndrew started for home. He shook hands with the boy and his father again, and made his way back into the trees; Clay went running after him.

"Mr. McAndrew!"

In the shade, the truck stopped, and the broomstick trainer got out. He walked from the dark to the light. He exhaled. "Call me Ennis, for Christ's sake."

"Okay, Ennis," and now Clay looked away. The pair of them were baked in sunshine, like kindling of boy and old man. He said, "You know—you know Carey . . ."—and it hurt just to say her name—"you know her bike?" Ennis nodded and came closer. "I know the combination for the lock—it's thirty-five-twenty-seven," and Ennis knew the number immediately.

Those figures, that horse.

He walked back to the truck in the shade.

"I'll tell Ted, I'll tell Catherine, okay? But I don't think they'll ever take it. It's yours when you come and unlock it."

And that was how he drove away:

He climbed inside the truck again.

He held a broom-hand, fleetingly, up.

He waved to the boy out the window, and the boy walked gradually back.

before first light had hit the house

So they gave her six months—and maybe that would have been better. It certainly would have hurt less, or at least shorter than her epic Hartnell job, of death but never dying.

There were all the sordid details, of course.

I pay them scant regard:

The drugs all sound the same in the end; an index of variations. It's like learning another language, I guess, when you're watching someone die; a whole new kind of training. You build towers out of prescription boxes, count pills and poisonous liquids. Then minutes-to-hours in hospital wards, and how long the longest night is.

For Penelope it was mostly the language, I think.

There was death and its own vernacular:

Her pills were called *The Chemist Shop*.

Each drug was an *oxymoron*.

The first time she'd said that was in the kitchen, and she'd studied them almost happily; all those stickered boxes. She read the names aloud, from Cyclotassin to Exentium to Dystrepsia 409.

"Hey," she said, and configured them; her first stab at a towering pharmacy. It was like she'd been duped (and let's face it, she really had). "They all just sound the same."

In so many ways, she'd found the perfect name for them, too, because they *did* all sound like anagrams, of *oxy* and *moron* combined. The ridiculous element, too—the moronic nature of fighting it—of killing yourself to survive. They really should come with warnings, like the ones on cigarettes. *Take this and slowly die*.

As futile as it was, there was still one operation, and the taste of warmed-up hospital.

See, don't ever let them fool you, when people talk of the smell of hospitals. There's a point where you go beyond it, when you feel it in your clothes. Weeks later, you're back at home, and something just feels like—it.

There was once, one morning, at the table, when Rory got a rash of the shivers. As they rose, then fell on his arms, Penelope pointed across.

"You want to know what that is?" she asked. She'd been staring at a bowl of cornflakes; the riddle of trying to eat them. "It means a doctor just turned in his sleep."

"Or worse," said Dad, "an anesthesiologist."

And "Yeah," said Rory, so willingly, as he stole from our mother's breakfast. "I hate *those* dirty bastards the most!"

"Hey—you're eating all my Goddamn cornflakes, kid."

She pushed the bowl at him, and gave him a wink.

Then the treatments came in waves again, and the first were wild and whip-like, like a body gone down in a riot. Then slowly more professional; a casual breaking down.

In time they came like terrorism.

A calculated mess.

Our mother, burning, falling.

A human nine-eleven.

Or a woman becomes a country, and you see her leaving *herself*. Like the winters of old in the Eastern Bloc, the threats came on more quickly:

The boils, they rose like battlegrounds.

They blitzkrieged over her back.

The drugs wreaked havoc with her thermostat; they scorched her, then froze, then paralyzed, and when she walked from bed she collapsed—her hair like a nest on the pillow, or feathers on the lawn, from the cat.

For Penny you could see it was betrayal. It was there in the green-gone eyes; and the worst was the sheer *disappointment*. How could she be let down like this, by the world and by her body?

Again, like *The Odyssey* and *The Iliad*, where gods would intervene—till something spiraled to catastrophe—so it was with *here*. She tried to reassemble herself, to *resemble* herself, and sometimes she even believed it. At best we soon were jaded:

The stupid light of hospital wards.

The souls of lovely nurses.

How I hated the way they walked:

The stockinged legs of matrons!

But some, you had to admire them—how we hated to love the special ones. Even now, as I punch what happened out, I'm grateful to all those nurses; how they lifted her in the pillows, like the breakable thing she was. How they held her hand and spoke to her, in the face of all our hatred. They warmed her up, put fires out, and like us, they lived and waited.

One morning, when the toll hit close to breaking point, Rory stole a stethoscope—taking something back, I guess—as our mother became an impostor. By then she was the color of jaundice, and never again the color she was. We'd come to know the difference by then, between yellowness and blond.

She held on to us by our forearms, or the flesh of our palms and our wrists. Again, the education—so easy to count the knuckles, and the bones in both of her hands. She looked out through the window, at the world so bright and careless.

It's also a thing to see, when you see your father change.

You watch him fold in different places.

You see him sleep another way:

He leans forward onto the ward bed.

He takes air but doesn't breathe it.

Such pressure all held within.

It's something fatigued and trodden-looking, and clothes that sigh at the seams. Like Penny would never be blond again, our dad would lose his physique. They were the dying of color and shape. It's not just the death of *them* you see when you watch a person dying.

But then—she'd make it out.

Somehow, she'd climb from all of it, and traverse the hospital doors. She'd go straight back to work, of course, though death was at her shoulder.

No more hanging from the power lines for that old guy.

Or draping round the fridge.

But he was always out there somewhere:

On a train or a bus, or footpath.

On the way back home to here.

By November she was miraculous.

Eight months and she'd managed to live.

There was another two-week hospital stint, and the doctors were noncommittal, but sometimes they'd stop and tell us:

"I don't know how she's done it. I've never seen anything so—"

"If you say *aggressive*," said our dad, and he'd pointed, calmly, at Rory, "I'm going to— See that kid?"

"Yes."

"Well, I'm going to tell him to beat you up."

"Sorry—*what?*"

The doctor was quite alarmed, and Rory suddenly awoke—that sentence was better than smelling salts.

"Really?" He was almost rubbing his hands together. "Can I?"

"Of course not, I'm joking."

But Rory tried to sell it. "Come on, Doc, after a while you won't even feel it."

"You people," said that particular specialist, "are totally out of your minds."

To his left there was Penny's laughter.

She laughed, then quelled the pain.

"Maybe that," she said to the doctor, "is how I've been able to do it."

She was a happy-sad creature in blankets.

On that occasion, when she came home, we'd decked out the entire house:

Streamers, balloons, Tommy made a sign.

"You spelt *welcome* wrong," said Henry.

"What?"

"It's only one *L*."

Penelope didn't mind.

Our father carried her from the car, and for the first time, she actually let him—and next morning we all heard it, before first light had hit the house:

Penny was playing the piano.

She played through the sunrise, she played through our fights. She played through breakfast, and then long past it, and none of us knew the music. Maybe it was a misspent rationale, that when she was playing she wasn't dying—for we knew it would soon be back again, having swung from wire to wire.

There was no point closing the curtains, or locking any of the doors.

It was in there, out there, waiting.

It lived on our front porch.

pact with the devil

When Clay ran back from McAndrew, our father was standing with Achilles.

He asked if Clay was okay.

He told him he'd really missed him.

"You didn't build while I was away?"

"No." He patted the mule, but cautiously. "There could be thousands of people working on this bridge, and the world could come to see it . . . but they'd all know who it belonged to." He handed him the lead of the animal. "You're the only one who can finish it."

For a long time, Clay stood outside.

He watched Achilles eating.

Evening would soon be upon them.

There was one thought overpowering him, and at first he didn't know why.

I think he just wanted to talk to him.

It was the legend of Pont du Gard:

> *Once, in France, which wasn't even France then—it was the ancient world—there was a river that proved unbeatable. That river, today, is the Gardon.*
>
> *For centuries, the people who lived there could never quite finish a bridge, or if they did, the river destroyed it.*

Then one day the devil strolled into town, and made an offer to the villagers. He said, "I can build that bridge for you easily! I can build it in a single night!"

And the villagers, they almost cried.

"But!" The devil was quite beside himself. "The first one who crosses the bridge next day is mine to do with what I please."

So a meeting was held in the village.

It was discussed and finally agreed.

They took up the devil's offer, and watched in total rapture, in the night, as he tore stones from up on the mountaintops, and anything else he came by. He threw and juggled the pieces, and made arches in twos and threes. He made that bridge and aqueduct, and in the morning, he awaited his payment.

He'd made his bargain; he'd lived up to it.

But the villagers, for once, had outsmarted him—and set a hare free over the top of it, as the first one to cross the river—and the devil was infuriated:

He picked up the hare and smashed it.

He flung it epically against an arch, and the outline is still there today.

While Clay and Michael Dunbar stood, in the field by Achilles and the river, he watched and spoke across to him.

"Dad?"

The insects were mostly silent.

There were always these bloodied sunsets here, and this was the first for Achilles. The mule, of course, ignored it, though, and went on with what he was born for; this field was made for the eating.

But Michael stepped closer and waited.

He wasn't sure how to approach Clay just yet, for the boy had seen so much—and then came something strange:

"Remember you asked if I knew it? The legend of Pont du Gard?"

Michael was caught, midanswer.

"Of course, but—"

"Well, I wouldn't."

"You wouldn't—what?"

Achilles was listening, too, now; he'd looked up from the grass.

"I wouldn't make a deal—for the bridge to be built in a night."

It was dark by then, well dark, and Clay kept talking on.

"But I would make a trade for *them*." He gritted his lips, then opened them. "I'd go to hell just to make them live again—and we could both go, you could go with me—one of us for one of them. I know they're not in hell, I know, I know, but—" He stopped and bent, then called again. "Dad, you have to help me." The darkness had cut him in half. He would die to bring them back again. Penelope, he thought, and Carey. At the very least, he owed them this.

"We have to make it perfect," he said. "We have to make it great."

He'd turned and faced the riverbed.

A miracle and nothing less.

the seven beers of penny dunbar

Somehow she stitched the days together.

She made them into weeks.

At times we could only wonder:

Had she made a deal with death?

If so, it was the con of the century—it was death that wouldn't stick.

The best was when a year was gone.

The months hit lucky thirteen.

On that occasion, out of the hospital, Penny Dunbar said she was thirsty. She said she wanted beer. We'd helped her to the porch when she told us not to bother. Usually she never drank.

Michael had her arms then.

He looked at her and asked.

"What is it? You need a rest?"

The woman was immediate, emphatic:

"Let's go down to the Naked Arms."

Night had hit the street, and Michael pulled her closer.

"Sorry?" he asked. "What was that?"

"I said, let's go down to the pub."

She wore a dress we'd bought for a twelve-year-old, but a girl who didn't exist.

She smiled in the Archer darkness.

* * *

For a very long moment, her light lit up the street, and I know that sounds quite odd, but that's how Clay described it. He said she was just so pale by then, and her skin so paper-thin. Her eyes continued to yellow.

Her teeth became old framework.

Her arms were pinned at the elbows.

Her mouth was the exception—or the outline of it, at least.

Especially at times like these.

"Come *onnn*," she said, she tugged at him. Cracked and dry, but alive. "Let's go for a drink—you're Mikey Dunbar, after all!"

Us boys, we had to skylark.

"Yeah, c'mon, Mikey, hey, Mikey!"

"Oi," he said. "Mikey can still make you clean the house, and mow the lawn." He'd stayed up near the porch, but saw it was pointless finding reason here, as she walked back down the path. Still, he had to try. "Penny—*Penny!*"

And I guess it's one of those moments, you know?

You could see how hard he loved her.

His heart was so obliterated, but he found the will to work it.

He was tired, so tired, in the porch light.

Just bits-and-pieces of a man.

As for us, we were boys, we should have been a sitcom.

We were young, and the dumb and restless.

Even me, the future responsible one, I turned when he came toward us. "I don't know, Dad. Maybe she just has to."

"Maybe *nothing*—"

But she cut him off.

A hollow, septic arm.

Her hand held out, like a bird paw.

"Michael," she said. "Please. One drink's not going to kill us."

And Mikey Dunbar eased.

He ran a hand through his wavy hairline.

Like a boy, he kissed her cheek.

"Okay," he said.

"Good," she said.

"Okay," he said again.

"You said that already," and she hugged him; she whispered, "I love you, did I ever tell you that?"

And he dived right down inside of her.

The small black sea of her lips.

When he brought her toward the car, his clothes looked damp and dark on him, and again, she wouldn't recede.

"No," she said, "we're walking," and the thought of it struck him cleanly. This woman's Goddamn dying—and making sure she takes me with her. "Tonight we'll walk together."

A crowd of five boys and a mother then, we crossed the expanse of road; I remember our shorts and T-shirts. I remember her girlish legs. There was darkness, then the streetlights, and the still-warm autumn air. The picture slowly forms for me now, but soon it comes to an end:

Our father stayed back on the lawn.

A part of him was foundering there, and the rest of us turned to watch. He looked so damn alone.

"Dad?"

"Come on, Dad!"

But our father had sat down, head in hands, and of course it could only be Clay:

He returned to our lawn on Archer Street, and approached that shadow-of-dad. Soon he stood beside him, then slowly, he dropped and crouched—and just when I thought he would stay with him, he was up again, he was behind him. He was placing his hands in that area, in what every man on earth has:

The ecosystem of each armpit.

He pulled our father upwards.

They stood, then swayed, and steadied.

* * *

When we walked, we walked at Penelope pace, so pale in every movement. We turned a few more corners, onto Gloaming Road, where the pub sat calm and shiny. The tiles were cream and maroon.

Inside, while the rest of us looked for a stool, our father went to the bar. He said, "Two beers and five ginger beers, please," but Penny had loomed behind him, all sweat and shown-off bones.

She put her hands on top of the beer mat.

She dug deep, through barren lungs.

She seemed to be reaching around down there, for something she knew and loved. "How about"—she called the question up, piece by piece—"we just make it seven beers?"

He was a young barman, turning already for the soft drinks. His nametag said *Scott*. They called him Scotty Bils. "Excuse me?"

"I said," she said, and she looked him square in the face. His hair was going missing, but he wasn't short of nose. "Make it seven beers."

That was when Ian Bils came over; the pulse of the Naked Arms. "Everything all right here, Scotty?"

"This lady," Scotty Bils said. "She's ordered seven beers." His hand in his fringe like a search party. "Those boys over there—"

And Ian Bils—he didn't even look.

He kept his eyes firmly on the woman in flux, who was bracing against his bar. "Tooheys Lights okay with you?"

Penny Dunbar met him halfway. "That sounds great."

The old publican solemnly nodded.

He wore a cap with a galloping mustang.

"Let's make it all on the house."

There are victories and there are victories, I guess, and this one still didn't come cheap. We thought she might let go that night, when finally we got her home.

Next day we all stayed in with her.

We watched her and checked for breathing:

Her naked arms and the Naked Arms.

She stank like beer and disease.

In the evening, I wrote the absent notes.

The best scrawl of our dad's I could manage:

My wife is quite sick, as you know. . . .

But I know I should have done this:

Dear Miss Cooper,

Please excuse Tommy for being absent yesterday. He thought his mum might die, but she didn't, and to tell you the truth, he was actually a bit hungover. . . .

Which technically wasn't true.

As the oldest, it was only me who made it through my drink, and it was quite an effort, I'm telling you. Rory and Henry had half each. Clay and Tommy managed the froth—and still, none of it mattered, not remotely, for we watched Penny Dunbar smile to herself; a girl's white dress and bones. She'd thought she might make men of us, but this was every woman for herself.

The Mistake Maker made no mistake of it.

She stayed till she'd finished them off.

the walking tour of featherton

When they spoke of Pont du Gard again, it was to herald the beginning of the end.

They walked and started work again.

They worked and Clay wouldn't stop.

As it was, Michael Dunbar counted a hundred and twenty consecutive days that Clay worked on the bridge, and very little sleep, very little eating—just a boy who could work the pulley, and heave stones he had no right to carry. "There," he would say to his father. "No, not there, up *there*." He'd stop only to stand with the mule for a while; Clay and the faithful Achilles.

Often, he slept in the dirt out there.

He was covered by blankets and falsework.

His hair was matted flat to him.

He asked if Michael would cut it.

It fell to his feet in clumps.

They did it outside by the bridge, in the looming shadows of arches.

He said thanks and went back to work.

When Michael would leave for the mines, he made Clay promise to eat.

He even called us here, to make sure we rang to check on him, and it was something I did religiously; I called him three times a week, and counted twenty-four rings till he made it in: the length of the sprint to the house.

He spoke only of the bridge and building it.

We shouldn't come, he said, till he'd finished.

The bridge and making it perfect.

Probably one of the best things Michael ever did was force him to take a break:

A weekend.

A whole weekend.

Clay, of course, was reluctant. He said he was going to the shed; he needed that torturous shovel again.

"No."

The Murderer, our dad, was final.

"Why not?"

"You're coming with me."

It was no surprise that Clay slept all the way in the car, as he drove him out to Featherton; he woke him when he'd parked on Miller Street.

Clay rubbed at his eyes and ignited.

"Is this," he said, "where you buried them?"

Michael nodded and passed him a coffee cup.

The country began to spin.

In the confines of the car, while Clay drank, our father gently explained. He didn't know if they lived there anymore, but it was a couple called the Merchisons who'd bought the place, though it seemed there was no one home—except for the three out back.

For a long time they were tempted—to cross that toasty lawn—but soon they drove on, and parked near the bank. They walked the old town and its streets.

He said, "This pub here's where I threw bricks up. . . . I threw bricks up to another guy throwing bricks up—"

And Clay said, "Abbey was here."

Oi, Dunbar, y' useless prick! Where are me Goddamn bricks?!

Michael Dunbar simply said, "Poetry."

* * *

After that, they walked till evening, right out onto the highway; and Clay could see the beginnings of things, like Abbey eating an Icy Pole, and his father and the dog called Moon.

In the town he saw the surgery:

Dr. Weinrauch's infamous chopping block.

Then the woman and resident boxer, who'd punched at the keys in the office.

"It's not quite how I saw it," he said, "but I guess things never are."

"We never imagine things perfectly," said Michael, "but always just left or right. . . . Not even me, and I used to live here."

By night, near the end, they procrastinated.

They needed to make a decision.

"Did you want to go over and get it?" said Michael. "Did you want to go dig up the typewriter? I'm sure those people won't mind."

But now it was Clay who'd decided. It was Clay who was firm and final. It was then, I think, he'd realized:

For starters, this story wasn't over yet.

And even then, it wouldn't be him.

The story was his, but not the writing.

It was hard enough living and being it.

merchants and swindlers

THE SEVEN BEERS WAS ANOTHER BEGINNING:

A timeline of death and events.

Looking back I can see how rude we were, and Penny herself, pure insolence.

Us boys, we fought and argued.

So much of the dying hurt us.

But sometimes we tried to outrun it, or laugh and spit toward it—and all while keeping our distance.

At our best we interrupted.

Given death had come to claim her, we could at least be difficult losers.

In winter that year I took holiday work with a local floorboard and carpet firm. They offered me a full-time job.

At school, by sixteen, I was both good and not-good at many things, and my favorite was usually English; I liked the writing, I loved the books. Once, our teacher mentioned Homer, and the rest made light and laughed. They quoted a much-loved character, from a much-loved American cartoon; I said nothing at all. They'd joked at the teacher's surname that day, and at the end of class I'd told her:

"My favorite was always Odysseus."

Ms. Simpson was a bit perplexed.

I liked her crazy ringlets, and her spindly, inky hands.

"You know Odysseus and didn't mention it?"

I was ashamed but couldn't stop. I said, "Odysseus—the resourceful one. Agamemnon, king of men, and"—quickly, I sucked it in—"Achilles of the nimble feet . . ."

I could see her thinking, *Shit!*

When I left, I didn't ask their permission:

I told my mother in her sickbed, and Michael Dunbar in the kitchen. They both said I should stay, but my mind was already set. Talking about resourcefulness, the bills were becoming flood-like—defying death had never been cheap—but that's still not why I did it. No, it just seemed right, that's all I can say, and even when Penny looked at me, and said I should sit up next to her, I felt completely certain and justified.

She struggled to hold a hand up.

She raised it to my face.

I could feel the hot-tin roof of it, as she ignited on top of the sheets; it was one of those *oxymorons* again—it cooked her from within.

She said, "Promise you'll still keep reading." She swallowed, like heavy machinery. "Promise me, promise, okay, kid?"

I said, "Of course," and you should have seen her.

She caught fire, beside me, on the bed.

Her papery face was lit.

As for Michael Dunbar, in the kitchen, our dad did something strange.

He looked at the bills, then me.

Then he walked outside with his coffee cup, and hurled it toward the fence—but he'd somehow got the angle wrong, and it landed amongst the lawn.

When a minute went by, he'd collected it, and the cup remained unharmed.

From there the door was flung open, and death came in from everywhere; it marauded all that was hers.

But still, she wouldn't allow it.

One of the best nights was late in February (nearly twenty-four months in total), when a voice arrived in the kitchen. It was hot and very humid. Even dishes on the rack were sweating, which meant a perfect night for Monopoly. Our parents were in the lounge, watching TV.

I was the top hat, Henry the car, Tommy the dog, Clay the thimble. Rory, as always, was the iron (which was the closest he'd get to actually using one), and he was winning, and rubbing it in.

Rory knew I hated cheaters, and gloaters more than anything—and he was doing *both*, way out in front, rummaging everyone's hair, each time we had to pay him . . . till a few hours in, it started:

"Oi."

That was me.

"What?"

That was Rory.

"You rolled nine but moved ten."

Henry rubbed his hands together; this was going to be great.

"*Ten?* What the hell are you talking about?"

"Look. You were there, right? Leicester Square. So get your ironing arse back one spot to my railway and fork out twenty-five."

Rory was incredulous.

"It was ten, I rolled *ten*!"

"If you don't go back, I'm taking the iron and ejecting you from the game."

"*Ejecting* me?"

We sweated like merchants and swindlers, and Rory struck out at himself for a change—a palm through the wire of his hair. His hands were already so hard by then. Those eyes gone even harder.

He smiled, like danger, toward me now. "You're joking," he said, "you're kidding."

But I had to see it through.

"Do I look like I'm Goddamn joking, Rory?"

"This is bullshit."

"Right, that's it."

I reached for the iron, but not before Rory had his greasy, sweaty fingers on it, too, and we fought it out—no, we *pinched* it out, till coughing was heard from the lounge room.

We stopped.

Rory let go.

Henry went to see, and when he came back in with a nod of okay, he said, "Right, where were we, anyway?"

Tommy: "The iron."

Henry: "Oh yeah—perfect, where is it?"

I was deadpan. "Gone."

Rory searched the board in a frenzy. "*Where?*"

Now, even deader-pan. "I ate it."

"No way." Disbelief. He shouted. "You gotta be kidding me!" He started to stand, but Clay, in the corner, silenced him.

"He did," he said. "I saw him."

Henry was thrilled. "What? *Really?*"

Clay nodded. "Like a painkiller."

"What? Down the hatch?" He burst forth with loudmouthed laughter—blond in the white-blond kitchen—as Rory turned fast, to face him.

"I'd shut up if I were you, Henry!" and he paused for a moment, then went out back, and returned with a rusty nail. He slammed it down on the proper square, paid his money, and glared at me. "There, you dirty bastard. Go try swallowing *that*."

But, of course, I didn't have to—for when the game started up again, and Tommy rolled the dice, we heard the voice from the adjoining room. It was Penny, part gone, part alive.

"Hey, Rory?"

Silence.

We all stopped.

"Yeah?"

And looking back, I love the way he called that now—how he stood, and was ready to go to her, to carry her or die for her if he had to; like the Greeks when called to arms.

And the rest of us sat, we were statue-like.

We were stilled, and remained alert.

God, that kitchen and its heat, and the dishes all looking nervous; and the voice came stumbling forward. It was on the board between us:

"Check his shirt. . . ." We felt her smiling. "Left pocket," and I had to let him. I let him reach over and in.

"I should give you a fucking nipple cripple while I'm at it, you bastard."

But soon, he'd managed to find it.

His hand reached in, he produced the iron, and he shook his head and kissed it; tough lips on silver token.

Then he took it and stood in the doorway, and he was Rory and just young and untough for a moment, the metal gone soft in an instant. He smiled, and shouted his innocence, his voice gone up to the ceiling.

"Matthew's bloody cheating again, Penny!" and the house all around us was shaking, and Rory was shaking with it—but soon he came back to the table, and placed the iron on top of my railway, then gave me a look that fell at me, then at Tommy and Henry and Clay.

He was the boy with the scrap-metal eyes.

He cared nothing, at all, for anything.

But that look, so afraid, so despairing, and the words, like a boy in pieces: "What'll we do without her, Matthew? What the hell are we s'posed to do?"

football in the riverbed

We did it in early December.

We all just got in my car.

Clay could say what he wanted, about waiting until he was finished. All of us, we'd all had enough of it, and I took out my tools and work gear; we reached in and righted the seats. Rosy came with us, too. Tommy tried also for Hector, but we said to him don't push your luck—and God, how we drove and thought of him.

Those reams of empty space.

We drove but hardly spoke.

In the meantime, the clouds were gathering, which meant one of two possibilities.

The storms would pass by, rainless; and they'd wait to be tested for years. Or the flood would come to them early, while they desperately worked to the finish.

Probably the greatest moment came when they took the molds out—the falsework—for the arches to stand alone. They were men of other terms then—of bridging as opposed to dying—and so they spoke of the strength of the spandrels, and the hopes they had for each keystone.

But then simplicity got the better of them, or of Michael, at least, in the riverbed:

"Let's hope the bastards hold."

It was like fins out in the ocean—you were sure they were only dolphins, but really, did you *really* know? Not till you saw them up close.

They knew in their hearts they'd done everything.

They'd done everything to make it perfect.

The sandstone gleamed in the mornings.

"You ready?" said Michael; Clay nodded.

As the truest of tests, he went below.

He said, "Clay, you stay there—stay out in the light," and he performed the final dismantling, and the arches were true, still standing; and then came his smile, and the laughter:

"Come here," he said, "here, Clay, *come under*!"

They embraced like boys in the archway.

When we got there, I remember us seeing it.

The bridge looked totally finished, and the sandstone deck rendered smooth.

"Christ," said Rory, "look at it."

"Hey," cried Henry, "there he is!"

He jumped from the moving car:

He stumbled and laughed, then ran and picked him up, and tackled him into the ground.

Again, just one more history.

How boys and brothers love.

In the evening we played football in the riverbed.

It was something that had to be done.

The mosquitoes could barely keep up with us.

The ground was brutally hard, and so we tackled, but held each other up.

There were also moments we stopped, though, and just looked, in amazement, at the bridge—at the monumental deck of it, and the arches, like twins, in front of us. It *did* stand like something religious, like a son's and father's cathedral; I stood by the left-hand arch.

And I knew it was made of him:

Of stone, but also of Clay.

What else could I make myself do?

There were still many things I didn't know yet, and if I had, I might have called sooner—to where he stood between Rosy and Achilles.

"Hey!"

And again:

"Hey!" I called, and I nearly called *Dad* but said *Michael* instead, and he'd looked at me, down in the riverbed. "We need you to even the teams."

And strangely, he'd looked to Clay.

This was Clay's riverbed, Clay's bridge; and hence it was also his football field, and he'd nodded and Michael soon came.

Did we have a good talk then, about uniting more strongly than ever, especially at times like these?

Of course not, we were Dunbar boys.

It was Henry who spoke to him next.

He gave him the list of instructions:

"You can run right through the arches, okay? And kick the ball over the top. You got it?"

"Got it"—and the Murderer smiled from years ago, if for only a split-second moment.

"*And*," said Henry, to finish things, "tell Rory to stop fucking cheating—"

"I'm *not* cheating!"

We played in the blood of the sun.

the world cup of dying

The clock hit two years gracefully.

Then awfully, two and a half.

She went back to work as a substitute.

She said, "This dying shit is easy."

(She'd just thrown up in the sink.)

When she did make it out to work, sometimes she wouldn't come back, and we'd find her halfway home, or the last in her car, in the car park. Once she was out by the railway line, laid back in her seat near the station, and trains passed through on one side, and traffic went by on the other. We knocked on the window to wake her.

"Oh," she'd said, "still alive, huh?"

Some mornings, she'd start to lecture us. "If any of you boys see death today, just send him over to me." We knew she was flaunting her courage.

On days she was too sick to leave, she'd call us toward the piano.

"Come on, boys, put one here."

We lined up to kiss her cheek.

Each time might have been the last.

Whenever there was lightness or buoyancy, you knew drowning wasn't far.

As it turned out, the third Christmas *was* her last.

We sat at the kitchen table.

We went to a hell of an effort; we made *pierogi*, and unspeakable *barszcz*.

She was finally ready, by then, to sing "*Sto Lat*" again, and we sang for the love of Penelope; and for Waldek, the statue, and no countries. We sang only for the woman in front of us. We sang only for all her stories.

But soon, it had to happen.

She was given a final choice.

She could die in the hospital, or die at home.

She looked at Rory in the hospital ward, then me, and all the rest of us, and wondered who should talk.

If it had been Rory, he'd have gone, "Hey, you there—nurse! Yeah, *you*, that's it—unhook her from all that shit." If it was me, less rude, but blunt. Henry would be too confident, and Tommy wouldn't speak—too young.

On short deliberation, she'd settled for Clay, and she called him close and whispered it, and he turned to the nurse and doctor; both women, both kind beyond measure.

"She says she'll miss her kitchen here, and she wants to be home for us." She gave him a jaundiced wink then. "And she has to keep playing the piano . . . and keep an eye on *him*."

But it wasn't Rory whom he'd pointed to, but the man with a hand on Tommy.

From the bed she spoke up outwardly.

She said, "Thank you both for everything."

Clay had hit thirteen back then, his second year of high school.

He was called into a counselor's classroom, after Henry had just walked out; he was asked if he needed to talk. Dark days before Claudia Kirkby.

His name was Mr. Fuller.

Like her, he wasn't a psychologist, but a teacher given the job, and a good guy, but why would Clay want to talk to him? He didn't see the point.

"You know," the teacher said. He was quite young, in a light blue shirt. A tie with a pattern of frogs, and Clay was thinking, *Frogs?* "Sometimes it's easier to talk to someone other than your family."

"I'm okay."

"Okay, well, you know. I'm here."

"Thanks. Do I just go back to math?"

There were hard times, of course, there were terrible times, like when we found her on the bathroom floor, like a tern who couldn't make the trip.

There was Penny and our dad in the hallway, and the way he helped her along. He was an idiot like that, our father, for he'd look at us then and mouth it—he'd go *Look at this gorgeous girl!*—but so careful not to bruise her.

Bruises, scratches. Lesions.

Nothing was worth the risk.

They should have stopped at the piano, for a break and a cigarette.

But there are no breaks for dying, I guess, it's relentless, and unrelenting. Stupid, I know, to put it like that, but by then you don't really care. It's dying at twice the rate.

There was forcing herself to have breakfast sometimes, to sit at the kitchen table; she never could master the cornflakes.

There was Henry once, out in the garage:

He was punching like hell at a rolled-up rug, then saw me and fell to the ground.

I stood there, helpless, hingeless.

Then walked and held out a hand.

It was a minute before he took it, and we walked back out to the yard.

Sometimes we all stayed in their room.

On the bed, or sprawled on the carpet.

We were boys and bodies, laid out for her.

We lay like prisoners of war.

And of course—it was *ourselves* we imitated later, on the day of the anniversary, when I read for a while from *The Odyssey*.

Only now it was Michael who read to us:

The sounds of the sea and Ithaca.

He stood by the bedroom window.

* * *

At regular intervals, a nurse came by and checked on her. She surrendered her to morphine, and made work of checking her pulse.

Or did she concentrate like that to forget?

Or to ignore what she was here for, and who and what she was:

The voice of letting go.

Our mother was certainly a marvel then, but a wonder of sad corruption.

She was a desert propped up on pillows.

Her lips so dry and arid.

Her body capsized in blankets.

Her hair was standing its ground.

Our father could read of the Achaeans, and the ships who were ready for launching.

But there was no more watery wilderness.

No more wine-dark sea.

Just a single boat gone rotten, but unable to sink completely.

But yes.

Yes, Goddamn it!

Sometimes there were good times, there were great times.

There was Rory and Henry, waiting outside Clay's math class, or science, just coolly leaning:

The dark-rust hair.

The swerving smile.

"C'mon, Clay, let's leave."

They all ran home and sat with her, and Clay read, and Rory spoke: "I just don't see why Achilles is being such a sook."

It was the smallest sway of her lips then.

She still had gifts to give.

"Agamemnon stole his girlfriend."

Our dad would drive them back again, lecturing at the windshield, but they could tell his heart wasn't in it.

* * *

There were the nights when we stayed up late, on the couch, watching old movies, from *The Birds* to *On the Waterfront* to things you'd never expect from her, like *Mad Max 1* and *2*. Her favorites were still from the '80s. In truth, those last two were the only ones both Rory and Henry abided; the rest were all too slow. She'd smile when they whined and moaned.

"Boring as bloody bat shit!" they'd crow, and it was safe, a routine.

A metronome.

And finally then, the morning I'm looking for, and she must have known she was close—and she came for him at three o'clock:

She carried the drip through the door of our bedroom, and first they sat on the couch.

Her smile was hoisted up by then.

Her face was in decay.

She said, "Clay, it's time now, okay?" and she told him the edits of everything. He was only thirteen years old, he was still too young, but she said the time had come. She told him moments way back to Pepper Street, and secrets of sex and paintings. She said, "You should ask your father to draw one day." Again, she lifted, and dropped. "Just ignore the look on his face."

After a while she said she was hot, though.

"Can we go outside to the porch?"

It was raining, and the rain was glowing—so fine it shone through the streetlights—and they sat with their legs out straightened. They leaned against the wall. She gathered him slowly toward her.

She traded her life for the stories:

From Europe to the city to Featherton.

A girl named Abbey Hanley.

A book by the name of *The Quarryman*.

She'd taken it when she left him.

She said, "Your father once buried a typewriter, you know that?" In perfect, near-death detail. Adelle and her starchy collar—she'd called it the ol' TW—and there was a time when they'd both traveled back there, to an old-backyard-of-a-town, and they buried the old great Remington—and it was a life, she said, it was everything. "It's who we really are."

By the end, the rain was even softer.

Her drip had nearly fallen.

The fourth Dunbar boy was stunned.

For how does a just-thirteen-year-old sit by and gather this up? And all of it falling at once?

But of course he'd understood.

He was sleepy, and also awake.

They were each like bones in pajamas that morning, and he was the only one of us—the one who loved their stories, and loved them with all his heart. It was him she fully trusted. It was him she'd imagined would go one day, and dig up the old TW. How cruel those twists of fate.

I wonder when first he knew:

He'd give those directions to me.

First light was still half an hour away, and sometimes good fortune is real—for the wind began to change. It came shadowing sideways through to them, and held them like that on the porch. It came down and wrapped around them, and "Hey," she said, "hey, Clay"—and Clay leaned slightly closer, to her blond and brittle face. Her eyes were sunken closed by then. "Now you tell the stories to me."

And the boy, he could have fallen then, and bawled so hard in her lap. But all he did was ask her. "Where do I even start?"

"Wherever," she swallowed, "you want," and Clay stalled, then helped it through him.

"Once," he said, "there was a woman, and she came with a lot of names."

She smiled but kept her eyes closed.

She smiled and slowly corrected him.

"No—" she said, and her voice was the voice of dying.

"Like this—" and the voice of surviving.

A momentous effort to stay with him.

There was refusal to open her eyes again, but she turned her head to speak: *"Once, in the tide of Dunbar past, there was a many-named woman,"* and it came a great distance from next to him, and Clay now called toward it; he had something to add of his own.

"And what a woman she was."

In three more weeks, she was gone.

portrait of a father as an older man

Soon there was nothing else left:

They finished but were never finished—for they knew there was something to come.

As far as building the bridge went, though, construction and cleanup were over; they watched it from every angle. In the evening it seemed to shine longer, as if charged by the heat of the day. It was lit, then faded, then gone.

The first one across was Achilles.

He looked ready to bray, but didn't.

Lucky for us no pacts had been made with bad or corrupting spirits; he walked gingerly first, examining it, but by the middle he'd taken ownership:

Backyards, suburban kitchens.

Fields and handmade bridges.

They were all the same to Achilles.

For a while they didn't know what to do with themselves.

"I guess you should go back to school."

But that time had surely passed. Since the death of Carey Novac, Clay had lost the will to count. Now he was just a builder, without a single certificate. The proof was all in the hands.

By the time a month had gone by, Clay came back to the city, but not before Michael showed him.

They were in the kitchen, with the oven—and this was no ordinary boy. People didn't build bridges this quickly, and certainly not of such magnitude. Boys didn't ask to build arches; but then, boys didn't do so many things—and Michael thought of the morning that flooded them, in the last of the waters to come.

"I'm going home to work with Matthew," said Clay, and Michael said, "Come with me."

First they went under the bridge, and his hand on the curve of the archway. They drank coffee in the coolness of morning. Achilles was standing above them.

"Hey, Clay," said Michael, quietly. "It's still not finished, is it?"

The boy by the stone said, "No."

He could tell by the way he'd answered, that when it happened he'd leave us for good—and not because he wanted to, but he had to, and that was all.

Next was something long coming, since Penelope, the porch and the stories:

You should ask your father to draw one day.

They were small by the bridge, in the riverbed.

"Come on," said Michael, "here."

He took him out back to the shed, and Clay saw now why he'd stopped him—when he'd gone for the torturous shovel that day, when he'd driven him out to Featherton—for there, on a homemade easel, and leaning slightly away, was a sketch of a boy in a kitchen, who was holding toward us *something*.

The palm was open but curling.

If you looked hard you could tell what it was:

The shards of a broken peg.

It was in this kitchen I'm sitting in.

Just one of our in-the-beginnings.

* * *

"You know," said Clay, "she told me to. She told me to ask you to show me."

He swallowed; he thought, and rehearsed:

It's good, Dad, it's really good.

But Michael had beaten him to it.

"I know," he said, "I should have painted her."

He hadn't, but now he had him.

He would draw the boy.

He would paint the boy.

He would do it through all the years.

But before that beginning was this:

the bright backyard

In the last weeks, for the most part, it was barely her shell that stayed with us. The rest of her, out of our reach. It was suffering, the nurse and her visiting; we caught ourselves reading her thoughts. Or were they thoughts long written in *us:*

How the hell does she still have a pulse?

There was a time when death had loitered here, or swung from up on the power lines. Or hung, slung-armed, round the fridge.

It was always here to take from us.

But now, so much to give.

There were quiet talks, there had to be.

We sat kitchen-side with our dad.

He said there were still a few days.

The doctor explained that yesterday, and also the morning before that.

Those days-before were endless.

We should have already had a stopwatch back then, and chalk to write the bets with; but Penny would just keep living. No one would win the winnings.

We all looked down at the table.

Did we ever have matching shakers?

* * *

And yes, I wonder about our father, and what it was like—to send us each morning on our way—for it was one of her dying wishes, that we all get up and leave. We all go out and live.

Each morning we kissed her cheek.

She'd kept it seemingly only for this.

"Go, sweet boy—get out there."

That wasn't Penelope's voice.

It also wasn't her face—that turning thing that cried.

That yellow pair of eyes.

She would never see us grow up.

Just cry and silently cry.

She'd never see my brothers finish high school, and other absurdist milestones; she'd never see us struggling and suffering, the first time we put on a tie. She wouldn't be here to quiz first girlfriends. Had this girl ever heard of Chopin? Did she know of the great Achilles? All these silly things, all laden with beautiful meaning. She had strength now only to fictionalize, to make up our lives before us:

We were blank and empty iliads.

We were odysseys there for the taking.

She'd float in and out on the images.

And I know now what was happening:

She'd beg him for help every morning.

The worst was each moment we left.

"Six months," she'd say. "Michael—*Michael*. Six months. I've been dying a hundred years. Help me, please help me."

Also, it was rare now—it hadn't happened for weeks—that Rory, Henry, and Clay would skip school and come home to visit. Or at least we were fools to believe it—because one of them often *did* come back, but was good at remaining unseen. He'd leave at varying time slots, and watch from an edge of window frame—until once he could no longer see her. He'd left school as soon as he'd got there.

Back home he walked the lawn.

He moved to their bedroom window.

The bed was unmade and empty.

Without thinking he took a step backwards.

He felt the blood and the hurry—

Something was wrong.

Something's wrong.

He knew he had to go in there; he should walk straight into the house, and when he did, he was hit by the light; it came right through the hallway. It belted him in the eyes.

But still he carried on walking—out the open back door.

On the porch, he stopped when he saw them.

From the left he could hear the car—a single but tuneless note—and he knew in his heart the truth of it: that car wasn't leaving the garage.

He saw his father standing, in the blinding light of the yard, and the woman was in his arms: the woman of long-lost piano, who was dying but couldn't die, or worse, living but couldn't live. She lay in his arms like an archway, and our father had dropped to his knees.

"I can't do it," said Michael Dunbar, and he laid her down gently to the ground. He looked at the garage side door, then spoke to the woman beneath him, his palms on her chest and a forearm. "I've tried so Goddamn hard, Penny, but I can't, I just can't."

The man kneeling, lightly shaking.

The woman in the grass was dissolving.

And he stood and he cried, the fourth Dunbar boy.

He remembered, for some reason, one story:

He saw her back in Warsaw.

The girl in the watery wilderness.

She was sitting and playing the piano, and the statue of Stalin was with her. He was whipping her knuckles with an economic sting, every time her hands dropped, or she made another mistake. There was so much silent love in him; she was still just a pale little kid. It was twenty-seven times, for twenty-seven musical sins. And her father gave her a nickname.

At the end of the lesson he'd said it, with the snow and its falling outside.

That was when she was eight.

When she was eighteen, he decided.

He decided to get her out.

But first he'd eventually stopped her.

He'd stopped her playing and held her hands, and they were whipped and small and warm. He clenched them, but did it softly, in the width of his obelisk fingers.

He'd stopped and eventually told her—

And the boy.

Our boy.

This young but story-hardened boy of ours, he stepped forward, and believed in everything.

He stepped forward and kneeled down slowly.

Slowly, he spoke to our dad.

Michael Dunbar didn't hear him coming, and if he was surprised he didn't show it—he was numb on the grass, unmoving.

The boy said, "Dad—it's okay, Dad," and he slid his arms beneath her, and stood, and took her with him. There was no looking back, our father didn't react, and her eyes, they didn't seem yellow that day; they were hers and always would be. Her hair was down her back again, her hands were crisp and clean. She looked nothing like a refugee. He walked with her softly away.

"It's okay," he said again, this time to her, "it's okay," and he was sure he saw her smile, as he did what only he could, and only in his way:

"Już wystarczy," he whispered quietly, then carried her through the translation. "That's enough, Mistake Maker"—and he stood with her under the clothesline, and it was then she'd closed her eyes, still breathing but ready to die. As he took her toward that note he heard, from the light to the smoke in the doorway, Clay could be totally certain; the last thing Penelope had

seen in the world was a length of that wire and its color—the pegs on the clothesline, above them:

As weightless as sparrows, and bright in the light.

For a moment they eclipsed the city.

They took on the sun, and won.

the hour of greatest water

AND SO IT WAS.

All of it led to the bridge:

It had finally been enough for Penelope, but for Clay it was one more beginning. From the moment he carried her away, it was life as he'd never known it. When he came back out to the clothesline, he reached up for the first of his pegs.

His father wasn't able to look at him.

They would never be the same again.

What he'd done, and what he became at that moment, would turn so fast to regret.

He never remembered the walk back to school.

Just the lightweight feel of the peg.

He was sitting down, lost in the playground, when Rory and Henry found him, and lifted him up and half carried him.

"They're driving us all back home," they said. Their voices like broken birds. "It's Penny, it's Penny, she's—"

But the sentence never had an end.

At home, the police, then the ambulance.

The way it all swam down the street.

It was well into afternoon by then, and our father had lied about everything; and that was always her plan. Michael would help her, then tell them he'd gone out briefly. It was Penny herself, so desperate—

But the boy had come home and he'd ruined it.

He'd come and he'd saved the day.

We would call our father the Murderer.

But the murderous savior was him.

In the end there was always the bridge.

It was built, and now for the flooding.

The storm never comes when it should.

In our case, it happened in winter.

The whole state was soon underwater.

I remember the endless weather, as the city was lashed with rain.

It was nothing compared to the Amahnu.

Clay was still working with me.

He was running the streets of the racing quarter, where her bike, surprisingly, stayed; no one had got out the bolt cutters, or managed to break the code. Or maybe they just didn't want to.

When the news came through of the weather, the rain started coming much earlier; Clay stood in the first drops of water. He ran to the stables at Hennessey.

He made the lock into all the right numbers, and walked the bike carefully away. He'd even brought down a small bike pump, and put air in the sunken tires. Cootamundra, The Spaniard and Matador. The courage of Kingston Town. He pumped hard with the names inside him.

When he rode out through the racing quarter, he saw a girl on Poseidon Road. It was right up top near the northern part, near the Tri-Colors gym and the barbers. The Racing Quarter Shorter. She was blond against blackening sky.

"Hey!" he called.

"Some weather!" she replied, and Clay jumped off the old bike.

"Do you want this thing to get home?"

"I'd never be as lucky as *that*."

"Well, you are today," he said. "Go on, take it." He put the stand out and walked away. Even as the sky started storming, he watched as she went and took it. He shouted:

"Do you know about Carey Novac?"

"What?" she cried back, then, "Who?"

The pain of shouting her name, but he felt all the better for it. "The lock!" he called, through the water. "It's thirty-five-twenty-seven!" and he thought for a final moment, and swallowed the pins of rain. "If you forget, just look up The Spaniard!"

"The *what?*"

But now she was on her own.

He watched her a moment, then gone.

From there, there was only more rain.

It wouldn't be forty days and nights.

For a while, though, it looked quite likely.

On the first of them, Clay walked out, for the next train to Silver, but the rest of us wouldn't allow it. All five of us, we piled in my station wagon, and Rosy, of course, in the back.

Mrs. Chilman looked after the rest.

In Silver, we were just in time:

When we drove across the bridge, we looked down.

The water bit hard at the arches.

From the porch, in the rain, Clay thought of them; he remembered upstream, and those tough-looking trees, and the stones and the giant river gums. At this moment they were all being pummeled. Debris was flailing downwards.

Soon the whole world was flooded, it seemed, and the top of the bridge was submerged. For days, the water kept rising. Its violence was something magnetic; it scared the absolute life from you, but it was hard to not watch, to believe it.

Then, one night, the rain stopped.

The river continued to roar, but in time began to recede.

There was no telling yet if the bridge had survived—or if Clay could achieve its true finish:

To walk across that water.

All through the days the Amahnu was brown, and churned like the making of chocolate. But at sunrise and sunset there was color and light—the glow, then dying of fire. The dawn was gold, and the water burned, and it bled into dark before night.

For three more days, we waited.

We stood and we watched the river.

We played cards in the kitchen with our father.

We watched Rosy curl up near the oven.

There wasn't room for all of us, so we laid down the seats in the station wagon, and Rory and I slept out there.

A few times, Clay went out back, to the shed, where Achilles stood guard, and saw more of the artworks in progress. A favorite was a loose-drawn sketch, of a boy in the legs of the eucalypts—until it happened, it came, on Sunday.

As always he woke in the dark.

Not long before dawn, I heard footsteps—they were running, they were splashing—and next I heard the car door open; and I felt the force of his hand.

"Matthew," he whispered. "Matthew!"

Then, "Rory. *Rory!*"

And quickly, I came to realize.

It was there in Clay's voice.

He was shaking.

The lights came on in the house, and Michael came out with a flashlight, and when he'd gone down toward the water, he soon came careering back. As I fought my way out of the car, he staggered but spoke to me clearly, his face shocked and disbelieving.

"Matthew, you have to come."

Was the bridge gone?

Should we be making attempts to save it?

But before I could take a step further, first light had hit the paddocks. I looked in the distance and saw it.

"Oh, God," I said, "Je-sus *Christ*." Then, "Hey," I said, "hey, Rory?"

By the time we were all assembled, on the concrete steps of the porch, Clay was down on the first of them, and heard himself speak, from the past.

I didn't come here for you, he'd said to him—to the Murderer, Michael Dunbar—but standing here now he knew different. He'd come out here for all of us. He just couldn't have known it would hurt this much, in the face of something miraculous.

For a second he watched the border collie, who was sitting, licking her lips—but abruptly he turned to Rory. It was years by then in the making—but he struck him back hard in the eyes:

"Shit, Tommy, does that dog have to pant so bloody loud?" and Rory, in turn, had smiled.

"Come on," he said to Clay now. The gentlest I'd ever heard him. "Let's go and we'll see it together."

Let's go to the river and see it.

When all of us made it down there, the sunrise was in the water. The expanded river was burning; it was alight with the plumes of dawn, and the bridge was still submerged—but intact, and made of him. The bridge was made of Clay, and you know what they say about clay, don't you?

Could he walk across the Amahnu?

Could he be better than a human, for a moment?

The answer, of course, was no, at least to that final question, and now we saw it up close.

* * *

In the last of our footsteps he heard them:

More words they'd said here in Silver.

I'd die to find greatness, like the David someday. . . .

But we live the lives of the Slaves.

The dream was now over and answered.

He would never walk over that water—a miracle made of a bridge—and nor would any of the rest of us; for in the fire the arches were set with, where the river and stone held him upright, was someone so true and miraculous, and something I'll never forget:

Of course, it could only be him.

Yes, him, and he stood like a statue, just as sure as he'd stood in a kitchen. He was watching and chewing, and nonchalant—with that customary look in the thatch of his face—flare-nostriled, controlled to the end:

He had water and dawn all around him; the level an inch up his legs—his hooves on river and bridge. Till soon he was moved to speak. His usual pair of questions, mid-chew, and a mulish grin:

What? he said, from the firelight.

What's so unusual about this?

If he was here to test Clay's bridge for him—if that was why he'd come—we can only agree and admit to it; he was doing a bloody good job.

after the end

the old tw,
revisited

In the end, there was one river, one bridge and one mule, but this isn't the end, it's after it, and here I am, in the kitchen, in the morning, with the bright backyard behind me. The sun is steadily rising.

As it is, I really couldn't say anymore:

Just how long it's been.

How many nights have I sat here, in this kitchen that's seen our lives? It's been a woman telling us she would die, and a father come home to face us. It's where Clay had the fire roared into his eyes, and that's just a few of many. Most recently it's been four of us; four Dunbar boys and our father, all standing, and waiting, together—

But then there's only *this* left; I sit, I'm punching away. After coming back home from Featherton, with a typewriter, a dog, and a snake, I've been here night for night, with everyone else asleep, to write the story of Clay.

And how can I even begin?

How do I tell you the after-parts, in our lives since the bridge was finished?

Once, in the tide of Dunbar past, he came home to us here on Archer Street, then left us, we were certain, forever; and the years brought many things with them.

In the beginning, when we left the river, Clay had hugged our father, and kissed Achilles's cheek. (That scoundrel out in his moment—he'd come back to us quite reluctantly.) For Clay there was uncharted triumph, such wonder at what he'd seen. Then incurable, bottomless sadness. Where did he go from here?

Even as he collected his things—his old wooden box of memories, and his books, including *The Quarryman*—he looked at the bridge from the window. What good was the mark of a masterpiece? It had stood to prove all he'd worked for, and saved absolutely nothing.

When we left, he'd held it out to our father:

The bronze and the pale-covered book.

"It's time I gave you this back."

As he walked toward my station wagon, there was a final father's last gasp; he ran up quickly, behind him. He said, "Clay—Clay!"

And Clay knew what he'd wanted to say to him.

But he knew he was leaving us all.

"Clay—the backyard—" and Clay cut him off with his hand. He said what he'd said to him years ago; a child and not yet a bridge:

"It's okay, Dad. It's okay." But he soon added something else. "She really was something, wasn't she?" and our father could only agree.

"Yes," he said, "she was."

When he got in the car, Clay watched us.

We all shook hands with our father.

There was talking, and Tommy calling Rosy, and Clay gone to sleep in the station wagon; his face against the window.

He slept through us crossing his bridge.

At home, it took most of a day and a night, as he and I sat in this kitchen. My brother had told me everything—of Penelope and Michael, and all of us—and all he had been with Carey. Twice I nearly broke down, and once I thought I'd be sick; but even then he'd talked on, he'd rescued me. He'd said, "Matthew, but listen to this." He told me how when he'd carried her, she was that pale and blond-backed girl again, and the last thing she'd seen was the pegs. He said to me, "Now it's you, Matthew. You have to go out and tell him. You have to go out and tell Dad. He doesn't know that's how I saw her. He doesn't know that's how she was."

When he was done, I thought of Penelope, and the mattress, The Surrounds. If only we'd burned it when we should have! God, I thought so many things. No wonder, no wonder. He was never the boy he'd been; he would leave now and never return. There was just too much of him left here: the carry of too much memory. I thought of Abbey Hanley, then Carey—and what she'd called him at Bernborough Park.

We'd lost our beautiful boy.

When he left, next day, there wasn't much said, you know by now how we are. It was Clay who did the most talking, I think, for he was the one who'd prepared.

To Rory, he said, "I'll miss our hart-to-harts," and there was rust and wire around him. They laughed to ease the ache.

For Henry, it was simple.

He'd said, "Good luck with your lotto numbers—I know you're going to win."

And Henry, of course, half tackled him.

He'd answered him, "One to six."

When he tried offering Clay some money, one last time, Clay just shook his head again.

"It's okay, Henry, you keep it."

And Tommy—young Tommy.

Clay put his hands on his shoulders.

"She'll meet you at the thylacine," and it was that that nearly finished us—until all who was left was me.

For me, he was able to wait.

Soon he'd walked between us, the way boys often do. We don't mind touching—shoulders, elbows, knuckles, arms—and now he'd turned and faced me.

For a while he said nothing at all; he simply made his way to the piano, and quietly lifted the lid. Inside remained her dress, and *The Iliad* and *The Odyssey*.

Slowly, he reached in, then handed the books to me.

"Go on," he said, "open the top one."

Inside were two separate notes.

The first was the letter from Waldek.

The second was a little more recent:

In case of an emergency
(like you keep running out of books)

There was the number, and signed, *ck*.

I almost said he should give it a Goddamn rest, but he got there, easily, first. "Read everything she gives you, but always come back to these." His eyes were fierce and firelit. "And then one day you'll know. You'll know to go out to Featherton, to dig up the old TW, but you'll have to get your measurements right, or you might dig up Moon, or the snake. . . ." His voice became a whisper. "Promise me, Matthew, promise."

And so it was.

He left us late that evening.

We watched him walk, down the porch, across the lawn onto Archer Street, and our lives were left without him. Sometimes we'd catch a shadow, or see him walk through the streets of the racing quarter—but we knew it was never Clay.

As the years climbed by, I could tell you so much:

We all had lives of our own.

Every now and then there'd be a postcard, from places he must have worked in—like Avignon and Prague, or later, a city called Isfahan—and of course they were places of bridges. My favorite was from Pont du Gard.

Here, we missed him with every minute, but we couldn't help being ourselves; the years spanned out to eleven—since the day our father had come, and asked if we might build a bridge.

For Tommy in that time, he grew up.

He went to university, and no, he isn't a vet.

He's a social worker instead.

He takes a dog called O to work with him (you should know by now what it stands for), and he's twenty-four years old. He works with tough, hard kids, but the lot of them love the dog. His pets all lived forever, of course, or forever until they were gone. First went the goldfish, Agamemnon, then T, the marching pigeon, then Hector, and lastly, Rosy.

Rosy was sixteen years old when finally she couldn't walk anymore, and all of us carried her off. At the vet it was Rory, believe it or not, who said, "I think she was holding out—waiting, you know?" He looked at the wall and swallowed. She was named for the sky and Penelope, that dog. "I think she was waiting for Clay."

It's only Achilles, in Silver, still alive now.

That mule is likely unkillable.

Tommy lives near the museum.

Then Henry.

Well, what would you guess for Henry? I wonder.

What to expect from brother number three?

He was the first of us to be married, and would always come up smiling. He went, of course, into real estate, but not before making a packet—on betting and all he'd collected.

During one of his Epic Books and Music Sales, a girl walked her dog up Archer Street. Her name was Cleo Fitzpatrick. For some people life just sails like that, and Henry is one such case.

"Oi!" he'd called, and first she ignored him, in cutoff shorts and a shirt. "Oi, girl with the Corgi-cross-shih tzu, or whatever it is!"

She put in a fresh piece of gum.

"It's a kelpie, dickhead—" but I was there, it was easy to see. It appeared in her black earthy eyes. Fittingly, she bought a copy of Dostoyevsky's *The Idiot*, and came back the following week. They were married the following year.

As for Rory, strange as it seems, he's the one closest to our father again, and goes out quite a lot to the bridge. He's still as rough as guts—or rough as bags, as people like Mrs. Chilman would say—and the years have taken the edge off, and I know how he always missed Clay.

It wasn't long after old Mrs. Chilman died, actually, that he moved to a suburb close by: Somerville, ten minutes north. He likes to come back and sit here, though, drinking beer, and laughing away. He likes Claudia, too, and talks to her, but mostly it's him and me. We talk about Clay, we talk about Penny, and the story is passed between us:

"So they gave her six months—a hundred-and-eighty-odd days. Did they have any fucking clue who they were dealing with?"

Like the rest of them, he knows what happened now, in the backyard that bright-lit morning; how our father couldn't do it, but Clay was somehow able. He knows what happened beyond it, with Carey and The Surrounds; yet, inevitably, we always come back to it—when she told us, in here, in the kitchen.

"What'd Clay say about that night?" he asks, and he waits a few beats for the answer.

"He said that you roared the fire in his eyes."

And Rory will smile, every time. "I pulled him from out of that chair you're in."

"I know," I say, "I remember."

And me?

Well, I did it.

It only took me several months, but I'd been reading Penelope's books—her immigrant Everests—and opening Waldek's letter; I'd memorized Claudia's number.

Then, a Tuesday, I didn't call the number at all, but walked straight into the school. She was there in the same room, marking essays, and when I knocked, she caught sight of the doorway.

She smiled a great smile of the living.

"Matthew Dunbar," she said, looking up at me. She stood at the desk and said, "Finally."

* * *

As Clay had asked, I did go out to Silver.

I went there many times, often with Claudia Kirkby.

Tentatively at first, my father and I traded stories—about Clay as both son and brother. And I told him what Clay had asked me to, about the last time he saw Penelope—as the girl she once had been. Our father was mostly astonished.

At one point I nearly told him; I nearly said it but kept myself back:

I know now why you left.

But like so many other things, we can know it but leave it unsaid.

When they tore down the Bernborough Park grandstand, and replaced the old red rubber track, we somehow got the date wrong, and missed the inglorious moment.

"All those beautiful memories," said Henry, when we went there to see the pieces. "All those gorgeous bets!" Those nicknames and boys at the fence line—the smell of never quite men.

I recalled the times Clay and I spent there, and then Rory and stopping him and punishment.

But of course, it's Clay and Carey there.

It's them I imagine best.

They're crouched together, near the finish line.

It was one more sacred site of his, left hollow without him in it.

On the topic of sacred sites, The Surrounds, however, remains.

The Novacs have long left Archer Street, for a life back home in the country. But as councils go, and construction work, too, The Surrounds hasn't yet been built on; and so Carey and Clay still own that place, at least according to me.

To be honest, I've grown to love that field, most often when I miss him hardest. I'll wander out back, usually late at night, and Claudia comes to find me. She holds my hand and we walk there.

We have two young daughters, and they're beautiful—they're regretless; they're the sound and color of being here. Would you believe we read *The*

Iliad to them, and *The Odyssey*, and that both of them learn the piano? It's me who takes them to lessons, and we practice back here at home. We're here together at the MARRY-ME keys, and it's me who watches, methodically. I sit with the branch of a eucalypt, and stall when they stop and ask me:

"Can you tell us about the Mistake Maker, Dad?" and of course, "Can you tell us about Clay?"

And what else can I do?

What can I do but close the piano lid, as we go in to face the dishes?

And all of it starts the same.

"Once, in the tide of Dunbar past . . ."

The first is Melissa Penelope.

The second is Kristin Carey.

And so it then comes to this:

There's one more story I can tell you now, before I can leave you in peace. To be truthful, it's also my favorite story, of the warm-armed Claudia Kirkby.

But it's also a story of my father.

And my brother.

And the rest of my brothers, and me.

See, once—once, in the tide of Dunbar past, I asked Claudia Kirkby to marry me; I asked with earrings and not a ring. They were just small silver moons, but she loved them, she said they were something. I wrote her a long letter, too, about everything I ever remembered, about meeting her; and her books, and how kind she had been to us Dunbars. I wrote to her about her calves, and that sunspot, center-cheek. I read it to her on her doorstep, and she'd cried and she'd told me yes—but next, she already knew.

She knew there would also be problems.

She could tell from the look on my face.

When I told her we should wait for Clay, she squeezed my hand, and said I was right—and like that, the years climbed by. They climbed by and we had our daughters. We watched everything form and change, and though we feared he would never come back here, we thought waiting might just bring him to us. When you wait you start feeling deserved.

When five years had passed, though, we wondered.

We'd talk in the night, in our bedroom, which had once been Penny and Michael's.

Eventually, we came to a decision, after Claudia finally asked me:

"How about when you turn thirty?"

I agreed, and again, the years went by, and she even gave me one extra; but thirty-one, it seemed, was the limit. There hadn't been a postcard for a long time by then, and Clay Dunbar could have been anywhere—and that was when finally I thought of it:

I got in my car and drove there.

I arrived in the night in Silver.

I sat with our dad in his kitchen.

As he'd often done with Clay, we drank coffee, and I looked at that oven, and its digits, and I stayed and half bawled and I begged him. I looked out across the table:

"You've gotta go out and find him."

As soon as possible, Michael left the country.

He took a plane to a city and waited.

Every morning he went out at dawn.

He got to the place at opening, and left in the dark at closing.

It was snowing there then, it was freezing, and he got by with some phrases in Italian. He looked lovingly up at the David; and the Slaves were all he had dreamed of. They were fighting and struggling, and turning for air, as they argued from out of the marble. The Accademia staff got to know him, and they wondered if he might be insane. Being winter up there, there weren't many tourists, so they noticed him after a week. Sometimes they gave him some lunch. One evening they'd had to ask—

"Oh," he said, "I'm just waiting. . . . If I'm lucky he might just come."

* * *

And so it was.

Every day for thirty-nine days, Michael Dunbar was in Florence, in the gallery. It was incredible to him, to be with them so long—for the David, those Slaves, were outrageous. There were times when he drifted off, too, just leaning as he sat by the stone. It was security who often woke him.

But then, on that thirty-ninth day, a hand had reached out for his shoulder, and a man was crouched above him. There was the shadow of Slave beside him, but the hand on his clothing was warm. His face was paler, and weathered, but there was no mistaking the boy. He was twenty-seven years old, but it was something like that moment, all those years ago—Clay and Penelope, the bright backyard—for he saw him how once he was. You're the one who loved the stories, he thought—and it was suddenly just a kitchen, as Clay called out, his voice so quiet, from the dark toward the light.

He kneeled on the floor and said, "Hi, Dad."

On the wedding day we couldn't be sure.

Michael Dunbar had done his best, but we hoped out of sheer desperation, more than any real hope at all.

Rory would be the best man.

We all bought suits and nice shoes.

Our father was with us as well.

The bridge was a constant build.

The ceremony would be in the evening, and Claudia had taken the girls.

In late afternoon, we assembled—from oldest to youngest: me, Rory, Henry, Tommy. Then Michael had come soon after. It was all of us here on Archer Street, suited up, but ties were loosened. We were waiting, as we had to, in the kitchen.

There were moments, of course, when we heard things.

Whoever went out came back.

Each time was met with "Nothing," but then, Rory, last hope, said:

"*That*."

He said:

"What the hell was *that*?"

* * *

He'd considered going mostly on foot, but he caught the train and bus. On Poseidon Road, he got out one stop early, and the sun was warm and friendly.

He walked and stopped, he leaned at the air—and quicker than he'd hoped or imagined, he stood at the mouth of Archer Street, and there was no relief, and no terror.

There was knowing he was here, he'd made it.

As always, there had to be pigeons.

They were perched up high on the power lines, as he came to our front yard. What else could he do but walk on?

He did and soon he stopped.

He stood on our lawn, and behind him, diagonally, was Carey's house, where she'd stood with the cord of the toaster. He almost laughed when he thought of our struggle here—the violence of boys and brothers. He saw Henry, and himself, on the roof, like kids he once knew and had talked to.

Before he realized, he'd said the word "Matthew."

Just my name and that was all.

So calm and so quiet—but Rory had heard—and we stood up, together, in the kitchen.

I'm not sure I can ever explain it, or have a hope or a Je-sus Christ.

God, how do I get this right?

So all I can do is punch harder here, to give you it all as it was:

See, first we all ran to the hallway, and ripped the fly screen clean from its hinges—and there, from the porch, we saw him. He was down on the lawn, dressed up for a wedding, with tears in his eyes, but smiling. Yes, Clay, the smiler, was smiling.

Amazingly, no one moved closer:

All of us, totally still.

But then, quite quickly, we did.

Me, I took a step, and from there it was suddenly easy. I said Clay, and Clay, and Clay the boy, and the gusts of my brothers swept past me; they jumped the steps of the porch, they tackled him down to the lawn. They were a scrum of bodies and laughter.

And I wonder how it must have looked then, to our father, a mess at the railing. I wonder how he must have seen it, as Henry and Tommy, then Rory, all finally climbed off my brother. I wonder how it must have been to watch, as soon they helped him up, and he stood and dusted himself off, and I walked the last meters to meet him.

"Clay," I said. "Hey, Clay—"

But there was nothing else now I could say to him—as this boy, who was also the man of this house, allowed himself finally to fall—and I held him, like love, in my arms.

"You came," I said, "you came," and I held him so hard, and all of us then, all men of us there, we smiled and cried, cried and smiled; and there had always been one thing known, or at least it was known to him:

A Dunbar boy could do many things, but he should always be sure to come home.

acknowledgments

There would be no Dunbar boys, no bridge, and no Clay without the toughness, laughter, and sheer collective heart of Cate Paterson, Erin Clarke, and Jane Lawson—all of them clear-eyed and truth-telling. All of them Dunbar boys themselves. Thank you for everything.

To my friends and colleagues: Catherine (the Great) Drayton, Fiona (Riverina) Inglis, and Grace (PP) Heifetz—thank you for hanging in. Thank you for your willingness to age a decade or so in those Spartan days of reading.

Tracey Cheetham: If 2016 could happen, so could this. The finest from across those bridges.

Judith Haut: Very few people have withstood my idiocy more than you. It's the Arkansas in your blood. Thanks always for your love and friendship, no matter the river or city.

William Callahan: You may never know what you are to this book. You were there to carry me up. You bribed me out of Hades.

Georgia (GBAD) Douglas: Ultimate penultimate. I'll miss our *hart-to-harts*. Infuriatingly right. T-shirts might yet be made.

Bri Collins and Alison Kolani: Both perennial saviors, both masters; irreplaceable.

To these stalwarts (a truly great word), thank you for helping this last decade, and in some cases more recently:
Richard Pine, Jenny Brown (the Kindest of All Time), Kate Cooper, Clair Roberts, Larry Finlay, Praveen Naidoo, Katie Crawford, Kathy (the fixer of *anything*) Dunn, Adrienne Waintraub, Dominique Cimina, Noreen Herits, Christine Labov, John Adamo, Becky Green, Felicia Frazier, Kelly Delaney, Barbara Marcus, Cat Hillerton, Sophie Christopher, Alice Murphy-Pyle, and (geniuses) Sandy Cull, Jo Thomson, and Isabel Warren-Lynch.

To these people, never underestimate the friendship and camaraderie you've given both me and this book:
Joan DeMayo, Nancy Siscoe, Mandy Hurley, Nancy Hinkel, Amanda Zhorne, Dana Reinhardt, Tom and Laura McNeal, Andy, Sally, Inge, Bernd, Leena, Raff, Gus, Twain, Johnny, and TW.

Special mention to:
Blockie: For walks with Floyd; for listening. *Picasso*. All roads lead to Huddart.
Angus and Masami Hussey: Game-changers, life-changers, the best of different continents.
Jorge Oakim: I'd climb any wall, anywhere. Thanks for everything.
Vic Morrison: Not only for music and piano-moving (and tuning) advice, but for a lifetime of art and risk, and the story that led to the Slaves.
Halina and Jacek Drwecki: For love and arguments over the ins and outs of Polish, and for stories of camps and cockroaches: *so big!*
Maria and Kiros Alexandratos: For first talks on bridge-building.
Tim Lloyd: For help and advice on all things equine, not least driving me around Otford, finding something approximating a mule.
HZ: For typically wry advice on roughing up the German language.

Zdenka Dolejskă: For that one line of Czech . . . Every little bit counts. Thank you.

Jules Kelly: Secret keeper extraordinaire.
The mysterious Frau H.
And Tim Smith: For all the inspiration, and for waiting in the water.

To the other mz: Decades don't just disappear. They disappear like this. Thanks for making me see what life would be like *without* finishing. As always, you were the difference.

Lastly, to all readers everywhere: It's nothing without you. Thanks for all of everything.

mz